THE WRONG MAN

DAVID ELLIS

Quercus

First published in Great Britain in 2012 by Quercus Editions Ltd
The paperback edition published in 2013 by Quercus Editions Ltd

Quercus Editions Ltd
55 Baker Street
7th Floor, South Block
London W1U 8EW

A CIP catalogue record for this book is available
from the British Library

PB ISBN 978 1 78087 791 4
EBOOK ISBN 978 1 78087 790 7

10 9 8 7 6 5 4 3 2 1

Printed and bound in Great Britain by Clays Ltd, St Ives plc

Typeset by Ellipsis Digital Limited, Glasgow

To Jonathan Lincoln Ellis, our little man

PROLOGUE

January

Something bad is going to happen to Kathy Rubinkowski tonight.

But at the moment she is preoccupied with the tight parallel-park job, navigating the tiny space available just a block from her apartment. She has no business fitting her Accord in the minute gap between the SUVs, but finding a spot within two blocks of her condo is as rare as a sighting of Halley's Comet, so the effort – and the inevitable dings from the neighboring vehicles – is worth it.

She looks about her before she kills the engine. Gehringer Street, this far north, is populated by gated walk-up condo buildings and the occasional single-family dwelling, usually awaiting a remake from the next yuppie couple that moves in. At a few minutes before eleven P.M., the street is empty and sleepy. The lighting is decent. A light fog clings to the streets, courtesy of the rising temperatures today. It is January in the Midwest, but this afternoon it peaked at forty-two degrees.

She exhales and stretches her limbs. She is bone tired. Eight hours of reviewing bills of lading and shipping invoices, followed by four hours of inorganic chemistry, listening to Professor Dylan drone on in that monotone about molecular orbital theory, has left Kathy a tired girl.

She grabs her backpack from the passenger seat and eases out of the car. She closes the door and beeps it locked. The temperatures have fallen over the last hour, like the city suddenly remembered that it was winter. Kathy does another quick scan of her surroundings. Everything seems fine. She goes around to the trunk and pops it open. She reaches in and grabs her gym bag. She'd given thought to working out in the school gym tonight, but she couldn't muster the energy. Maybe she'll do twenty minutes on her treadmill tonight, though she doubts it.

She doubts it because she has something else to do. Not a work assignment. Not a school assignment. Not an assignment at all. Something nagging at her. Something that may be nothing, but the more she thinks about it—

She closes the trunk. A soft, quick gasp escapes her and she stumbles backward against the grille of the SUV behind her. A moment ago there hadn't been anyone on the street. Now there is. She takes a breath.

'Sorry,' she says, aware of her frazzled reaction. 'You startled me.'

In less than five seconds, a bullet enters her skull between her eyes. The bullet is a straight front-to-back, shattering the sphenoid and ethmoid bones and the orbital plates and lodging in her brain stem. It creates a shock wave that propagates through her brain, causing instantaneous loss of consciousness. Only a moment before she lacks any capacity to do so, Kathy remembers that tomorrow is her twenty-fourth birthday.

She collapses to the street in a dead fall. Blood pours from her nose and mouth, fueled by a heart that does not yet realize

4

it should stop pumping. Her blackening eyes do not see the man's hands maneuvering her purse off her arm, removing the cell phone from her waist holder, yanking the necklace off her neck.

She does not hear the echo of the man's shoes on the pavement, scurrying away from her lifeless body.

Detective Frank Danilo watched through the one-way mirror. The offender was talking to himself, his lips in constant motion, his hands curled up but his fingers wiggling.

The prints taken at the booking had come back to a Thomas David Stoller. Age twenty-seven. Discharged from the Army Rangers twenty-three months ago. Domiciled officially on Van Hart Way, but from the looks of it, Stoller called Franzen Park his home.

'He hasn't stopped talking.' Detective Mona Gregus sipped her coffee. 'Couldn't make out a frickin' word if my life depended on it.'

'Because he's mumbling or because he's incoherent?'

Gregus shook her head. 'Maybe both.'

'Is he for real?' Danilo asked. 'Because you see where this is gonna go.'

'Yeah, I do, Francis, but it's not our problem. Let's get a statement and let the ACA take care of it.'

Danilo nodded. He tapped her arm with the back of his hand. He picked up the evidence box, and they entered the interview room.

The smell hit them first, powerful body odor. Tom Stoller had matted dark hair that went in every direction. A heavy beard that had collected assorted debris. He was wearing two layers of clothes on top, a ratty undershirt, and a stained, ripped, long-sleeved shirt with lettering so faded it was indecipherable. He'd been found in these clothes. That was odd only because he lived and slept outside, and this amount of clothing was no match for the freezing temperatures.

Stoller had bags under his dark, unfocused eyes. His cheeks bore scars and an uneven complexion. He was unnaturally thin. Stoller's shoulders curled in upon the detectives' entry into the interview room, but otherwise he showed no signs of recognition.

Detective Danilo was in role now, but he couldn't help but pause a moment. An Iraqi war vet, now homeless. He wasn't officially the victim here, but that didn't mean he didn't have his own share of tragedy. That was always the worst part of the job for Danilo, when you felt just as bad for the offender as you did the vic.

Danilo flicked on the video camera and looked through the lens to make doubly sure it covered the chairs at the table. Of course it did, but still – there'd been that incident eighteen months ago in Area Two, when the camera somehow got moved and the detective hadn't checked. Judge Mulroney hadn't been amused at seeing a camera filming a blank wall and hearing audio only; he kicked a perfectly good confession on a double homicide.

The detectives took their seats at the table across from the offender. 'This is Detective Francis Danilo. With me is Detective Ramona Gregus. The interviewee is Thomas David Stoller.' Danilo ran through Stoller's Social Security number and last known address as well as the date, time, and location of this interview.

'Mr Stoller, I'm Detective Frank Danilo. This is Detective Mona Gregus. Can I call you Tom?'

Stoller kept up with the mumbling, but now he had tucked his chin and lowered his voice. Gibberish. Incoherent babble.

'Tom, can you look at me?'

The offender peeked up at him, then straightened his posture.

'Tom, you have the right to remain silent. Anything you say can and will be used against you in court. You have the right to an attorney. If you can't afford an attorney, one will be appointed to represent you. Do you understand these rights, Tom?'

The offender looked back and forth between the detectives. His head nodded all the while. The video camera would capture the nods. The Supreme Court never said the consent had to be verbal.

'Tom—'

'You got . . . water?' Stoller asked, his voice rough with phlegm. First contact.

'You want some water, Tom? We can get that for you.'

Detective Gregus left the room. Danilo waited. Technically, he could continue, but a defense attorney could play with any statement made while Stoller waited for his water. No court would find coercion, but the right jury, with the right lawyer, might buy that Stoller thought he wouldn't receive basic sustenance unless he gave the coppers what they wanted.

A moment later, Gregus put two large foam cups of water in front of Stoller. He drank them each down in single gulps, water escaping the sides and dripping from his dirty beard. He smacked his lips and nodded.

'I'm hot,' he said.

8

'Okay,' said Danilo. 'We can get you a blank— You're *hot*?'

'I'm hot.'

Must be nerves, Danilo figured. Internal thermometer rising due to anxiety. It happened sometimes. It was hard to imagine this guy wouldn't have a permanent chill with his lack of clothing and the outside temp in the twenties, but he'd been inside for several hours now.

'Tom, do you know why you're here?'

Stoller didn't answer. He'd stopped his mumbling and seemed to be listening.

Danilo opened the evidence box and lifted the bag holding the murder weapon, the Glock 23 semiautomatic pistol.

'That's my gun,' Stoller said, as Danilo dangled it before him.

Danilo snuck a peek at Gregus. Jesus. That was easy.

'This is your gun, Tom?'

Stoller reached for it. Danilo pulled it back.

'That's my gun,' Stoller insisted, as if wronged.

'We need to hold on to it, Tom. Okay? Keep your butt in that chair.'

'It's mine.' Stoller stared down at the table. 'It's mine.'

'Where did you get this gun, Tom?'

Stoller didn't answer. Like maybe he didn't hear it. Danilo repeated the question and still got no response.

'Where do you live, Tom?' he asked.

The suspect's eyes danced, a crooked smile appearing briefly. 'Where do I . . . live?'

'Okay, sleep,' said Danilo. 'Where do you sleep?'

'Park.' Stoller chuckled.

'Franzen Park?' The answer seemed obvious enough. Franzen Park was the name of the surrounding neighborhood, a yup-and-comer, where some high-end townhouses were sprouting up amid apartment buildings where students like Kathy Rubinkowski lived. But Stoller clearly spent his nights in the park itself.

Stoller shook his head, but he didn't seem to be responding.

'West side of the park, Tom.' Danilo tried to sound casual. 'A street called Gehringer. You know that street, Tom?'

No answer. A slow buildup didn't seem to be getting Danilo very far. The detective drummed his fingers and thought for a moment.

'Why'd you run from the cops, Tom?'

The police had found Stoller in Franzen Park, behind the park district's main building, huddled between two dumpsters, inventorying a purse later identified as belonging to Kathy Rubinkowski. He threw a two-by-four at one of the cops, knocking away his flashlight, and ran for a good three blocks before the uniforms, with the help of an additional patrol car, cut him off.

Stoller stopped his fidgeting. His eyes darted about. Fresh heat, fresh odor came off him. His forehead had broken out in sweat. His hands came off the table, poised in midair. He seemed to be lost in some world other than this one.

Detective Danilo waited him out. But Stoller didn't seem ready to spill. So Danilo repeated his question about running from the police tonight. He tried some others, too. *What did you do last night, Tom? Where'd you get this purse, Tom?*

'Tom.' Danilo slammed his hand down on the table.

Stoller winced at the sound but didn't turn to Danilo. Like he heard a sound but couldn't place it. His lips moved quickly, but damned if Danilo could make out a single word.

'Tom!' he repeated, slamming his hand down again.

Detective Gregus retrieved a file folder from the evidence box. Crime scene photos. She pushed them over to Danilo and nodded.

Right. Probably the right time for this.

Danilo slid a photo across the table. Kathy Rubinkowski, lying dead on the street by her car, amid a pool of blood.

The suspect glanced at the photo and looked away, whipping his head around, his eyes squeezed shut.

'You did this, Tom, didn't you? You killed this woman.'

The table rocked on its legs as Stoller pushed himself away, jumping from the chair.

'Tom, did you shoot this woman?'

Standing away from his chair now, Stoller shook his head violently and tugged at his hair with both hands.

'Tom, if you don't explain this to me, you're going to be charged with first-degree murder.'

'No.' He shook his head so hard, so uncontrolled, Danilo thought, he must be hurting himself.

'Tell me how it went down, Tom, or you'll spend the rest of your life—'

'Put it down!' Stoller barked in a low, controlled baritone. 'Drop it! I said *put it down!*'

The detectives looked at each other. Neither of them was holding anything they could put down. What was he—

'Put it down!'

Danilo steeled himself. Security was one concern. But there were no loaded weapons in this room, and they could hit the emergency button under the table, alerting the stationhouse of the need for emergency assistance, if things got out of control.

11

The camera was another concern, but the suspect would still be within the camera's sight line, and the volume of his voice was more than sufficient.

Stoller braced himself, feet spread, and continued to shout his command: 'Drop the weapon! Drop the weapon right now! Put down your weapon!'

His eyes were closed the whole time. He was essentially shouting at the wall.

Tense silence followed, a few seconds. In a careful voice, Danilo asked, 'Did she pull a weapon on you, Tom? Is that how it happened?'

'I told you to put it down!' Stoller's posture eased. His voice lowered from a stiff command to a plaintive plea. 'I told you . . . I told you to put it down. Why didn't you . . .'

Stoller collapsed to the floor. He let out a wretched wail, somewhere between an anguished, girlish squeal and a guttural animal cry.

'Wake up!' he whined. 'Please don't . . . don't die . . . please, God, don't die . . .'

Stoller burst into uncontrolled sobs.

Detective Danilo pinched the bridge of his nose and let out a long sigh. Sometimes he hated this job.

BOOK ONE
October/November

1

Deidre Maley held her breath until she left Courtroom 1741. A proud woman who took care to contain her emotions, she waited until she had a small portion of the corridor to herself before she burst into tears.

She'd felt so helpless. So angry and confused and helpless. Watching her nephew Tommy in that prison jumpsuit, those vacant eyes staring at the floor as the judge matter- of-factly issued rulings that she couldn't completely comprehend, and that Tommy surely couldn't follow in his current condition. Their lawyer, a public defender, was a nice man who seemed to care about what he was doing, but he always had so many cases going, he was always so hurried, always promising that there was plenty of time to prepare for the trial, even though it was less than *two months away*.

After a while, Deidre collected herself. Crying about it was never going to solve anything, her mother always said. Her nephew Thomas didn't have a mother, not anymore. She was all he had now.

She saw a couple of men who looked like reporters – if carrying notepads and handheld tape recorders was any indication – rush into the neighboring courtroom, 1743. Not being in a particular hurry to return to work, she followed them inside.

A trial was obviously in progress, the antiseptic silence and formality coupled with tension. Dread filled her chest. In just a few short weeks, her Tommy would be on trial just the same.

Deidre took her seat and watched. In the center of the room, a lawyer in a gray suit stood with a pointer in his hand, next to a blow-up photograph that rested on a tripod and was turned toward the jury. From what she could see, it was a photograph of a gas station and a street.

'Now, Ms. Engles,' the lawyer boomed, 'are you confident that you had a clear and unobstructed view of the shooting?'

'Yeah.' In the witness stand sat a young, pretty African-American woman, mid-twenties at best.

'This truck.' Turning to the blow-up photograph, the lawyer aimed his pointer at a truck parked at the gas station, parallel to the street and perpendicular to cars that would be pumping gas, except that there were no cars in the photograph. 'This truck did not obstruct your view?'

'No. We were on the far end. You could see the street around the truck.'

'For the record, the far west end?' The lawyer used that pointer again. 'The furthest-west end of the gas station?'

'Right.'

'The furthest-west row of gas pumps?'

'Yeah.'

'And you were on the west side of that last row of gas pumps?'

'Yeah.'

'And showing you People's Twenty-four, previously introduced.' The lawyer moved to a second photo, a second tripod.

16

'Does this photograph accurately depict your point of view, sitting in the driver's seat of your automobile, while your car was parked on the west side of the farthest-west row of gas pumps on the night of the shooting?'

'Yeah, that's how I saw it.'

'And you can easily see straight ahead to the street, which would be south, without obstruction from that gas truck?'

'Yeah, real easy.'

'And you are certain, Ms. Engles, that the person you saw fire a weapon and kill Malik Everson is sitting in the courtroom today?'

'Yeah, it was Rondo.'

'By "Rondo" you mean Ronaldo Dayton.'

At the defense table, the lawyer nudged an African-American man sitting next to him. That man stood up.

'That's Rondo right there,' said the witness.

'The record will please reflect that the witness identified the defendant, Ronaldo Dayton.' The prosecutor nodded with satisfaction. 'Nothing further,' he said.

Deidre sighed. The prosecution had so many resources. An army of police officers and lab specialists and doctors, fancy blow-ups and diagrams, everything that defendants like her Tommy lacked. It was such an unbelievably lopsided fight. Unless you had money.

Or you got really lucky with a good defense attorney.

'Afternoon, Ms. Engles.' The defense lawyer strode into the center of the courtroom. Her first full look at him, he wasn't what she'd expect in a lawyer. He looked more like a football player. Tall with broad shoulders. A formidable person. Judging from the expression of the witness, she held the same opinion as Deidre.

17

'My name's Jason Kolarich. Can I call you Alicia?'

'Yeah, okay,' she said. 'Can I call you Jason?'

She giggled a bit. So did a couple of jurors.

'Sure, why not?' he said. The lawyer didn't have any notes with him. He stood just a few feet away from the witness, angled toward the jury. 'Alicia, you have a relationship with a guy named Bobby Skinner, don't you?'

'Yeah.'

'Bobby is the father of your daughter.'

'Yeah.'

'And Bobby, he's a member of a street gang, right? The African Warlords?'

'Not no more.'

'Well, we might disagree on that, but – we *can* agree, at least, that Bobby used to be a Warlord.'

'Yeah, used to be.'

'And he still has friends there. He still hangs with them, doesn't he?'

'He's got some friends, yeah.'

'And my client, Ronaldo Dayton, he runs with the Black Posse. Isn't that your understanding?'

'Yeah, Rondo's with the Posse.'

'And the Posse and Warlords, as far as you understand it, they don't get along so well, do they?'

'No, they don't get along.'

'It would be just fine with the Warlords if a member of the Posse went down for this shooting, wouldn't it?'

'Objection,' said the prosecutor.

'Sustained,' said the judge, an attractive woman with long gray hair.

'Your boyfriend, Bobby, told you to make this story up, didn't he?'

'Objection.'

'The witness can answer.'

'Bobby didn't tell me that,' the witness protested.

This lawyer, Jason Kolarich, seemed to have already moved on, expecting the denial. He nodded and shifted a step to his right. The jury seemed to be paying close attention to him. He had a commanding presence in the courtroom, a quiet confidence that seemed to draw everyone in.

'You testified that you bought gas at the Mobil station at about a quarter to two in the morning.'

'Yeah. Yeah, see, 'cause I left my friends and I's low on gas and I didn't wanna get gas the next morning before work 'cause I wouldn't a had time.'

Kolarich nodded. 'The attendant at the gas station – he didn't see who shot Malik Everson, did he?'

'Don't know about that.'

'You're the only eyewitness.'

'Don't know about *that*, neither.'

Kolarich smiled amiably enough. 'That's fair. Now, when you first told the police that you witnessed the shooting, you weren't real clear on where your car was positioned – which row of gas pumps you were using. Correct?'

'I – I don't think we talked about it.'

'Okay, but you didn't say, "I was on the furthest-west row of gas pumps." Nothing like that.'

'Not right away, but they didn't ask, y'know.'

'Right. I know.' Kolarich looked over at the prosecution. 'It was only *after* you were shown the photograph of that gas truck blocking virtually the entire view of the street that you and

19

the cops came up with a story that your car was on the far-west row of gas pumps.'

'Objection.'

'Sustained,' said the judge. 'That question is stricken. Mr Kolarich, we've discussed this.'

'We have, Your Honor. But Alicia, I have the chronology right, don't I? It was only after you saw that photograph of that huge gas truck blocking the street view that you told the police your car was parked at the *only* gas pump from which you could've had a view of the street.'

The witness shrugged. 'I'm not sure. I think maybe that's right.'

Kolarich went to the table and lifted a document. 'I can have you review the police report chronology if you like.'

'No, I'll take your word for it,' the witness said.

'Good enough.' Kolarich paused, looked at the ceiling, stuffed his hands in his pockets. 'And – you said you were driving a 2006 Pontiac Grand Prix. That was the car you filled up at the gas station.'

'Yeah. I got the receipt from the credit card.'

'You have a receipt that someone using this card bought gas. That's all it says. True?'

'I don't . . . I don't get you.'

'The receipt doesn't say what car received the gas, or what person pumped it.'

The witness still seemed perplexed.

'Isn't it true, Alicia, that your Grand Prix was parked *outside your house* at the time of the shooting?'

This time, the witness didn't answer so quickly. 'My car—'

'If I told you that your neighbors will testify that your

Grand Prix was parked outside your house at the time of the shooting—'

'Objection, Judge! Objection.'

The judge raised a hand. 'The objection is sustained. Mr Kolarich, you know better. Ladies and gentlemen of the jury, please disregard Mr Kolarich's last question. He just stated "facts" to you that haven't been established as facts.'

'Not yet,' said Kolarich.

The judge turned on Kolarich. 'Counsel, you will not interrupt this court, and you are not doing yourself any favors here. This is not the first time I've given you this warning. But it will be the last. Are we clear?'

'Yes, Judge.'

'Ladies and gentleman, you are not to believe so-called "facts" just because a lawyer says he has these facts. You will only consider the evidence presented. Now, Mr Kolarich, see if you can behave yourself.'

'I was driving Bobby's car,' the witness blurted out.

Kolarich turned to her. 'I'm sorry?'

'I just forgot which car, is all. I was driving Bobby's car. Bobby's got him a Mercedes he bought. A used one. He's real proud of it.'

Kolarich paused for a long moment. He raised a hand, as if trying to work it all out. 'You drove Bobby's car.'

'Right. It's also kinda small like the Grand Prix. I just got mixed up on the car. But it don't change what I saw.'

'I see. I think I have that record somewhere.' Kolarich trudged back to his table and opened a folder. On the other side, the prosecutors were flipping through some papers themselves. 'Okay, here it is. Bobby Skinner drives a 2006 Mercedes C280 4matic. License plate KL-543-301. Does that all sound right?'

'Yeah, I think so. That's the license plate, and it's a Mercedes. He parks it in the garage, so that's why the neighbors wouldn't a known if it was parked there or not.'

The witness sat back in her seat and seemed pleased with herself, as if she were winning a debate. It sure seemed like she was, from Deidre's viewpoint.

Kolarich threw the slip of paper on his table, looking exasperated and disappointed, and turned around to face the witness. 'But you're *sure* you were in the driver's seat, having just pumped gas, when the shooting occurred. Isn't it possible you remember that wrong?'

'No, I'm sure about it,' said the witness, with renewed animation.

'And you were staring straight forward, looking south at the street where the shooting occurred. You're sure you weren't facing north?'

'I'm sure, Jason,' she said, smiling. She really was a cute young lady.

'And you're still *sure* you were positioned at the farthest-west end of the gas station, the last row of gas pumps, and on the west side of that last row?'

'Yeah.' She was feeling better now, having recovered nicely from a brief slipup.

'So from your position in the driver's seat of the car, if you looked to your left, there was the gas pump you were using. Forward was the street where the shooting occurred. And to the right were no gas pumps, just open space and the restaurant next door?'

'Yeah, that's right. See, I never thought about it from, like, which car 'cause I drove away as soon as I seen the shooting

22

and that part about which car, it didn't matter. Grand Prix or Mercedes, I wasn't thinking, y'know.'

'Well, I guess that makes sense,' said Kolarich. 'Because the shooting would have stuck out in your mind more than the car you were driving.'

'Yeah, right.'

'Mercedes, Grand Prix, they're roughly the same size – you just slipped up in your memory.'

'Right, yeah.'

'Okay.' The lawyer sighed. 'But just for the record, you're *sure* now that it was your boyfriend's car, the 2006 Mercedes C280 4matic, that you were driving. Not the Pontiac Grand Prix.'

'Yeah, I mean, now that you say it and all. Yeah, I'm sure.'

The lawyer let out an audible sigh and shook his head, seemingly defeated. Maybe beneath the impressive surface, Deidre thought to herself, he wasn't that great a lawyer, after all.

The judge said, 'Anything further, Mr Kolarich?'

'Oh, just one more thing, Judge,' he said. 'Alicia, how did you pump the gas?'

'How did I – what?'

'How did you pump the gas?'

'I – same way you always do, I guess . . .'

The lawyer moved away from the table, back toward the witness. 'No,' he said. 'What I mean is, if you pulled the driver's side of the car up to the gas pump, as you've repeatedly testified, how did you fill the tank? When the gas tank for a 2006 Mercedes C280 is on the *passenger* side?'

The witness froze.

Jason Kolarich smiled.

And so did Deidre Maley.

23

2

My client, Ronaldo Dayton, looked better than I'd ever seen him as the sheriff's deputy escorted him from the defense table to the county lockup. I promised him I'd stop by later to review the case before tomorrow, but I already knew that I wasn't going to put on a defense. We would rest, and closing arguments would follow. I didn't want to give the prosecution any time to try to rehabilitate their star witness, who hadn't turned out to be such a star, after all.

'Mr . . . Kolarich?'

I turned around and saw a woman standing with her hands clasped together, as if in prayer. She was on the high side of middle-aged, gray and weathered, wearing a troubled expression. That wasn't exactly surprising. There weren't a lot of happy faces in the criminal courts building.

'My name is Deidre Maley,' she said.

'Pleasure to meet you,' I said. My mother raised a polite boy. His name is Pete, my brother. But I have my moments, too.

'That was . . . impressive,' she said. 'Do you mind if I ask: How did you know she wasn't driving the Pontiac?'

The courtroom had filtered out. The jury was long gone, and the prosecutors had left, too.

'I didn't,' I said. 'I just knew she was lying.'

She considered me. She probably couldn't decide if she was impressed or disgusted.

'My nephew needs your help,' she said.

Okay, put her down for impressed.

'He's been charged with . . . felony murder, they call it. He has a public defender for a lawyer, but I'd like someone else.'

I asked, 'Who's the P.D.?'

'Bryan Childress.'

'Sure. He's good.' I knew Chilly back from law school. He'd been with the P.D.'s office since graduation. But he was about to leave. I wondered if she knew that.

'He's good, but he's about to leave,' she said.

Check.

'And I think . . . I'd like you to represent him, Mr Kolarich.'

The P.D.'s office gets a bad rap. Most of them are actually quite good. But they're overworked, so sometimes clients feel like they're not getting special treatment.

'I don't have very much money,' she said. 'But if you could be patient – I promise I'd find a way to pay you.'

She was probably in her sixties, so her earning potential wasn't exactly at its peak.

'Tom is a sweet boy. He's sick. He came back from Iraq a different person. I tried to keep an eye on him, but I just couldn't. My husband, you see, suffers from multiple sclerosis, and I couldn't take care of Tom like I should have. I can't help but feel like this is all my fault.'

And I couldn't help but feel like I was being played. Aunt Deidre was laying it on pretty thick. I was waiting for her to collapse so I could catch her in my arms.

'His parents are deceased,' she added. 'I'm all he has for family.'

Did he rescue drowning orphans, too? But lucky for her, she caught me in a good mood.

'I'll meet him,' I said. 'After that, no promises.'

3

Don't ask me why I do the things I do.

But I was bored. And this one sounded interesting.

The Madelyn R. Boyd Center was two blocks south of the criminal courts building. I finished a preliminary hearing I had before Judge Basham on a B-and-E and met Bryan Childress in front of Boyd at eleven sharp. We were both surprised that I was on time.

Childress wore a gray suit and black tie. Cheap stuff. Chilly never cared much for clothes. Back in law school, he never cared much for anything at all except which bar we'd hit that night.

'So, Ronaldo Dayton,' he said to me. 'Well done. I heard the jury came back in four hours?'

Three, actually. Rondo was probably still celebrating as we spoke.

Chilly whistled. The state had really wanted that one. It wasn't that they cared so much about one gangbanger killing another, but Ronaldo Dayton was a chief with the Black Posse, and they wanted him bad.

We went through the doors up to the front desk. 'Hey, Chilly,' said one of the guards, a younger guy, meaning my age. Looked familiar.

'Jimmy, you remember Jason Kolarich? From the gym.'

He nodded at me. 'Sure. I caught one or two of his elbows.'

Right. Now I placed him. We played hoops together a couple weeks back. 'I was trying to teach you the three-second rule,' I said.

He seemed to like that. 'You guys going up to the penthouse?'

Childress nodded. I showed my bar card. Jimmy the guard took down my information and handed me a piece of paper with instructions. I knew the drill. I'd been here a couple times when I was a prosecutor and was trying to flip a gangbanger.

Jimmy followed us into the elevator and slipped a key card into a slot, the only way you could punch a button for the penthouse. Nobody was supposed to go up there by accident.

I looked over the instructions on the sheet of paper.

DO <u>NOT</u>:

- Touch the glass partition

- Pass the inmate anything that has not been placed in the visitor's container at the guard station

- Accept anything the inmate tries to pass to you

- Pass <u>anything</u> through the speaking holes

- Turn off any lights

THE TRANSFER OF CONTRABAND TO AN INMATE IS A VIOLATION OF SECTION 2-16 OF THE CODE OF CORRECTIONS AND IS PUNISHABLE BY UP TO 6 YEARS IN PRISON.

When I looked up from the piece of paper, Chilly was smirking at me. He was almost my height, with reddish-blond hair and a spray of freckles across his rosy cheeks. He looked like a leprechaun on human growth hormone.

'So you met Aunt Deidre,' he said. 'She's a persistent one.'

I folded the instructions and put them in my jacket pocket. The door opened on six. The guards, a man and a woman, sat behind a desk. Above them, in a thick, boxy font, were the words:

DEPARTMENT OF CORRECTIONS
PRETRIAL DETENTION SERVICES
SEGREGATION UNIT

The walls were painted a dull orange, with a large clock and a photo of our governor, Edgar Trotter, smiling broadly. Three windows allowed mid-morning sunlight that angled across the tile floor. It had the sedate, antiseptic feel of a medical facility.

Bryan, who was counsel of record, filled out the paperwork. Case name, docket number, relationship to inmate, that kind of thing.

'We had you down for an interview room,' the female guard said to Chilly. 'If he's not counsel of record, it's no contact.'

'Right. That's fine.'

They made me sign a form indicating I understood the visitation etiquette and a waiver absolving the state of any liability for any damages resulting from this visit. We emptied all of our pockets and gave up our cell phones and wristwatches.

'Anything you want to transfer to him?' the guard asked.

Chilly looked over at me. 'You want to give him your business card?'

29

I slipped one out of my pocket and into the round plastic container. The guard made sure that was all we wanted and then closed it up.

The male guard stood up. 'You gentlemen have any questions?'

We didn't. The guard handed us visitor badges and walked us down a hall. We passed through a metal detector and another guard picked us up.

'Our guy was an Army Ranger in Iraq,' said Bryan. 'First lieutenant. An honorable discharge, nothing indicating any problems, nothing but good stuff on his record. When he gets home, he has a break with reality, as they say. He drops out of college, can't hold down a job, and finally goes to ground. He's arrested a couple of times on vagrancy and shoplifting, nothing that really sticks. But as far as anyone can tell, he's been living on the street for over a year when the murder happens.'

'Combat fucked him up,' I said.

'It would fuck *me* up.'

Me, too. 'So he shoots a woman getting out of her car in Franzen Park,' I said, recalling Bryan's summary yesterday. 'On Gehringer near Mulligan, by that shoe store. And your guy says this was post-traumatic stress? A flashback? He thought the woman was some soldier in Iraq and he opened fire?'

'Basically.'

'And our client told the cops that the victim pulled a gun on him?'

'In the interrogation, he committed to it. He said he told her to put the gun down. He said it over and over again to the detectives. "Put it down. Drop the weapon. Put it down."'

'But you don't buy it?'

30

Chilly let out a low moan. 'The victim didn't own a gun, and there's no evidence she had one. No GSR on the victim, no embedded bullets found at the scene, other than the one in the vic's skull. Point being, if she had a gun, there's no trace of it.'

'But if he was flashing back, it was just him hallucinating, anyway. So who cares if he was accurately perceiving events?'

'That's the argument, Counselor. It just would have been nice if she actually had a gun. It would make the whole thing feel more real to the jury.' Chilly hit my arm. 'Oh, and I haven't told you the best part: Our guy told the cops he apologized to the victim. "Please don't die," "I'm so sorry," that kind of thing.'

It was my turn to moan. Seek forgiveness and you might spend your afterlife in heaven. But you'll spend your mortal life in a state penitentiary. Our state followed the modified ALI on insanity. The defendant had to show that he suffered a mental defect that prevented him from appreciating the criminality of his conduct. Basically, that means he has to prove he didn't know what he was doing was against the law.

It's a bit difficult to claim you didn't know you'd done something wrong when you immediately apologized to the victim after you shot her.

We reached the room. The guard unlocked the door and reminded us that we'd be monitored at all times with video but not audio.

The room was partitioned with thick glass. On our side, besides a dingy floor and peeling paint, there were two chairs and a shelf that ran along the partition. The smell of bleach hung in the air.

We sat in the chairs and waited for the arrival of Bryan's client.

'There's a wrinkle,' he said, his voice lowered.

I looked at him. 'What's the wrinkle?'

And then the door on the other side opened, and in walked Thomas Stoller.

4

Tom Stoller was led in by an unarmed guard. He moved awkwardly, as if the guard were helping him put one foot in front of the other.

'Hey, Tom,' said Bryan.

Stoller was wearing a gray pullover, blue jeans, and slippers on his feet. He had hair to his shoulders, an unshaven and scarred face. His eyes were unfocused and his expression was, well, void of expression.

'How's it going, Tom?'

Stoller rolled his head back and forth. He licked his lips incessantly, his tongue playing peekaboo.

'They had eggs this morning,' he said.

'Yeah? That's good. You look like you could use a good meal.'

He nodded at Bryan's comment and looked off in the distance.

'Tom, this is Jason Kolarich. Remember we talked about this lawyer I wanted you to meet?'

Stoller was on the young side, probably not even thirty, and the bright redness of his lips from his persistent licking made him look even younger. He was gaunt, but he had wide shoulders and looked like it wasn't so long ago that he was in pretty good fighting shape. If he was an Army Ranger, he must have been.

'Tom, you remember I told you that I was leaving the public defender's office? That I'd need someone to take the lead on your trial?'

Stoller's eyes dropped for a moment, like he was concentrating. After a time, he said, 'You told me you weren't gonna be my lawyer anymore.'

'That's right. But I wouldn't turn over the case unless I found a really good replace—'

'You were . . . wearing that tie with stripes. Red.'

Bryan paused for a moment. He seemed to be accustomed to disorganized conversations with his client.

'Was I? I don't—'

''Cause I said I liked it. And you said your mom bought it for you.' Stoller scratched his jaw.

Chilly sighed and put his hands on the table. 'Okay, Tom—'

'You think it's okay if I wear a tie at my trial?'

'Yes, Tom, but listen to me, okay? Can we talk about the case for a minute?'

The client's eyes wandered again. He didn't answer.

'I wanted you to meet Jason. He's a lawyer like me.'

Stoller was in full motion now, licking his lips and rubbing his hands together. This guy was suffering from more than post-traumatic stress disorder.

'It's hot in here,' he said. 'I take off my clothes at night to sleep, but they don't like it when I do that. I'm hot all the time.'

'Lieutenant Stoller,' I said with some force. I can make my voice count when necessary.

His eyes popped up to meet mine. He stopped fidgeting.

'I'll be your lawyer if you want. Is that okay with you? It's your choice, Lieutenant.'

He broke eye contact after a moment; it was too much for him. He went back to his habitual comforts, his tongue stabbing out and his hands in constant motion. 'I just want this to be over,' he said. 'Can you make it colder in here?'

I looked over at Bryan, who nodded toward the door.

'Think about it, Lieutenant,' I said. 'You don't have to decide now.'

'I'll come back soon, Tom,' said Chilly. He stood and motioned to the video camera in the corner of the room. A moment later the same guard came through a door to retrieve Stoller.

'I don't care who my lawyer is,' he said, as the guard touched his arm. 'I just want this over.'

We watched him walk out through his door. Then we left through ours.

'A *wrinkle*,' I said to Chilly out in the hallway. 'What's the diagnosis?'

'Schizophrenia. Disorganized schizophrenia. They think it was triggered by the PTSD.'

'Disorganized is right.'

'Aunt Deidre didn't mention any of this?'

'No,' I said. 'She said he was sick. She wanted me to see for myself, I think.'

Chilly put his hand on my shoulder. 'You surprised me in there, Counsel. I thought this was just a feel-out session. I didn't expect you to offer your services.'

So Tom Stoller suffered from post-traumatic stress disorder and disorganized schizophrenia. He admitted to apologizing to the victim after he shot her, so an insanity defense was an uphill climb. Self-defense was a sure loser; it would be hard to believe that a young woman would appear to be a threat to a homeless man.

This case was a d-o-g.

'He said he's hot in his room,' I told the guard at the front desk.

'This ain't the Four Seasons,' the male guard said, reading some document.

I stared at the guard, but he wasn't looking at me. Staring at someone doesn't impress your point if they don't know you're staring at them. I wanted him to know. So I slapped my hand down on the table in front of him. Now he knew. He looked up at me, momentarily startled and then offended. He was the guy with the gun, after all.

I said, 'This isn't one of your behavioral cases. This is a guy who's mentally ill. This is a guy who served two tours in Iraq and came back broken. He put his ass on the line for his country and paid a pretty steep price. Now whaddaya say we check on that temperature?'

'We'll check on it,' said the woman. 'Dial it down a notch or we'll put you in cuffs.'

We got into the elevator.

'So?' Chilly asked me as we rode down. 'Why'd you take the case?'

I shrugged. 'Aunt Deidre got to me.'

'Yeah, but you wanted this case, didn't you?' He wagged a finger at me. 'And I'll bet everything you learned up there made you want it even more. I mean, it looks like a dog, no?'

I shrugged. 'You said yourself. With you leaving, there's nobody available on your staff who could do it without wanting another continuance. And I'm not that busy.'

We reached the ground floor and the doors parted. 'Okay, well, this is great, Jason. Thanks. Tom's a good guy and he deserves the best.'

He'd have to settle for me. I had fifty days to be all that I could be for First Lieutenant Thomas David Stoller.

5

Judge Bertrand Nash is one of these larger-than-life legal figures in this city who seems like he's been on the bench since the dawn of mankind. Word is that he once served as the county attorney – the top local prosecutor – but I'm not sure anybody is alive today to actually attest to that fact. If you looked up the definition of 'judge' in the dictionary, you'd expect to see his picture: the broad, weathered face; the thick mane of silver hair; he even has a baritone voice belying his age.

He is imperialistic and stubborn and gregarious. He spares absolutely no one his wrath, which may come in the form of a stinging rebuke or withering sarcasm, always to the acclaim of the spectators in the courtroom, most of them lawyers well trained in the art of laughing uproariously at every tidbit of humor offered by the man in the robe.

He treats his courtroom like a treasured jewel. He tolerates no informality, no breach of etiquette circa 1890 or whenever he cut his teeth as a practitioner in the courts. You don't approach the witness without permission. You don't dare utter a sound after an objection is made until he's addressed it. You don't address the court unless you're on your feet, and only then if he invites you. You don't ask for an extension of time on a response to a motion unless your reason for doing so involves death or serious bodily harm. And you are never, ever late to court.

Cancer took a bite out of him two years back, but he's slowly rebounding, growing that wide face back into the loose-fitting skin around his eyes and jowls. The guy is probably going to live to a hundred, if he isn't already there.

This morning, Judge Nash looked over his glasses and down at me. 'You're a bit late to the game, Mr Kolarich,' he said.

'Yes, Your Honor. As Mr Childress indicated—'

'I can read, Mr Kolarich. Mr Childress is moving on to greener pastures, I see?'

'I'll be joining Gerry Salters's firm, yes, Judge,' said Bryan, standing next to me.

'Mr Salters is a fine attorney. A lousy golfer, but a fine attorney.'

Like a laugh track in an old sitcom, the courtroom burst out in amusement.

Judge Nash looked over at the prosecution team, led by a woman named Wendy Kotowski. 'Do the People have any objection?' he asked.

I moved to the side so that Wendy could approach the microphone. Judge Nash handled his courtroom more like the federal courts, where the lawyers spoke from a lectern into a microphone.

Wendy said, 'We would only object to a continuance at this stage, Your Honor.'

The judge looked alternatingly at me and Childress, then back to Wendy.

'I didn't ask you if you objected to a continuance, Ms.

39

Kotowksi. I asked you if you objected to substitution of counsel.'

Wendy should have known better. This wasn't her first time in front of this guy.

'We do not object, provided that it will not delay this proceeding,' she clarified.

'What about that, Mr Kolarich? Will you be seeking to move this trial date?'

'Your Honor—'

'It's a one-word answer, Mr Kolarich. Do you want to move this trial date? We're scheduled for trial six weeks from now.'

'Judge, my answer depends—'

'That's more than one word, Counsel. I said one word. And I gave you your choice of yes or no. These are basic words of the English language.'

The judge looked over our heads at the gallery. We were first up, which you never wanted to be in front of Judge Nash. He was playing to the crowd.

'Maybe,' I answered.

'*Maybe?*' The judge rotated his head. The courtroom went silent, waiting for the volcano to erupt.

'Maybe,' I said.

The judge's eyes narrowed. 'Well, how about this, Counsel: This case has received several continuances, and I don't want another. Mr Childress has undoubtedly prepared this case for trial, and the parties are prepared to try this matter on the scheduled date. If your entry into this matter requires a continuance, keeping in mind that Mr Childress is perfectly capable of staying on as lead counsel, I will have to think very hard about your motion. Now,' he said, leaning forward, 'does that change your answer?'

'No,' I said.

The judge blinked. He didn't like my response. A defendant's right to counsel of his choice is sacred in the law. It transcends virtually all other rights. It is not without limits, but a judge runs very close to that word he dreads the most – *reversal*, an appeals court overturning his ruling – when he tells a criminal defendant he can't have his chosen lawyer.

The judge had been trying to box me in, and I'd called his bluff.

After a moment, a twinkle appeared in his eye and one side of his mouth moved. Judge Nash loved the artistry of the courtroom. He respected someone who was willing to play the chess game.

'I'd like to hear from the defendant,' said the judge.

Tom Stoller was seated in the holding pen to our right, staring at the corner of the courtroom, seemingly oblivious to all of us. A guard had to walk over and get him to stand up. He was wearing a canary-yellow jumpsuit befitting an inmate in solitary lockup pending trial.

'Mr Stoller, do you understand that the purpose of the proceeding today is that Mr Kolarich is seeking to become your lawyer instead of Mr Childress?'

Tom wouldn't look at the judge and kept up with the same tics, the tongue popping in and out of his mouth and the wiggly fingers, even though his hands were cuffed in front of him. 'Okay,' he said.

'You understand that, sir?' The judge's tone had softened. He liked beating up on us lawyers, but an individual defendant got kinder, gentler treatment. Plus the courts of appeals in this state were big fans of the Sixth Amendment, and no judge wanted to be viewed as denying someone the counsel of their choice.

'Yeah.'

'And this is something you agree with, Mr Stoller? You want Mr Kolarich to be your lawyer?'

Tom's eyes bored into the floor. 'Okay.'

'Well, I want it to be more than "okay," Mr Stoller. This isn't my request. This is *your* request. You want to change lawyers? Because Mr Childress here is a fine, experienced attorney who has handled your case for some time. And the law firm that's going to hire him can wait for him, if you'd prefer to keep him.'

'Okay,' Tom said.

The judge sat back in his chair, exasperated. 'Mr Kolarich also is an excellent attorney. He's appeared before me many times, and I have no qualms about his abilities. But he's coming into this trial very late. I'm not sure your case is that complicated, but he's still late. And I want you to understand, I am going to be very reluctant to move your trial date. So before you choose, you need to understand that. Now,' he said, 'do you understand what I'm saying?'

'Yeah.'

I was pretty sure Tom was having a different conversation inside his head right now.

'Who do you want as your lawyer, Mr Stoller?'

Tom looked at both of us. Then he pointed at me. 'Him,' he said.

'You are indicating Mr Kolarich?'

'Okay.'

The judge took a deep breath. 'Even though he's only going to have about six weeks to get ready for this trial? I am very unlikely to move this trial date.'

'I don't wanna,' Tom mumbled.

'Say that again, Mr Stoller?'

'I don't wanna move it. I want this over.'

The judge studied Tom for a moment, concern arching his eyebrows.

'May I be heard, Judge?' I asked.

'You may.'

'My client doesn't want a continuance, Judge. But I very well may. My client is mentally ill, and I think he should take my advice. So far, he hasn't. I'm not prepared to move for a continuance at this time, but I may do so.'

'You'll carry a heavy burden,' Judge Nash warned me. He granted the motion allowing me in as lead counsel and called the next case.

I looked back at Deidre Maley – Aunt Deidre – who was watching her nephew walk out of the courtroom, tears brimming in her eyes. When he was gone, she turned her eyes to me.

Thank you, she mouthed to me, showing a bit more hope in that expression than I'd previously seen.

I sincerely hoped that it was warranted.

6

Don't ask me why I do the things I do.

The part about being at Vic's until closing – that part's easy. The vodka helps me sleep. And I don't like drinking alone, even if I don't know anyone else in the bar.

The part about the girl, though. That's the don't-ask-me-why part.

I watched her for three hours at the end of the bar. Came in alone about ten, maybe ten-thirty. Thin and dirty-blond and pretty. But not like a Barbie doll. Petite face, slightly crooked nose, but a look about her more than anything. Like she's seen a lot.

Character, they call it. That's what I like, a face with character. I don't trust Barbie dolls. I prefer women who don't realize how attractive they are.

Ten-thirty, we'll call it, she came in. Kept to herself. Looked my way once or twice, but that was due more to the fact that we were opposite bookends of the wraparound bar, so I was directly in her line of sight.

She wasn't the problem. The yuppies and middle-aged burn-outs in their work costumes, talking big and making their moves, they weren't the problem, either.

44

The two guys in the corner booth, they were the problem. Swarthy Italians with thick manes of hair and even thicker necks.

They sent over the first drink to the lady at about midnight, when the population had dwindled from thirty to single digits. A glass of pinot. She turned and smiled and looked away before she could see the two men in the corner, raising their glasses of scotch to her in response.

The second drink came at half past midnight, when there was a finger's worth remaining in her glass. She said something to the bartender that I couldn't make out. Maybe that's because I was on my fourth vodka, but the volume of her voice seemed to match her petite build.

The bartender personally delivered the next round of scotch to the goons in the corner, and his voice was a little stronger than the lady's.

'She said thanks, guys, but she's not in the mood for company tonight. She said no offense.'

'Ho!' cried one of the Italians, wounded.

The peppy adult-contemporary music had changed to soft, boozy jazz. Cologne still lingered in the bar. I was getting tired and figured I could sleep well now, but something told me to stick around.

Besides, I could use the exercise. In the week-plus since I'd entered Tom Stoller's case, I'd gone through all the evidence the prosecution had turned over and everything that Bryan Childress and the public defender had gathered on Tom's behalf. I'd spoken again, with little success, to Tom himself. I didn't get much out of him besides the meal plan for that day and the temperature of his room. I hadn't gone for a run for nine days straight, and our recent mid-October ice storm hadn't helped matters any. Either way, the lack of exercise had left my muscles itchy.

The woman fiddled with her smart phone for a moment. She didn't seem like the smart-phone type. Not the aggressive, corporate sort, this one, not if I was reading her correctly. But what did I know? All I could really figure was that she was nursing some sort of wound, and she could hold her liquor. Counting how she started plus the ones courtesy of the Sicilians, that made six wines, which would tip me more than four Stolis.

The seventh came courtesy of the goombahs again. I don't know why the bartender didn't run interference for the lady, but he served her up. That was it for the lady. She pushed it away and pushed herself off the bar stool.

She didn't even acknowledge the corner boys, which might have been a smart move. Save them some face. Italians are like that. Lost every war they ever started but still think they're the toughest guys going.

'Ho!' one of them called out.

I settled up and threw on my coat.

Both men stood up. They weren't tall, but they were wide. Weight lifters, the muscular shapes of their shoulders and arms notable, even through their winter coats.

'That's no kinda polite,' thug number one said. 'All those drinks and not even a hello?'

The woman, who had thrown on her long white coat and gathered her purse, turned to the man. 'Hello,' she said. 'And good-bye.'

'No, no, no.' They picked up their pace as she left the bar.

So did I. When I pushed through the door, the three of them

46

were standing outside. One of them, the beefier one, was holding the lady's arm by the biceps as she tried to yank it away.

'—your name,' he said. 'Least you can do is tell me your name. I bought you all those drinks.'

'I didn't *tell* you to buy me any drinks,' she protested. Her voice wasn't so weak, after all. She seemed like someone who could take care of herself under normal circumstances.

'Just let her go,' said the second goombah.

'I'll let her go when she tells me her name and thanks me for the drinks.'

All at once, everyone seemed to notice me. Maybe that's because I cleared my throat really loudly. The woman caught my eyes. Both goons turned and looked at me. Our breath lingered in the frozen air. This is where the protocol called for me to de-escalate the situation.

'I'm the one who should be upset,' I said. 'I sat there the whole night and you didn't buy me a single cocktail.'

'This don't concern you,' said the one holding the woman's arm.

'A wine spritzer, something,' I said. 'Throw me a bone.'

Goon number two squared off on me now. 'How 'bout I throw you my fist?'

'Clever. Good comeback. Listen, fellas,' I said.

Don't ask me why I do the things I do. As awkward as it was, my presence was eventually going to be enough to make them release this woman. And a smooth diplomat like me could have gotten these men on their way without fisticuffs. A lot of braggadocio and threats – face-saving – but not fisticuffs. The guy was too close for me to throw a punch, anyway.

47

So I threw him an elbow. I'm right-handed, but for some reason I can throw a stronger left elbow. Go figure. Like my brother's a righty but swings a golf club lefty.

The elbow caught him in the soft part of the skull at the temple. I can't take total credit for knocking him over, as there was a decent patch of ice on the sidewalk. Anyway, he lost his feet and fell hard on his left shoulder, and his head collided with the ice.

Maybe it's unresolved aggression. Reliving my childhood or something. My mother always told me I couldn't solve problems with my fists.

But like I said, it was an elbow.

'That had to hurt,' I said to the other goon. 'I'm Jason, by the way. What's your name?'

'Now, what'd you do *that* for?' said he. Sounded like a rhetorical question. He was playing it tough, but from my take, the wariness in his eyes, he didn't want to escalate the situation. More bark than bite. Once again, protocol dictated I give him an out to save face.

'You still haven't told me your name,' I answered. 'I'll get you started. It ends in a vowel.'

The other guy got to his knees. His shoulder was bothering him. He probably had a headache, too. This ice is a bitch.

'Not the last time we'll be seeing each other. Understand?' This from the first one, who released the woman and went over to help his buddy.

'I'm here most nights,' I said.

It took them some time to leave. Number two got to his feet, cussed a few times, and mumbled some aggressive thoughts. But they were leaving. The threat was over.

The woman could have been on the next block by now if

she'd wanted to be. But she stuck around. Watched them leave, waited until they were well out of sight.

Then she turned on me. 'I can fight my own battles, thank you.'

'You had that situation under control, did you?'

'Dealing with jerks has become my specialty.'

Present company excluded, I'm sure. She smoothed her hands over her white coat. Frozen breath trailed out of her mouth. Her heels looked vulnerable on the ice.

'Safe travels,' I said.

She walked away without another word.

7

I made it to my law firm the next morning by nine. I kept my own hours, and on days when I didn't have court in the morning, I often worked out in the morning and arrived late. But today I wanted to finish up my notes on the prosecution's evidence in *Stoller* and get them typed up for the beginnings of a crude database.

I pushed through the door bearing the stenciled lettering of TASKER & KOLARICH and smiled at our young receptionist, Marie, who majored in archaeology and minored in the avoidance of productive labor.

'Hold all my calls,' I said. 'I'm on with the Pentagon in ten minutes.'

She hardly looked up. There was definitely a document in front of her, so she must have been working very hard on it. 'You have a ten-thirty.'

Right. I'd forgotten. Some guy who called a couple days ago and was vague about why.

My partner, Shauna Tasker, had a young couple in her office. My guess, a real estate closing for a husband and wife. Shauna was good about diversifying. She preferred litigation but took on all sorts of transactional matters, too, from real estate sales to corporate formations to employment agreements to falling asleep from boredom.

'What up, old man?' said the third member of our team, Bradley John, as he passed the office with a cup of Starbucks in hand.

'Hey, Rock Star.'

I'm only seven years older than Bradley, for the record. He's been out of law school for three years and joined up with us three months ago. I like the kid but try not to let him know it.

I had court this afternoon on a state drug possession, and another appearance in federal court on a gun case. The drug possession was a guy running pills, including a couple that hit Schedule I and therefore could get the kid six years inside, even for a first offense. The gun charge was an arrest by city cops but was scooped up by the feds, who can kick the sentence on a gun crime into the stratosphere compared to state guidelines. I have a decent chance on that one, because the kid dumped the gun during the chase, but nobody saw the dumping.

All fine, they've paid up front and both will probably go to trial, which is the only thing that keeps my heart pumping these days. But my ten-thirty, from what I gathered between the lines over the phone yesterday, might be a homicide.

The guy's name was Lorenzo Fowler. He was of medium height, thick across the middle, with heavy bags under his bloodshot eyes. He was wearing a dress shirt open at the collar and a cheap wool sport coat. He wore too much cologne – any cologne is too much – and shook my hand too hard when he sat across the desk from me.

He smoothed his hands over the arms of the chair and tapped his feet. Nerves. That's not unusual in my line of work.

'So this is attorney-client, right?' he asked.

'Are you an officer of a publicly held corporation?'

He cocked his head. 'What? No.'

'Are you going to tell me about a crime you plan to commit in the future?'

'No. Nothing like that.'

'Then everything you tell me is confidential.'

He nodded.

'I've got some, uh, legal problems,' he said. That distinguished him from absolutely nobody who entered my office.

'Tell me about it,' I said.

'It's not important.'

Interesting response. 'You wanted to hire me, what, to cater your kid's birthday party?'

His eyes narrowed as he considered me. I don't think he thought I was funny.

'They're looking at me for something. Something maybe I did, maybe I didn't do.'

I nodded along. 'You need a lawyer.'

He shook his head. 'No, I got a lawyer for that other thing.'

I was done trying to coax him. He'd get there eventually.

'Anyway.' He took a nervous breath and looked around the office. 'If it ever gets hot, I'm thinking – see, I've got something I could trade. I know something about another case.'

I put my hands on the desk. Thus far, this conversation hadn't called for copious note-taking. 'Mr Fowler, if you're represented by counsel, talk to him. Or her. Not me.'

His head bobbed for a minute. He wet his lips and looked around the walls of my office, the cheap artwork and diplomas. Nerves flaring up again.

'This would be something I wouldn't talk to him about.'

Something wasn't connecting. Unless. There was only one way this made sense.

'Who do you work for?' I asked. 'The Morettis? The Capparellis?'

He cocked his head, then smiled. I wish he hadn't. He hadn't received stellar dental care over the years.

'Capparellis,' he said.

Right. Fowler worked for the Mob, the Outfit, whatever remained of the old crime syndicate since the feds have taken a massive bite out of their organization. Not what they once were in this city, but still formidable. Guns and girls and gambling, plus drugs and protection. Rico Capparelli was the top guy of the family and went down on a federal racketeering charge – RICO, ironically. His brother, Paul, is presumed to be running things these days, though I know that only from press accounts. When I was a prosecutor, I focused on street gangs, not the Mob.

Whatever that other thing was that Lorenzo Fowler maybe did, maybe didn't do, he was represented by the Mob's lawyer. A Mob lawyer's first loyalty is to the Mob, not the person he's defending. Fowler had something to trade, but he couldn't do it through his current attorney. Which meant he was going to sell out somebody higher up on the food chain.

'You want legal advice,' I said. 'You want an idea of what kind of deal you could cut.'

'That's it.'

Okay, that's it. 'What's the thing you maybe did, maybe didn't do?'

He hitched one shoulder. 'Guy who owns Knockers. The strip club over on Green? He mighta taken a beating last week. He might not survive it.'

'Sorry for his troubles.'

'Not if you knew the asshole, you wouldn't be.'

I thought it was possible that I could learn to like Lorenzo Fowler.

'Okay, so it's an aggravated battery, maybe an attempted murder,' I said. 'And one day soon it could be a murder.'

Fowler shuddered at the thought.

'What do you have to trade?' I asked.

That made him shudder all the more. His shoulders closed in. 'Maybe there was another murder. A whole different kinda thing. And maybe I know about it.'

'Maybe you know who did it?'

'Say I do.' His expression didn't betray his thoughts. It was probably a trait he'd developed over years of slinging bullshit.

'Okay, say you do. You can solve a murder for the police? That would be worth something. Probably not immunity, but something.'

He was listening very closely. 'I wouldn't walk?'

'From beating the strip club owner? I doubt it. An aggravated battery, if this guy lives? And murder if he doesn't? It would be a stretch. It all depends on the circumstances.'

'Even if the name I'm trading is Gin Rummy?'

I didn't catch the reference. I could see from the expectant look on his face that he thought I'd recognize the name.

'Who's Gin Rummy?' I asked.

A brief smile crossed over his mouth. 'There's five people in the world that know that. You wanna be the sixth?'

I shook my head. 'That's up to you. I take it Gin Rummy is somebody significant?'

'To the coppers? Oh, yeah. The federal types, too. And to Paulie, for sure.'

Paul Capparelli, presumably, the top guy in the crime family now.

'Paulie always says, "Gin Rummy's the man."' Fowler laughed to himself.

'Gin Rummy's a hit man?' I asked.

Fowler stared at me for a long time. Finally, he said, 'Close enough.'

'An assassin,' I said.

'Right.'

'You see a difference between "hit man" and "assassin"?' It wasn't a helpful question I was asking, but this guy was starting to annoy me.

Enough of the cat-and-mouse. 'Is that it, Lorenzo? Just Gin Rummy's real name? Or do you have proof that Gin Rummy committed this other murder?'

He showed those hideous teeth again. 'I got proof.'

'What kind of proof?'

'Proof,' he said.

I was a few years out of date in what little knowledge I possessed, while a prosecutor, about the Mob and its assorted characters. But it sounded like this Gin Rummy was significant. And that could mean special consideration.

'You're wondering about witness protection, that kind of thing?' I asked.

'Right. Problem is, this thing, this other murder I got information on, it's stateside. Not federal.'

The state doesn't really do witness protection programs per se, but the feds will cooperate with the locals if the payoff is good enough. I told Lorenzo all that.

'Oh, it'll be worth it,' he assured me.

I'd have to take his word for it for the time being. 'You're not ready to pull this trigger yet, I take it?'

'Right. But here's another question. If I wanna do this, can I go through you and keep it quiet and all?'

'I think we could work that out, Lorenzo.'

He leaned forward in his seat. His skin was flush. 'And this thing we're talking about, you won't repeat it.'

'It's a privileged conversation, if that's what you're asking.'

'I'm not *asking* nothin'.' His eyes went cold. He had quickly resorted to the bravado of the Mobbed-up thug. 'I'm tellin'. You won't repeat this. We understand each other?'

I have this thing where, whenever I get agitated, I try to count to ten before speaking. On occasion, I've been known to say inappropriate things, and it was a New Year's resolution of mine to get along better with people. But that was two New Years ago, and it didn't take.

I got all the way to four in my count. 'Don't threaten me, Lorenzo, and don't ever contact me again,' I said. I got out of my chair. 'And *now* we understand each other.'

Lorenzo Fowler turned right when he left his appointment and stood at the curb to hail a cab. He gave up after a few minutes and decided to walk through the commercial district.

From across the street, Peter Ramini stood with his hands in his coat pockets. Always, these days, with his hands in his pockets. He watched Fowler disappear down the block. No need to follow. It didn't matter where Lorenzo was going next. All that mattered was where he'd just been. Ramini carefully removed his cell phone and punched a speed-dial button. Within four minutes, a black town car pulled up at the curb.

He got in the backseat, next to another man named Donnie.

He stuffed his hands back in his pockets. He waited until the Lincoln moved into traffic before he spoke.

'That appointment Zo made with that lawyer,' he said. 'Name of Jason Kolarich. Well, he just had the meeting. Ask Paulie what he wants to do about Zo.'

Donnie was a big man with deep-set eyes and a midsection that looked like he was hiding an inner tube under his shirt. 'Anything else?' he asked.

Ramini thought for a moment. 'Yeah,' he said. 'Ask him what he wants to do about Jason Kolarich, too.'

8

Dr Sofian Baraniq leaned back in his chair in our conference room. He was on the young side for an expert – his CV put him at forty-four – but he looked distinguished, with the gray that peppered his hair and his thick beard. He looked foreign but had not the slightest trace of an accent, which suggested he was American-born. Either way was fine with me. I didn't know his ethnicity, but the origin of his name suggested India or someplace Middle or Far Eastern, and most juries tended to give weight to experts with such backgrounds. Call it reverse racism or favorable racism or ignorance, but it seemed to matter. Juries were less likely to find bias with, and more likely to respect, experts who were Asian or Indian. Like any lawyer, I would take whatever advantage I could grab.

'It's a complicated case,' said the doctor. His dress shirt was stained and his tie was drab. 'He suffers from PTSD and schizophrenia. The accompanying symptoms of either could have manifested themselves at the time of the shooting.'

I was ready for that. Bryan Childress had discussed it with me. Tom Stoller could have been experiencing a flashback to Iraq from PTSD or a hallucination brought on by his schizophrenia.

'Does that matter, for your purposes?' he asked me.

It was the right question to ask. 'I have to prove a mental defect,' I said. 'Both are recognized mental defects. In theory, I could say that it was either PTSD or schizophrenia, take your pick. But that doesn't look good to a jury.'

I really wanted PTSD. Because it gave me license to tell the jury all about Tom's harrowing experience as a combat veteran in Iraq. But I didn't want to say that to Dr Baraniq.

'I've far more experience testifying in the field of PTSD,' said the doctor. 'But the problem is that I can easily diagnose Tom as a disorganized schizophrenic. It doesn't matter what he and I talk about. I can observe him and I can read the observation and lab reports. The state is treating him with antipsychotic and mood-stabilizing medications, which is consistent with my diagnosis. So I feel comfortable with my diagnosis. But PTSD? I have to know what was happening to him at the time of the shooting. And I have to know what happened to him in Iraq. And for that, Tom has to talk to me. He has to talk about that night. He has to talk about Iraq. And he won't.'

I deflated. Childress had given me a sense of this problem, but hearing it firsthand from my expert was like a needle through my balloon.

'You can testify generally about PTSD,' I said.

'Of course I can.'

'I think we all could presume that combat in Iraq was less than enjoyable.'

'Especially for an Army Ranger, yes.'

'And the night in question – Tom won't talk about that, but you have his videotaped interrogation.'

'Yes. And I believe we saw an episode of PTSD there.'

59

I nodded, feeling a head of steam. 'And it's fair to presume that because he was looking at the victim's photograph, you could infer he suffered the same PTSD episode when he shot her?'

The doctor looked at me. So much for the steam.

'It's . . . certainly a real possibility that he did,' said the doctor. 'But can I say to a reasonable degree of scientific certainty that Tom was suffering from PTSD when he shot that woman?'

He didn't answer his own question. Which was an answer in itself.

Shauna Tasker cleared her throat. 'You said the state is medicating Tom as if he were a schizophrenic?'

'I said the medication is consistent with that diagnosis.' Dr Baraniq smiled, as if apologizing. 'I'm not trying to split hairs. They are using antipsychotic medication that would have the effect of controlling delusions and hallucinations. They are using mood-stabilizing drugs that essentially tranquilize him. This is how I would medicate a disorganized schizophrenic. But these drugs are used in other contexts as well. So they are not necessarily conceding that he is schizophrenic.'

Shauna nodded dutifully, thinking this over. In my experience, it could be frustrating to talk with medical experts, who qualified almost everything they said. You needed a flowchart to follow their reasoning. It was how most people felt after talking to a lawyer.

'Has Tom suffered delusions or hallucinations at Boyd?' I asked.

Dr Baraniq shrugged. 'Not that I know of. But that doesn't mean he hasn't. It means he might have but didn't share it with anybody. Disorganized schizophrenics are typically very withdrawn individuals. Tom could be sitting in a chair, listening to you talk, and inside his mind is racing in a hundred directions. Then, throw in the medications he's taken, which essentially suppress his emotions, and the symptoms probably wouldn't manifest.'

'Especially if no one's looking for them,' I said.

'Exactly.' Dr Baraniq pointed at me. 'The correctional system, especially at the pretrial stage, wants him to be sedate and compliant. They aren't interested in solving his problems.'

'They're not curing Tom,' said Shauna. 'They're just putting Band-Aids on the wounds.'

'Absolutely. Tom needs medication, but he also needs psychotherapy. He needs social and vocational training. He may need electroconvulsive therapy.' The doctor shook his head. 'He's not getting any of that in pretrial detention. Almost by definition, pretrial lockup is a temporary thing. The state doesn't commit resources to long-term treatments.'

It was a tragic truth. I'd heard it for years. But right now, I had more immediate concerns on my mind. 'Back to the shooting,' I said. 'Is it possible that, rather than an episode of PTSD, Tom suffered a hallucination spawned by his schizophrenia? And *that* was what caused him to shoot Kathy Rubinkowski?'

'In theory, yes,' said the doctor. 'But as I said, I can't sit here and say that Tom has suffered *any* hallucinations. Nor could I tell you the nature or magnitude of them.'

I sighed.

'And I also have to tell you,' said the doctor, 'that if I'm testifying in the abstract about a symptom that hasn't manifested itself to our knowledge, as opposed to testifying about the specifics of Tom's case, I would be forced to admit that most violence carried out by schizophrenics is violence to themselves. It's not like what you see on television.'

Shauna tapped her pen on her pad of paper. 'But PTSD,' she said. 'A violent outburst in the context of PTSD is normal.'

'It's common. More common than violence to another person caused by schizophrenia.'

I looked at Shauna. We were both trying to decide which route was the least shitty.

'Tom suffers from PTSD,' said the doctor. 'I know the state will contest that opinion, but I'm very comfortable with it. It's the best explanation for what happened. We have an instance of it caught on tape, in my opinion. And his behavior suggests it. No, he won't tell me about Iraq, which isn't helpful – but in one way, it is. His avoidance of it shows me his level of discomfort. And has he complained to you about the heat?'

I nodded. 'Yeah, he did.'

'The heat reminds him of Iraq. A sticky room in a prison hospital has nothing on the deserts of the Middle East, but it's a reminder. He avoids everything that reminds him of it.'

That made sense.

'And he has a general disinterest. He's fatalistic, in fact, wouldn't you agree?'

'He told me he didn't care who his lawyer was, he just wanted this to be over,' I said. 'I've met with him twice now, and the predominant themes are that he won't talk about anything related to the night in question or his military experience. And he won't agree to a continuance of his trial.'

Silence. Lawyers taking in information, processing it, trying to fit it within a legal argument that could save a client. An art, not a science. Facts go in different directions. They don't necessarily line up in one neat, tidy explanation.

'PTSD,' said Shauna.

I took a breath. 'PTSD,' I agreed.

'PTSD, but we need him to fill in some blanks for us,' said the doctor. 'Otherwise, I'm testifying in the abstract about that night.'

'Got it.' I breathed out. This was more complicated than I'd expected.

'Your trial date is still December the first?' the doctor asked me.

'Right. For now, at least.'

'Do you have an idea of when you'll call me to the stand?'

'Right now? Not really. December one is a Wednesday. We'll pick a jury, then the prosecution's case will go in over a few days. Less than a week, would be my guess. So I would shoot for . . . probably the eighth or ninth?'

'Okay, that would work. The seventh wouldn't.'

I sighed. 'Doctor, I need you to be flexible here.'

'This is why I raise this. The seventh I cannot do. I have a religious obligation.'

'Okay, well – what religion is that?'

'Islam,' he said.

'Oh.' That stopped me. 'That's . . . interesting.'

'Why is that . . . interesting? Because I'm testifying about a man who served in a military operation that occupies a predominantly Muslim country?'

Something like that, yeah. I'm not good with political correctness. It's not that I give a rat's ass about someone's religion. I'm not even sure how I feel about my own religion. But I'm not good with sensitivity.

Dr Baraniq laughed at my awkwardness. 'You can relax, Mr Kolarich. Muslims in America learn to have thick skin.'

They'd have to. I remembered when they built that gigantic mosque a couple of miles west of our downtown commercial district. It was billed as the largest mosque in the Midwest. They finished construction in the summer of 2001, only weeks before the September 11 attacks. And to make matters worse, the name of the mosque was Masjid al-Qadir, which bore an unfortunately close resemblance to the name of the terrorist group that attacked us. Back then, when I was a prosecutor and single, I passed the mosque every day on my way to work. There were protests and death threats and daily pickets for months. Finally, the mosque agreed to take down the big sign bearing its name, but they didn't change the name.

The way it ultimately turned out, the mosque was credited – by those willing to give it any credit – with cleaning up that neighborhood, which had been populated with gangs and drugs and plagued by drive-by shootings. They hold monthly food and clothing distributions and have done a decent job of assimilating.

All of this got me thinking. Dr Baraniq's religion could be helpful at trial. If I could somehow sneak in a mention of it during his testimony, it would only bolster his credibility. The last thing a Muslim psychiatrist could be accused of is a bias favoring an American soldier.

He wagged a finger at me. 'We need Tom to talk, Mr Kolarich. He won't talk to me. He won't talk to the state's doctor.' He stared at me.

'You think he'll talk to *me*?' I asked.

'He'd better.' Dr Baraniq lifted his coat off the back of his chair. 'Or we have no chance of winning this case.'

9

'The key to this trial is sympathy,' I told the conference room. 'Tom Stoller gave everything for his country. It destroyed him. It gave him PTSD, which triggered his schizophrenia. Things went south from there. A tragedy happened. But Tom Stoller is a victim every bit as much as Kathy Rubinkowski.'

'Well, maybe not every bit as much.' This from Joel Lightner, my private detective. His tie was pulled down and his feet were on the table. Joel joins me occasionally for drinks, by which I mean about three times a week. He is a two-time loser at marriage, a rabid skirt-chaser, and a happy drinker.

'What happened to insanity?' Bradley John, our young pup, asked. Unlike Joel, young Bradley was hoping to learn a thing or two.

'Insanity is our legal theory,' I said. 'We argue it with everything we have. But it's a tool. We use it to give the jury his background. To sympathize. So they won't want to put one of our nation's brave soldiers in the penitentiary for life. We have to prove insanity by clear and convincing evidence, and I'm not sure I could even get a preponderance. Tom knew right from wrong. He told the victim he was sorry. And he stole her purse, phone, and necklace afterward. So I'm under no illusion

65

that we can make that case. What I do believe is that in the process of attempting to make our case, we put the jury in the frame of mind that they want to acquit.'

'But he was flashing back to Iraq, right?'

Lightner turned his head lazily – read: condescendingly – toward young Bradley. 'You think he apologized to the Al Qaeda guerrillas when he shot them?'

'Maybe he did.' Shauna was smartly dressed today for court. Her blond hair, which she'd grown out some, curled around the curves of her face. And she had the naughty-librarian black horn-rimmed glasses that made Joel squirm. 'Seriously,' she said. 'Maybe he felt bad about killing people. What's odd about that? I mean, isn't that why war screws people up so much?'

I raised my hands. 'That's all fine, people. I agree. We use that. We embrace what he told the police in the interview. But at the end of the day, the jury's looking at an instruction that says that we have to prove that his mental defect prevented him from appreciating that what he did was a crime. We have to make them disregard the law and walk him because they view him as a victim.'

I paced the room for a while. I would have preferred to have a football in my hand, but I'd misplaced it in my office. 'Joel,' I said. 'I need fresh interviews on everybody who served with Tom overseas. I need someone to testify about what kinds of things happened over there. And anything specific to Tom. If Tom won't tell us, maybe they will. Hopefully – and I can't believe I'm saying this – hopefully he killed some people over there.'

'And I assume the home run would be if he killed a woman in her twenties while she pulled a gun on him after getting out of her car?'

'Yeah, Joel, that'd be super.' It was a reminder of what a stretch this case would be. PTSD flashbacks, according to Dr Baraniq, were typically spurred by circumstances similar to the traumatic event in your past. It was hard to see how encountering a petite, well-dressed young woman could have flashed Tom Stoller back to Iraq. But it was all we had.

'Bradley,' I went on. 'Hit the books. I want every court decision ever published on PTSD. The PD's office did some research, but I want you to double-check it. I want to know what factors can vitiate the defense, the use of hypotheticals versus actual firsthand accounts, anything. I want examples where the defendant refused to talk about the event but still managed to pull this off. Keep in mind some jurisdictions follow M'Naughten or irresistible impulse, not the modified ALI. Preferably, I want something on point in a jurisdiction following ALI like us. But I'm not greedy.'

'Got it. Got it.' Bradley seemed pumped for this case.

'Shauna,' I said. 'Take a look at the forensics and the blood spatter and the medical examiner reports. We don't have to accept that the shooting happened exactly the way the prosecution claims. If we need to hire that guy – what's his name, Peters? – then let's talk and we can do it.'

'And when you're done, Shauna,' said Joel, 'come over to my place. We'll open a bottle of wine and talk about it.'

Shauna rolled her eyes and nodded at me. 'What's your assignment?'

'Me?' I stretched my arms. 'I'm going to get Tom Stoller to talk to me,' I said.

10

Lorenzo Fowler was a married man, so when he visited Sasha, he had to go to her place. It was more accurately described as *his* place, as he bought the condo and paid the utilities and assessment. It was one of the ritzier places on the blossoming near-west side of the city. Sasha could have had her pick of spots, but she fancied herself an artist and liked the feel of this part of the city.

Fowler parked his car down the street, got out, and pulled up his coat collar. It was dark and cold, and before he trudged forward, he took only a quick look about him for immediate threats.

He didn't see any.

He didn't see Peter Ramini, sitting in a different car down the street, his hands stuffed into his coat pockets.

It was nine-forty when he arrived at Sasha's condo. Anyone trying to predict Lorenzo's movements would estimate that he would spend about four hours at her place before returning home. He always returned home. He never spent the night at Sasha's.

Just over four hours later, Lorenzo emerged from the elevator in the building's lobby. He nodded to the man at the front desk with no trace of embarrassment or guilt. He always felt better after an evening with Sasha. For a Ukrainian gal, she could make a plate of sausage and peppers. And in the bedroom, she performed feats of gymnastic agility that could earn her a gold medal in the Olympics. He was a bit lightheaded after a half-bottle of wine and the food and the sex. It was a welcome break.

The early-morning air was a harsh return to reality. Things had been tough for Lorenzo of late. That strip club owner Lorenzo had disciplined with an aluminum baseball bat had died two days ago. The police had come looking for Lorenzo today at the lumberyard. They'd be back again tomorrow. Paulie would be nervous.

Paulie was always nervous these days. It wasn't like how it used to be. The feds had always been around, but the surveillance was so good these days that it was impossible to know where you were safe. Nowadays, Paulie wouldn't communicate with anybody other than a whisper directly into his ear.

So what would Paulie think of the cops wanting to talk to Lorenzo about a dead strip club owner?

Lorenzo shuddered. He thought about his conversation the other day with that lawyer, Kolarich. He seemed like the sort that wouldn't shy away from helping him. Some lawyers, they heard the Mob was involved, they'd back off. Kolarich seemed like the kind of guy who would get off on it. And the kid had brass; Lorenzo hadn't met that many people who, knowing that Lorenzo worked for the Capparellis, told him to fuck off. Despite what he'd said, Kolarich would be there for him, he figured, if he needed him.

Trading the identity of Gin Rummy could do it, he felt certain. The feds would jump in and walk him on the strip club owner's death and probably anything else for which they charged Lorenzo. You take away Gin Rummy, you take away Paulie's best muscle. You take away one of the few people Paulie still trusted. It was valuable information. Lorenzo would be able to write his own ticket. Someplace warm, that much was for sure. An apartment for Sasha, too, if she'd come. Would she?

And then something felt wrong, and all at once Lorenzo felt exposed. Nothing he could put his finger on, but it wasn't an accident he'd managed to stay alive for fifty-two years, thirty-four of them with the Capparellis.

He slowed his pace and removed his Beretta from the back of his pants so that he was holding it at his side. The streets were empty. The nearest bars were two blocks away. Other than a couple on the corner who appeared to be engrossed in each other, Lorenzo felt reasonably sure he was alone.

Still, he widened his approach to his parked car, so that he could see into the backseat before he got too close. Okay, the backseat was empty, good enough. As he kept walking around his car, he saw something on the ground, a single flower and a note. It stopped his movement for just a moment, while he focused on the ground behind his automobile.

In that brief window of time, a bullet threaded his windpipe and sent him staggering backward against the chained-up door of a used bookstore. He tried to hold himself up, tried to raise his gun, but the signals weren't reaching their intended targets.

A second bullet shattered Lorenzo's left kneecap. A third did the same to his right.

Lorenzo crumpled into a heap at the door of the used bookstore.

He tried to scream, but no sound came except something warm and sticky through the hole in his throat.

You had your chance, he told himself, as the lights went out.

11

I was back at Vic's, a bar I adopted as my preferred choice when I couldn't find drinking buddies. You hit your mid-thirties and most of your friends have wives and kids, like I once did, and while five martinis at a fine local establishment on a Monday night might sound appealing, they usually have higher priorities. I did, too, once upon a time.

I took my usual seat, on one end of the wraparound bar, drunker than usual, because I'd forgotten to eat anything for dinner. The place had filtered out by now and it reminded me of that time a few days ago when I'd made the acquaintance of those two idiots bothering that lady.

I thought about Tom Stoller and my three failed attempts, thus far, to get him to open up to me. Shauna was working with our expert, Dr Baraniq, but whichever way you cut it, we had holes in our defense. I'd reconciled myself to that. In the end, it was like I'd said to my team – if we did our job, they wouldn't let the technicalities of an insanity argument get in their way. Either the jury would want to acquit him or they wouldn't.

I was tired. Today was the deadline in the Stoller case for the defense and prosecution to share any remaining discovery

– information to be used at trial – and witness lists. No matter how much you planned, it was always a rush at the end to get it done. And with Judge Nash, you didn't want to omit anything. If it wasn't turned over in a timely manner, it wouldn't be admitted at a trial where he presided.

I raised my empty glass for a fifth Stoli. I wasn't an alcoholic – which, of course, is what every alcoholic says. But I was different (a lot of them say that, too). I wasn't trying to hide from anything or blur reality. I was coping with reality pretty decently these days, thank you very little. I still missed my wife and daughter so desperately that it sucked oxygen from my lungs, but I'd learned how to coexist with it.

No, I drank so I could fall asleep at night. I'd lost that ability to let my mind settle into that calm transfer from wakefulness to dreams. Once I'm down, I stay down, but I can't find that equilibrium to get me there.

The bartender, not the normal guy, shoved a glass of wine in front of me filled with ice cubes and slices of lemon and lime. I stared at it for a long time.

'The fuck is that?' I asked.

'A wine spritzer. From the lady.'

I turned back to the far corner of the bar. The lady from the other night, again with the white coat, was sitting in a booth. Somehow I'd missed her coming in.

She walked over to me. I'd fancied her a bit from afar the other night. 'Intrigued' was probably a better word. Up close now, she looked pretty much the same, the petite build and girlish features, but now with the details filled in. A crooked mouth, cautious eyes, nice pale skin with a dusting of freckles high on her cheeks. She smelled pretty damn good, too.

'That cocktail you wanted,' she said.

'Great.'

She still hadn't taken a seat. She seemed to be debating with herself.

'You want to thank me but you don't know how,' I said. 'You're a lady who can take care of herself and you don't appreciate men acting like they're rescuing the damsel in distress.'

She listened to me with a trace of amusement.

'On the other hand,' I went on, 'those two big goombahs were a bit of trouble for you. Maybe you'd underestimated them. So you were relieved when I came out and offered some assistance. You appreciated and resented the gesture at the same time.'

She worked her mouth a bit as she watched me. Waiting for me to go on, but at the moment I was spending some time on that mouth of hers and letting my imagination move to places dark and steamy. I was in what you'd call a dry spell, you see. I made Mohandas Gandhi look like Hugh Hefner.

'How'm I doing so far?' I asked.

'In your mind?'

'We can start there, sure.'

'You're doing great,' she said. 'You're charming and insightful and oh-so-confident.'

'Don't forget I rescued you, too.'

'How could I?'

I gestured to the chair. 'Have a drink with me.'

She paused, the mirth disappearing from her eyes. 'I did want to thank you.'

'There'll be plenty of time to do that between sips. I'll even let you buy, if that'll make you feel better about it.'

'But you're making it hard. To thank you.'

'I'm rough around the edges to mask my sensitive, vulnerable side.'

'You're also married,' she said. She nodded in the direction of my left hand resting on the bar. 'No ring tonight, though.'

She was right, you could still see the pale outline on my ring finger. I finally took the ring off a few months ago, but I guess the impression hadn't yet worn off.

'Then I guess you better be on your way,' I said.

The bartender put down a Stoli next to the wineglass. I turned away from the lady and went to work on the drink. A few minutes passed and she didn't move.

'It was nice of you to help me the other night,' she finally said.

'Think nothing of it.'

'I'm not used to people trying to help me.'

I didn't answer. I drained the Stoli and felt the effect immediately.

'You're not married, are you? I was wrong about that.'

I put down my glass. 'I'm not married anymore.'

'You have a pen?'

Did I have a pen? No, I didn't. But the bartender did, along with another glass of Stoli for me.

She handed me a slip of paper. It had the word 'Tori' and a phone number.

'If you want to call me sometime,' she said.

'Good to know,' I said, but Tori was already headed for the door.

12

The room they let us use at the Boyd Center reminded me of a large playroom for children. There were stations for board games and a sitting area around a television and a desk with chairs. The walls were painted with that same orange color, and the carpeting on the floor was thick, if a little dingy. Not the traditional setting for an attorney-client visit, but budgets were tight, and this was also the room for family visits.

Tom Stoller was in limbo. He needed serious psychological assistance from the state, but he wasn't getting it, because this was the same 'state' that appeared in the caption *State v. Thomas Stoller*, the same 'state' that wanted to put Tom in prison for life, the same 'state' that didn't want to concede that Tom suffered a mental defect at the time of the shooting – or at all, for that matter.

I sat across the room and observed Tom with Shauna. They weren't discussing the case. They weren't probing his troubled mind. They were playing checkers. I'd brought Shauna along today because she was good with people, far more adept than I at establishing bonds and adjusting to the nuances of inter-personal relationships.

Sitting across from Shauna, a checkerboard between them,

Tom showed the same tremors I'd seen every time I visited. His tongue was peeking in and out of his mouth. His eyes were blinking rapidly. His fingers wiggled constantly. Side effects, Dr Baraniq had said, of the antipsychotic medication. Tom appeared to be contemplating his next move in the board game, but for all I knew he was in a faraway place, envisioning himself as Sir Lancelot to Shauna's Guinevere.

You'd think that his mere presence at Boyd was an acknowledgment of Tom's mental illness, but it wasn't. The state wasn't stupid. Boyd housed all kinds of people who presented problems to jailhouses, ranging from patients with communicable diseases, such as HIV, to notorious individuals deserving of segregation, such as gang leaders or police officers, to those with your basic 'behavioral' problems.

Tom Stoller fell into the last category. He wasn't mentally ill. He was a 'behavioral' problem. Yeah. Sure. Once they convicted him, he'd go to a penitentiary and receive somewhat decent psychological services. But for now, especially with an insanity defense looming, the state wouldn't treat him as anything but a problem inmate who could be kept compliant if they drugged him up.

Tom double-jumped two of Shauna's checkers. 'Ooh, I was hoping you wouldn't do that,' she groaned.

Tom looked up at her and stared, expressionless, in the inappropriate way of a child. Even when Shauna smiled and broke eye contact, as would any adult, he held his stare on her.

Shauna dutifully jumped one of Tom's checkers. 'Take *that*,' she said.

'I had girlfriends,' Tom said. I almost jumped out of my chair. It was the first time Tom had ever volunteered anything personal.

'I'll *bet* you did.' Shauna winked at him. Bless her heart, she likewise recognized the significance of the moment but played the whole thing casually.

Tom stared back down at the checkerboard, and Shauna snuck a peek in my direction. Before too much time had passed, and the moment was entirely lost, she said, 'Was there one in particular? Usually there's one special one.'

'Jenny. Jenny, but she didn't want to . . .' Tom dropped his head and started mumbling.

Shauna waited for a moment. 'She didn't want—'

'I can't think of the name of the movie.' Tom shook his head harshly, like he was removing cobwebs. 'In Somalia. She didn't like it.'

'The mov—'

'It made her sad. She didn't like . . . suffering.'

I knew what he meant. It was a graphically violent film about the American Special Forces operation in Mogadishu that went south and got a bunch of our elite soldiers killed.

'*Black Hawk Down,*' I said, from across the room.

Tom whipped his head around at me. With one violent thrust, he jumped up and backhanded the checkerboard clear across the room. Instinctively, Shauna pushed her chair backward, and I got to my feet. I raised my hand toward the security camera to indicate we didn't want or need intervention by the Corrections guards.

Tom stood, frozen, his gaze lost somewhere in a memory. He slowly turned and walked over to the corner, where he took a seat and sat silently, stoic except for the familiar tremors. Shauna and I looked at each other, speechless.

'She didn't want me to fight,' he finally whispered.

13

The Starboard Room in the city's Maritime Club was at full capacity over lunch, thirty tables with eight guests at each, as the U.S. Secretary of Labor droned on about reform of collective-bargaining laws and diverse workplaces in the 'New America.'

New America is right, thought Randall Manning, president, CEO, and sole shareholder of Global Harvest International, a privately held company located eighty miles south of the city. Normally he wouldn't give the time of day to a speech on the topic of diversity, of all things, but he needed to be in town on other business and welcomed the excuse. And he couldn't deny enjoying the prestige of the invitation, a seat among the elite. He could allow himself that much; he hadn't experienced a great deal of enjoyment in his life of late.

As the labor secretary continued through his speech, Manning leaned over to the man sitting next to him, his lawyer, Bruce McCabe. 'Where,' he said in a controlled whisper, 'is Stanley?'

Stanley Keane, he meant, the owner of SK Tool and Supply, located in the small downstate town of Weston.

'Don't see him,' said McCabe. McCabe, a principal at the law firm of Dembrow, Lane, and McCabe, was outside counsel to Global Harvest.

Manning put his hand on the back of McCabe's chair and spoke into his ear. 'Stanley needs to be here,' he said. 'He needs to be seen here.'

'He understands that.'

'Does he, Bruce? It was your job to make sure he understood.'

'He'll show up,' McCabe insisted.

He never did. When the speech and luncheon ended, Randall Manning mingled with other business executives. He shook their hands and listened to their stories and told some of his own. He laughed at their jokes and told some of his own. He waited in line for a photograph with the labor secretary and swallowed his loathing and forced a smile on his face for the photographer.

When it was over, Manning had his driver take him to the Gold Coast Athletic Club, where he met the president of a pharmaceutical company – one of Global Harvest's biggest clients – for a game of squash. At five o'clock, he met a local alderman and a state senator for drinks to discuss a tax-incentive proposal for a freight yard that Global Harvest was considering building inside the city limits. At seven o'clock, he had a steak at one of the city's best joints, enjoying a view of the river in the process.

At nine o'clock, he returned to his hotel. He took the elevator up to his room, changed his overcoat from a charcoal one to a beige one, donned a fedora hat, and took the elevator back down to the fourth floor, a transitional floor that allowed him to access a different bank of elevators that, in turn, allowed him to exit the hotel onto a cross street, different from the one he'd taken to enter the hotel. He never broke stride into a waiting town car and settled in for the drive.

They drove to a town called Overton Ridge, several miles outside the city limits to the south and west. The car passed the Good Shepherd Methodist Church on the corner of Wadsworth and Pickens, bearing a small magnetic sign that read: WHOSOEVER SHALL CALL UPON THE NAME OF THE LORD SHALL BE SAVED.

The car stopped in an alley behind the church, where two large, armed men stood by the back door. They showed Randall Manning down a set of stairs to the basement, then to a back room.

When that door opened, six men stood at once. They included Manning's lawyer, Bruce McCabe. They included Stanley Keane of SK Tool and Supply, who hadn't made it to the luncheon today.

On Manning's motion, the six men took their seats at a long rectangular table. At one end, where a seat remained vacant for Manning, was a .38 revolver. Manning picked it up and pointed it at the man sitting immediately to his right.

'Are you prepared to give your life for the cause?' he asked.

'I am,' said the man, young and powerful like a football player in his prime, with a severe haircut and militant eyes. 'I understand that the cause is greater than the individual. I understand that sacrificing this life for the cause will open up a new and richer life in the hereafter. I understand that—'

'Good.' Manning lowered the weapon to his side and walked around the table to Stanley Keane's spot. 'And you, Stanley?'

Stanley shrunk amid the scrutiny. 'I am,' he said. 'I understand that the cause is—'

'Enough,' said Manning. He positioned the revolver against

Stanley's left ear. 'Did we not agree that it was necessary for you to attend the luncheon today?'

'We did, sir.'

'But you did not.'

'It was a scheduling issue, sir—'

'A scheduling issue? We have to cover our tracks, Brother Stanley, if you hadn't noticed. If anyone is wondering why I'm here in the city today, I can point to the lunch with the labor secretary, I can point to a meeting I had with elected officials, I can point to a game of squash with a pharmaceutical company president who is a valued client. You, Stanley? What can you show?'

Manning cocked the weapon, and Stanley broke into a series of apologies. 'I got a late start and I wouldn't have made more than the last few minutes, sir, and by then—'

'Stanley,' Manning said with an icy calm. 'We have a unique opportunity here, do we not?'

'We do, sir. We have an opportunity to return this—'

'And this opportunity is made particularly unique by the standing of the members of our Circle, true?'

'Yes, sir.' Sweat trickled down Stanley's cheek.

'And keeping up appearances is paramount, yes?'

'Paramount, sir.'

'If we travel to a meeting of the Circle, we do so at the risk of calling attention to ourselves, do we not?'

'Yes—'

'And as I'm standing here at this moment, Brother Stanley, I am aware of no particular cover story for why you are here. If anyone were to inquire. *Because you missed the luncheon.*'

'I apologize, sir. I have no excuse.'

82

Manning braced himself, and thus Stanley did as well. The entire room did.

Then Manning uncocked his weapon and held it at his side. 'We are close, brothers. The closer we get to our goal, the higher the risks, the graver the danger.' He moved around the table to his rightful place at the head. 'We have survived many challenges. We are so close now. Now is not the time to let down. Now is the time to recommit.

'Brothers, have I made myself clear?'

'Yes, sir,' they replied in unison.

'Very good.' Manning took a seat and bowed his head. 'Now, we pray.'

14

'So he shoots Kathy Rubinkowski, he walks over to her dead body and he steals her purse, cell phone, and necklace.' Shauna tucked a strand of her hair behind her ear. 'How is that consistent with PTSD? He's reliving a moment in Iraq, he shoots her, and then he *robs* her?'

Lying flat on the couch in the corner of my office, I threw my football up in the air and caught it coming back at my face. 'I saw a movie once where a soldier stole a cigar out of the pocket of the dead enemy soldier. The spoils of war, I guess.'

'I guess. It takes a little sympathy out of your sympathy argument, though.'

'Don't forget, Tom apologized to her.'

'Yeah, that's great. "Sorry I shot you, really I am, but as long as I'm here, no sense in letting all that money in your purse go to waste." That's a real crowd-pleaser, kid.'

She winked at me. Shauna was my best friend. She was my lifeline. It wasn't so long ago that she pulled my head out of my ass and forced me to share office space with her. I was on track to throw my legal career into the dumpster after I lost my wife and daughter. I'll always wonder what I would have done for a living. Maybe an astronaut. The rodeo circuit would have been cool. Though I've never ridden a horse, much less a bronco.

I continued my one-man game of toss. 'It's worse than that. It's not even impulsive. Tom didn't have any blood on him. Right? That's what the police report said. And you saw that pool of blood around the victim's body.'

Shauna leafed through the photos of the crime scene. 'You're right. He took her purse, her cell phone, and yanked the chain off her neck without getting any blood on himself. That would have taken some work.'

'I know. So it makes our sell tougher. We convey this image of a soldier in the heat of battle, and then he's carefully helping himself to her possessions.'

'Maybe soldiers really *do* rob their enemies,' she said. 'We need to find somebody who'll testify to that.'

'Already on my list. Lightner's working the witnesses right now. Those that aren't still in Iraq.'

'Whoa. A Mob shooting,' Shauna said.

'Huh?' I looked over at her. She was fondling the mouse to my computer, checking the Internet. Then a light went on and I sat up, popping to attention. 'Who was it?' I asked.

She shrugged. 'Let me pull it up.' Her eyes moved along the computer screen. 'Lorenzo Fowler? Hey, wasn't he—'

'Shit.' I jumped off my couch and read over Shauna's shoulder. Lorenzo Fowler, age fifty-two, reputed lieutenant in the Capparelli crime family, found dead on the 2700 block of West Arondale. The article was complete with a photograph of poor Lorenzo slumped against a glass door that read TATTERED COVER NEW & USED BOOKS.

'A bullet through the throat and one through each kneecap,' Shauna moaned. 'Ouch.'

I revisited our meeting. Lorenzo was in the soup, or so he thought, for the beating of a strip club owner. He wanted to make a trade with the prosecutors, if it ever came to that – the name of the Capparellis' assassin of choice.

'Do you have an alibi for last night?' Shauna asked me.

'Wow. Lorenzo Fowler.'

'Seriously, Jason. Did he tell you anything that would be helpful to the police?'

'Sure,' I said. 'I'll just run over there and give a full interview with the police and breach the attorney-client privilege. While I'm at it, I'll stop by the state supreme court's chambers and turn in my law license.'

Shauna turned back to look at me. 'I'm your law partner, pal. The privilege holds. Did he give you anything?'

Poor Lorenzo. Sounds like his fear was well-founded.

'He gave me Gin Rummy,' I said. 'The name of a Mob hit man. Actually, he didn't like that term. He preferred "assassin."'

I read through the article again. Gunshots to the throat and knee-caps. The throat was the only one they needed. The shots to the kneecaps would have been gratuitous. It was punitive.

A message, delivered along with the kill.

15

I met Tori outside Deere Hall, the primary building in the city campus of St. Margaret's College. She was wearing the same long white coat, a gray wool cap, and a backpack slung over her shoulder. She appeared amid a flood of students through the Gothic arched doorway, caught my eye, and bounded down the stairs. She didn't smile – I hadn't yet seen her smile – but it wasn't an unpleasant expression, either. Guarded, in a word.

Daylight was evaporating, and it was growing cold as we walked down the street. There were still patches of ice mixed with dirty slush on the walk.

'What do you study?' I asked.

She looked at me. 'Math.'

'What do you do with a math degree?'

'You teach. At least, I will.'

'What age?'

'Oh, probably young kids,' she said.

'You like kids?'

She didn't answer. It was a dumb question. Why would she want to teach kids if she didn't like them?

'You have any kids of your own?' I tried.

'No kids.'

I took a breath. It hit me that there could be a return volley, the same question put back to me. But she didn't ask. She just looked me over for a moment as we walked.

'What do you do?' she asked.

'I'm a lawyer.'

'What kind?'

'I represent criminals. Sorry, people accused of crimes.'

'Is that hard?'

'It can be. The prosecution has a lot more resources at its disposal. It's usually a lopsided fight.'

She was quiet for a moment. 'That's not what I meant.'

'I know. You meant does it bother my conscience?'

She turned to me again. 'You like to tell people what they're thinking, I've noticed. That's a very male thing. Very alpha male.'

'Is it? Am I asserting control?'

'Something like that, yes.'

'Maybe you should be majoring in psychology, Tori.'

'I was thinking the same thing about you.'

'Experience is the best psychoanalysis,' I said.

'Who said that?'

'I just did. I'm the only one walking next to you.'

'That's not what I m—'

'I know. You meant who was I quoting?'

She shook her head in bemusement. She had just passed a test. The test was whether she could tolerate my bullshit. For at least a couple minutes, apparently, she could.

It was the time of year when the weather couldn't make up its mind, and people took advantage of any halfway warm and clear day to get out and enjoy themselves before the gloomy blanket of winter took over. Parents were hustling their children across busy streets. Students were loitering like the aimless souls they were, laughing and smoking and chatting into their cell phones. I felt like an outsider, an observer, in every way. I didn't have anyone to shop for, and I had little in common with young people, with their egocentric cluelessness about the world.

But I wished I did. I wished for all of that. Even the part about being clueless. Sometimes I wished I didn't understand people.

'You like being a lawyer?' Tori asked me.

A fair question. Should be an easy answer.

'He pauses,' she noted.

'I like competition,' I said. 'I liked prosecuting criminals more than defending them. But defending them is harder. More of a challenge. I like the challenge.'

She thought about that for a moment. 'It's not about helping people?'

'That can be a fringe benefit.'

We stopped at an intersection, waited for the light. She probed me with those big brown eyes. Her dishwater-blond hair was curling out of her cap. Cute, which didn't really fit her. She was older than most college kids, probably late twenties, which meant there was a story there. Usually that story's not a happy one.

'Have you ever defended a killer?' she asked.

'I've handled some murders, yeah.'

'Were they guilty?'

I nodded. 'Most of the people I represent are guilty, Tori.'

The light changed. Everyone else entered the crosswalk. Tori didn't move. She turned and looked up at me. This would be the moment in a movie where she kissed me. Or told me what a swell guy she thought I was. Or told me to fuck off.

'Who sits at a bar all night drinking alone?' she asked.

'You,' I said.

'I did that once. You did it at least twice, and you and the bartender seemed to know each other pretty well.'

'I don't sleep well. The vodka helps.'

'You don't have to go to a bar to drink vodka.'

'But if I drank at home, it would feel pathetic,' I said.

She raised her eyebrows at me.

'More pathetic,' I clarified.

Her eyes narrowed to a squint. She was studying me, psycho-analyzing me. I'm not a big fan of that kind of thing, generally speaking, but for some reason it didn't bother me with her.

She let out a sigh. 'I think you're an interesting guy,' she said. 'I think it would be fun to hang out with you. But I'm not looking for romance. That's just not happening with me right now.'

'What a coincidence. It hasn't been happening with me, either.'

She threw me a look. 'Is that your macho way of saying you agree to my terms? Because I'd understand if you didn't.'

'I agree to your terms, Tori. On one condition.'

She raised her eyebrows again. 'Let's hear it.'

'You entertain the possibility down the road – just the possibility – of a hand job.'

For the first time, Tori let out a real, honest laugh.

16

'Tom,' I said. 'Tom, we have to talk about this.'

I'd spent the last ninety minutes with my client, trying in vain to get him to consider the list of witnesses we planned to call at trial. Thus far, I had obtained from him an in-depth recitation of the entire week of meals served by the Department of Corrections, including last night's disappointing chili – disappointing, in his eyes, because it had onions, but probably disappointing in several other respects, too – and blow-by-blow descriptions of two *Seinfeld* episodes he'd watched.

Tom was wearing nothing but a T-shirt on top in a room that was set in the mid-sixties at best. It reminded me of what our shrink, Dr Baraniq, had said, that Tom avoided any sensation of heat because it reminded him of the war.

'I don't care about witnesses,' he said, motioning to my file. 'I just want this over.'

Dr Baraniq had also complained to me yesterday that he'd spent an entire day with Tom without gaining any insight whatsoever. My expert was going to be left with nothing more than a hypothesis of what might have happened.

'It's going to be over soon, Tom. Whether you look at this

witness list or not. Don't you want it to be over in a way that we win?'

Tom did what he always did, avoiding eye contact and wiggling his fingers and licking his lips with violent tongue thrusts. The skin around his mouth was chapped so badly that he vaguely resembled Heath Ledger as the Joker.

'I'm not gonna win,' he said.

'We *can* win, Tom. Just—'

'Don't wanna.'

'You don't wanna what? You don't wanna *win*?'

Tom looked up at the ceiling and smiled. Then he started laughing. First time I'd seen that emotion from him. Dr Baraniq had said inappropriate emotional reactions were a symptom of disorganized schizophrenia.

'Win? *Win*? How'm I supposed to *win*?'

'You win,' I said, 'by showing that you were suffering from your illness when you shot that woman.'

Tom shook his head furiously. 'That's not . . . that's not . . . winning. No, no, no.' He got up from his seat and started walking toward the door.

'What *is* winning to you?' I called out. 'Tom—'

'There's no *winning*. I can't win.' He stood facing the wall, his head shaking more quickly with each passing minute. 'I can't . . . It doesn't go away. It doesn't go away.'

'Hey,' I said.

Just like that, Tom dropped to the floor and began mumbling to himself. The words were inaudible but delivered with violence, with anguish.

'Tom,' I said.

But he wasn't listening. He rocked back and forth on the floor, lost within himself.

A guard entered the room and looked at me with a question.

'Go ahead,' I said, and sighed. Tom was gone for now. He was probably gone for good.

I had to find a way to help him. But I couldn't do it without him helping me first.

When I got back out to the registration desk, they handed me my cell phone. I saw three messages from the cell phone of Joel Lightner. When I got out of the elevator, I dialed him up.

'I found something,' he said to me, breathless. 'Get ready to be happy.'

17

Take the house, they tell you. It doesn't matter what happened last week. It doesn't matter what happened to your best friend. Take the house, they tell you, so you do it.

It was a tip, you hear, but last week was a tip, too – a bogus one, a setup. Three Rangers and two Marines blown up within thirty seconds of entering.

That's what you're thinking as you're standing outside the house. It's just past two in the morning, but you aren't thinking about how tired you are. You aren't thinking about how lonely you are. You aren't thinking about how hot you are, the thickness of the desert air, the burden of the forty pounds of gear you're wearing. You aren't thinking about the questions you have about your mission, this whole fucking quandary.

You're thinking only about that door, and what's behind it.

You look to your left, to your lieutenant. Lew looks more like a robot than a human in his combat fatigues and night-vision goggles and gear, bracing the M-14 rifle. But he is a human being, and you know his heart is hammering against his chest the same as yours.

The call comes, and you follow Lew through the front door

with a rush. There is a back door, too, and simultaneously your team has entered from that direction as well. You call out your orders, but there is nobody in the front room, a parlor room with a couch and two chairs and an overhead light that looks like a cheap lamp upside down and suspended from the ceiling.

The smell of tobacco smoke is fresh. A cigarette still burns on the small table in front of the couch, smoke lingering in the thick air. You look at Lew. He sees the cigarette, too.

Only moments ago, somebody was sitting right here on this couch.

Gunfire erupts from the back of the house. Lew breaks down the hallway to the right. First door is a bathroom. You follow him in. Secure. Nobody here. Lew slaps your chest and points to the tub of the shower. You would have missed it, but not Lew. A nylon strap protruding from the bottom of the shower basin. Lew tells you to hold security on the bathroom. He approaches the bathtub cautiously, shuffle step by shuffle step. He reaches his hand inside the tub and in one motion yanks on the strap and jumps as far away as he can, awaiting an explosion.

No explosion, but a large section of the basin lies askew in the tub. A hidden door to a hidden bunker.

They wait a beat before Lew pulls again on the loose piece, yanking it free and clear of the exposed hole, a near-perfect square. You crane your neck and barely make out the outline of a swinging ladder before gunfire erupts through the hole. Instinctively, as Lew jumps back, as bullets bounce off the tiled walls, you aim the M-14 toward the square hole and open fire.

The initial gunplay dissipates. Lew tosses a grenade down the hole, and you both retreat into the hallway as it detonates.

You call for help, and several Rangers come down the hall. You recall the initial gunfire in the rear of the house and, vaguely, the commotion, but your attention has been focused on this bathroom. When you look back into the bathroom, you see that Lew is already halfway into the hole.

It's a ladder of rope, the rungs uneven. Your foot slips through at one point and you almost fall headfirst. You right yourself and ultimately climb down about ten feet to soft footing, maybe cinder. It is dark, but your night-vision goggles show, very nearly up ahead, two tunnels, left and right.

'Put it down!' you hear Lew shout. 'Drop it! I said *put it down*! Put it down!'

You start running, thinking the noise is coming from the right tunnel.

'Drop the weapon! Drop the weapon right now! Put down your weapon!'

Automatic gunfire, a short burst and awful silence. Your heart pounding so fiercely that your vision is spotty, the fear so thick in your throat you can't speak, you make a decisive right turn into the tunnel, your M-14 raised and ready—

Lew is bent over, on his knees. For a moment you think he's been hit, lower torso probably—

'I told you to put it down! I told you . . . I told you to put it down. Why didn't you . . .'

Your eyes predominantly focused forward, you peek down and see in Lew's arms a tiny face. You see a tiny arm, a tiny open hand. On the cinder below, you see what appears to be a water pistol, a toy weapon.

Gunfire scrapes the walls a few feet in front of you. The tunnel has a slight angle so they don't have a straight shot. You fire back to let them know what's coming if they advance.

'Lew!' you yell. 'Lieutenant!'

It comes again, gunfire spraying the wall closer still as they advance. You and several other Rangers who have joined you open fire in return. Smoke and dust fill the enclosed space, rendering your night-vision goggles of little use.

Lew doesn't move throughout the cross fire, cradling the young girl in his arms, rocking her, speaking into her ear.

'We're getting the fuck out of here!' calls your company commander. 'Move out! Move!'

'Lieutenant!' you call. 'Lieutenant Stoller! *Tom!*'

You reach down and grab him by the arm and drag him. He offers no resistance. The two of you are thick in the cross fire now.

'Get the fuck up, Tom!'

Belatedly, Lew gets to his feet and you retreat to the ladder. The last to leave the tunnel, filled now with smoke, you toss a grenade to keep the enemy at bay. Your last vision is the little girl, sprawled lifeless on the cinder, the grenade rolling in her direction.

18

Bobby Hilton's eyes looked out over the park, empty this time of year, save for two children trying to scrounge up what little wet snow remained.

'You know the insurgents use children,' he said. 'Sometimes as shields. Sometimes they strap suicide vests to them. Sometimes they give them a weapon and tell them to open fire. You don't know. You don't fucking know.'

'I believe you,' I assured him. 'I don't doubt it for a second.'

Hilton picked at his teeth, trying to calm himself, wrench himself free of a memory that had an obvious effect on him.

'Whatever came of it?' I asked. 'I didn't see anything about this on his record.'

Hilton shook his head but kept that aimless gaze. 'We called in Spooky. A gunship.' He looked at me. 'An air strike. Fired five or six rounds into the house. Obliterated the house and most of the bunker and the insurgents with it. I wasn't part of the team that went back in.' He grimaced. 'But that little girl would've just been part of the wreckage. Hate to say it, but she was probably blown to pieces. I think there were seven dead, all in, maybe eight.'

'And how was Tom afterward?'

Hilton shrugged and leaned forward on the park bench. It was a frosty day, but these returning vets don't seem to mind the cold so much. 'Whatever happened to him, he kept it to himself. Yeah, maybe he was a little slower on the draw, maybe he talked a little less, but he was never a real open sorta guy or anything. He kept doing his job. We did more missions. He kept it all inside. For a while, at least.' He looked at me. 'Y'know, that tunnel he discovered, we didn't know anything about it. Our intel in Mosul at that point was for shit. Turned out it was part of a network of tunnels smuggling in foreign fighters. They figured we destroyed a couple thousand rifles, over a hundred kilos of heroin, and we closed down a major network for smuggling terrorists. All because of Tom. But instead of walking out of there thinking of himself as a hero, he had to live with the fact that he shot an unarmed little girl. I mean, I heard him calling out to her to drop her weapon. He just – he didn't know it was a damn water pistol. You can't know. You're on the spot, and it's them or you. You don't have time for conversations.'

Robert Edward Hilton had just ended his second tour in Iraq only two months ago. He was a short, stocky guy in his mid-twenties with an acne-scarred face and prematurely receding dark hair. The public defender's investigators hadn't interviewed him because he was still in the war theater, but Joel Lightner had found him now that he'd returned to his home in Racine, Wisconsin.

Joel, seated next to me – a prover, in case Hilton got reluctant on me at trial – was keeping quiet but taking notes.

'So Tom shot some woman here in the city. Goddamn.' Hilton crossed his legs and put his arms across the back of the bench. 'Post-traumatic stress? I mean, he was reliving Mosul?'

'It sounds like it,' I said. 'You watch the interrogation video and you hear him playing out that scene. "Drop the weapon, drop the weapon, why didn't you drop the weapon?" I mean, it's uncanny.'

'Aw, Tom. The poor guy—'

Hilton's eyes filled. He was uncomfortable with the emotion, as if he possibly could be faulted.

'Tom shot this woman with a Glock 23,' I said, hoping to focus Hilton away from the pain and onto something technical. 'He ever use a gun like that?'

Hilton blinked away his tears. He wiped his nose with the back of his hand and breathed out. 'In the military? Not that I remember. Tom bought a Glock?'

'I don't know if he bought it, or how he got it. He's a homeless guy. Maybe traded for it or something. Maybe took it off somebody. The serial number was scratched off.'

Hilton thought about that. 'Your investigator said he hit her between the eyes?'

'Right.'

'From how far?'

'They found the shell casing about ten feet away.'

Hilton smirked. 'That's good shooting, with a gun like that.'

Joel Lightner had thought the same thing. Something stirred inside my brain. A connection forming, maybe.

'I need you to testify,' I said. My heart skipped a beat as I envisioned the reaction on Judge Nash's face. Discovery was due thirty days before trial. We were now twenty-seven days away. I'd need the court's permission for the late submission. And the judge had no sense of humor in such matters.

Hilton blew out a sigh and got off the bench. 'That's up to Tom,' he said.

'Tom won't open up.'

'Listen, guys.' Hilton seemed to become aware of the cold. He stuffed his hands into his pockets. 'I'm talking to you because you said Tom wouldn't. Or can't. You should have this information. Maybe it will jar him or something. But I'm not talking about this in court unless Tom says okay.' He nodded presumptively. 'Okay?'

This was what I was waiting for. It wasn't perfect. Kathy Rubinkowski was a white, mid-twenties, unarmed woman, not a pre-teen Iraqi girl with a water pistol. She was shot between the eyes with a handgun, not through the chest with a rifle. And on the surface, at least, a quiet city street in January was nothing like a hotbed of danger in the scorching heat of an underground tunnel in Iraq.

Some of this could be explained away as circumstantial, like the weapon – M-14 rifles weren't exactly readily available to a guy like Tom – but still, it was far from perfect.

Regardless, it was as close as I was going to get. And more important, even to a cynic like me, it was what really happened. It was the truth.

And that, more than anything, is what rocked me as I sat in that park: the truth. The truth is not usually something a defense attorney seeks. Where the government seeks to construct a case, the defense lawyer seeks to tear it down. Where the government tries to clarify, the defense lawyer obfuscates. It was like I'd said to Tori: Most of my clients were guilty. There was something liberating about that. I'd still try my damnedest to win the case, but when I couldn't, no matter how much I hated losing, it didn't penetrate my shield. At some gut level, I knew that my clients had gotten what was coming to them.

But not now. Now I knew that my client really did suffer an episode of PTSD the night of the shooting. It wasn't an argument. It wasn't a theory.

Tom Stoller, by all rights, should be acquitted. And whether he went to prison or a hospital when this was over would be entirely up to me.

19

Bobby Hilton's knees bounced as he stared through the thick glass. He looked over at me and seemed like he wanted to say something.

This was a guy who not so long ago was storming houses where high-powered weapons awaited him on the other side of the door. A guy who knew that any road down which he traveled could be laden with an improvised explosive device. A guy who worked in a place where the majority of the people there resented him at best, and wanted him dead at worst.

But here he was, nervous as a schoolboy, and all he had to do was say hello to an old friend.

'You think this might – bring him out of his shell?' he asked me.

'Don't worry about that,' I said, as the door from the other side of the glass opened. 'Just talk to him.'

The guard led Tom Stoller to the seat on the opposite side of the glass. I was permitted to sit in the same room with him, as his attorney, but anyone else got the no-contact visitation room.

'Hey, Lew,' said Hilton, his voice shaky. He put his palm against the glass.

Tom looked the same to me as always, disheveled and detached, the vacant eyes, the nervous tics from the medication. But Sergeant Robert Edward Hilton had known him in a different context altogether.

I moved to the corner of the room, some attempt at privacy for the two of them, though I could still hear everything.

Tom didn't seem to realize who Bobby was until he took the seat, at which point he locked eyes with his comrade for a few moments before retreating to his detached gaze.

'Hey,' he managed.

'How ya – how's – I mean . . .' Hilton didn't know how to start. There was no obvious introductory small talk when your pal is in lockup for murder.

'Hey,' Tom said again. 'Hey . . . Bob.'

'You doing okay in here, Lew? I mean, best as possible?'

'It's – hot. It's hot.' Tom stared into his lap.

'You look like you need to get some food in here,' Hilton said. 'Gotta be better than the MREs, right?' He chuckled, but it fell flat. Tom was unresponsive.

'The vegetables taste like dirt,' Tom said. I thought all vegetables tasted like dirt.

'Hey, Clap and Rush said hey. I told them I was seeing you.'

'Okay.' Tom's eyes moved everywhere except to his visitor.

Hilton was unsure of himself. Tom wasn't exactly a sterling conversationalist these days. And more to the point, he was an entirely different person than the one Hilton had come to know in Iraq.

'Lew,' he said, 'I told your lawyer about the tunnel. I told him about it. I told him that if it was me, I'd have done the same thing. That you tried to warn her and you couldn't have known. . . .'

104

Tom turned his head, like he was responding to a sound to his left. He held it there, his gaze steadied on the wall.

'Lew, you got a good lawyer here, don't you think? He wants to help you. You gotta let him. Can you talk to him about what happened the night that woman was shot?'

It was like Tom's mental computer had frozen up. He didn't move an inch. Save for the rise and fall of his chest, it was hard to tell if he was dead or alive.

Hilton dropped his head. He was talking to a man who had once been his superior officer, who had commanded his respect and admiration, to hear him tell it. How devastating it must have been to see Tom so utterly broken now. And that was to say nothing of whatever internal demons Hilton carried himself. Nobody would walk away from a war experience without scarring.

'I don't remember,' said Tom, words as lucidly delivered as any I'd heard from him.

Hilton straightened. So did I, slouching in the corner. Dr Baraniq had warned me that it was not uncommon for someone experiencing PTSD to have amnesia over the episode. But I'd been counting on Tom being able to recount at least some detail of the night Kathy Rubinkowski was shot – for Dr Baraniq and for the jury.

I had no occurrence witnesses whatsoever. Tom couldn't speak to what happened. There was nobody that heard Tom yelling to Kathy Rubinkowski to *drop the weapon, drop the weapon,* or anything to that effect. Nobody to testify that the victim posed any perceived threat to Tom whatsoever. No triggering event to which I could point that would explain why, at that moment, Tom Stoller suddenly fell into the grip of a PTSD episode.

I had nothing. Nothing but a hypothesis from a doctor.

Getting nowhere with Tom, Bobby Hilton returned to lower-key material. He told Tom how he was going to work in his father's pizzeria in Racine with an eye toward taking over the place. He talked about how he was engaged now. He repeatedly asked Tom if he needed anything, but got nothing but one-word responses. Tom kept his head turned to the left, looking off in the distance, for the remainder of the conversation. It was painful to watch.

'Take care, Lew,' said Hilton. He placed his hand on the thick glass again before he walked past me and out the door.

I approached the glass. 'Tom, I'll see you tomorrow,' I said.

My client didn't answer. He was gone for the moment. No sign of recognition or emotion, save for a tear that formed and ran down his cheek.

When I walked back out in the hallway, Sergeant Bobby Hilton was on the floor, head in his hands, sobbing like a child.

He looked up at me with a tear-streaked face. 'Tell me . . . what you need me to do,' he said to me, struggling. 'I'll do anything.'

20

Detective Gary Boxer led me into an interview room. He had a file folder in his hand and a small notepad. He dropped them both down on the desk and motioned to me.

'So what's your interest in Lorenzo Fowler?' he asked.

'He came to see me a few days before he was murdered. Legal advice. I didn't take the case, but we talked. I wish I could tell you what he said to me.'

Boxer opened his hand. He was probably just over forty, with a rash of blond hair and deep-set eyes. A toothpick moved freely in his mouth. 'He's dead,' he said to me. 'He's got no worries at this point.'

'But he's got the privilege. It survives his death.'

'Okay, so you can't tell me what he told you. So why are you here?'

'Thought I might ask you some questions.'

'You're gonna ask *me* questions.' He eyeballed me for a moment. 'Okay, shoot. Not saying I'm gonna answer.'

'You know a strip club called Knockers?'

He kept with the poker face for a moment before relaxing. 'So maybe we liked him for that murder. We sweated Lorenzo pretty good two days before he died. You probably know that, right?'

'Not saying I do, not saying I don't,' I answered.

Boxer tapped his fingers on the table. 'You're not the Capparellis' lawyer. So if he's coming to you, it means he wanted out. He wanted an independent lawyer.' He nodded as he thought this over. 'Lorenzo was thinking about a trade. Turning state's evidence. We figure the Capparellis hit him, right? He was becoming a liability. Maybe he was trying to find a way out of the whole business. Stop me if I got it wrong.'

I didn't stop him.

'And that's the very reason the Capparellis would want him out of commission,' he continued. 'A liability, like I said.' He worked the toothpick expertly from one side of his mouth to the other. 'This isn't exactly stuff I didn't know.'

Right, but he was going to take his time extracting information from my silence.

'Might Lorenzo have given you some valuable information?'

'He might have,' I said. 'He might not have.'

'He might have, he might not have.' Boxer was going to wait me out.

'You play cards?' I asked.

He shook his head. 'Used to play poker. You?'

'I like a different game,' I said. 'I prefer gin rummy.'

A wry smile crept across the detective's face. Boxer got it. 'Funny,' he said. 'The Capparellis have a guy who goes by that nickname.'

'What a coincidence,' I said.

'We don't know his identity. There's some people in the brown building downtown who'd sure like to, though. So would some of my colleagues.'

'So would I,' I said.

Boxer frowned. He'd gotten his hopes up. 'So Lorenzo didn't tell you.' He drummed his fingers again. 'Was that gonna be the trade?'

'I'd be breaching my privilege if I answered that.'

'Sure. Right.'

'From the papers, Lorenzo's murder sure read like a Mob hit,' I said. 'One in the throat. One in each kneecap.'

'They're not subtle, these guys.'

'Maybe you can't answer – but does it look like Gin Rummy?'

Boxer shrugged and sighed. Couldn't tell if he was debating whether to share with a civilian or if he didn't know the answer. 'Hard to say, Counselor. Whoever it was, he was a damn good shot. These were precision shots, and not from close range.'

'Shell casings?' I asked.

'No, no. Nothing like that. Trajectory of the windpipe shot, lack of tattooing or charring or anything. Wasn't close up. The offender shot out the kneecaps while Lorenzo was up against the door of the bookstore, and the offender wasn't on the sidewalk or the curb or the street, either. Two eyewitnesses on the corner said so.'

'The shooter was, what – across the street? Bent down between cars?'

Boxer smiled. He was done sharing, but it seemed like I'd guessed right. He leaned in toward me. 'I'm gonna ask you straight, just so there's no misunderstanding with these games we're playing. Do you know who Gin Rummy is?'

'No.'

'Then I'm out of time for you.' He slipped me a card. I slipped him one of mine. Then I slipped out of the police station.

21

Tori, Joel Lightner, and I strolled along Arondale Avenue as the sun threatened to sink beneath the real estate. We didn't get any snow last night, but it was forecasted, so I wanted to do my due diligence before the weather clocked me out.

West Arondale was becoming the new Boystown, and wherever the gay population moved in, the city became a mecca for nightclubs and cafés and art shops and boutiques, some of the risqué variety. Bars advertised specials on chalkboards along the sidewalks. A clothing store featured a mannequin dressed in leather bondage.

When I was a kid, anything on Arondale Avenue that was west of Coulter was off-limits. Think the red-light district in Amsterdam, except the women weren't displayed in windows. The strip clubs stayed around until the early nineties, when the gentrification began and the city started strong-arming them through zoning changes that were litigated in court for years. James Madison probably never thought that his beloved First Amendment would apply to a nude woman grinding herself in the lap of a middle-aged man for twenty bucks.

'You sure know how to show a girl a good time,' Tori said to me as we reached the 2700 block of West Arondale.

'You wanted to know what it's like to defend criminals,' I said. 'This is what it's like.'

Lightner looked over the two of us. 'This is your second date?'

'It's not a date,' Tori and I said together.

'Hey, okay, excuse me.'

'Our first date,' I said, 'Tori informed me that she found me interesting in a purely nonsexual way.'

Joel said, 'You have good taste, Tori. Except for the part about finding him interesting.'

Tori seemed to enjoy the back-and-forth. I can always count on Joel for subtlety and discretion.

'I never said my interest was nonsexual,' she clarified.

'Okay, now we're getting somewhere.' Joel rubbed his hands together.

'I just said the sex wasn't going to happen.'

'Oh. So, what – you're just going to be friends? That doesn't work.'

'Lightner, for Christ's sake,' I said.

'Well, if you're ever in the mood for a more mature gentleman like myself—'

I stopped. Joel did, too, belatedly. 'What'd I say? You're all sensitive these days?'

'I'm not sensitive, Lightner. I just figured, if we're here to investigate a crime scene, I don't know – maybe we shouldn't walk right past it.'

'Good point.' He turned and looked across the street at the Tattered Cover bookstore. A huge mat had been thrown down in front of the store where Lorenzo Fowler had bled out.

'Witnesses say they didn't see anybody in the street,' I said. 'And he wasn't shot at close range. So he was shot from across the street, where we're standing, basically. I'm thinking he crouched down between two cars and waited for Lorenzo. Sounds like Lorenzo was coming around the back of his car and he got one in the windpipe.'

We waited for a couple of cars to pass and then hustled across the street. The bloodstain on the street was still apparent. 'Lorenzo stumbled backward from that shot, all the way back against the door of the bookstore. Then he took one in each kneecap.'

'The shooter is still across the street at this point?' Lightner asked.

'Yeah. Must have been. The witnesses say there wasn't anybody in the street walking toward him or anything like that. They didn't see anybody.'

'And he used a Glock?'

'A semiautomatic handgun. A Glock or something similar, probably.'

I thought about all of this, taking it in now that I was at the crime scene itself. It was always different seeing it in person, versus case-file photographs or witness accounts.

In my peripheral vision, I noticed that Lightner was watching me carefully. I glanced at him and broke eye contact. We were both thinking the same thing: Two cases of absolute precision shooting, from a considerable distance, with a handgun?

We were standing at the curb now, directly in front of the Tattered Cover bookstore. A faint bloodstain was still visible from the point on the sidewalk where the first bullet blew through his windpipe. 'Why does Lorenzo walk around the back of the car?' I asked. 'He's walking eastbound. That's what the witnesses said. So most people would go around their car from the nearest side. In this case, around the front.'

'Maybe his car was close up against the car in front of it,' said Lightner. 'Maybe there wasn't room.'

'Or he was being careful,' Tori chimed in.

I looked at her and pointed.

'A woman walking alone wants to check out her car before she gets in it,' she went on. 'She walks around the car so she can see into the backseat and make sure nobody's waiting for her. She circles the car and then gets in.'

'And Lorenzo was definitely paranoid,' I said. 'I can attest to that.'

Tori nodded. 'So you think whoever shot him knew he'd act that way?'

I looked at Joel. 'Lightner, what do I need you for? Tori here's a natural. You're right,' I said to her. 'This was a Mob hit. Lorenzo was about to get pinched on something, and the Capparellis were afraid he might start looking to cut a deal and spill some secrets.'

'And this is a case you're working on? That's pretty cool. More interesting than quadratic equations.' She looked me over. 'So this is why you defend criminals.'

'He believes passionately in the Bill of Rights,' Lightner said. 'He doesn't do it for the money. Just like he doesn't hang out with beautiful women for the sex.'

Tori paid attention to that, the use of the plural.

'You should see his law partner, Shauna,' he explained. 'Another knockout, strictly platonic.'

Joel doesn't have a filter. It was hard to believe that neither of his marriages worked out.

We were walking now, returning to our car. 'Lightner,' I said, 'nobody born after 1960 uses the term "knockout."'

'I was born after 1960.'

'Not by much.'

'But I'm a kid at heart.'

Tori shook her head. 'Do I even need to be here? Neither of you needs a girlfriend. You just bicker with each other.'

We stopped the next block down at a bar advertising a Bloody Mary special. That sounded good to me, but minus the tomato juice and celery stick and whatever else polluted the vodka. Tori excused herself for the bathroom and Lightner admired her exit.

'I like her,' he announced.

'What are you, my dad?'

'If I were your dad, you'd be better-looking.'

Fair enough. Lightner lifted a glass of scotch off the bar and hit my arm.

'I thought this was just idle curiosity on your part,' Joel said. 'Y'know, this guy Lorenzo comes to visit you, then he gets popped, you're curious to see it all. Isn't that what you said to me – "Just curious"?'

'I'm a curious sort.'

'Yeah, and then you bring Tori along, so I figure you want to impress her. Otherwise, why would you interrupt a planned dinner with her to visit a crime scene?'

'You got it,' I said. 'I was trying to impress her.'

'Bullshit. Bullshit. Could this be a coincidence?' Joel asked. 'Two shootings with a small-caliber handgun from an intermediate distance with spot-on results?'

He was right, of course. I raised my glass of Stoli, so Joel wouldn't feel awkward drinking alone.

'Now I have to figure out what all this means,' I said.

22

Judge Bertrand Nash peered over his glasses at me as I sat in the first row of the courtroom. Even before they called my case, he had singled me out for disapproval.

'*State versus Thomas Stoller,*' the clerk belted out.

The prosecutor, Wendy Kotowski, wore an indignant expression as well, as she joined me at the lectern. She was playing to the judge. She knew what made him tick.

'Mr Kolarich,' the judge boomed before I'd opened my mouth. 'There are two motions before the court today, each of which seeks to excuse you from the normal preparation that I demand of every lawyer who appears before me. Now, you've appeared before me on several matters, mostly in your previous role as a prosecutor. Have you not?'

'I have, Judge.'

'And what is the typical batting average of people who think that the thirty-day discovery cutoff doesn't apply to them?'

'Not one that would get them into the major leagues.' I happened to know that he was a particular aficionado of the national pastime.

'Or the *minors*,' he said.

'Your Honor—'

'Mr Kolarich, did I not specifically warn you that if you were going to be a late entry into this matter, you couldn't use the excuse of lack of time to prepare?'

Words to that effect, I guess. No need to quibble. 'Judge—'

'Counsel, if your predecessor, Mr Childress, had made this motion, I'd have said to him that this witness, this . . . Robert Hilton, he's been discharged from the military for two months. That's two months where Mr Childress knew about him and could have tried to contact him to determine whether he had any relevant information.' The judge leaned forward. 'Are you about to tell me that you should get special consideration because you came into this case late?'

'No,' I said. The best way to get your chance with this judge is to say as little as possible until he's done with his ranting. It is essentially the same approach, I'm told, used by parents to deal with their toddlers. He was going to have to let me make my record, so better if I let him resolve his anger first.

The judge waved a hand. 'It's your motion, Mr Kolarich.'

'Judge, there was an initial round of witness interviews and a follow-up by my office, with my investigator. As soon as we located Sergeant Hilton, we contacted him. As soon as we talked to him, we disclosed him to the other side. Less than twenty-four hours. At that time, we were twenty-six days out from trial. Four days late. If Your Honor were inclined to balance the equities, balance those four days against the fact that Mr Hilton's testimony is absolutely crucial to the defense. This is our whole case.'

The judge adjusted his glasses. 'And—'

'My client won't talk to me, Judge. He's borderline catatonic. You've declared him fit for trial and I can't do anything about that. But he's suffering from disorganized schizophrenia and

I can't get him out of his shell. Sergeant Hilton has opened a very important window into what happened in Iraq, and it speaks directly – and I mean directly – to our defense. If the jury doesn't hear this testimony, Tom Stoller doesn't get a fair trial. Now, I know your rules are important, but I've never known you to exalt them over a defendant's right to a fair trial.'

I'd counted about two dozen people in the courtroom before I stepped up. With Judge Nash, that's usually a bad thing, because he likes to skewer lawyers in front of an audience. But I was laying it on pretty thick now – truth be told, I *have* seen Judge Nash exalt his rules over the Seventh Amendment – in the hope that he'd be shamed into showing me some leniency.

'The People object,' said Wendy Kotowski, when asked. 'The defense had ample opportunity to disclose this witness, even while he was still in the military. They've known about him for almost a year. They may not have spoken with him, but they could have told us about him. They didn't. They've waited until after the discovery cutoff in the clear hope of trying to gain an advantage.'

'That's ridiculous,' I protested, jumping in without invitation, usually a no-no for this judge. 'Your Honor, I could have just littered my witness list with everyone Tom Stoller ever served with in the military. I would have been within my rights. And if I did that, the prosecution would be here complaining that I abused the disclosure process. But I didn't do that. And now the prosecution is saying that I *should* have named Sergeant Hilton as a witness even at a point when I had no idea if he was remotely relevant to the case.'

'Your Honor?' Wendy said, doing it the right way, asking

permission. He gave her the floor. 'Your Honor, the bottom line is that your rule protects both sides from gamesmanship, and it should do so now. We both have to live with this rule. And I would note that Mr Kolarich has coupled this motion with a request for a continuance in the hope that you'll split the baby, so to speak.'

She was right. That's exactly what I was doing.

The judge nodded. 'I did notice that, Mr Kolarich. You make a request you know I'm likely to deny and couple it with a lesser request. "Splitting the baby," as Ms. Kotowski said. You think I'm going to split the baby, Mr Kolarich? Do you think I'm King Solomon?'

Don't ask me why I do the things I do. Call it a gut reaction, I guess, an instinctive read of the situation.

'No,' I said, 'but I heard you taught him everything he knew.'

There's that old saying that you could have heard a pin drop. I would say that for one beat of a moment in Courtroom 1741 on Wednesday, November 10, at 9:22 A.M., you could have heard the blood circulating through an ant's scrotum.

And then the old man reared his head back and burst into laughter. My theory is that a guy accustomed to everybody sucking up to him enjoys catching a little shit once in a while.

The rest of the courtroom followed suit like lemmings. Everybody thought I was funny. But he still hadn't decided my motion.

After a time, the judge removed his glasses, wiped at his eyes, and calmed down. 'Why do you want a continuance, Mr Kolarich?'

I paused a beat. I had to be careful here. I was unlikely to win this motion. The odds of Judge Nash moving this trial were slim. And if we were going to a jury in three weeks, I didn't want to show my hand to the prosecution. I wanted to maintain the element of surprise.

No, I decided. It wasn't worth the risk. I'd have to stick with the same bullshit I put in my written motion. 'Judge, the information from Sergeant Hilton has opened up a new line of evidence for us. We'd like to pursue it. Now that we know the event that my client was reliving, we want to interview the servicemen and servicewomen with whom he worked for evidence of the effect it had on him. The prosecution is contesting the presence of a mental defect, and how he responded to this event in Iraq is part of the factual underpinning my expert needs.'

The judge looked down over his glasses at me. He glanced at the prosecutor but didn't ask for a response. 'The court finds that the defense exercised reasonable diligence in securing the information from Mr Hilton and in disclosing his testimony to the prosecution. The court will deem the defense's disclosure of Mr Hilton to be appropriate. But you're not getting your continuance, Mr Kolarich.' He nodded presumptively. 'See you in three weeks.'

23

'I need you to focus on me, Tom,' Shauna said, pointing to her own eyes.

I'd brought Shauna back because she seemed to be the only person he would respond to. But so far today he'd been playing with a deck of cards, organizing them by numbers, then by suits. To look at him, you'd think he had the brainpower of a young child. But he didn't. His intelligence hadn't diminished any. Dr Baraniq had said that Tom would seek comfort from his demons by doing things that required no difficulty what-soever. Boring, said the doctor, would be fine with Tom. Boring was comfortable.

'I know you don't remember what happened when that woman was shot,' she tried, in that soothing voice that had been used on me, too, on occasion. 'But can you tell me how you got the gun?'

He didn't answer. He kept playing with the cards. I looked at my watch, except I'd left my watch with the front desk, so all I saw was the pale outline of it on my wrist. I was growing impatient. I had work to do, especially if this case was going in the direction I thought it was.

'Lieutenant,' I said, which always seemed to draw his

attention, at least momentarily. I used my grown-up voice. I walked over and lorded over him. 'Stand up, Lieutenant. Stand up!'

I'd held his eye contact, which was promising. I didn't know if this approach would work, but I had nothing to lose.

Tom stood up and faced me. His eyes didn't stay locked with mine, but they remained in the ballpark. It was as good as I would get.

'Where did you get the gun?' I asked. 'Did you steal it?'

He turned away. I grabbed him by the shoulders and kept him where he was.

'Did . . . you . . . *steal* it?'

'No.' He shook his head, staring into my chest.

'Then how'd you get it?' I asked. 'How?'

'I . . . found it.'

'Where? Where did you find it?'

'I . . . I don't know where I was sleeping. I try to stay warm but not too warm. Not too warm. It's so cold, but then it gets so hot and then I have to take off my coats because it's so hot—'

'The purse,' I tried. 'The woman's purse? Where did you get that?'

'The . . . purse.'

'The purse, Tom! The victim's purse and the gun? How did you get them?'

I shook him fiercely. I expected him to wilt, but instead he righted himself and in one motion raised both of his hands and swept my arms off his shoulders. Expertly done, the result of training. His eyes grew dark, and he moved his legs apart to anchor himself.

I wasn't sure what would come next. Something was

happening, that's all I knew. He was out of his shell. For all I knew, he was going to come at me.

'I don't think you killed Kathy Rubinkowski,' I said. 'I think somebody killed her and tried to make it look like a robbery. They dumped the gun and her possessions, and you found them.'

He didn't move. He just watched me.

'I don't think you were confessing to her murder in that interrogation room,' I said. 'You were confessing to killing that girl in the tunnel in Mosul. Tell me I'm wrong.'

He remained stoic, other than a reddening of his cheeks.

I pushed him with everything I had, but he kept his balance. He grabbed my right forearm, twisted it behind my back, and drove me to the floor. In the space of three seconds, the ex-Ranger had subdued me.

'No!' I called out as the door burst open and guards entered. 'It's okay. I have to do this!'

'It's okay,' Shauna repeated to the guards. 'Really.'

That stalled them momentarily. As long as things didn't escalate, they might give us a few moments.

'I . . . don't . . . remember,' Tom whispered harshly into my ear.

Tom released my arm and stood up. The guards came over and handcuffed him behind his back. I looked up at Tom, whose limp posture showed that he had immediately regressed to his normal state of detachment.

But he resisted when they tried to move him, twisting his body back toward me, looking in my direction, his lips parting but nothing coming out. I raised my hand to the guards, who seemed to understand.

'It's too late,' Tom finally said. The guards turned him toward the door and marched him out.

Shauna looked at me. 'Did he say he doesn't remember?'

As the doors closed and my client disappeared, I said, 'Happy Veterans Day, Tom.'

24

'Okay, everybody, stop what you're doing on *Stoller*. A new game plan, and we don't have much time. Twenty days, to be exact.'

Bradley John, Joel Lightner, and Shauna Tasker had joined me in the conference room. It was time to dole out new instructions for a sprint to the finish.

'Bradley, I want case law on the prosecution's burden of proof in insanity cases and inconsistent defenses. I know it's out there and I know what it says, but I want the most recent case law and I want a memo I can convert to a brief if need be.'

'Got it,' said Bradley.

'Joel, do background on the victim, Kathy Rubinkowski. I'll look through the discovery, but we already know it's light. They got their man the first night, and since he was a homeless guy with a screw loose, they must have figured they didn't need motive. I have nothing on this woman. That's what you have to find me. Who gained from Kathy Rubinkowski's murder?'

'Who's drafting the subpoenas?' he asked.

I shook my head. 'No subpoenas. This is under the radar.

Whatever you can get through your charm and good looks. Shauna,' I said. 'Take whatever research Bradley's come up with on the insanity defense on the use of hypotheticals and amnesia and turn it into a motion in limine.'

'I thought *I* was doing that,' said Bradley.

'Man up, kid. I don't have time for a learning curve right now.'

'You're not seriously going with inconsistent defenses,' Shauna said.

'They're not technically inconsistent,' I said. But what a defense strategy I was putting together. *Tom didn't kill her, but if he did, he was insane.* But it probably wouldn't get that far. I'd see what the next twenty days would bring and pursue a defense of innocence as far as it would take me. I could always fall back on insanity. Point was, I didn't have to make that decision yet. I could wait until the defense put on its case if need be.

I clapped my hands together. 'Get me good stuff, people.'

Everyone scattered. It was mid-afternoon now, the morning having been spent at the Boyd Center with my client. I took the discovery file on Kathy Rubinkowski and started to read.

25

At five-thirty, my intercom buzzed.

'*Tori Martin?*' said our receptionist, Marie.

Shit. I'd forgotten. 'Here or on the phone?'

'*Here.*'

'Send her back.'

Dinner tonight had been my idea. The other night, when we'd visited the scene of Lorenzo Fowler's murder, my mind had turned to other things, and Lightner was there, anyway, so we had a couple of drinks and scratched on dinner. This was the rain check.

I wasn't really sure why I was pursuing this. She'd made it clear that she wasn't interested in anything other than a platonic relationship. It's not like I was looking to get married or anything, but I guess I wanted something, though if pressed I couldn't define what.

'Hey. Nice offices.' She couldn't have meant that, at least not my office. With the well-worn couch and a desk I'd picked up at a garage sale, half-empty bookshelves, and a desk full of disheveled papers, it looked more like a bachelor pad.

She brightened the place up, though. I couldn't deny the attraction. She put herself together nicely. The long white coat was expensive, and she dressed fashionably, with the caveat that I knew absolutely nothing about women's fashion. And truth was, Tori Martin would look hot in a cloth sack.

'Sorry, something's come up,' I said. 'I should have called.'

'That's okay. Should I – we can reschedule.'

'Sit a minute,' I said. I came around the desk and picked up the football in the middle of the room. She lifted her purse off her shoulder and sat on the couch.

'A case just heated up,' I said.

'The one about Lorenzo? That crime scene?'

'Not exactly. Kind of.'

She cocked her head. 'Really.' She was interested. Most people, on a superficial level, would be. Cops and robbers. Cool stuff. But she didn't pursue it. It was one of the things I liked about her. She had a natural reserve, bordering on aloofness, but I preferred it to the nosy type.

Said differently, she reminded me of me.

'I have a case going to trial in three weeks,' I said, 'and we've just decided to change our theory.'

'What kind of case?'

'A murder trial.'

'Cool.' Her expression lightened. 'That's exciting, right?'

'That's one way to describe it.'

'Can you tell me about it, or do you have some privilege or something?'

'No, I can.' I sighed. 'You want a bottle of water? Or something stronger?'

'Water's fine.'

I had a small refrigerator in the corner of my office, near my desk. 'My client's accused of murdering a woman in

127

Franzen Park last January,' I said. Inside the fridge were three bottles of Sam Adams, a small bottle of Stoli, and one bottle of nature's finest. I considered taking a small break and opening up a cold one, but one would probably lead to more. I figured I'd let Tori make the call. If she wanted a drink, that meant she wanted dinner, and maybe I could use a few hours to clear my head. 'You sure you just want *agua*?'

She didn't answer, so I glanced back at her. She looked like she'd just swallowed a bug. I sometimes forgot how this worked. People thought crime and justice were interesting to hear about and read about and watch on television, but when it got close to home, the idea of defending somebody who murdered a fellow human being was not for everybody. There are a lot of people – other lawyers as well as laypersons – who don't have the stomach for it. I might not, either, had I not first been a prosecutor and grown somewhat inured to death and violence. A lot of prosecutors become true believers and form a deep-seated antipathy for their opposing counsel. Me, I never saw the world that way, maybe because I spent a good part of my youth putting minor dents in the law myself. There are a lot of people from my neighborhood who would say that if I didn't have some size and the ability to catch a football and run like hell, I'd have wound up serving time in prison instead of sending people there.

On top of that, the murder victim was a woman; she was Caucasian; and she lived on the north side. People aren't supposed to be murdered up there. People are supposed to die violently on the south and west sides. When it happens to someone in the nice neighborhoods, especially a white woman, it's usually headline news.

I handed Tori the sweaty bottle of water. She probably

wanted to put it against her forehead as much as drink from it. Hell, she probably wanted to head for the exit.

'Cat got your tongue?' I asked, trying to shake her out of her funk.

'He . . . killed her?'

'He's accused of killing her,' I said, but this cute little game of *allegedly* sounded a lot less cute when applied to a real-life case.

Tori looked away. Disgust, I think, or maybe fear. Yep, I thought, she was seriously second-guessing any interest she had in me.

I took one of the chairs in front of my desk, flipped it around, and sank in it. 'This is what I do, kid.'

She took a deep breath and looked up at me. *How could you do this?* she seemed to be thinking. *How could you defend someone who killed a defenseless woman?*

'Why did he kill her?' she asked.

I shrugged. 'You ask me a week ago, I'd say this guy's an Army Ranger who lost his mind when he got back from Iraq. He suffered post-traumatic stress that triggered a dormant case of schizophrenia. He killed her because he thought he was in wartime. He was out of his mind.'

That seemed to make a difference with Tori. My client was a sick war veteran, not an evil monster.

'I just got this case a few weeks ago,' I said. 'It was a straight insanity defense, the shrink was already lined up, no eyewitnesses. It was pretty much a battle of the experts.'

'And?'

'And now I think my client didn't do it at all.'

She thought about that for a moment. Judging from our conversations to date, I had the sense that she enjoyed the

129

mental calculations of the law, using a different part of her brain. She had to balance that against her obvious revulsion.

The truth was, I had no idea what was running through her mind.

'You think he's innocent? And you said it's "kind of" related to that thing you took me to? That crime scene?'

'It might be. I'm not sure, but I think so, yeah.'

Tori kicked off her heels and brought her knees up on the couch. I watched her intently. It was the first time she'd removed an article of clothing in my presence. Sure, it was only a pair of shoes, but baby steps, right? Without dreams we are nothing.

I framed my hands. 'What you saw on Arondale – that was Lorenzo Fowler. He was a mobster. That murder was a professional job. The guy used a semiautomatic handgun from long distance. And he sent a message with the kneecap shots. And picked up the shell casings.'

'Does that mean something – the shell casings?'

'It means he knew what he was doing. A pro picks up the shell casings to prevent a match to his gun. That was a hit, no question.'

'Okay. I'm following.'

'So now we have my client, and the murder in Franzen Park. The theory was that he had a flashback to Iraq and shot this woman from a distance of about ten feet. He shot her with a Glock, which is probably the same model used on Lorenzo.'

She watched me carefully. I don't know if she was listening to the details or if she was reconsidering whether she wanted anything to do with me. But it helped me to articulate this out loud, to bounce it off somebody who wasn't an invested member of the defense team.

'Two murders with a handgun used from a pretty good distance, and landing with such precision,' I said. 'Kathy Rubinkowski took one between the eyes, and with Lorenzo – every shot landed perfectly, the windpipe and the kneecaps.'

'So everything was the same?' she asked.

'Well, no,' I said. 'They recovered the gun and the shell casing in the Franzen Park shooting. The shell casing is how we know the approximate distance of the shot.'

'So it's not the same.'

'Not exactly, no. He robbed her, too.'

'He robbed this woman he shot?'

'Right. They found her purse, cell phone, and necklace on my client.'

'That – sounds very different,' she said.

'I agree. Which makes me think that the murder was premeditated, and the robbery was to throw everyone off the scent. To make it look like a garden-variety robbery-homicide.'

'You think the same person shot both people? Lorenzo and this woman?'

'That's the thought.'

Tori chewed on that for a while. So did I.

'So you're saying the fact that these two things seem different is actually proof that they're the same,' she said.

I laughed. It probably wasn't what a mathematician would call linear thinking. 'They're not that different, Tori.'

'So you think you have an innocent client? A for-real innocent client?'

I sighed. 'If you'd asked me a few days ago, no. But now? Yeah, I do think he's innocent. I think if my client were halfway in control of his brain at the moment, he'd tell me that he

131

didn't lay a finger on the victim. I'd wager he's never laid *eyes* on her.'

'Wow.' Tori curled her toes into the cushion of the couch. 'If your client is innocent, that must be a lot of pressure on you.'

'Especially when someone reminds me of it.'

'Sorry.' She pulled a strand of hair out of her mouth. I enjoyed anything related to her mouth. Whatever women put on their lips today, it made hers shiny and full. I may have mentioned something about a dry spell.

'So – what's the idea?' she asked. 'Why would someone shoot this mobster guy and some innocent woman?'

'That's what I have to find out.'

'Do you have any idea at all?'

'No,' I said. 'Other than knowing who killed them both.'

'Oh.' She tripped over a laugh. 'You know who killed them?'

If knowing the nickname, but not the identity, of the killer counted, then yes, I thought I had a reasonable idea who pulled the trigger in each case.

'Gin Rummy,' I said.

She looked at me with a blank expression. 'What?'

'It's a person. Gin Rummy. He's a Mob hit man. Or an assassin, Lorenzo said. You know the difference between a hit man and an assassin?'

She shook her head. 'Is this a riddle?'

'No,' I said. 'But Gin Rummy is. Lorenzo was going to trade the identity of Gin Rummy for a get-out-of-jail-free card from the feds. And now I don't have to wonder why Lorenzo picked me, of all people, to confess his sins and seek advice.'

'I'm not following.'

'I think Gin Rummy committed the murder in Franzen Park,

the murder of Kathy Rubinkowski,' I said. 'And I think Lorenzo was there, or somehow knew about it, and was prepared to testify against Gin Rummy. And now I know why Lorenzo picked me to confess his sins to and get a little advice. He came to me after I'd filed an appearance in the case. He knew I was the lawyer for the man accused of killing Kathy. So he knew that I, more than anybody, would help him talk to the feds and cut a deal. I'd want the information to exonerate my client.'

That seemed to make sense to her. 'Then it sounds like you need to figure out who Gin Rummy is,' said Tori, stating the obvious. 'Is there any way I can help?'

I smiled. 'We are a little shorthanded,' I said.

26

Kathy Rubinkowski's parents lived in the northwest suburbs in a townhouse community of mostly retirees. The community was constructed around a man-made lake. The homes were all built with the same red-brick, white-wood pattern, a Stepford-wives feel to it that gave me the willies. To a guy like me who grew up in the city, the suburbs were a nonstarter. My wife, Talia, had mentioned them once, back when she was pregnant with our daughter, and I just about went into convulsions – probably because I knew I'd be swimming against the current on that one and would probably relent one day, about the time we were on child number four or five and we were priced out of the city housing market.

I'd wanted to bring Shauna with me to this appointment because of her soft touch, but she was swamped with other cases and needed to clear them out so she could work on *Stoller*. So I dragged Lightner with me, who didn't normally have a deft touch but could turn it on when he was on the job.

I rang the doorbell, and Lightner and I instinctively stepped back from the door, a nonthreatening posture. It was midday, and we were in full view of twenty other townhomes, but we were still two sizable guys showing up at a door.

A man's voice came through a speaker next to the door. '*Yes?*'

'Mr Rubinkowski, it's Jason Kolarich.'

I'd called ahead and talked my way into an appointment. Ray Rubinkowski hadn't been happy to hear from me, but he'd been polite enough to hear me out.

He answered the door in a plaid shirt and blue corduroys. Classic retired-dad wear, I would think, though I was hardly an expert. My father's wardrobe these days was limited to a gray jumpsuit, courtesy of Marymount Penitentiary.

Age had weakened Rubinkowski's voice and added ten pounds to his midsection, but he was clear-eyed and handsome. He bore some resemblance to his deceased daughter, his only child. I knew from background research that he'd been an accountant until his retirement two years ago.

He took our coats and showed us into what he called the parlor. I didn't think people used that term anymore. His wife, Doreen, was sitting on a couch with her hands in her lap. She could just as easily have been in a dentist's reception area awaiting a root canal. She probably would have considered that more enjoyable.

'We made coffee,' she said, the extent of her greeting.

'We're fine,' I answered for both of us. Joel and I took a seat.

'What you said on the phone – it – was a surprise,' said Ray. 'You said there were questions about how . . . how it happened?'

I'd been careful with my words over the phone. I didn't want the family to call the prosecutor and tell her that the defense was changing its theory. That might be unavoidable, ultimately, but I wanted to keep as many cards as close to my vest for as long as possible.

'Mr and Mrs Rubinkowski,' I began.

'Ray,' he said. 'And Doreen.'

He was being more generous than I'd have been, were the roles reversed. 'We have questions. I'm new to the case. I just came in less than two months ago, and maybe seeing things with fresh eyes makes a difference.'

They didn't respond to that. They seemed confused.

I asked, 'Can you think of why anyone might have wanted to hurt your daughter?'

Kathy's mother drew back, placing a hand over her heart like she was about to recite the Pledge of Allegiance. Her husband patted her knee.

'From what little information I have,' I said, 'your daughter was an ambitious young woman who was working her way through a master's program and had a bright future. So it seems weird to me to have to ask this question, but I feel compelled to do so.'

'You're saying this like we don't already know who shot her,' said Ray. 'Your client shot her. So why the hell would you ask us a question like that?'

By now silent tears had fallen down Doreen's cheeks. She turned her head to look out the window, a defense mechanism, while her husband glared at me.

I shrugged. 'I'm just trying to paint a picture for myself.'

'You want to smear Kathy,' he said through a clenched jaw. 'Is that it? You want to make her look like someone who deserved what happened to her.'

'No, sir,' I protested. 'I'm just—'

'You're trying to get your client off,' he interrupted. 'You'll say whatever you need to say to win the case. That's your job, isn't it? You don't care if what you're saying is right or wrong. You'll say whatever you need to say. You'll say bad things about

136

Kathy, if that's what it takes. And now you want us to be a part of it?'

'Ray—'

'Are you telling us that your client didn't kill our daughter?' Ray was growing more upset with every word. 'Because that would be the first I've heard of *that*.'

I sighed. I could tell him the truth, that I seriously doubted that Tom Stoller shot her, but once again I had to balance a lot of considerations. If Ray Rubinkowski had something very important and relevant to tell us, then it was worth disclosing my change in defense strategy to Ray, and therefore, inevitably, to the prosecution. But if I didn't think my odds were good, I was better off not showing my hand.

I'd hoped it wouldn't come to this. I'd hoped that the Rubinkowskis would just answer a few of my questions and let me be on my way. In hindsight, it was foolish of me. You can't walk into the home of bereaved parents and expect them to take a loaded question, like the one I asked, lying down.

Plus, I didn't want to do that to them. I knew what it was like to deal with a loss like theirs. You learn the facts, gruesome and incomprehensible facts, and you try to find a way to process them and ultimately coexist with them. Over time, the repetition, the constant replaying of the sordid information in your mind, has the effect of blunting it. On day one, you couldn't possibly utter the words – *my wife and daughter died in a car accident; my daughter was shot by a homeless man* – but over time the wounds scar over. Then someone like me comes along and says, That horrific pain that you've managed to store away? Well, it's all wrong. We have to rip open those scars. We have to reexamine everything. You have to relive this.

137

'No, I'm not saying that,' I answered. 'We're still pleading insanity.'

Ray and Doreen consoled each other. I waited them out. On the mantel of the fireplace was a shrine to their only child. Photos of Kathy Rubinkowski with a cap and gown at high school graduation, as a toddler sitting atop a horse, at the kitchen table, smiling into the camera with a mouthful of braces.

I looked at Lightner, who motioned toward the door. But I wasn't ready to go yet.

'Again, Ray, Doreen, I was just trying to get a big picture here. I didn't mean to upset you. I just have one more question, if I may.'

Finally, Ray composed himself and turned to me again. His jaw was clenched, his face reddening with frustration.

'Did you give anything to the police or the prosecutors?' I asked. 'I didn't see anything in the discovery.'

Ray, who had been ramping up to bawl me out again, was disarmed by the innocuous question. 'I – I don't think so.' He looked at his wife. 'Dor, did we give Wendy anything?'

'That legal document,' said Doreen. 'From the FedEx.'

'Oh, right. There was one thing,' he said to me. 'But I don't think there was anything to it. Wendy didn't seem to think so.'

I looked at Lightner. I had nothing to lose at this point.

'Did you keep a copy?' I asked.

27

Randall Manning smoothed his hands over his oak desk at the headquarters of Global Harvest International. It was the desk his father had when he ran GHI years ago, back when there was no 'I' in the initials, when the company was simply selling fertilizer products in a three-state region. The desk was largely empty. There was a computer monitor and mouse, which he considered garish but necessary, and on the right a line of family photographs. His wife, Bethany. His son, Quinn, with his wife and their daughter, Cailie.

Manning prided himself on a clean desk. It gave the impression of control. Sometimes Manning wondered if that was a misimpression.

'Go ahead, Richard,' he said in a calm voice.

'Mr Manning, it's Patrick Cahill. Again,' he added. Richard Moore was GHI's head of security. He was a former state trooper who cashed out after his pension fully vested and took a job with GHI. He was a reliable employee, in Manning's opinion, but in this case a nuisance.

'Insubordination, in a word,' Moore explained. 'Cahill wouldn't take direction from his supervisor. This particular supervisor is African-American. The supervisor directed Cahill to lock up one of the sheds, and Cahill refused. They almost came to blows, sir. They had to be separated. When it was all said and done, according to three separate witnesses, Cahill was heard saying – this is a quote – "I'm not taking directions from no . . ." and then he used the N-word.'

Manning closed his eyes. He squeezed the rubber stress ball in his hand. Squeezed it until it caused pain. 'What's your recommendation, Richard?'

'One-month suspension, sir. And probation. One more incident and he's gone.'

'But you've not instituted that yet?'

'No, sir. I have your clear instructions on Cahill. No discipline without your approval.'

Manning had personally hired Cahill and had explained to Moore, at the time, about Cahill's difficult upbringing and the need to give second chances to individuals in life. The background story had been largely false. The justification for hiring Cahill was entirely bogus.

'If I may say so, sir.' Moore cleared his throat. 'This will become a morale problem if we let him skate on this.'

'I understand, Richard. I have no intention of letting him "skate." I only wonder if there are other ways to handle this.'

'Sir, if I—'

'That will be all, Richard. I'm going to speak with Patrick, and I'll let you know.'

Moore paused, a delay that bordered on insubordination, before he nodded curtly and left the room.

Twenty minutes later, Patrick Cahill was standing at attention in Manning's office. Cahill was age twenty-seven, built like a truck, with a penetrating stare and a natural scowl to his face. He'd flamed out of the military, failed to qualify as a local cop, and bounced around personal-security firms and gigs as a bouncer at various bars. Virtually all of them had ended badly, insubordination and fighting being the principle causes.

He was an unstable and violent personality. He was a terrible choice for an employee.

But he was a perfect choice for the Circle.

'Patrick,' Manning said, standing face-to-face with Cahill. 'What am I going to do with you?'

'Sir—'

'Racial epithets, Patrick? Are you out of your *mind*?'

Cahill kept his eyes forward, military posture.

'You are never to call attention to yourself. *Never*. Understood?'

'Understood, sir.'

Manning shook his head in exasperation. 'Now I have to discipline you, Patrick. Because if I don't, I'll be calling even more attention to you.' He pointed to the door. 'Richard Moore wants to suspend you for one month. But I can't do that, can I, Patrick?'

No, he couldn't. Because a one-month suspension would take Cahill out of commission until December 15. And Randall Manning needed Patrick on the fence before then.

'I'm going to dock you a month's pay,' Manning said. 'I'll have accounting shave it off your weekly wage over six months' time. And then I'm going to pay you out of my own pocket, so you're made whole. But Patrick, this is your last chance. If you screw up again between now and the operation, I'm going to be impatient.'

Manning moved to within an inch of Cahill's face.

'Who took you in when you had nobody?'

'You did, sir.'

'Who gave you a job and a place to live?'

'You did, sir.'

'Who has given you the opportunity to change the world?'

'You, sir.'

'This is a war, Patrick, and very soon everyone's going to have to take a side. Make sure you're on the right side. No more mistakes. Now go.'

Patrick Cahill turned on his heel and marched out of the office.

28

Joel Lightner and I listened to the footfalls of Ray Rubinkowski, the arthritic clicking of his ankles, as he came back downstairs. Neither of us really understood what he was about to show us. When Ray came back into the parlor room, he handed me a two-page stapled document.

'I don't know if this means anything to you,' he said. 'Wendy said it didn't to her.'

That was the second time he'd said that.

It was a legal document. The heading said *Exhibit A: Response to Interrogatory #2*. In the header of the document, right-adjusted, was the name of a lawsuit and a docket number: 09 CH 1741. That told me the lawsuit was a civil action in state court that was filed in 2009.

The lawsuit was styled *LabelTek Industries Inc. v. Global Harvest International Inc.*

I didn't recognize LabelTek or Global Harvest International. Nothing in the document told me the subject matter of the lawsuit.

'This is a discovery document in a lawsuit,' I explained. 'Kathy was a paralegal, so discovery would be her primary responsibility.'

'That's right, it's what she did,' said Ray.

Each side in a lawsuit gets to ask questions, and request documentation, from the other side to get ready for trial. We call this 'discovery.' When a party submits written questions to the other side, they are known as 'interrogatories.' I consider this aspect of being a lawyer 'boring' and 'unbearable.'

But maybe not this one time. The document I was holding was a response to an interrogatory. The answer was long, so the party answering this interrogatory had apparently made its response a separate exhibit. For all I knew, that was standard. But I didn't really know. Discovery was largely for civil litigants. I avoided civil litigation like I avoided raw vegetables.

The response to the interrogatory listed a number of companies. The list filled two pages, with forty-seven companies. There were a couple of recognizable Fortune 500 companies on this list but mostly names I'd never heard.

I looked up at Ray Rubinkowski, who was watching me closely. 'Kathy gave you this?' I asked.

Ray nodded. 'A couple of days after Kathy died, I got a FedEx package. It was a birthday card for me, a gift-wrapped sweater, and this document.'

I didn't see the relevance of this document to anything I wanted to know.

'For all I knew, it was accidental,' he said. 'It fell in or something. I've been known to misplace an item now and again, and I figured she probably did just that.'

Sure, that was possible. 'So she mailed this a day or two before her death?'

'Yeah.'

It was hard to believe that was a coincidence. 'It was for your birthday – the package, I mean.'

'Yeah. My sixty-first birthday. Our birthdays were the same week. I turned sixty-one, she would've turned twenty-four. She wasn't going to make it out here to see us until the following weekend, so I suppose she wanted to make sure I got my present on time before my birthday. That would be like her.'

Okay, so maybe a coincidence. 'Do you still have the FedEx package?'

He shook his head no. That was okay. We knew the approximate date it was sent and the sender and recipient. If we needed proof of the delivery, we'd get it.

'On the back,' Lightner said to me.

I turned to him. 'What?'

'The back of the document,' he said.

I flipped the document over. There was handwriting. A grand total of four letters, followed by two question marks:

AN

NM

??

'I have no idea,' Ray said, when I asked him if the initials AN or NM meant anything to him.

'Did Kathy say anything about sending you something in the mail?' I tried.

'Not that I can remember. No, I don't think so.'

'Did she say anything about her job near the time she died? Anything about trouble she was having at work or anywhere else, for that matter?'

Ray jabbed a finger at me. 'You're doing it again. You're trying to dig up dirt on my little girl.'

I raised my hands. 'I wasn't. But never mind.'

Kathy's parents stared at me for a long time. It was clear that I'd reached my limit.

I thanked them profusely and left their house with the document in tow. When we reached our car and were well out of earshot of the Rubinkowskis, Joel and I looked at each other.

'Probably nothing,' I said.

'Yeah, probably,' he agreed. 'But the timing sure is interesting.'

29

The conference room in our law firm had become the unofficial war room for the Stoller trial. We had blow-up photos of the crime scene on tripods in one corner. A television rested in another corner, with a DVD of Tom Stoller's interrogation ready to play at any time. A few boxes rested on the conference room table.

The room was more than we needed. As these matters go, this wasn't a document-intensive case. Most of the paper was the physical evidence and forensic reports concerning the same. At the moment, there wasn't much for witnesses, either. We had Dr Sofian Baraniq and Bobby Hilton, the Army Ranger buddy. Then there was a guy named Sheldon Pierson who lived right by where the murder occurred on Gehringer Avenue. He estimated that he was probably outside during the time of the murder, but he couldn't add much because he couldn't hear or see a damn thing.

But I thought he could add a lot for me.

I was reviewing the responding police officer's write-up while Bradley was poring through the case file of *LabelTek Industries Inc. v. Global Harvest International Inc.* Yesterday, after my interview with the Rubinkowskis, I'd told Bradley to pull the entire file from the circuit court.

I was about to check on his progress when Shauna burst into the room like she had news.

'Yes, Ms. Tasker?' I said.

She held up a document. 'Motion from the prosecution. You're not going to like it.'

'Are you sure I'm not going to like it?'

'Pretty darn sure, yeah.'

'She's moving to bar the insanity defense,' I said.

Shauna cocked her head. 'How did you know *that*? Did she tell you?'

'No, but it's what I would have done.' I nodded and held out my hand for the document. 'She's claiming lack of cooperation, right?'

'Right.' She handed me the motion.

I was actually surprised Wendy Kotowski had waited this long. When you plead insanity, you place your mental condition at issue, and you must permit the government's shrinks to evaluate you. Tom had been as stingy with the prosecution's doctors as he had been with Dr Baraniq – and with me. The state was arguing that the defendant was making it impossible for them to fully evaluate him, and, thus, he should not be permitted to assert the insanity defense.

Bradley grabbed Shauna's copy and read it over. 'What does Nash do with this?' he asked.

'Grants it, probably,' I said.

'And you're calm about this.'

'Does it help if I freak out?' I read the motion in its entirety. It was well done. Wendy was always a good writer. Before she started first-chairing in the felony courtrooms, a lot of the

148

other ACAs would turn to her for help on briefs. There is a 'brief bank' in the county attorney's office where samples of various motions and briefs are kept, and many of them were penned by Wendy Kotowski.

Besides, she'd had plenty of time to draft this thing. She knew months ago she was going to argue this. Why not? It's a free shot on goal. Knock out the defendant's legal theory and he's left with nothing. And even if you lose, you tie up defense counsel on the eve of trial, make him scramble to respond to this motion instead of preparing for trial testimony. Wendy knew full well how thinly staffed we were at the law offices of Tasker & Kolarich.

'If she wins on this, she goes after Hilton next,' I said. 'She argues that there's no relevance to his testimony because if PTSD is out of the game, it doesn't matter what kind of shit Tom went through in Iraq. His war experience is irrelevant.'

'And then we're fucked,' said Bradley.

I tossed my football in the air, putting some English on it. 'Not necessarily,' I said.

'Why not necessarily?'

'For one thing, we can revisit fitness.'

'Fitness – for trial? What does that have to do with this?'

'Young Bradley, what is the standard for fitness for trial?'

'Fitness for . . . The defendant is able to . . .' He paused. 'The defendant has to be able to assist his lawyers in the preparation of his defense.'

'Correct. And what's his defense, young Bradley, in this case?'

'Well, insanity.'

'And if he won't talk to me about the case, is that assisting me?'

Young Bradley paused. I winked at Shauna. 'Wait for it,' I said.

'Oh,' Bradley said. 'Oh, so now the prosecution's saying the same thing as us.'

'There you go.'

Shauna piped in. 'So we join with the prosecution in arguing that Tom won't talk about the case. We renew our motion that Tom isn't fit to stand trial, and now we have Wendy Kotowski corroborating our position.'

'We do.' I threw the football too high in the air and almost didn't reach it coming back down. 'This will play right into Nash's wheelhouse. He loves to see lawyers tie themselves in knots with their own words.'

'And this does what?' Shauna asked. 'It just buys us time, right?'

'Right. It buys us time so my brilliant team of lawyers and investigators can discover hidden jewels of information that will reveal the innocence of our client.'

Shauna took a seat and looked at me crosswise. 'So that's why you wanted to keep the insanity notice on the books. Even though you didn't like it. You didn't plan on using it. You just wanted to bait the prosecution.'

I waved her off. 'Hey, before we break our arms congratulating ourselves, we have one very big variable,' I said. 'That obstacle goes by the name of Bertrand Nash.'

30

Tori stopped by the law office around eight-thirty with some work product for me. I'd deputized her, put her to work on summarizing some of the background evidence into abstracts that I could quickly reference if necessary. She'd wanted to help, and I'd warned her that it was grunt work, the lowest of the low – background summaries of Tom Stoller and the others with whom he'd served in Iraq. I'd probably never use them, but I'd rather have the information and not need it than need it and not have it.

Shauna had taken some work home with her, which was too bad, because I wanted her to meet Tori.

Tori looked glum. Not an uncommon reaction of a woman in my presence, and Tori wasn't exactly a ray of sunshine on a good day.

'This is really sad,' she said. 'He had schizophrenia hidden inside him and the post-traumatic stress unleashed it?'

'Yeah, it's a bitch of a thing, no question.'

'But you're not going to say that at his trial? That he had a flashback or whatever?'

I shook my head. 'I think I have a stronger case on reasonable doubt.'

'That's too bad,' she said.

I didn't follow.

'I mean, it's a compelling story,' she said. 'If I were on the jury and heard about war and that tragic thing that happened in Iraq with that little girl, and now he has post-traumatic stress, and on top of that, a mental illness, I'd feel sorry for him. I wouldn't want to convict him.'

That was a savvy observation, I thought, for a math major. She was right on the money.

'I'm going to try to get that information in front of the jury, anyway,' I said.

'Oh, good. You really should.' Tori strolled the conference room, looking at the exhibits. She stopped on the blow-ups of the crime scene, the dead stare of the victim, the pool of blood, but then quickly turned away.

'You get used to that,' I said.

She looked at me. 'To what?'

'The violence. The blood and gore. You have a problem with that, don't you?'

'Why do you say that?'

'Your reaction, the other day. When I told you I was defending someone accused of killing a woman in Franzen Park. You looked like you were about to vomit.'

She stared at me. I had a hunch that she didn't like being analyzed. I didn't, either. I was beginning to think we were made for each other.

'Well, I don't like violence against innocent people,' she said. 'I don't like it when people are minding their own business, trying to make a living and support their family and all the right things, and then someone comes along and

152

senselessly kills them. That turns my stomach, yes. And I wouldn't *want* to get used to it.'

Fair enough. A good reason to stick to mathematics. Plus, she would make a room full of male high school algebra students very, very happy. She removed her long white coat to reveal a black turtleneck and jeans. She looked better every time I saw her.

'But if you're a criminal or something,' she continued. 'If you're doing something bad. If you're a drug dealer or whatever and someone kills you – honestly, I don't have much sympathy for that. If you're in that game, you live with the risks.'

'You play in mud, you get muddy,' I said.

'Exactly.' Tentatively, she looked back at the crime scene blow-ups. 'So which one was she?'

'She – you mean the victim? Kathy Rubinkowski?'

'Yes. Which one was she? Was she an innocent victim? Or was she muddy?'

Interesting. Very interesting. It was really helpful to inject some fresh blood into this process, a layperson unschooled in the law but with brains and common sense, plus a nice ass.

It hadn't occurred to me to think of Kathy Rubinkowski as anything but a victim. If Tom shot her as part of a PTSD episode, the answer was easy, she was a random, innocent victim. But even if it were a Mob hit, I'd been working on the assumption that she had stumbled on something at work, that kind of thing, and she was murdered before she could expose it.

But Tori, unpolluted and viewing this from a fresh perspective, had made a good point. Why was Kathy necessarily an innocent player? She could have been involved in something shady herself. I made a note to mention something to Joel

Lightner. He was probably pursuing that angle, anyway, but it never hurt to make the comment.

'Maybe while you're majoring in math, you could minor in pre-law,' I said.

'Not for me.' She walked across the room to where I was sitting. My heart did a two-step. The faint scent of flowers followed with her. I knew – meaning my brain fully comprehended – that nothing was about to happen. She wasn't going to sit on my lap or disrobe or any of the images that swam through my head. But I found her approach provocative no less.

It was a humbling feeling. I still didn't really know how to do this. Even before I met my wife, I was never good at the initiation stage of a relationship. Since her death, I've never felt like I had my legs under me when it came to navigating this kind of thing.

'But I do want to help,' she said. 'I don't have any legal training, but I can do summaries or abstracts or whatever. I'd really like to help this poor guy.'

I narrowed my eyes. 'Are you sure this isn't your detached way of trying to spend more time with me?'

She watched me for a moment, then allowed for a small smile. 'Always that cocky exterior,' she said, shaking her head.

Yeah, okay, but I was breaking through with her, even just a little.

'You can help,' I said. 'Let's start by figuring out if Kathy Rubinkowski was clean or muddy.'

31

The clock was ticking – booming, actually – on the Stoller trial, but despite my attempts to clear my schedule as much as possible, I still had some other matters that required my attention. This morning, I had to cover a prelim on a residential burglary, a high school senior who broke into a neighbor's basement to steal part of his gun collection. The kid was eighteen, so there was no question on the adult transfer, but he'd been released to his parents on a fifty-thousand-dollar bond.

The preliminary hearing, where the government establishes probable cause to charge the defendant with a crime, took less than an hour. It was always the same, a one-sided affair where the prosecution gets to ignore virtually every rule of evidence, and the judge is directed by law to find probable cause as long as the prosecutor doesn't fall to his knees, burst into tears, and admit that the defendant is innocent.

My client's parents wore crestfallen expressions, an upgrade from their initial reactions of utter shock. Shock because they couldn't believe their boy would break into someone's house, and shock because of the swiftness and perceived mercilessness of a criminal justice system that doesn't make an exception for their precious child.

Three weeks in, they'd now resigned themselves to the circumstances, but they were no less perplexed and clearly heartbroken. They peppered me with questions, prodded me for assurances, and left the courtroom clutching their son.

When it was over, I went up to the sixth floor and asked the man at the reception desk for Wendy Kotowski. After making me wait for ten minutes, Wendy appeared down the hallway, waved me back, and started toward her office. Not exactly a first-class escort, but we had history, and informality between us was customary. In the end, we were good friends and held each other in high regard.

'Kolarich, you're a piece of shit, you know that?' she said as I entered her office.

Okay, maybe not *high* regard.

Wendy had enough seniority in the office to have walls and a door but no window. With her time in and her talent, she should be even higher up on the chain by now. But with the economy like it was, there wasn't much movement out of the county attorney's office these days, so the ones who'd been around longest were sticking around.

I liked her. She shot straight and kept everything in perspective. She was fair to the defense beyond what was minimally required, at least in my opinion, but when she got into a courtroom she was fierce.

'How are the twins?' I asked, nodding to the photos on her desk. Two boys, they'd be twelve or thirteen by now, if my memory was right.

'Good, they're good,' she said, and sighed. 'They just got their drivers' licenses, so I'd advise against driving in the city until they're off to college.'

Okay, I was off a few years.

'Why am I a piece of shit?' I asked. 'Your voice mail wasn't specific. There could be any number of reasons.'

Wendy looked around her office for something. From the stacks of paper covering her floor, it was no simple task.

'I understand you had a nice visit with the Rubinkowskis,' she said.

'It was very nice, thanks for asking.'

She dropped her head and leveled a gaze on me. 'Are you trying to get between me and the family?'

'Wouldn't dream of it.'

'No, of course not. "Can you think of why anyone might have wanted to hurt your daughter?" What the hell was that about?'

I played innocent. 'Hey, you're moving to bar my insanity defense, kid. I need a plan B.'

'Yeah, and a plan C, too, apparently. "Did you give Wendy any documents?" You think I don't know what you're doing?'

'What am I doing?' A nonanswer. Wendy watched me for a long time.

'I know you, Kolarich. When you filed your appearance in this case, I told Connor—'

'How is Connor?'

'Good. Getting divorced, but good.' She nodded. 'I told him, here comes a fucking headache around the corner. I knew you'd start pulling shit here.'

She looked tired in the eyes. Her unmanageably curly hair had a dark tint to it, bloodred, which told me that gray must be creeping in and she was going with a bottle. Bad choice, in my opinion. Maybe she was dating again. She'd divorced when the twins were fairly young, and during the years we were in the office together, she'd basically surrendered any thought of

157

romance, focusing on keeping those boys on the straight and narrow and putting criminals in prison. Different time, different situation, I might have even gone for her myself.

'There's a case you may have heard of called *Brady versus Maryland*,' I said.

'Bullshit. Bullshit, and you know it,' she said. 'That document isn't remotely exculpatory. It doesn't have anything to do with this case. Especially an insanity case.'

But back when Tom Stoller had been indicted, the assistant public defender, Bryan Childress, had pleaded both not guilty and not guilty by reason of insanity. It was a formality, the dual plea, but technically my defense extended beyond insanity to a straight NG.

Even so, she was right – that document that Mr Rubinkowski had given me wasn't telling me much of anything, at least not on the surface. There was no particular reason why Wendy would think this would be favorable to me. When I was a prosecutor, I always erred on the side of disclosure. I gave the defense pretty much anything and everything. It was one part strategy and one part ethics: If I gave them everything, they could never tag me with a *Brady* violation, and it also allowed me to inundate the defense with unnecessary material so that anything particularly good for the defense would not stick out.

Wendy waited me out. When I didn't speak, she finally said, 'So?'

She wanted to know if I was going to try to fuck her on this.

'So what?' I asked.

'Are you gonna try to fuck me on this?'

'The thought never crossed my mind.' I kept a poker face,

then laughed. 'Wendy, I wouldn't do that,' I said. 'I sincerely believe that at the time, you thought this document was not exculpatory. You had no idea how explosively relevant that document would turn out to be.'

She rolled her eyes. 'Explosively relevant,' she repeated back.

'A bombshell. A game-changer.'

'Sure.' She framed her hands. 'Just when you think Tom Stoller shot Kathy Rubinkowski, you learn that – horrors – she was a paralegal who helped prepare responses to discovery requests!'

I smiled again. I didn't smile much, but I did around her. I missed my fellow prosecutors. I missed this office. 'I'm sure you're right,' I said. 'In fact, the more I think about it, that document holds no relevance whatsoever. I wouldn't even give it another thought if I were you. Really.'

Back to playing poker with her. She knew the dance. I think she found it amusing. I used to be able to punch her buttons. I once had her in stitches in a courtroom, still laughing hard as her case was called, and she narrowly avoided a contempt citation.

'You have a copy of that document, then?' I asked.

She nodded. 'Ray faxed me a copy back when he received it.'

'Good enough. And I trust there are no other documents you've brazenly withheld?'

'Not that I can think of at the moment.' Wendy watched me for a time, then her smirk slowly disappeared. 'You're not going to ask for an extension based on this – this innocuous piece of written discovery?'

'No,' I said.

Her posture softened. She looked up at me again. 'So – how are you doing these days? You got your feet back under you?'

'Sometimes I pinch myself,' I said.

'That good, eh?'

'No, I just like pinching myself.' We were done. I pushed myself out of the chair.

'Loser buys dinner,' I said.

'Deal. Someplace with a white tablecloth.'

She didn't have to agree so quickly.

32

Bradley John all but pounced on me when I returned to the law firm. He was still young and eager, which I was hoping would rub off on me, at least the 'eager' part. Bradley did three years as a county prosecutor in one of the collar counties, which meant he got good experience up front, but he tired of the reverse commute and wanted to work in the same city where he lived. He'd just turned thirty but still did the social-barhopping thing, still viewed his law career as completely in front of him, and overall seemed like a guy who was happy to be part of the team.

He had something to show me and beckoned me to the conference room, the war room. Once there, I picked up the document that Ray Rubinkowski had given me and flipped it over to the back, which had the cryptic handwriting:

AN

nm

??

'You figure who AN and NM are?' I asked.

'Working on it,' he said. 'But I did figure out those symbols below the initials. They're question marks. It means she had a question.'

'That's first-class work, Bradley. And just for your own knowledge, it would be very helpful if AN and NM were the initials of the two people who murdered Kathy Rubinkowski.'

'Got it.'

'And if you could get their confessions, too. That'd be great.'

'No problem, Boss. Next on my list.'

Bradley had taken little time becoming comfortable with my sarcasm. It was one of the few endearing qualities he possessed. That and being industrious and talented.

'*LabelTek Industries versus Global Harvest International,*' he said, the name of the case that was in the header of the document Kathy Rubinkowski had sent to her parents. Presumably, that told us that Kathy had been preparing answers to written interrogatories related to that lawsuit.

I settled in for an explanation.

'Global Harvest International sells fertilizer and related products to commercial interests,' Bradley said to me. 'LabelTek designs labels. They claim that they designed the label for a product that Global Harvest was selling called Glo-Max. It's some kind of commercial-grade fertilizer. Anyway, they're claiming Global Harvest took their design and used it and screwed them out of a royalty. So they're suing, right?'

'The American way.'

'Right. They're saying they are owed a royalty for every bag of Glo-Max that was sold. They estimate damages in the lawsuit to be in excess of three million dollars. So in this lawsuit, they issue all the standard discovery – interrogatories, requests for production of documents – all that normal bullshit flurry of paper.'

He pointed at the document that Ray Rubinkowski had given me. I flipped it over from the back, with the handwritten initials, to the front, which bore the heading *Exhibit A: Response to Interrogatory #2.*

'So what was interrogatory number two?' I asked.

'LabelTek asked for a list of every company that had purchased Glo-Max fertilizer.'

I looked down at the paper. Sure. This was the response to that question. Forty-seven different companies had purchased Glo-Max fertilizer.

'This is where it gets interesting,' said Bradley. He reached into a box and removed a thick stack of documents attached to a green folder, bound at the top. This was part of the court file. For cases that are no longer active, the clerk's office will let licensed attorneys check out a court file for twenty-four hours. But you mess with the order of the documents or remove one and forget to replace it, the Supreme Court gets testy. 'I found Global Harvest's answer to that interrogatory,' he said.

'I have it right here, right? The one Ray Rubinkowski gave to me.'

'Wrong.' Bradley suppressed a smile. He was right – this was getting interesting.

He had a document ready for me. He'd already made copies from the court file and replaced them in the file. He slid it in front of me. It was the entire set of Global Harvest's responses to the many interrogatories issued by LabelTek. The first page bore the court clerk's file stamp, which made it official. I leafed through to the back of the document, because I knew the response to interrogatory number two was appended as a separate exhibit due to its length.

'The draft response to interrogatory number two that you got from Mr Rubinkowski had forty-seven names on it,' said Bradley. 'The one they filed had forty-*six*.'

I did a quick check, but Global Harvest's lawyers had made it easy for me by numbering the list. Sure enough, the response listed forty-six companies, one less than the draft answer that Kathy Rubinkowski had mailed to her father.

'And you're going to tell me which one was missing,' I said.

Bradley nodded. 'It was a company called Summerset Farms Incorporated. It was number thirty-eight on the draft response Kathy sent her parents. It doesn't appear in the final version filed in court.'

Okay. That might be something. Or it might be nothing. Global Harvest didn't list Summerset Farms as one of the purchasers. So what?

'Who is Summerset Farms?' I asked.

'There isn't much online about them. Looks like they're a local company that grows wheat and makes a granola and a cereal they sell locally.'

'Okay. Is that it?' I asked.

'Nope.' He shook his head vigorously, full of pride in his discovery. He slid another document in front of me. 'Here is a subpoena that LabelTek issued to Summerset Farms.'

I looked it over. It was a subpoena duces tecum, meaning a subpoena for records only and not for a personal appearance. It requested 'copies of any and all contracts, invoices, shipping orders, correspondence, and any other like documents pertaining to the purchase of Glo-Max 2.0 Fertilizer from Global Harvest International or its subsidiaries or agents.' It also requested the name of the individual at Summerset Farms 'most knowledge-able about any transactions involving Glo-Max.'

A lot of legalese, but I got the drift. 'Somehow,' I said, 'the lawyers at LabelTek had reason to know about Summerset Farms, even though Global Harvest didn't mention them.'

'Right, and it took me a day to figure out how.' Bradley was enjoying himself. The thrill of a discovery, a breakthrough, which I certainly hoped this was.

'The sale of certain fertilizers are governed by state and federal regulations. I'm not going to pretend to know the full extent, but I do know that our state's Department of Agriculture, maybe in concert with the feds, maybe separate—'

'Bradley, cut to it.'

'Okay. The state agriculture department requires that companies report sales of certain kinds of fertilizer. The state tracks the sales and movement.'

'So if someone looked it up, they could see that Global Harvest sold Glo-Max fertilizer to Summerset Farms.'

'Something like that,' Bradley said. 'The database doesn't include all the information. You don't know for sure which brand of fertilizer was purchased from reading the public portion of the database. But you can see that Summerset Farms is listed as a purchaser, yeah.'

Bradley showed me another document. Another subpoena. This one was issued to the state Department of Agriculture.

'Same day that LabelTek subpoenaed Summerset Farms,' he said, 'January fifth, they also sent a subpoena to the state Department of Agriculture.'

Right. Same date, January 5. Same basic information requested. They wanted to know if the state had any records of Summerset Farms purchasing the Glo-Max product.

'Okay,' I said. 'The lawyers for LabelTek weren't going to trust their opponents in litigation to list all their customers. I mean, the more sales Global Harvest made, the more money LabelTek can claim as royalties, right? So they subpoenaed Summerset Farms and the Department of Agriculture. That makes sense. That's what I would have done. Take a shot. See what you find.'

'Right,' said Bradley.

'And – what did they find?'

A wide grin spread across Bradley's face. 'Nothing,' he said.

'Okay, I'll bite. Why did they find nothing, Bradley?'

He slid another document in front of me. The caption read, 'Motion for Voluntary Dismissal and for a Good-Faith Finding.'

I was no expert in civil litigation, but I knew what a voluntary dismissal was – it meant the lawsuit was being dropped. I was vaguely aware, through Shauna, that settlements had to be approved by the court. The court had to find that the settlement was made in 'good faith.'

Okay, fine – the parties settled. Civil lawsuits settle far more often than they go to trial. That's one of the myriad reasons I loathe civil litigation.

'Check the date,' Bradley said.

The motion for voluntary dismissal was filed on January 8.

'Interesting,' I said.

'Three days after the subpoenas were issued,' said Bradley. 'And that includes the time to actually reach a settlement. Look at the signed settlement agreement. The date is January seventh.'

He was right. The settlement was signed on January 7 by someone named Randall M. Manning, CEO and president of Global Harvest International.

'And factor in that it takes at least a few conversations to reach a settlement,' I said. 'And then draw up the papers.'

Bradley was nodding enthusiastically. 'That means they settled the lawsuit almost immediately upon seeing those subpoenas.'

Okay, but we were still missing something. I hadn't read these documents, but Bradley obviously had.

'How much was the settlement?' I asked.

This kid couldn't stop grinning. 'Remember I said that LabelTek estimated damages at three mil?'

'I do.'

'They settled for *four* million, plus over a hundred thousand in attorneys' fees.'

'Wow.' I got up from my chair and started pacing. I wished I had my football. 'So Kathy Rubinkowski, preparing draft answers to written discovery in the lawsuit, makes a list of Glo-Max purchasers that includes Summerset Farms. Then somebody, ultimately, removes Summerset from that list. Then the enter-prising lawyers representing LabelTek check the state database, take a shot, and issue subpoenas to Summerset and the Depart-ment of Agriculture.'

'Yep.'

'And basically before sundown the next day, Global Harvest has completely laid down. Not only do they settle, but they settle for *more* than LabelTek was requesting, and they pay their attorneys' fees. That's got to be the first time in recorded history that a case settled by giving the plaintiff every dollar they asked for, *plus* an additional third, *plus* fees.'

'And the case had only just begun,' said Bradley. 'They hadn't even taken depositions yet. It's not like a witness turned on them or something. This is totally bizarre.'

'You forgot the best part,' I said. 'Kathy Rubinkowski was murdered on January thirteenth.'

Bradley kicked up his feet onto the conference room table, his performance completed.

'You believe in coincidences, Boss?'

My young associate deserved a gold star. He'd found a thread. Now we had about two weeks to see how hard we could pull on it.

'I don't believe in coincidences,' I said. 'But I do believe in cover-ups.'

33

The law firm of Dembrow, Lane, and McCabe was twenty
lawyers, covering the gambit for its corporate clients. They
had a bankruptcy practice and an intellectual property group,
but their bread and butter was serving the everyday needs of
large companies, from labor and employment to regulatory
compliance to transactional work to litigation.

A quick Google search told me that the firm laid off ten
lawyers, a third of their workforce, just over a year ago. Corporate law firms rose and fell with the fate of their clients, and
therefore with the economy. Some of these midsize firms were
successfully using the economic downturn as a marketing tool
– *big-firm representation at a small-firm price*, that kind of thing
– but apparently not so for Dembrow, Lane.

Their offices were what you'd expect, designed to impress but
not impressive. The conference room to which they led us on
the thirty-second floor had a view of the commercial district,
which was buzzing on a Friday morning.

I was alone. I'd thought about bringing along Bradley John,
who had uncovered this information two days ago. And it
would have been nice to have Shauna here, who can read

people with the best of them. But the more I thought about it, the more I thought it was better just the two of us.

Bruce McCabe entered the conference room at nine forty-five – fifteen minutes late – without apology. He was about six feet tall and a little soft in the midsection. He had a high-and-tight haircut and dark, deep-set eyes. I knew from the bio on his firm's website that McCabe started in the military, serving in the JAG Corps, before he moved to the private sector some twenty years ago. What the bio didn't say, but what I caught as a vibe from the moment he entered the room, was that Bruce McCabe was a humorless man, with an intensity bordering on anger.

He made a point of checking his watch before he even offered his hand to me. 'My morning is full,' he said. 'I made some time for you but not much.'

'I appreciate you doing that,' I said.

'You didn't exactly ask nicely.'

That was true. When I couldn't even get him on the phone, I threatened his secretary with a subpoena. Then I repeated the threat to him. It was an empty threat, in fact. A subpoena would have tipped the prosecution to my strategy. My case wasn't all that good on innocence, so I needed to at least keep the element of surprise. But he didn't know that. The subpoena threat got his attention. That told me something, right there.

'Fifteen minutes,' he said.

'I represent Tom Stoller, the man charged with Kathy Rubinkowski's murder.'

'You said that on the phone.'

'We have some questions about her death.'

'You said that on the phone, too. Are you going to tell me something new?'

I fixed my glare on him. Okay, asshole. Here's something new: 'Kathy Rubinkowski was working on a lawsuit filed by LabelTek Industries against one of your clients, Global Harvest International. We were wondering if Kathy had ever expressed concern with you over anything related to that case.'

McCabe studied me for a long time. Then he said, 'I thought you were conceding that your client shot Kathy. I thought this was only about insanity.'

'We're exploring options,' I said.

'I see.' He drummed his fingers on the countertop of the conference room table. 'Well, the answer is even if she did express concerns to me, I wouldn't tell you.'

That's the same answer I would have given. Probably the only one he *could* give.

'I see that the case settled,' I said. 'Not six months into it, before depositions, just after the New Year in January.'

McCabe opened his hands. 'Is there a question?'

'The question is why,' I said.

'You couldn't possibly expect me to tell you why my client chose to settle a lawsuit.'

'If the case settled for thirty cents on the dollar, no. Or fifty cents. Or even eighty cents. But a hundred and thirty cents? Plus attorneys' fees? Global Harvest gave LabelTek everything they asked for and much more.'

McCabe drilled a stare directly through me. He was the lead counsel on the case. At best, I was telling him he got his ass kicked. But we both knew I was suggesting something else – that he laid down, that his opponent was sniffing a little too close to something sensitive, and they paid a king's ransom to make them go away.

'Since you seem to know so much about that case,' he said,

'and because it's a matter of public record, I don't mind reminding you that LabelTek only *estimated* damages at three million dollars. In fact, it turned out that their information showed that number to be much higher.'

'C'mon, Counsel. Neither of us is stupid.'

McCabe chose to channel his anger into a forced smile. I do that sometimes, too. 'Is there anything else, Mr Kolarich?'

'Did you like Kathy Rubinkowski?'

'Of course I did. Everyone did. We were devastated by the news.'

'Then I would think you'd want to bring her killer to justice.'

'Of course I do. But I'm not going to abrogate the attorney-client privilege so you can go on a wild-goose chase.'

I nodded and thought for a moment. McCabe began to push himself out of his chair.

'You know anything about Summerset Farms?' I asked.

He settled back in his chair and looked out the window. 'Summerset . . .'

'The company that was served with the subpoena just before you settled the lawsuit, Bruce. It was also the subject of a separate subpoena issued the same day to the state agriculture department. You haven't heard of Summerset?'

'I . . . don't recall anything about . . . about a Summerset Farms.'

'That's odd,' I replied. 'Because you're their lawyer.'

It's hard to keep a poker face when you're busted that badly. McCabe wasn't very good at it. He could have played it off any number of ways. He could have said yes, of course he was Summerset's lawyer, he meant only that he couldn't remember the subpoena.

Bradley John had made that connection yesterday. Summerset Farms was incorporated in this state, and every corporation has to designate someone as its agent for service of process and other matters. They named Bruce McCabe. That was strange, actually. Normally, you'd name one of the corporate officers or some employee. Summerset had named its outside counsel. It was another question I would try to answer, starting today.

'This meeting is over, Counsel.' McCabe got to his feet.

'Good enough,' I said. 'I understand your position. You don't hold the privilege. So I'll have to go to the person who does.'

He blinked twice. 'What's that?'

'I'll have to subpoena Randall Manning. The big guy at Global Harvest. The one who signed the settlement agreement.'

McCabe paused. 'Just because he signed the settlement agreement doesn't mean he has knowledge of the settlement.'

'Then he can tell me that. After I subpoena him.'

'I'll quash that subpoena.'

'You mean you'll *try* to quash it. You'll fail. You ever met Judge Nash?'

McCabe grew tense. He was considering his options. I was learning more and more as I went along here. 'I could speak to him about a limited waiver,' he suggested. 'Maybe he'll let me discuss this in more detail.'

I made a show of weighing that option. 'Nah, my curiosity is piqued. I'm going with the subpoena.' I got to my feet. 'Thanks for your time. I'll copy you on the correspondence.'

'Wait,' he said.

I stopped at the door.

'What if I were to arrange something? You and Mr Manning and I could have an informal discussion. There's no need for a subpoena.'

'That's the spirit, Bruce.' I tapped the door. 'First thing next week, or I issue that subpoena.'

34

Randall Manning stood in the office of his lawyer, Bruce McCabe. Being one of the name partners at Dembrow, Lane, and McCabe meant a corner office with enough room for a conference table as well, with impressive views to the west suburbs and south of the industrial flats.

But the shades were drawn out of an abundance of caution, notwithstanding that they were thirty-two stories above ground. Stanley Keane was smoothing out the map on the conference table. Bruce McCabe was waiting to present his information.

Manning watched each of them. His eyes wandered to Bruce's impressive walnut desk. Like Manning himself, Bruce McCabe lined his desk with photographs of his family, in particular his oldest son, James.

Invariably, Manning's attention turned to his only son, Quinn. Manning had always known that his son was smarter than he. He remembered the summers when Quinn would intern at the company that he was destined to take over one day, the fresh perspective he brought even as a high school kid, the insightful comments. It had been Quinn's idea, not so long ago, to expand aggressively overseas. He'd done an entire workup without solicitation, projections and figures and strategies. 'It says *Global* Harvest on the door, right, Dad?' he'd said. 'And what does "International" mean to you?'

And Randall Manning had made the biggest mistake of his life. He'd agreed to let Quinn explore the opportunities.

'Okay, here we go,' said Stanley Keane.

Bruce McCabe had a yellow highlighter, which he poised over the map of the city's commercial district and near-north side. He drew on the map as he spoke. 'The procession starts at noon on South Walter Drive next to the Hartz Building,' he said. 'It will move north up Walter and wind around with the river. It will cross the Lerner Street Bridge. And once over the river, it's only three blocks to the federal building.'

Manning nodded. That's where the procession would end, at the north end of the federal building, known derisively as the 'brown building' for its drab color and unexceptional architecture. It was home to the federal courts, the U.S. attorney's office, and more than thirty agencies of the federal government. It was in the federal plaza that, immediately following the march, a brief outdoor commemoration would take place.

'Last year,' said Stanley Keane, 'it took thirty-eight minutes to reach the federal plaza for the commemoration.'

'And the commemoration lasted how long?'

'Thirty-six minutes.'

'So one P.M. would be a safe target time.' Manning looked at Stanley.

'Yes, sir. That's the plan.'

Manning nodded. 'What about security?'

'Security.' Stanley Keane groaned. 'You know how it is these days, Randy. They keep that stuff pretty close to the vest. All we can say is what happened last year.'

'Refresh me,' said Manning, though he didn't require a refresher. He knew every aspect of the security from last year's event. He just wanted to gauge Stanley Keane's preparation.

Stanley used a pencil and marked up the map. 'It was primarily a perimeter formation,' he said. 'City police on foot, about six for every city block, lining the curb on each side. Vehicle blocks on each end, but only sporadically blocking the cross streets. Mostly the east-west streets were simply barricaded with traffic horses. It's kind of a scaled-down version of what they'd do in a full-blown parade. I mean, it's the middle of winter and all. Most people don't care all that much about Pearl Harbor Day.'

They will now, thought Manning. He asked, 'And what about the state police?'

Stanley shook his head. 'I don't know, sir. I'd imagine they'd stay very close to the governor as he walks at the head of the pack. But I don't know. The governor didn't participate last year.'

But he would this year. Governor Trotter, plus one of the state's U.S. senators and the city's mayor, would be walking in the front row of the procession. They would be joined by a former brigadier general who lived in the city and who served in World War II. He was, in fact, serving in Pearl Harbor on the day it was attacked.

Manning looked out the window, through the drawn translucent shade, colored by the rays of the afternoon sun. He thought about what was going to happen nineteen days from now.

What had President Roosevelt said about December 7, 1941? *A date which will live in infamy.*

And what would be said about December 7 of this year? A

different time, a different event, but no doubt similar proclamations, teeth-gnashing denunciations, self-righteous indignation.

But one day, Manning was sure, history would thank him.

'All right. Bruce, your turn,' said Manning. 'Tell me about this visit you had this morning. Tell me about Jason Kolarich.'

35

'The trial begins on December first,' I said to Joel Lightner. 'That's eleven days from now. Anyone mention that to you yet?'

'Did anyone mention to *you* that the FBI has tried to come up with the identity of Gin Rummy for the last *three years* and drawn a blank?'

We were walking down Gehringer Street. It was Saturday, early evening, and the Franzen Park neighborhood was alive. The taverns and restaurants we passed were full. The sidewalks were crowded with people. Everyone was having a good time. Everyone but me.

To everyone else, Saturday meant the weekend, time with family, drinking and socializing and relaxing. To me, it meant people were harder to find, government offices and professional workplaces were closed. And after the weekend, it would be a short week for Thanksgiving. People would be halfway out the door by noon on Wednesday. And then forget it, there's no chance of finding anybody until the following Monday.

And the Monday after Thanksgiving was November 29 – two days before we started selecting a jury.

Joel Lightner had spent the last week trying to nail down

the Gin Rummy question. He'd tapped all his connections at the local, state, and federal levels and come up empty.

'Just the last three years?' Tori asked. Yes, I'd brought her along. She'd visited the other crime scene with us, why not this one, too? Besides, she'd shown a real interest in this case and her non-lawyer, lay perspective had proven helpful on more than one occasion thus far.

Clearly, then, I had several reasons for bringing her along. It wasn't like I was trying to impress her or win her over. Good. Glad that was settled.

'The name Gin Rummy first came over a wiretap about four years ago,' said Joel. 'Second-rate sources. Not Paulie Capparelli or anybody at the top. So the FBI, they jot the name down, but they don't think much of it. Right? I mean, these guys, they all have about five nicknames, anyway.'

'Okay,' said Tori, though she probably had no idea.

'But then there's a prison tap. Rico Capparelli, the top guy, who's inside for life now, he mentions the name. So now the FBI is paying attention. As best they can tell, Gin Rummy has about ten hits to his name over the last couple of years. Remember Anthony Moretti?'

I did, in passing, at least. The Moretti family, which had connections out east in New Jersey, was the principal rival of the Capparellis. About a year ago, Anthony Moretti, the capo, was shot in his bed. Two bodyguards in the apartment were found dead, too.

'That was Gin Rummy?' I asked.

'That's what everyone thinks.'

Tori looked at me. 'So you're messing with a pretty big guy.'

'I like to keep things interesting. But I have to *find* this guy first.'

We crossed Mulligan at the crosswalk and passed a shoe store that Talia used to love.

'I love this store,' Tori said. It stood to reason, fashionista that she was. I can't believe the word 'fashionista' was even in my vocabulary. The boys back home would be ashamed. Maybe I was getting soft.

We got halfway down the block on the west side of the street and stopped. Lightner fished out copies of the photographs from a manila envelope.

'Here,' he said, pointing to a tree that had been planted in the middle of the sidewalk. I didn't understand why the city bothered. Regardless, this time of year, the branches were naked, leaving it looking more like a gigantic, ugly weed.

'The shell casing was found in the dirt at the base of the tree,' said Joel. He took a couple of steps to his left, which put him almost up against a tall privacy fence that served an apartment building. Behind that five-foot privacy fence was a condo building where a witness, Sheldon Pierson, was prepared to testify that he was outside, untangling Christmas decorations, during the interval of time in which the medical examiner estimated the murder occurred, but unfortunately he didn't hear a thing or obviously see anything.

On the opposite side of the street were walk-up three-flats and some single-families. Some were renovated in the last decade and some looked like they'd barely survived an aerial bombing. A neighborhood in progress, halted by the economic downturn.

Joel extended his right arm and made a gun with his hand. 'So he shot her from here. The casing probably landed straight in the dirt.'

Using one of the evidence photos as a guide, I walked over

to the curb and found the spot where Kathy Rubinkowski had fallen dead. There was a diagonal crack in the curb that I could use as a reference point from the photographs. Plus I pretty much knew it, anyway, as this wasn't my first trip to the crime scene. It's absolutely vital that you visit the crime scene. It's almost as important that you visit it a second time, and a third. You have to see things up close. You have to play out the scene. Otherwise, you could miss something that could make or break the case.

'Last time I walked it, it was ten feet,' I said, measuring the distance from Joel Lightner to me.

'That's highly accurate shooting,' Joel said, not for the first time.

'He shot her right between the eyes?' Tori asked. 'So she was looking right at him?'

I looked at Tori. 'What's your point?'

She was her typically put-together self in the long white coat with black knee-high boots. 'If someone pointed a gun at me, I'd run. Or duck.'

'That's what you think,' said Joel. 'But in fact, humans center their eyes on danger. There are studies on this. People want to predict the danger, so they focus on whatever is the source of danger. If Kathy saw the gun, odds are that she'd fix her eyes directly on it, and she'd turn so she was seeing it head-on.'

Tori listened, then shook her head. 'I'd duck. I wouldn't stare at the gun.'

'That would be your secondary response,' said Joel. 'Your initial response would be to focus on the weapon. Remember, this probably happened in the space of a second or two. Maybe given more time, maybe the outcome would have been different.'

181

'This is all very fascinating, folks,' I said. 'When this over, let's write an article together. But for now, how about we figure out how to acquit our client of murder?'

Peter Gennaro Ramini watched Jason Kolarich and the others as they reenacted the shooting of Kathy Rubinkowski. He'd had little trouble following them, using the cover of the festive crowd on a Saturday night. He didn't need to get too close at this point. He knew what they were doing. So he stood at the intersection of Gehringer and Mulligan, half a city block away, leaning against the door of a bank, his hands stuffed in his pockets as always – his signature, at this point.

Kolarich and company seemed to have the details of the shooting basically right, the distance and the angle, the position of the victim's body. The latter detail would have been easy to gather from the photographs. The accuracy of their distance measurement surprised him initially. Once you got past a space of four feet or so, it was difficult to pin down the distance of a gunshot with any particularity.

But then he remembered the spent shell casing. That must have been how they measured it. There had been no need to be concerned about the shell casing, from his perspective, because it didn't matter if the casing traced back to the murder weapon; the murder weapon was going to be found, anyway. Besides, if the shell casing wasn't left behind, it would look like a professional job. It wouldn't look like an amateur robbery-turned-homicide, which is how he'd wanted it to appear.

But the flip side of that was now obvious to him: It gave a distance. And that distance was meaningful, a pretty long distance for a Glock to be fired with such precision. It gave

Kolarich an argument he wouldn't otherwise have – that the shooting was carried out by someone of superior skill. A pro. A hired gun.

He watched them until he knew all he needed to know. And then he went home.

Tomorrow, there would be a conversation.

36

The black town car picked up Peter Ramini at precisely nine in the morning, as Ramini exited the drugstore. He got into the backseat and quickly returned his hands to his coat pockets.

Next to him, Donnie ate a bagel lathered with blueberry cream cheese, more than a little of which found resting places on his chin or his ever-expanding stomach. The guy was like a beached whale. But he was the only person Paulie Capparelli trusted, the only person in the world who could lean down and whisper into Paulie's ear and receive advice back the same way.

'Whaddaya got, Pete?' Donnie grunted.

'I got a problem, that's what I got.'

'Tell Donnie. Donnie will make it all better.'

Ramini glanced over. Sometimes Donnie forgot that he was the courier, not the decision maker.

'You remember this thing back in January, almost a year ago, with that lady at the law firm.'

Donnie grunted again. That meant yes. 'Polish name.'

'Rubinkowski, right.'

'A beautiful piece of work, my friend. They pinched some

other guy, and the fucknut actually *confessed* to it.' Donnie had a good chuckle with that. 'He says he was insane, right?'

'That's right, Don. But listen. So we just had this other thing – the one with Zo.'

Donnie grew quiet with the change in topic. Of course he recalled that. Lorenzo Fowler, at one time, had been one of those guys who could whisper in the capo's ear, only then the capo was Rico Capparelli, not Paulie. Still, even with the transition, Zo had been considered a trusted member of the inner cabinet – trusted, that is, until the problem with the strip club owner. Nobody had told Zo to take a baseball bat to the guy, and then, of all things, he fucking *died* from the injuries.

Lorenzo had been feeling the hot breath of law enforcement on his neck, and it wasn't hard to see the nerves getting to him. Enough so that Paulie ordered a close watch over Lorenzo.

So when Lorenzo made a phone call to set up a meeting with Jason Kolarich – not one of their Mob lawyers but a total outsider – Paulie knew about it within ten minutes. And he didn't like it.

'You remember how Zo called that attorney,' said Ramini.

'Yeah. Right. We figured he was gonna cut and run. Use an outside lawyer so we wouldn't know.'

'Right. So remember this lawyer's named Jason Kolarich.'

'Right.' Donnie took a mountainous bite of his bagel. 'Kolarich. What is that, Russian? Bulgarian?'

Ramini breathed in, breathed out.

'Romanian? No, Hungar–'

'Don, how the fuck should I know? He's from . . . Paraguay, okay? He's from fucking Antarctica. I fucking care.'

'Petey–'

'I'm trying to make a serious point here. I got a problem here, all right?'

'Okay, Petey.' Donnie patted Ramini's knee. 'Listen, I know this already. Lorenzo goes to see the lawyer. We're afraid he mighta told him things. Lots of things. But then you took care of Lorenzo. So that erases the lawyer from the equation. He's got nobody to worry about after Lorenzo was in the ground. Problem solved, right?'

'Wrong. Because this guy Kolarich, he's not some random lawyer. We figured Lorenzo picked just anybody. Like outta the phone book or whatnot.'

'Right.'

'Right, but it turns out Kolarich isn't just some random guy. Kolarich is the lawyer who is defending the guy they pinched on the Rubinkowski thing.'

Donnie stopped in mid-bite. His head slowly turned to Ramini, cream-cheese chin and all. 'The guy who says he's crazy?'

'Right. Tom Stoller is his name. But whatever. Point being, Zo wasn't just talking to some stiff. He was talking to the guy trying to figure out who killed Kathy Rubinkowski.'

Donnie wasn't sure what to say, which was hardly surprising. When Donnie fell out of the tree, he hit a few stupid branches on the way to the ground. Undying loyalty was in his job description. Smarts, not so much.

'So taking care of Zo doesn't automatically take the lawyer outta the equation,' Ramini said. 'If Zo told this lawyer how the Rubinkowski thing really went down—'

'Did he?'

'I don't know, Don. But here's the thing. Sounds like this lawyer isn't so much going with this insanity thing anymore.'

186

'How do you know that?'

'Because remember the guy who hired us on Rubinkowski?'

Donnie thought for a moment. This could take a while. 'The industrial guy. Moneybags from bumblefuck.'

'Manning. Randall Manning,' said Ramini. 'Manning pays me a visit the other day. He says this lawyer Kolarich is sniffing around him. Asking questions that don't sound so much like he's pleading insanity anymore. More like he's trying to solve a puzzle. And sounds like he's getting pretty fucking warm. Warm like a fucking blowtorch.'

Donnie moaned.

'I just watched this lawyer Kolarich,' Ramini went on. 'I just watched him last night, looking over the scene, trying to figure the thing out. The whole time, I'm thinking, he's looking at this like it's a pro job.'

'Oh, motherfuck,' Donnie moaned.

'I know all about this Kolarich. I did good intel back when Zo paid him a visit. He used to be a prosecutor, and now he thinks he's a cowboy. You remember this thing our last governor had with the feds?'

'The governor?' Donnie turned to him. 'That was Kolarich?'

'He was right in it, yeah. A fucking crusader, this guy.'

'So this crusader,' said Donnie. 'This guy who ain't afraid of nobody. Does this crusader got a family?'

Donnie might not be a rocket scientist, but he knew a thing or two. It was the right question to ask.

'Not really. Wife and daughter died in a car accident. His dad is upstate on a fraud pinch. But dad and kid are on the outs, anyway. He's never visited him, far as we know. There's also a brother, but he's fucking around in the Cayman Islands.'

'That's no help.'

'Hey, Mooch, turn right up here,' Ramini hollered to the driver, Donnie's brother. If it was possible to be less talented than Donnie, his brother was it. 'I'm going to the gym.'

'Whaddaya do, like the treadmill and Nautilus and whatnot?' Donnie asked.

'Ah, they got a track. I run, mostly.'

'I've been thinking about doing that myself.'

Ramini looked over at his three-hundred-pound friend. 'Yeah, you might want to think about that, Don.'

The car pulled up to the gym.

'Talk to Paulie, Don,' said Ramini. 'Talk to him today.'

'So nobody? C'mon, Petey, nobody we can tie to this lawyer? No one he cares about?'

Peter Ramini thought for a moment. He thought about watching Kolarich and company reenacting the crime scene. This could get complicated very quickly.

'He's got a lady friend,' he said.

37

Tom Stoller stared at his feet, his tongue moving a hundred miles an hour over his lips. I couldn't see his hands, but I knew the fingers were twitching as well. I knew he was living in his own world right now, thinking about a hundred things that had nothing to do with this court appearance or even this criminal case, quite possibly having to do with military service in Iraq.

And the state, part of the country that sent this guy to do its dirty work thousands of miles overseas, that put him into a dire situation, fucked him up, and abandoned him when he returned, now wanted a judge to strike his insanity defense from the case.

The docket clerk called our case. Tom didn't even move at the mention of his name.

Today was Tuesday. We were in the final stages of trial prep. All the distractions – other clients, meetings, court appearances, depositions – were over for all of us. It was all hands on deck. Shauna was working on the experts. Bradley was preparing pretrial motions. Joel Lightner was hunting down everything he could find on Gin Rummy and Summerset Farms and Global Harvest. There was something there, I was sure. Kathy Rubinkowski had stumbled onto something.

But in the meantime, since I had no assurance I would be

able to find anything in time, I had to also prepare for an insanity defense. Shauna would handle our shrink, Dr Baraniq, and I'd probably cross their expert. Unless, of course, Judge Nash struck the insanity defense, at which point he would have no choice but to give me more time to prepare a retooled defense. That, as Shauna had noted, was one of my real motives here – to let the judge bar the insanity defense so he'd give me more time to pursue my strongest case, that Tom was innocent.

Judge Nash peered down at us over his glasses. He was in a foul mood today. He had abused the lawyers in the three cases coming ahead of us on the docket. I didn't mind his mood or his abuse, but it made him unpredictable – read *more* unpredictable than usual.

'Ms. Kotowski,' he boomed. 'It's your motion.'

Wendy dove into it, arguing the inability of her experts to perform an analysis of Tom Stoller because he refused to talk about the events of the night in question. She cited case law, which I could not distinguish, that gave the judge the authority to bar a defense based on mental state when the defendant refused to cooperate with the government psychiatrists.

She had another argument as well. And it was her best one. 'On the one occasion where the defendant even remotely engaged the state's expert, Dr Ramsey,' she said, 'the defendant indicated that he had no memory of Kathy Rubinkowski's murder. Your Honor, the law is clear that a defendant seeking excuse by virtue of a mental condition must lay a foundation that this defendant simply cannot lay. He can't claim a PTSD defense when he doesn't even remember what happened.'

Tom had said the same thing to me, more of a whisper, when he tackled me in the visitation room. He'd also mentioned it to Bobby Hilton, his war buddy, in my presence.

'So, Mr Kolarich.' The judge turned to me. I approached the lectern, but he kept talking. 'Your client won't talk to the state's experts?'

'That's what they claim, Judge. I'm not in a position—'

'Has your client talked to *your* expert?'

I paused. 'My expert plans to testify—'

'Is that a no, Counsel? It sounds like a no.'

'He hasn't provided detail to Dr Baraniq,' I conceded.

'Okay, well, does your client *remember* the events of that evening?'

'Judge,' I said, 'I'd rather not give the prosecution a preview of my case.'

The judge frowned. 'You'll have to if you want to assert this defense, Counsel. You don't get to sit back on the Fifth Amendment while asserting insanity. You know that.'

'Judge, I bear the burden of proof on this issue. The defense. All the state has to do is rebut my case after the—'

'Mr Kolarich.' He shook his head. 'The state is correct. The defendant can't sustain a defense of post-traumatic stress disorder if he can't recall the events of the crime. I've read the submission of the state's expert that the defendant said he doesn't remember what happened. And I haven't heard any denial from you.'

'Judge—'

'Counsel, you can tell me, your client can tell me, if he'd like to testify – but this is your last chance. Does your client remember what happened on the night in question or doesn't he?'

'Judge, as far as I am aware, no, he can't recall, but my expert is prepared to testify that—'

'No,' said the judge, shaking his head. 'No. I'm striking your affirmative defense of not guilty by reason of insanity. The prosecution's motion is granted.'

I paused for a moment, as if absorbing this expected development. The judge would have been correct to bar the insanity defense on either of the grounds Wendy asserted.

But I had a plan B, and it was time to assert it. 'Judge, the problem the prosecution has with my client is the same one I have. He's unresponsive. He can't talk to me. He can't help me. He is totally unable to assist me in my defense. And you don't have to take my word for it. The prosecution is basically making my case for me. Tom Stoller is not fit to stand trial.'

'Wait a second,' Wendy protested.

'Hold on, Counsel,' said the judge. 'Mr Kolarich, you're talking about *fitness* now? Your client has had two fitness hearings provided at state expense. He's been declared fit twice.'

'He won't – he can't talk to me, Judge. How is that assisting me in my defense? That's the very definition of being unfit to stand trial. The prosecution agrees with me. You have no party standing before you that *doesn't* think he's unfit—'

'Counsel, your client won't talk to the state's expert. That doesn't make him unfit. You seem to have had the ability to gain some knowledge from him, not that you volunteered that information to the court. We are not holding a third fitness hearing, and that's that.'

'Your Honor—'

'We're done, Counsel. We are done.'

'Then I move for a continuance,' I said, panic rising within me. I'd expected to win on plan B. This was plan C. 'You've stricken our affirmative defense only eight days before trial. We need time to reassemble and put on a defense.'

The judge didn't appear moved. 'You've had months to prepare, Counsel.'

'To prepare an *insanity* defense, Judge. Not a defense of reasonable doubt. I'll need a minimum of ninety days—'

'Mr Kolarich, you knew the risks. You knew the defendant wasn't cooperating, and you knew your client couldn't remember the events of the crime. And you knew Ms. Kotowski would file this motion. You didn't just fall out of a tree.'

'No,' I said. 'No, Judge. It's the *prosecution* that waited far too long to make this motion. They could have made this motion months ago. They waited until—'

'They were trying to get your client to cooperate, Mr Kolarich. And he wouldn't. That's not the state's fault. Now, I've made my ruling and I will not entertain further argument on it.'

'I understand your ruling on the state's motion. I'm moving for additional time to prepare in light of that motion. You can't possibly expect me to be ready on a reasonable-doubt defense in eight days.'

'Counsel,' he said, wagging a finger, 'I told you—'

'This is a total ambush, Your Honor. A total am—'

'Counsel, you do *not* interrupt the court. You do *not*.'

I had violated the first rule of Judge Nash's courtroom. And everyone knows that once you get on his bad side, if you don't make amends, it only gets worse.

'Your motion is denied. We start the trial December first, as planned. The clerk will call the next—'

'Judge, you can't do this. If you'll—'

'Mr Kolarich, that's twice you've interrupted me. Another word and you'll join your client in lockup.' The judge paused, as if to dare me to do it. I held my stare on him but didn't say a word. He couldn't hold me in contempt for staring.

'The clerk . . . will call . . . the next case,' he said.

Deep down in the soul of a defense attorney, the thought that visits him in the dead of night is not that he'll lose a case, or even that an innocent person will go to prison on his watch. What haunts him more than anything is the fear that he'll make a mistake, a gross miscalculation that will single-handedly be responsible for the loss of his client's freedom.

That it will be his fault.

I didn't care much for the insanity defense in this case. In all likelihood, I wasn't even going to use it. But at this moment I realized, more than ever, that I was counting on it to give me either a win on Tom's fitness to stand trial or a continuance, either of which would buy me more time, that Judge Nash would give that to me as a consolation prize after striking the defense. And I'd been wrong. The judge had made a mistake here, in my opinion, but when could you ever be sure a judge would rule correctly?

I looked over at my client. Tom was still staring at the floor, seemingly oblivious to what was taking place, his nervous tics in full swing. He caught my eye for one moment before the guard led him out of the courtroom.

'What does this mean?' Aunt Deidre grabbed me by the arms as the court took up the next case.

'We'll figure this out,' I assured her, moving her toward the exit. 'We'll figure something out.'

Never had I delivered words with such certainty that I didn't feel. I had outsmarted myself, failing to account for the unpredictability of a judge, and it wouldn't be me who would feel the weight of that miscalculation.

38

Peter Ramini kept his head down as he navigated the restaurant on the west side. Could be that he'd know some of the regulars, and he wasn't in the mood for small talk. He stayed along the bar, avoiding the diners. The smell of espresso hit his nose and caused him physical pain. It had been more than four years now since his diagnosis, and caffeine was absolutely forbidden. He'd tried the decaf espressos and it was like muddy water. It was worse than forbearance.

He managed to avoid any hellos and made his way back to the kitchen. Inside, Donnie was stirring a pot of tomato sauce and chatting up the staff. Jesus, if this guy wasn't eating, he was cooking.

Donnie caught Ramini's eye and met him in the corner. It was private enough, and this conversation wasn't going to take long.

'Always with your hands in your pockets,' said Donnie, sizing Ramini up. 'You're among friends, Petey.'

Ramini frowned. 'Anyway,' he said.

'Anyway, I talked to Paulie, like we said.' Notwithstanding the clanking of pots and pans and the shouts among the chefs,

Donnie knew the rule. You could never be too careful. He leaned into Ramini as best he could with his girth.

'Take out the lawyer,' he whispered. 'And his lady friend. And don't come back with more problems.' Donnie cupped his hands over Ramini's cheeks. 'His words, not mine, Petey.'

Ramini nodded. His stomach did a flip. But it was the right call. There was nothing more to discuss. He left the restaurant the same way he came.

39

Randall Manning was seated in the same conference room where his lawyer Bruce McCabe met with Jason Kolarich last week. Manning was dressed in a charcoal suit and a bright yellow tie. He checked his watch. It was almost nine in the morning. He had many things to do in the city today.

Tomorrow was Thanksgiving. He used to love that weekend, the food, the football, most of all the family time. But that was over now. Things were different. Now he dreaded the day.

Jason Kolarich walked into the office a few minutes after nine. He was big. Well over six feet and stocky. An athlete, presumably. And more than that. Edgy. Like he almost didn't belong in a suit. Like you wouldn't want to face him in a dark alley, much less a courtroom.

They shook hands. A good, strong grip. Solid on eye contact. But he revealed very little in his face. Certainly no hint of warmth. He probably intimidated a lot of people. But not Manning. That switch had already been flipped. Nothing, at this point, could scare him.

As Kolarich took his seat, he pulled an envelope out of his coat pocket. 'This is a subpoena for you to testify in court,' he said. 'I haven't decided if I'm going to serve it yet.'

Manning didn't respond. But it was a nice opening move by Kolarich. Reminding everyone of his leverage. Play nice, or I haul you into court. This Kolarich could be a problem.

'It's your dime,' said Manning. He looked over at Bruce McCabe, who had a pen poised over a lined yellow notepad.

'You married, Mr Manning?'

'I'm a widower, Mr Kolarich. As are you.'

In his peripheral vision, Manning detected a frown from Bruce McCabe. Manning knew better. It was pure ego, a power game, letting Kolarich know that they were looking at him, just as he was at them. Manning knew better. But he couldn't help himself.

Kolarich, however, revealed nothing. 'Glo-Max fertilizer,' he said. 'Did Global Harvest sell Glo-Max 2.0 fertilizer to a company called Summerset Farms?'

'We did, I believe.'

'Summerset Farms is wholly owned by Global Harvest, isn't that true?'

'Yes, we purchased the controlling stock.'

'You purchased *all* the stock,' said Kolarich.

Manning paused for a moment, as if in thought. 'That could be true.'

Kolarich didn't quibble with the equivocation. Probably because he already knew the answer. And they weren't in court. Not yet.

'You recall being sued by a company called LabelTek Industries?'

'Yes, I do,' said Manning.

'Do you recall that you were served with written interrogatories by LabelTek's lawyers?'

Manning opened a hand.

198

'Written questions,' said Kolarich. 'You signed the affidavit answering them.'

'If you say so.'

'One of the questions LabelTek asked was who bought Glo-Max 2.0 from you. And your answer didn't include Summerset Farms. I'm wondering why.'

'That's ridiculous,' said Bruce McCabe. 'You can't expect Mr Manning to remember that kind of detail.'

A brief smile came to Manning. 'I don't remember that.'

'Well coached,' said Kolarich to McCabe. Then, to Manning, he said, 'Did you know that Mr McCabe here is outside counsel to Summerset Farms?'

Manning looked at McCabe. 'I may have known that.'

Kolarich sat back in his chair. 'Your company owns over twenty-five companies in this state and around the country. Do I have that about right?'

'You do.'

'And of all those companies, Bruce McCabe has been outside counsel only to Global Harvest and Summerset Farms. Is that your understanding?'

So Kolarich had been doing his homework on GHI and its subsidiaries. 'Yes,' he said.

'No,' said Kolarich. 'There's one other company. SK Tool and Supply.'

'My client is not required to be an expert on the companies I represent,' McCabe objected.

Kolarich never took his eyes off Manning. He had an imposing stare. He probably got a lot of people to talk just by glaring at them.

'Global Harvest purchased the stock of Summerset Farms in June 2009,' said Kolarich.

Manning nodded. 'That sounds about right.'

'And it purchased SK Tool and Supply that very same month. Does that sound about right?'

Manning glanced over at McCabe. 'Something like that, yes.'

'Two companies within a month.'

'Yes, Mr Kolarich.'

'No other companies within eighteen months on either side.'

'Is there a point here, Counsel?' asked McCabe.

'You settled the LabelTek litigation for four million dollars plus attorneys' fees,' said Kolarich. 'You gave them more than they wanted. And you did it only days after LabelTek sent subpoenas to Summerset Farms about its contracts with Global Harvest.'

Manning looked at his lawyer. 'Did I even know this?' he asked. Of course he did, but now was the time to play the corporate CEO who doesn't bother with the details.

'No, you didn't,' said McCabe. 'I'm not sure *I* even knew it.'

McCabe, of course, knew it as well. Manning could still recall McCabe's breathless phone call when he got wind of the Summerset Farms subpoenas.

'Then why'd you lay down in the lawsuit? The case was in its infancy, and you gave them everything they wanted and more. You've done very well in life, Mr Manning, and I assume you've become quite a skilled negotiator. What kind of negotiation ends up with you giving your opponent in litigation one hundred percent of what they wanted plus more?' Kolarich shook his head. 'Something was troubling you. Was it the subpoena that LabelTek issued to the state Department of Agriculture? Was that it?'

'That's ridiculous. This is ridiculous.'

200

'Why didn't you want anyone looking at your sales records with Summerset Farms?'

'That's simply not the case,' said Manning.

Kolarich sighed. 'Then I suppose you won't mind turning them over to me.'

Kolarich slid the envelope across the table to Manning.

'The subpoena includes records. Prove it to me, Mr Manning. Right now. And I'll go away.'

Manning stared at the envelope. Kolarich was bluffing, he thought. But it was a pretty damn good bluff. 'If it's really so important to you, Mr Kolarich, I suppose I could arrange—'

'No,' said Kolarich. 'Do it right now. Pick up the phone and make the call. Have them faxed here. I'll wait.'

'This is completely ridiculous. This courtesy we've extended you is over.' Bruce McCabe stood up. 'This is a ridiculous wild-goose chase. Mr Manning has been more than generous with his time.'

'He has. He has.' Kolarich nodded to Manning. 'Just make the call, Mr Manning.'

'It's time for you to leave,' said McCabe.

Kolarich kept his eyes on Manning but waved at McCabe. 'Sit down, Bruce. Don't get your shorts in a knot. I'm almost done.'

McCabe looked at his client. Manning nodded at him. McCabe took his seat, emasculated.

'You know someone named Lorenzo Fowler?' Kolarich asked.

Manning didn't. 'No, sir.'

'What about someone who goes by Gin Rummy?'

Manning chuckled. 'Can't say I do.'

'Paul Capparelli?'

Manning went cold. 'Paul . . . Cap – the mobster?'

'The very one. You know him, Mr Manning?'

'Of course not.' Manning shuffled in his chair, uncrossing one leg and crossing the other. It was a nonverbal tell, he realized, that he was becoming anxious. A mistake on his part.

It wasn't hard to see where this was headed. Kolarich seemed to know that there was more to the murder of that paralegal, Kathy whatever, than met the eye. Somehow – God knows how – he'd found out about the LabelTek lawsuit, and the subpoenas would have been public records in the court file. Now Kolarich was looking squarely at Manning, wondering whether he'd hired someone to silence that paralegal. And he even knew about *Paul Capparelli*?

He was much farther along in the information he'd gathered than Manning could have possibly imagined.

'Pick up the phone and have those sales records faxed here,' said Kolarich. 'Sales of Glo-Max 2.0 fertilizer to Summerset Farms. Do it, and I go away.'

Kolarich was smart. He was boxing Manning in. Manning considered doing it. There wasn't much to hide on the face of the documents, not unless you really knew what to look for. But it would show his fear, his concern, and that might be more telling to Kolarich than the records themselves.

McCabe held his tongue, presumably unsure of what his client wanted to do. This would be Manning's call, and he had to make it on the spot without equivocation.

Manning shook his head in amusement. 'Mr Kolarich, as much as I've enjoyed this conversation, and as happy as I'd be to comply with any subpoena you issue, I'm not going to let some low-rent lawyer dictate who I call and when. It doesn't work that way, son. Surely you can understand.'

'Sure, I understand,' Kolarich answered with mock sweetness. 'By the way, Mr Manning. My client? He's accused of killing a paralegal at Mr McCabe's law firm. He's an Army veteran who put his life on the line for his country. He's mentally ill as a result, and fucked up in ways you and I couldn't possibly fathom. And on top of that, he's being accused of a crime that he didn't commit. Somebody framed this poor guy for murder, and whoever did that is going to burn in hell. You believe in God, Mr Manning?'

'Don't talk to me about God,' Manning snapped. 'And don't talk to me about hell.'

'Fair enough. I'm leaving now.' Kolarich got to his feet and nodded at McCabe. 'But I'm not going away, Randy.'

Kolarich left the room. Manning glanced over at McCabe, who looked like he'd lost some of the color in his face.

'When does that trial of his start?' he asked.

'December first,' McCabe answered. 'A couple of days after the Thanksgiving weekend. A Wednesday.'

'When will he call me to the stand?'

McCabe shook his head. He didn't know. 'Picking a jury will take some time. Then the prosecution's case goes in. My guess is jury selection will take a day or so. Maybe the judge won't even begin opening statements until the following Monday, which would be—'

'December sixth,' said Manning. He had that portion of the calendar committed to memory long ago. For eighteen months, he'd been looking at one single day on the calendar: Tuesday, December 7. Recognized officially in the United States as Pearl Harbor Day.

'Bottom line, it's too much of a question mark,' said Manning.

'I wonder what our friends the Capparellis would say about this,' said McCabe. 'They have a vested interest as well.'

'I don't even know if I can trust the Capparellis.' Manning pushed himself out of the chair and moved to the window overlooking the commercial district. No, he decided, he couldn't trust the Capparellis. They might have the same agenda, they might not. If they perceived Kolarich as a threat, they might move to eliminate him.

But they might move against Manning as well, to cover all the bases. Better that this particular assignment be handled in-house.

'I need my best for this,' he said. 'I need Patrick Cahill.'

40

I looked around the room at my team. Each of them had their assignments, and each of them was giving me their all. Shauna had rescheduled all of her work and even turned down a couple of clients to help on the Stoller case. Bradley John was focusing on nothing else. Joel Lightner, who had a three-person shop, was doing what he could, even though there was little to no promise of payment for doing so. And Tori, who had provided more help than I would have expected, was devoted to the cause as well.

When I was a prosecutor, we had a phrase for how everyone was feeling right now: tired and wired. Everyone was motivated but suffering from sleep deprivation, and no matter how charged up you were, your brain worked less efficiently on little sleep. And mistakes were made.

'Shauna,' I said.

'We're looking at three companies,' she said. 'Global Harvest International, which produces a number of commercial-grade agricultural products. And then two companies that GHI purchased in June of 2009: SK Tool and Supply, and Summerset Farms. We know from the LabelTek lawsuit and those sub-poenas that GHI sold fertilizer – Glo-Max 2.0 – to Summerset

Farms. And we think it's a sensitive point for GHI, and the reason they suddenly settled that lawsuit before the subpoenas could be effectuated.' She shook her head. 'Everything I can see from public information tells me that Summerset Farms is just a small little local company that grows wheat and sells granola and bread to local grocery stores. They have no dings from any federal or state agency, no citations or lawsuits or anything like that. They're on good paper with their certificates of incorporation and all that.'

'So there's nothing,' I said. 'Other than the fact that in June of 2009, GHI bought two companies.'

'That's not all that happened in June of 2009,' she said. 'That month, GHI also called off a plan to go public.'

Interesting. 'Global Harvest is privately owned,' I said.

Shauna nodded. 'It was handed down from Oliver Manning to his son, Randall. It's grown substantially during Randall's tenure. But he runs the place flat-out. He owns one hundred percent of the stock. They were going to take the company public. Randall stood to make tens of millions. Then, in June of 2009, he called it off.'

'Okay, so why would he do that?'

'You go public, you have stockholders,' said Shauna. 'You have a board of directors. If people don't like what you're doing, they throw you out on your ass. Or the shareholders can file derivative suits.'

'You surrender control,' I said.

'Right. You own it outright, privately, you call the shots. Nobody questions you.'

Good. That was a good thing to know. There was something significant about June of 2009, I assumed. Randall Manning decided to keep a firm control on his company, and he purchased two other companies.

'If there's anything there, I'll find it,' said Shauna, when I pointed this out.

I threw my football in the air and caught it. 'Anything else before we move on?'

'There's one more thing. Summerset Farms. It wasn't really a preexisting company that GHI purchased. Summerset Farms was a farm, owned by a farmer, who sold his wheat output to commercial entities.'

'I thought GHI purchased the stock of an existing company.'

'Technically, yes, Jason, but listen to what I'm saying. The farmer incorporated, like any large farm should do. But he didn't make granola or bread. He just grew wheat and sold it. GHI came along and bought him out. They kept the corporate name, Summerset Farms, but turned it into a different operation. They expanded their operations, too. They purchased more acreage. They bought out a number of neighboring farms. They have several square miles of land in the southwest in unincorporated Fordham County.'

I threw my football up in the air again. 'So why would a corporate giant like GHI want to get into the local grocery business?'

Shauna shook her head. 'Oh, GHI owns all kinds of companies. They're incredibly diversified. They're the principal shareholder in a chain of sporting-goods stores down south, believe it or not. They own outright a personal storage company called We-Hold-It or something like that. They own a men's clothier out east, a billboard company in California – I mean, it doesn't end.

'But the better question is, if they did want to get into the local grocery business, why wouldn't they buy an existing company that's already *in* that business? That's their M.O. They started Summerset Farms basically from scratch.'

'Is that necessarily odd behavior?' Tori asked.

It was a good question. Nobody in the room had ever worked for a corporate giant. Shauna had done lots of corporate legal work, and Lightner had done investigative work for large companies, but none of us knew a thing about strategic planning for an international company.

'There's gotta be big money in commercial-grade fertilizer,' said Joel Lightner. 'Wherever there's money, there's ways to skirt things. Maybe somebody at Global Harvest and Summerset Farms was doing something hinky off the books. Maybe this character Randall Manning was embezzling or something. You said he was sensitive about the sales records between GHI and Summerset?'

'Oh, yeah, there's something there,' I said. 'No question. This guy would've rather had a proctology exam than talk to me about Summerset Farms.' I nodded to Shauna. 'What about this other company GHI bought at the same time – SK Tool and Supply?'

Shauna tucked a strand of hair behind her ear and looked at her notes. 'I don't have much on them yet. They were a preexisting company, though. SK Tool and Supply was owned by a guy named Stanley Keane, thus the SK. They're strictly B-to-B—'

'Translation, please.'

'Sorry, business-to-business. SK sells industrial-grade power tools and all sorts of other equipment to all kinds of industrial clients.'

'Stanley Keane has no criminal record,' Joel Lightner chimed in. 'That's all I know about him so far.'

'And that's all I know about the company so far,' Shauna said. 'They're clean with the feds and state, their corporate papers are all in order. From what I can tell, there's nothing there.'

I pointed to her. 'Did SK Tool and Supply ever sell anything to Summerset Farms?'

'I don't know yet. There's no way to know who they sell their products to. That's not inherently public information. For what it's worth, I put in three calls to them today and got no return. I even called their lawyer, Bruce McCabe, who as you know isn't inclined to be much help.'

'No, he isn't. You couldn't go visit them, Shauna? A face-to-face?'

'They're more than two hours away, J. We just started looking at them. I just haven't had time.'

'And tomorrow's Thanksgiving. That's four more days we lose. And then it's three days to trial.' I moaned. 'Bradley, I take it that SK Tool and Supply doesn't sell fertilizer?'

'Not according to the Agriculture Department's database, no.'

'So if they're connected to Summerset Farms, it's through something else. Something that we don't know, and that will be almost impossible to discover before the trial starts a fucking week from today.'

Tori cleared her throat. 'Can I ask a question?'

'Shoot,' I said. Tori's outside perspective had proven helpful in focusing me.

'Why would there necessarily be a connection to Summerset Farms?'

'I'm not sure there is,' I conceded. 'But GHI bought both companies at the same time, in June of 2009. And all three of them have the same lawyer, Bruce McCabe. And GHI was pretty damn sensitive about disclosing its dealings with Summerset Farms. So sensitive that it handed out a ridiculously generous settlement to LabelTek and, if my theory is correct, murdered a paralegal who was asking too many questions.'

It was good to say it aloud. It sounded plausible. If I could fill in some blanks, it was a workable theory at trial. It gave me a needed boost.

'Is that it, Shauna? Anything else?'

'Well, I had been working with Dr Baraniq. But I guess that's over.'

'The hell it is. Bring him in on Friday.'

She made a face. 'Judge Nash barred him from testifying.'

'He struck the insanity defense,' I clarified. 'He didn't say anything about Dr Sofian Baraniq testifying or not testifying.'

'That doesn't make any sense, J. How does Dr Baraniq help us?'

I had an idea about that. But there was no need to get bogged down now. 'Let's talk about that later. Let's move on. Bradley,' I said.

'I have subpoenas prepared for the Department of Agriculture, SK Tool and Supply, Summerset Farms, Stanley Keane personally. . . . Let's see, you already served Randall Manning and GHI in person. You want me to send the other subpoenas out?'

'Not yet,' I said. 'The minute we serve them, we have to show the prosecution. I don't want to tip my hand just yet.' In fact, it occurred to me that I might momentarily forget that I served Randall Manning with that subpoena. For the time being, it might slip my mind to tell the prosecution.

'And what about Judge Nash?' Shauna asked. 'You haven't

disclosed any of this, and you're way past the discovery order cutoff. Isn't he going to deny all of this?'

I sighed and tossed the football in the air. 'I already have that problem, whether I disclose it now or a week from now. But I've laid a pretty good record here, I think. He fucked me on the insanity defense and fucked me on the fitness argument, and then when I said I was now being stripped of my defense on the eve of trial and needed additional time to prepare, he fucked me again. He's a stubborn old goat, but he's not stupid. If he doesn't give me a little slack on what I can show the jury, he runs a real risk of being reversed on appeal.'

'But you can't bank on that. With Judge Nash, you said you never—'

'I know I can't bank on it, Shauna. I've got a ruling from that piece of shit sticking out of my ass right now. You think I don't know that?'

'Hey, easy.' Shauna raised her hands.

'What other choice do I have, Shauna? We follow the leads and hope we come up with something that's compelling enough that Judge Nash can't possibly say no. I'm out of backup plans here, okay? This is the only hope we have.'

'Okay, everybody, let's turn it down.' Lightner patted the air with his hands. 'Deep breaths, everyone.'

'And what value have *you* added, Lightner?' I asked.

'I'm trying to find the mysterious Gin Rummy, pal. Someone not even the esteemed FBI can—'

'Some fucking hotshot P.I. you are. You couldn't track a bleeding elephant through the snow. You couldn't find a Jew in Israel. You couldn't locate oil in Saudi—'

Bradley John burst into laughter. So I turned on him next.

'And what about you, Bradley? Other than having two first

names and listening to "Panic! at the Disco" on your iPad and having Justin Bieber's haircut? You got anything else for me, sport?'

He raised his hands and tried unsuccessfully to suppress a smile. 'We exchanged motions in limine today,' he said.

'Great. That's great! And remind me again what we filed, Kid Rock. A motion to have our asses kicked at trial? A motion for a mattress to be placed in the courtroom so that when the judge is finished slapping me around for discovery violations, I have a soft landing?'

Bradley ticked off his fingers. 'Motion to exclude witnesses, motion—'

'I know what motions we filed, Hip-Hop. I was filing pretrial motions when you were feeling up Betty Lou in the bathroom at junior prom. Get me draft responses to the prosecution's motions by Saturday.'

I picked up the document that Ray Rubinkowski had given me, with the handwritten scratch on the back:

AN

NM

??

'Last I checked, you were supposed to figure out who AN and NM were.'

Bradley, who was only now losing his smirk, flipped back a page in the notebook in front of him. 'There's no lawyer at Bruce McCabe's law firm with either set of initials, so it's not someone Kathy Rubinkowski worked with. None of the companies listed in the answers to interrogatories Kathy was drafting have those initials. None of the companies listed on the Agriculture Department's database have those initials. I even tried to find a staff directory for LabelTek to see if they have anyone with those initials. I'm still looking. I won't stop.'

'Um, excuse me.' Shauna raised her hand like a polite school-girl. 'I think what you've been meaning to say is that you know how hard all of us are working and you appreciate it, and you know that we share your frustration.'

I tossed the football in the air. 'That's what I meant,' I sighed. 'It may have come out different.'

'A little different, yeah.'

'Okay, listen, everybody,' I said. 'You all need some rest. Get some tonight. Have a nice turkey day. Clear your mind, eat a lot of food, watch football, and come back Friday bright and early and ready for the final stretch.'

Bradley and Lightner headed out, neither of them real pleased with me at the moment. Shauna came over and lightly punched my arm. 'Sure you don't want to stop by tomorrow?' she asked. 'We eat at three. My parents will be happy to grill you on why I'm not married yet.'

I stretched my arms. 'I'm good,' I said. 'Sorry about just now.'

She waved me off. 'You could use a day off, too, Counselor. Clear your head. You're not going to be alone tomorrow, are you?'

'No, no. I'm fine.'

Shauna cast a glance at Tori. She probably figured that Tori was going to be the one keeping me company tomorrow. I couldn't tell how Shauna felt about that. The two of them had only recently met, had hardly said more than two sentences to each other. Shauna wasn't really the catty type, but she was protective when it came to me.

213

She forced a smile and said, 'Have a happy Thanksgiving, Tori.'

Tori replied likewise. It wasn't the most affectionate exchange I'd ever seen. The Alaskan tundra produced more warmth.

Then Shauna left, and it was just Tori, smirking at me from the corner.

'I'm just glad you didn't go off on me, too,' she said.

'Don't tempt me.' I ran my fingers through my hair. 'Let's get out of here,' I said.

41

I drove Tori to her apartment. I wasn't good company. I was off-balance. I'd never felt so out of control in my time as a lawyer. I had to climb a hill to climb another hill so I could use a telescope to locate my chances at an acquittal for Tom Stoller.

'Can I make a suggestion?' she said to me as I drove.

'Sure.'

'I'm not trying to tell you how to do your job.'

'It sounds like you're about to.'

'Well, that's what I mean. I can shut up if you want. If you told me how to teach differential equations to a class of grad students, I'd be annoyed. So I'd understand—'

'Tori, just tell me. Every time you've said something, it's helped.'

She was quiet for a moment. I think she appreciated that comment.

'Okay,' she said. 'Well, did it ever occur to you that maybe you're casting too wide a net?'

I pulled up to a red light and turned to her. 'What do you have in mind?'

She shifted in her seat to face me. 'You think there's

215

something dirty with this guy at Global Harvest and these other companies. And you're finding this out late in the game, so you're stretched thin, and you have Shauna and Bradley doing Internet searches and making phone calls and things like that to learn more about these companies. Which is fine, except wouldn't your private investigator be better at that?'

'Sure, but he's busy on other stuff.'

'Exactly. You have him trying to find this mysterious hit man, Gin Rummy. I'm just wondering if that's time well spent.'

The light changed and I started driving again, but she had me thinking.

'I mean,' she went on, 'what's your best-case scenario there? Let's say Joel can do better than the FBI and figure out who this person is. Okay, then what? You call him to the witness stand and what?'

'He denies everything,' I said. 'He takes five. He refuses to talk. I see your point. He could assert the Fifth and never even take the stand.'

'What if you build a case against this guy who works at Global Harvest – Manning? Can't you do that without trying to prove who actually pulled the trigger?'

I played it all out. I'd wanted to find Gin Rummy and put him on the stand and go after him on the similarities between the murders of Lorenzo Fowler and Kathy Rubinkowski. I was counting on my ability to tie him in knots and get something out of him – not an outright confession, of course, but enough to make the jury wonder.

But beyond my inability to even find this asshole, I also had to deal with Judge Nash, who would make me build a pretty damn strong evidentiary link before he'd let me parade witnesses before the jury who were not previously disclosed to the prosecution. The chances were good he'd never even let me put this guy on the stand.

'Jesus, you're right, Tori,' I said. 'With the amount of time I have left, that's a much cleaner approach. Fuck Gin Rummy. I don't need him. I show the jury that Randall Manning or Bruce McCabe or both had something to hide, then I make the case that the murder of Kathy Rubinkowski was a professional hit, not an amateurish robbery gone bad.'

'That's all I was thinking,' she said.

'That's all you were thinking? Then keep thinking, kid, because that's very helpful. Really, Tori. I could kiss you.'

I picked up my cell phone and dialed Joel Lightner. 'Hey,' I said, and then listened while Joel blew off some steam. 'I know, I deserve that, Joel. I deserve that, too. Okay, that was a little overboard. Listen, Joel, stop with this Gin Rummy shit. Focus on Randall Manning and Bruce McCabe and that other guy, Stanley – the SK Tool and Supply guy. Keane, Stanley Keane. Look for anything you can. I mean anything. Right, I know. I know, Joel. Yeah, the bleeding elephant, that was a low blow. No, I know, and to set the record straight, I *do* think you could find a Jew in Israel. I'm sure of it.' I looked over at Tori and rolled my eyes. 'I get it, Joel. You've put all this information together on Gin Rummy. Okay, so send it to me, and then move on to these other guys. We're out of time otherwise. Full throttle on those three guys and their damn companies. So are we still sweethearts? Tell you what, when this is over, manicures and pedicures are on me. Yeah, she's here. I'm driving her home. I'll ask her.' I turned to Tori. 'Joel wants to know if we're going to sleep together tonight.'

'No,' she said.

'She said no.' I listened and then turned to Tori again. 'He wants to know, if I don't do it for you, does he have a shot?'

Tori laughed.

'She thought that was funny, Lightner. She actually laughed at the notion of sleeping with you. Okay, bye.'

I punched out the phone. 'Underneath that rough exterior is a cuddly teddy bear,' I said.

'I know. I like Joel.'

'I meant me.' I pulled up to the curb. Tori lived in a high-rise on the near-north side, about ten blocks southeast of me. Her apartment on the eighteenth floor, which I'd never seen, probably offered a breathtaking view and the approximate space of a shoe closet.

Tori shifted again, so she was facing me. 'Oh, I've got you all figured out, Kolarich.'

I put the car in park. 'Do tell.'

'You're a do-gooder. A crusader.'

'Perish the thought.'

'Perish the thought? You told me you liked the competition. The challenge. That's what you said. I'm not buying it.' She wagged her finger at me. 'Let me ask you a question. How much are you getting paid for this case?'

'Objection,' I said. 'Irrelevant.'

'Irrelevant. You aren't getting paid a dime, are you?'

This lady was getting way too far into my head. It was a dangerous place to be.

'Aunt Deidre, she has problems of her own,' I said. 'Her husband's an invalid. She can barely scratch together a car payment each month. And Tom doesn't have squat for money.'

'Hey, I'm not criticizing you. I think it's very noble. You're expending all these resources and not getting anything back.

218

You're tearing yourself up over a client who isn't paying you. You're actually *losing* money and you seem to be losing your mind, too.'

I sighed. 'I've still got my health.'

Smart-ass comebacks weren't going to do it for her, not this time. She held her stare on me. With the tortured look on her face, I was beginning to expect her eyes to well up. But tears weren't really Tori's thing, not so far as I could tell. She'd built an impenetrable wall between herself and hurt, whatever that hurt might have been.

Still, she was feeling some of the tension I was experiencing. This math major, who spent her days with impersonal numbers and equations and theorems, was buying into this criminal defense case. And I was beginning to think she was buying into me, too.

'You're not what I expected,' she said.

I had several clever responses in tow. That was my trademark, right? Everything's a joke. But I wanted to give her a real answer. I wanted to talk to her. I wanted to find out what made her wait until age twenty-seven to start college, what had happened to her. And what had made her restart her life, what kind of hope must be propelling her beneath her defensive façade.

But before I could say a word, she pushed the door open and got out.

Peter Ramini watched the whole thing from his car, parked on the cross street to the high-rise building. He didn't need to bother tailing Kolarich tonight. He knew where the girl lived – her street address and her apartment number, 1806 – and he figured Kolarich would end up here with her.

But Kolarich didn't go in. She got out of the car alone and walked up the ramp into her building. Kolarich's SUV drove away into the night.

Ramini coughed and cleared his throat. He wasn't looking forward to what would come next. But his instructions from Paulie, via Donnie, had been clear enough.

How had this become so complicated?

42

Tom Stoller happily chowed down on turkey, gravy, mashed potatoes, and split-pea soup. Aunt Deidre spent little time on her food, deriving her own pleasure from Tom's.

We were in the visitation room. Deidre had charmed the guards over the eleven months Tom had been here, and when she mentioned there would be plenty of her home cooking left over, and she sure didn't want to haul it all the way back home, they were putty in her hands. Deidre, I thought, was pretty good at getting what she wanted.

It was paper plates and plastic cutlery, but to look at my client's contentment, you'd think he was sitting around the family kitchen table. I knew very well that Tom had a low opinion of the cuisine at the Boyd Center, as it was about the only thing he was willing to freely discuss.

The levity was severely undercut by the circumstances, naturally. This was in many ways like a last meal for Tom. But for God's sake, if they could manage to find some enjoyment for an hour or two, let them.

I wished I had my cell phone. I was coordinating with Tori, whom I was going to pick up in an hour. We had a field trip scheduled.

Deidre left Tom to his chomping and pulled me to the far end of the room. 'Do you have someplace you have to be, Jason? It's okay. It's Thanksgiving, after all.'

'I'll need to be running in a bit here, yeah.'

'Are you seeing your folks?'

I laughed out loud. 'No, ma'am. My mother's deceased and my father isn't close by.'

She cocked her head. 'You're all alone on Thanksgiving?'

'Not at all. I'm with you and Tom. That's enough for me. It's nice to see Tom enjoying something.'

'It is, it is. You should have seen him when he was a boy. His mother couldn't keep enough groceries in the house.'

Then Aunt Deidre looked at me. She just stared at me for a long time and didn't say a word. She didn't need to say any words. I knew what she wanted.

'Deidre, we have a rough road ahead. You understand that.'

She finally broke eye contact. Her brain knew this. Her heart was hoping against hope for something different.

'I'm throwing a lot of darts at the board and hoping something sticks,' I continued. 'I haven't given up hope. And if we get a bad result, I think we have a pretty good appeal issue already, out of the gate, with the judge striking our insanity defense and not giving me more time. Most judges aren't nearly so strict with discovery deadlines as Judge Nash. I think a higher court will be sympathetic.'

She nodded, trying to make this less difficult for me. It didn't. It made it worse.

'The state has a circumstantial case,' I said. 'I can drill some holes. Don't give up.'

She didn't look at me, but she rested her hand on my arm.

222

'Whatever happens, whatever we get, it will be better with you than anyone else. I'm sure of it, Jason.'

She was putting undue faith in me. She was expecting something I was pretty sure I couldn't deliver. It was a weight beyond what I normally carried on a case. I wasn't sure how I was going to handle losing this trial.

I left on that note. I said good-bye to Tom, but he only looked up briefly, mashed potatoes and gravy on his chin, before he resumed his feast. I was going to remind him that I'd be back tomorrow, that we'd have to go over some things, but I didn't want to ruin the small measure of enjoyment he was experiencing.

If things continued as they were, it would be the last home-cooked meal he'd ever eat.

43

The truck pulled up in the dirt at a red flag and stopped. *'Number One at Rovner Street. Stand by for the five-minute.'*

Randall Manning watched through binoculars and listened through his earpiece.

'Green light at Rovner, that's the five-minute,' the voice crackled through the earpiece.

The truck started moving again. Manning followed along with his binoculars. Good so far. Wait for the green light.

'Number Two at Rovner Street.'

Good. Just about right. Manning's pulse was steady. This wasn't the first time they'd run through it. It was, in fact, the twentieth.

'Number One at Dodd Street, stand by for the two-minute.'

Manning moved his binoculars to the second red flag, four hundred yards to the south, coming toward him. It was an approximation in terms of timing. It wasn't intended to be precise. It didn't need to be precise. They weren't in the city's downtown, and they were nowhere near Rovner Street or Dodd Street. They were out in the country – the 'boonies,' to most people. They were in unincorporated Fordham County, surrounded on all sides by farmland purchased by Summerset Farms following its acquisition by Global Harvest International.

'Green light at Dodd. That's the two-minute.'

Manning had driven the real route dozens of times. Dodd Street was actually far less than two minutes from the target, but Manning had built in an extra time cushion to account for unpredictable traffic.

The truck continued south, coming toward Manning. He was inside a dome he'd constructed more than a year ago for this purpose. A few hours ago, this dome had housed all sorts of farm equipment – tractors and plows and backhoes – all of which had been emptied out for this exercise.

He watched out the window from his position on the second-level balcony as the truck drove through the open double doors into the vast dome. He turned to face inside the dome and watched as the truck picked up speed and drove toward the makeshift building, consisting of only a front façade and door.

'Red light at Dayton, doesn't fucking mat-ter!'

The truck stayed at a speed of twenty miles an hour and pulled up just short of the front door of the building.

The rear door of the truck burst open, and Patrick Cahill jumped out. The driver, Ernie Dwyer, also jumped out. Each of them was wearing state-of-the-art body armor and a helmet with a face shield. They raised their black AKM assault rifles and backed away from the faux building.

'Pop the targets,' said Manning.

Standard tactical training, about which Manning knew absolutely nothing eighteen months ago. But he'd learned a thing or two since then.

Targets popped up like characters in a children's picture

book, the shapes of humans, in various spots around the faux building. From the distance he'd created, Cahill and Dwyer unloaded their assault rifles on the targets, knocking them flat. To the extent they missed the targets – though Manning doubted that the two of them had missed even once – their bullets hit a bulletproof tarp that had been placed floor-to-ceiling behind the building façade.

Randall Manning looked at his stopwatch.

'Good,' he announced. 'Well done. Now clean up. Then we eat, and then target practice.'

The ammo would be the first phase of the cleanup. Every shell casing would be collected. The bulletproof tarp would be lowered and scrapped. The roof would be opened to air out the place of the smell of gunfire. Then the tractors and other farming equipment would be brought back in.

Within an hour, tops, this dome would look like nothing more than a warehouse for farming equipment again.

Manning looked over at Bruce McCabe, who was standing next to him, looking a bit flushed.

'What's bothering you, Bruce?' he asked.

44

I stopped by my office to pick up the dossier that Joel had built up on the legendary Gin Rummy, because I knew he was pissed that I'd taken him off that assignment – actually, he was pissed that he hadn't succeeded in finding the guy – and I knew that he'd be in my office bright and early on Friday, and if he still saw the file in the same place on my desk, he'd think I wasn't paying attention to it. I wasn't, not at the moment, but Joel didn't need to know that. He had pretty thick skin, but he had a sensitive streak when it came to his professional abilities.

Then I picked up Tori at her condo. A cool wind whipped inside my car, and she closed the door quickly to keep it out. The temperatures were falling. It wasn't going to be a white Thanksgiving, but it was going to be a cold one.

She had her trademark long white coat and nice boots, always nice threads, but that was the only thing about her that looked normal. Her eyes were hooded and her face drawn. She looked like she hadn't slept well at all.

'I didn't,' she said, when I commented. 'And thanks for noticing.'

'Big math test coming up?' I asked, even though I was aware

that she had finished her last final exam a couple days ago. She was off until mid-January now.

She looked at me. 'Is that you making fun of me? You got something against math?'

'No, hey – I love math. Math is the greatest thing since . . . science.'

'Because that sounded like condescension. And that's about the only thing I can't take from someone.'

I had obviously struck a nerve with her that I hadn't seen coming. 'Tori, I'm sorry. That's not how I meant it.'

It was the first time I'd seen her get her back up about something. She was basically a cool customer, aloof, in control. Something had put her on edge.

Our relationship was odd. I really didn't know that much about her, and she didn't know much about me. We kept the topics safe. We kept each other at arm's length. All I knew was that the more time I spent with her, the more time I wanted to spend with her. Maybe it was her aloofness itself. I'd considered that possibility. I'd never been in a relationship where I was the pursuer. When I was in school, I was a jock, and girls followed athletic success like day followed night. Not necessarily the kind of girls you'd settle down with, but who the hell wanted to settle down?

Then there was Shauna, but she'd started as a pal, so that just sort of happened for a brief spell before we decided that our friendship worked better than romance. And then there was Talia. Even Talia took the first step with me.

I'd never felt like I was more interested than the lady. Until now.

Tori said, 'I was working on your case, if you want to know what I was doing. And I found something.'

228

'Okay, great. What?'

'Kathy Rubinkowski has a Facebook page.'

'Oh – okay. Facebook. Okay. Did you find anything interesting?'

'No, because we're not "friends."'

'Well, obviously you and Kathy weren't friends.' I looked over at her as I drove.

'Do you know anything about Facebook?' she asked.

'Sure. I know some shithead stole the idea from two other shitheads, or something like that. And there was a movie about it where everybody spoke in incredibly intelligent, fluid sentences.'

'You are hopeless. She has to invite me to her page, and she obviously can't now. So I can't get on her page, is my point. But if someone could find a way in, I'll bet you could find her e-mail address on her "information" page.'

'Ah, e-mail. I know e-mail. Okay, I get it. If we can get her e-mail address, we can hack her e-mail and see if anything was on her mind.'

'That's what I was thinking. You think Joel is able to do something like that?'

Interesting. He probably could. 'There might be some ethical challenges there, yes?'

'Technically,' she conceded.

'Technically? Tori, I'm seeing another side of you.'

'You're seeing a side that doesn't want some poor, sick kid to take the fall for something he didn't do. That's what you're seeing. This is hardball, not softball – isn't that what you always say?'

It was. I hated it when people used my words against me.

'Shit, where are those Mapquest directions?' I patted the

229

seat around me and looked down at the floor. 'Look in the back,' I said.

She did. 'I don't see it. There's some big file.'

'That's the Gin Rummy dossier Joel put together.'

'You're still spending time on that?' she asked.

'No,' I said. 'You were right. It's a waste of time. Even if I find Gin Rummy, he won't admit to anything. But Joel went to all this trouble, and I'm not even paying him for this shit. So I'll try to read it. I mean, he has biographies and background material. It's like an encyclopedia. I'll get to it at some point.'

'Whatever,' she said. 'I'll just pull the directions up on my iPhone.'

'You can do that?'

'You're really a dinosaur, aren't you?'

'I prefer "old school," Tori. You can pull up directions on that thing?'

'Sure. I'll just type in the name, get an address, and then set the GPS.'

'Great,' I said. 'So type in the name "Summerset Farms."'

45

'Tell me, Bruce,' said Randall Manning.

'Nothing's wrong.' McCabe shrugged. 'Just general nerves, I guess.'

'Identify it, Bruce. Tell me specifically.'

Below them, inside the dome, the cleanup was already under way. Shell casings were being collected, dust was being swept, the bulletproof tarp was being pulled down.

McCabe looked at Manning. 'It's the lawyer, Kolarich. The whole thing.'

Manning nodded. 'He won't figure this out in time, Bruce.'

'But he'll figure it out eventually. He'll connect us to this. And if we take him out now, isn't that a red flag? He clearly has his sights trained on us, and suddenly he winds up dead? We thought we had complete anonymity, Randy. There was no way any of this was going to connect to us.'

That was never a certainty in Manning's mind, or anywhere close to it. He had planned this well and chosen the operatives well, but he had no illusions. He knew that the odds were quite decent that he, personally, would be caught. He'd always told his men that they had to be willing to die for this mission. He preached it to them. McCabe was part of the Circle, of course, but he wasn't one of the operatives. He did the necessary legal work to get everything set up to put the mission in place. But that was all.

And now things were coming to a head. It wasn't just an idea now. It was happening.

'I think we'll get away with it,' said Manning. 'And then we'll lie low and wait for another opportunity. But yes, Bruce, there are risks. Surely this isn't the first time you're realizing this?'

McCabe wasn't dumb. Of course, he had to have been aware of the risks. But he'd placed trust in Manning, perhaps more than Manning had realized. And he hadn't had to get his hands dirty. He wouldn't be putting his life on the line on December 7. Maybe it was only now dawning on him what, exactly, they were going to do.

Perhaps it had been a mistake to bring Bruce here today, to see up close a dry run of the operation.

Or maybe it had been a good thing, in the end. If McCabe was going to go south on them, better that Manning knew that now, not afterward.

'I think we should abort,' said McCabe.

Manning put a hand on McCabe's shoulder. 'Let's go eat, Bruce. Everyone's tired and stressed and hungry. Let's have some turkey and think this over. Go on ahead. I'll be there in a minute.'

Manning watched his lawyer walk out the door. Then he dialed his cell phone.

'Patrick,' he said, 'wait five minutes and then come up to see me.'

46

Traffic was nonexistent on Thanksgiving afternoon. We got off the interstate and followed the local roads. The housing was sparse and modest, and there wasn't much for commerce besides gas stations, bait shops, and an occasional diner. Nothing was open today.

We found the street we were looking for, aided by a small sign that said Summerset Farms with an arrow pointing to the right. I turned right and drove down a paved road.

We pulled up to a long metal gate blocking the road. On the gate was a sign reading Summerset Farms is closed.

We got out of the SUV, if for no other reason than to stretch our legs after more than two hours in the car, and walked up to the gate. Down the road, there was a long ranch-style house and a gigantic barn, all painted red. And behind that housing was farmland as far as the eye could see. Shauna had mentioned that when Global Harvest purchased the farm, it bought up neighboring farmland.

'You didn't expect it to be open, did you?' Tori asked me. She looked like a fish out of water, a well-dressed, cosmopolitan woman in farm country. I suppose I didn't look much like the town, either.

And no, I didn't expect Summerset Farms to be open on Thanksgiving.

'Why the gate?' I asked.

'Who knows? Maybe vandals or robbers.'

'Yeah, maybe.' The gate was fastened to a post. It didn't appear to be hydraulic. I pushed on it, and it moved. So I kept pushing, and it kept moving, until I had cleared a path for my vehicle.

'I'm not the lawyer,' said Tori, 'but I do believe this would be trespassing.'

'Hardball, not softball,' I reminded her. 'You don't have to be a part of it. You want to go for a drive and come back in an hour?'

She thought that was amusing. 'I'll stick. It wouldn't be the worst thing I've ever done.'

With the gate out of the way, we returned to the SUV and drove up to the small parking lot. We got out and walked up to the ranch house. The front door was locked, as expected. There was a window, and I peered into the place. Not much to see for my purposes. It was a reception area with what appeared to be standard office space behind it. I guess they didn't sell their products to walk-up customers, or if they did, it didn't happen here.

We walked over to the barn. The main door, which was taller than me, had a gigantic padlock securing it. There were no other windows.

'Okay, that's what I figured,' I said.

Tori peered up at me, squinting into the sunlight. 'We came all this way just for this? You discover that the place is closed for Thanksgiving, try the door, peer into a window, and that's—'

'That's not it,' I said. 'That's just it for here.'

We returned to the SUV and retraced our steps past the gate. I closed it back up and drove down the road, following the fence line of the property. On the other side of the fence was a pretty weak-looking set of wheat crops, stubbly things, but I knew as much about wheat crops as I did astrophysics, so for all I knew the crop was doing quite well.

The land was pretty flat around here. I finally came upon a hill to my left. I followed a dirt path, which I was pretty sure was a road, up the hill and then stopped the SUV.

'Glove compartment,' I said to Tori.

She opened it and removed a fancy camera that I'd taken from Joel Lightner. She handed it to me.

I got out of the vehicle and climbed onto the hood. I helped Tori up, then helped her climb to the roof. Then I joined her.

'This is . . . unusual,' she noted.

The camera was something a good P.I. like Lightner would use, a high-powered lens attached to the camera that could get a decent image from over a mile away.

Through the camera, I looked out over the Summerset Farms acreage. The crops were sparse, stubbly, and brownish-green, like a neglected summer lawn. As I moved beyond the borders of the property line, the crops became even more sporadic and then nonexistent, just a bunch of dirt as far as the eye, assisted with this high-powered device, could see.

'That's a lot of acreage Global Harvest bought that they aren't using for wheat,' I said.

'Let me look,' said Tori.

'Hang on.' There was a large metal structure with a domed top. I didn't know what it was. Some kind of a warehouse or silo.

Then I saw something that didn't look like farming at all.

It looked like a bunch of guys shooting assault rifles at targets. The distance was such that I could barely register the sound of gunfire, but my eyes didn't lie.

'Check this out.' I kept the camera in position and motioned for Tori to take it. It moved a little when she grabbed it, but it didn't take her long to find the same thing I found.

'Oh my God,' she said. 'What are they doing? I mean, I know what they're doing. But . . .'

In my peripheral vision I saw a pickup truck barreling down the road toward us with a yellow siren flashing on top. The truck skidded to a stop down the hill from us. The truck's side panel was emblazoned with SUMMERSET FARMS SECURITY.

The man who got out was wearing a green uniform with a brown leather jacket over it. A firearm hung from his hip holster.

'Can I ask what you folks are doing?' he said.

'Sure,' I said.

He stared at me. I stared at him. We stared at each other.

'What are you doing?' he asked.

'None of your business.'

'It's our business, all right.'

'I'm exercising my First Amendment rights,' I said. Just like, apparently, they were exercising their Second Amendment rights, but I didn't say that.

He didn't think I was funny. He was built like a tank, plus he had a weapon.

'I want to see some identification,' he said.

'And I want to see peace in the Middle East, but neither one is going to happen today.'

'Get down, sir, and get into my vehicle.'

'As tempting as that sounds, I'm gonna pass,' I said.

The guard ably removed his sidearm and trained it on me.

'God, Jason,' Tori said to me under her breath. 'Let's get down.'

That made sense. The guy with the gun aimed at us wanted us to get down, so we got down. We climbed down to the hood, then I jumped off and helped Tori do the same.

'Get behind the wheel,' I whispered to her.

'Now get into my vehicle, both of you.' With the hand that wasn't holding a gun, the guard snapped a photograph of us with his cell phone.

I walked toward him, showing the palm of my right hand (the camera was in the left) to indicate I was no threat. I put myself approximately between the sight line of his gun and Tori. I heard the SUV's door open and close. Good. Tori had gotten in. The car was still running, so all she had to do was put the car in drive and take off if she were so inclined. If I were her, I might be tempted to do just that.

'She's not going anywhere,' the guard said. 'Neither of you are.'

'Take it easy, Deputy Fife,' I said. 'Before you hurt somebody with that gun.'

'Hand over that camera and get in my vehicle.' The guard was beginning to understand that I wasn't in a compliant mood.

'I'm a lawyer,' I said. 'I'm an officer of the court trying to serve a subpoena. It's against the law for you to interfere with me.'

'That's a helluva way to serve a subpoena, on the roof of a car.'

'I'm creative.' I turned so that my back was to the man. 'I'm

237

getting into my car,' I said. 'You're going to have to shoot me in the back to stop me.'

I moved slowly but without pause. They were ten of the longest steps I'd ever taken. But what could this guy do? How could he explain putting a bullet in my back?

'You're not driving away!' he called out. 'You're not leaving with that camera.'

If only he knew what I knew. I'd screwed up. I hadn't snapped any photos. I'd handed the camera over to Tori, and then Deputy Dawg here showed up. That was a miss on my part. A big miss. Lack of sleep = mistakes.

But at least I got into my car.

'Drive,' I told Tori.

And she did. She'd had time to adjust the seat so that she could reach the pedals. The gas pedal definitely worked. We took off over the hill in a burst. Smart move by Tori. She didn't retrace our steps and risk passing the guy. She drove up over the hill and out of sight.

'He seemed like a nice guy,' I said to Tori as we headed back to the interstate.

Tori looked behind us through the rearview mirror. I shifted in my seat and turned around. Nobody followed us. Once we were on the interstate, Tori stopped looking behind us.

'You picked today because you thought you'd have some freedom to look around the place,' she gathered. 'And because you thought if something illegal was going on here, today might be one of the days those illegal things would be happening.'

'Plus, it seemed like a nice day for a drive,' I said. 'No, you're right. Maybe now we know why Randall Manning is so sensitive about his sales records with Summerset Farms. Maybe fertilizer isn't the only thing being transferred from Global Harvest International to Summerset. Maybe they're running guns.'

'Is that all they were doing?' she asked. 'Then why were they shooting them, too?'

'Maybe checking the merchandise. Making sure the weapons work okay.'

She looked at me. 'Is that what you really think?'

I was trying to downplay what I'd just seen. But it wasn't going to work. Tori saw it for what it was.

'No,' I admitted. 'It looks like they're training for something.'

47

Randall Manning and Bruce McCabe walked along the floor of the domed building. Everything had been restored to normal, the shell casings picked up, the farm machinery returned to its rightful place. The men were finishing up their shooting practice outside.

Manning had considered having the target practice inside to maintain cover, but decided against it. The operation would take place outside, and he wanted the men accustomed to the elements. If it was sunny, he wanted them used to shooting with the sun in their eyes. If it was raining, they had to be prepared for that. Today the sky was clear and the sunlight was strong. Three weeks ago, they'd practiced in wind and snow.

Everyone had eaten. It had been a full Thanksgiving feast that Manning had catered in. Like Manning himself, none of these men had anyplace else to be. None of them had family to speak of. That was no accident. It was why they'd been chosen. It had been a slow, methodical search for months, finding just the right candidates – disaffected, angry, violent individuals with no familial connections and either national-istic or outright racist views. Finding them, to Manning's surprise, had been the easy part. It was winnowing them down to the best among them that had taken more of his time.

'I need you to take me seriously,' said McCabe, a little looser after a couple glasses of wine. The soldiers hadn't touched the alcohol, but McCabe and Manning had.

'I'm taking you very seriously, Bruce.'

'We have a chance to do this right, but this lawyer Kolarich is a threat.'

'Then we deal with the threat.'

'We deal with the threat and then we wait and let things pass,' McCabe insisted. 'We can't get rid of him and then turn around days later and carry out this thing.'

'We didn't choose the timing, Bruce.'

'But we did, Randy. I understand the symbolism of December seventh. I do. But there are other dates that could work. We shouldn't do this now.' McCabe stopped walking and waited for Manning to do the same. Manning turned to face him.

'I'm deadly serious, Randy.'

'What about your wife, Bruce? What about her?'

McCabe frowned. Color came to his face. 'Don't tell me about my wife. I'm not saying we shouldn't do this. I'm saying *not now*.'

Behind McCabe, Manning saw movement. Patrick Cahill, one of Manning's recruits, slipped out from behind a large tractor.

'Okay,' said Manning. 'Okay, Bruce.'

'Really? You mean it?' McCabe breathed out. His posture relaxed.

Then Patrick Cahill moved in. He used a rope, snapping it over McCabe's head and around his throat in one fluid motion. Manning heard a sickening crunch and desperate, gargling pleas from McCabe. McCabe struggled, his hands first going for the rope and then vainly swinging out behind him. But he was no match for Patrick Cahill, who lifted McCabe off his feet while he squeezed the life out of him.

Manning watched the whole time, until the last twitch of McCabe's leg, until his body went entirely limp and Cahill dragged him away. He was surprised at the numbness he felt. Bruce had been a friend, after all. A friend who had sworn an oath to the cause and then gone back on it, but a friend no less.

Manning had come a long way in eighteen months.

Then his cell phone rang, and he answered it.

'Mr Manning,' said the head of security. 'We had visitors today.'

48

Tori and I went back to my law office and worked for most of the rest of the evening. She was doing research online while I worked through the witnesses and wrote up an outline of my closing argument at trial. A trial lawyer, after assessing the evidence, starts his case preparation with a closing argument. That's the last thing you say to the jury, your final pitch, and you think about all the things you want to be able to say to them in that closing. Then you work backward, making sure that you put into evidence all the things you wanted to say, the individual bricks for the completed house you show them in closing.

My closing argument was now changing dramatically. This was no longer an insanity case. It was an innocence case. And most of the closing was going to be about things and people having nothing whatsoever to do with First Lieutenant Thomas Stoller. And most of it I didn't yet know. So the whole exercise devolved into a series of questions that I had.

Which meant I was back to being pissed off and flustered at day's end.

'I need more time,' I said to Tori as I drove her home. 'I

know there's something here, but I don't have the time to figure it out. I'm letting this kid down.'

'You're not. You're giving him your best, Jason.'

'It's not enough. It's not even close.'

She didn't answer right away, but I sensed she was watching me.

'What?' I said, not hiding my irritation.

'A lawyer I know once said that you do your best for your client, and when you go to bed at night, you sleep, because all you can do is your best. And in the end, it's your client, not you, that will do the time.'

'I don't know what kind of an asshole would say that.' Again, she was quoting my words back to me. 'I'm clocked out, Tori. I have a client who wants to go to prison, who wants to be punished, not for killing Kathy Rubinkowski but for shooting that girl in that tunnel in Mosul. He's no help to me. He doesn't remember anything about that night. So I'm left trying to convince a jury of something not even my own client will say, which is that someone else committed this murder and framed him. Isn't that grand? My argument is my client was framed, but my client won't even testify to it. And I have next to no proof of it. I have questions, and I have theories, but unless I can link them in some kind of tangible way, Judge Nash isn't even going to let the jury hear about—'

'Jason, slow down. You're feeling overwhelmed.' Tori touched my arm. 'There's still time. There's still a chance.'

I took a deep breath and tried to relax. She was right. I was letting the situation get the better of me. It wasn't like me. This was when I was usually at my best.

I made great time through the deserted city streets. I pulled up to her condo. Then I dropped my head against the steering

244

wheel and closed my eyes. There had to be something I was missing.

Tori took my hand and held it. Her hand was small and warm, and it felt good to connect with her. We sat like that for what must have been ten, fifteen minutes. I was tired and wired. I needed sleep, I knew, but this case wasn't going to give me that kind of peace. What lay ahead was nights of fitful sleep, eyes popping open in the middle of the night, tossing and turning.

'I used to be married,' Tori said to me.

I snapped out of my funk and looked at her. I wasn't sure why she was telling me this right now. An intimate moment, I guess.

'When did it end?' I asked.

'Five years ago,' she said. 'Five years ago today. November twenty-fifth, 2005. It was a Friday that year. The day after Thanksgiving.'

Funny that she'd know the date. But I guess it was tied to a holiday.

But a marriage ended with a court order dissolving the marriage. And you'd be hard-pressed to find a court open on the Friday after Thanksgiving.

Tori let go of my hand and stared out the window of the car.

'That's the day I killed him,' she told me.

I wasn't sure I'd heard her correctly. Other than alluding to the fact that her father was deceased, she'd never told me a thing about her family. And now she was telling me . . .

Did she just tell me she killed her husband?

'He was abusive,' she said mechanically. 'He knocked me around for years. One day, I decided I wasn't going to let it

245

continue. I didn't try to leave. I didn't try to get him in counseling. I just bought a gun and I shot him. He'd hit me a couple of times the night before. He got drunk at Thanksgiving dinner with his family, and when we got home, he used me for a punching bag. I woke up the next morning bruised and sore, and I felt like the oxygen was sucking out of my lungs. I felt completely trapped. He'd eventually apologize to me and make me believe that he could change, and then he wouldn't, and the cycle would repeat itself. I just couldn't do it anymore. Something just snapped. I got my gun out of the closet and I walked downstairs into the kitchen. He yelled at me because I hadn't made coffee. I shot him in the chest. He bled out right in front of me on the kitchen floor.'

I wasn't sure where to start, or whether I should say anything at all. I remembered the first time I met her, when those goons were hassling her, the one grabbing her arm outside. And I remembered how she reacted when I first mentioned I was defending a man accused of killing a woman.

'If I'd called for an ambulance right away, they might have been able to save him. But I didn't. I didn't want him to live. I wanted him to die.'

'Tori—'

'When the police came, they took one look at little ol' me and this bruiser of a husband, and I think they wanted to help me. They had some woman detective talk to me. She kept asking me what happened right before he shot me. I told her the truth. He was bitching about not having any coffee. And she said, "Is that when he hit you?" And I started to tell her, no, he'd hit me the night before. But then I realized that nobody would understand. The only way I could get away with this would be if they thought he was beating me up right then

246

and there. So I lied. I said he punched me that morning. I said I was in fear for my life. I lied because I was afraid they'd put me in prison otherwise.'

Slowly, she turned her head and locked eyes with me.

'So you wanted to know more about me, Jason. Now you do. Nice to meet you. Most sane men would turn and run.'

'Is that what you want me to do? Turn and run?'

She stared at me, her jaw tight and defiant, but tears formed in her eyes, the first crack in her shell. 'I don't know,' she said. 'Maybe.'

'Then you're going to have to push me away,' I said. 'I'm not running.'

I took her hand and held it for a long time. I didn't move toward her. She didn't move toward me. She'd opened up to me, but it was going to come in tiny steps. That was okay. I could wait. It was, in many ways, a terrible time to confide this secret to me, given the task I had before me and my time constraints. But it was an anniversary of sorts for her and it was on her mind. And she'd been watching me moan and groan like a little boy, suffering, and that somehow made her feel sufficiently at ease to share this thing.

There was plenty of time, I thought. Once this trial was over, Tori and I had plenty of time.

Then I thought to myself, Screw that, and I said, 'I'm coming upstairs with you,' and she said, 'Okay.'

49

I would imagine that Tori had a nice apartment, if I saw much of it. We barely made it through the door before we were undressing each other. I'd spent many hours dreaming of unbuttoning that long white coat and running my hands inside it. Many hours imagining her naked except for those black knee-high boots, but she kicked them off as we stumbled backward together.

I went first. I like foreplay. I liked watching her become more aroused as we progressed. I liked lying next to her on the bed, not letting her touch me, as my hands ran over her body. I liked caressing the inside of her legs as she moaned with expectation, almost tickling her, before my fingers slid inside her. I liked watching her free herself, unleash something primitive from within, break down that façade she always kept up. I liked watching her blush and bite her lower lip and squeeze her eyes shut. I liked that she gripped my hair tightly as I removed my fingers and replaced them with my tongue.

She was so light. She had such a petite but firm body. I lifted her up and onto me and our eyes met, wide open, gazing into each other, for just a moment before she closed them again. She ran her hands down my back as we bobbed up and down.

Her breath came in halted gasps, high-pitched, resembling sobs in some way. I'm usually pretty quiet, but I found myself grunting, and I knew this wasn't going to last long.

It didn't. But it was worth it.

She climbed off me and fell onto the bed. I did the same. She opened her eyes now and watched me, like she was observing me in some clinical fashion, trying to discern what or whom I was. Or maybe, I thought, she was wondering about herself.

And then her eyes welled up with tears. She silently fought them back and broke eye contact with me. After a moment she brushed the back of her hand over her eyes.

'I'm sorry,' she said.

'That's okay. A lot of women cry after they sleep with me.'

She allowed herself to laugh, and then a tear escaped and rode down her nose.

'This doesn't have to be a big deal,' I assured her. 'I'm not proposing marriage.'

She offered a smile that evaporated almost immediately. She didn't know how to handle this, or me, or something.

'Okay,' she said quietly.

50

On the Friday morning after Thanksgiving, Patrick Cahill stretched his calves and his quads, rolled his ankles, and ran in place to keep warm. To his right the sky over the lake was an intense pink, anticipating the rising sun. His breath lingered before him. It was probably just a hair above freezing, if that.

He was at an intersection, with his eyes trained six houses down the block. He wished he weren't so conspicuous, but he had no choice. His intel was vague at best.

He runs, he was told. *Jason Kolarich runs along the lake every morning, rain or shine.*

Not being particularly familiar with the city, Cahill had mapped it out last night. He had Kolarich's address. So that was point A. But the lakefront – point B – was another matter. The lake spanned the entirety of the city's east border. And there were a dozen different ways that Kolarich could access the lakefront from his townhouse. He'd have to go about three blocks east from his house. That was the easy part. But he could go north or south, and he could cut through a park or take a main artery. If Cahill were able to predict the spot at which Kolarich would reach the lakefront, it would be a simple matter of waiting for him. But since he couldn't, he had no choice but to follow him from his home.

There. Kolarich walked out of his townhouse at about a quarter to seven. He was wearing a sweatshirt and running shorts. He was a big guy, bigger than the photograph could convey. He jogged down the five stairs, opened the gate, and immediately took off to his left, eastbound, toward the lake, like he was shot from a cannon.

Cahill had to give him space, naturally. He receded into the shadow of the first house across the street. Kolarich paid him no heed, didn't even look in that direction. He crossed the street and ran north.

Good. He was probably headed to Ash. That was the most logical route. It was a major east-west artery that ran all the way to the lakefront.

Also good that he knew where Kolarich was heading, because Cahill was going to have a hell of a time keeping up with him. This guy was practically sprinting. Cahill was in good shape and liked his chances with him one-on-one – even better two-on-one – but he couldn't possibly run that fast.

'He's coming to Ash, I think,' he said into the microphone that was tucked under his shirt collar. 'Faded red sweatshirt and black shorts. Headphones in his ears and an iPod on his waist.'

Through his earpiece, he heard: '*He's coming to Ash, you THINK?*'

'He's a fast fuck. I can't keep up with him,' Cahill managed through halting breaths, sprinting after Kolarich.

It was two city blocks north, then three east. Cahill lost him and felt a flutter of panic before the words came through his earpiece.

'*Got him. He just headed south on the lake path. You're right, he is a fast fuck.*'

Cahill calmed a bit. Up ahead he approached the lakefront, which at Ash meant taking a ramp down to a tunnel that ran beneath the highway along the lakeshore. He caught his breath as he walked down the ramp. The sun was just beginning to appear over the lake, casting fluorescent pink and orange color across the skyline.

Then he was in darkness inside the tunnel. It ran the length of the four-lane highway above it and then some. The floor was a flat concrete. There were puddles of water and even a little ice. Other than the flat floor, the remainder of the tunnel was the typical tube shape, the highest point about ten, maybe twelve feet. There appeared to be overhead lights, but they were inoperative. Two homeless people slept against one side, huddled in blankets and layers of clothing with a grocery cart full of their possessions next to them. The chill helped stifle the odor, but it still reeked of urine.

When Cahill reached the end of the tunnel, a running path of cinder forked to the left for north or the right for south. Straight ahead and you were ten yards shy of the beach and the lake.

To the right, the land rose up at a forty-five-degree angle until it met the outer barriers of the highway. A 'grassy knoll' if there ever was one. The perfect ambush site. Kolarich would leave the tunnel, follow the cinder path to the right, and not even think to crane his head upward and to the right to look up the hill.

Just what his partner, Dwyer, was thinking. He was standing halfway up that hill, checking on angles down toward the mouth of the tunnel. He nodded at Cahill.

Dwyer was part of the Circle, too. He was ex-military like Cahill, though he was dishonorably discharged after serving five years in the stockade for sexual assault. Dwyer was bad news, but when it came to carrying out an exercise, he showed a steely discipline.

Cahill had demanded a partner for this job. You want to ambush someone while on a jog, you needed two people to be sure.

'He went south,' said Dwyer, slowly descending the hill. 'Like a bat out of hell.'

Cahill looked up the hill again. 'So it would be a tough shot from the hill.'

'I can hit a human target from ten feet away no matter how fast he's running,' he said. 'So can you.'

'But it's not supposed to look like sniper fire,' Cahill said, looking around. 'Manning said they'll be suspicious when this lawyer goes down. It has to look like a robbery. It has to be convincing.'

'Who robs a guy while he's jogging?'

Cahill sighed. It was a problem. True, people had been killed for less than an iPod or expensive running shoes. But it wasn't usually by a gun. It was more hand-to-hand stuff. A knife, maybe. Cahill had used a rope on Bruce McCabe, but that was different. Still, a good old-fashioned strangulation or blow to the head was the best way. Make it look like a struggle ensued, a grab-and-run gone bad – someone tried to swipe his iPod, he resisted, there was a fight, and he ended up dead. Theoretically, sure. But this guy Kolarich? He wouldn't be an easy drop.

'We could disappear him,' Dwyer suggested. 'Shoot him and cart him off. You pull the car up to the ramp. Two minutes, the whole thing's over. And we have a dark tunnel for cover.'

But that wouldn't look anything remotely like a robbery. Plus, that would require privacy of at least five minutes – not the two Dwyer was suggesting – in a very public area.

Another runner, an elderly man, slowly jogged past them. A couple of bicyclists flew by as well. The sun had risen now, and the men had to squint as they looked around.

The lakefront wasn't terribly crowded at dawn in the middle of winter, but it wasn't entirely deserted, either. And if they were going to take Kolarich out in a sniper-style ambush, they needed total privacy.

Every option posed risks. Some would look more like a robbery than others. But in the end, Manning had left Patrick Cahill with one final instruction:

Don't fuck it up. Make him dead.

'See you tomorrow morning, Kolarich,' Cahill said.

51

Peter Ramini got into the backseat of the town car and didn't even look at Donnie. He smelled him, though. The whole backseat reeked of fried food. An Egg McMuffin wrapper and plenty of crumbs lay on the floor at Donnie's feet. A cup of coffee rested in the cup holder near Ramini's feet. He missed coffee desperately.

'So I don't even need to tell you why the visit,' said Donnie.

Ramini looked at the driver, Donnie's brother Mooch, who was watching Ramini in the rearview mirror.

'No, you don't.'

'Paulie said to ask: What wasn't clear about his instruction?'

'It's not a matter of clear, Don. The guy pretty much works round the clock right now. He's got that trial. There's no way to get to him up there in that office.'

'He don't go home at night?'

'Yeah, he goes home.' Ramini's frustration was growing. And his fear, too. When instructions weren't followed, there were consequences. He knew he was running out of rope with Paulie Capparelli.

'Hey, you know how it goes,' said Donnie, his tone less amicable than normal. He was delivering an icy message, and they both knew it. 'So Paulie said to say, someone's gonna die. It's either gonna be Jason Kolarich or Gin Rummy.' Donnie looked over at Ramini.

Ramini bristled at the nickname. 'It'll get done right away,' he said. 'No more delays. Tell Paulie it's my word.'

Donnie put a greasy hand on Ramini's arm. Ramini, of course, had his hands stuffed in his pockets. 'I got a soft spot for your family, old man, you know that. I told Paulie, I said, "Gin Rummy's gonna take care of everything." Don't make me a liar, my friend.'

Ramini slid out of the car and watched it drive away. He knew he was out of warnings with Paulie Capparelli.

Jason Kolarich had to die right away.

52

After my morning jog, I ate some eggs and made it to my law firm by eight-thirty. I was feeling pretty good, all things considered, after last night with Tori. It seemed like she had some remorse afterward, but I was getting used to baby steps with her, and that was okay by me. Especially because I had this one thing going on, this murder trial, that required some attention.

It was the day after Thanksgiving, but by nine-thirty Bradley and Shauna and Marie were there, and we'd been on the phone several times with Joel Lightner from his office. At three-thirty in the afternoon, my expert on post-traumatic stress disorder, Dr Sofian Baraniq, arrived.

At one time, Dr Baraniq had been my entire case. That was back when my client was pleading, in essence, insanity, and the case would rise or fall on whether the jury believed Dr Baraniq. That part of the case was gone now, and to some people's minds, that meant Dr Baraniq was no longer relevant to the case. But he was. I still planned on using him. And while my case no longer rested entirely on him, he was still crucial to our defense.

He was in a conference room with Shauna. I stopped in to

say hello. I liked this guy. He had a boyish face but was book-ish, too, with his glasses and trim beard and precise manner of speech. He had a sense of humor and self-deprecation that would make him credible but not arrogant to a jury. Most important, he could break down technical testimony into something that was accessible to lay jurors. A good expert is a teacher, and he spent most of his time teaching grad students.

'Good to see you again, Doctor.'

He was on his cell phone but quickly got off. He extended a hand. 'Hello again, Mr Kolarich.'

'Might as well call me Jason.'

'I understand the court has entered a ruling on my testimony.'

'The insanity defense is out, yes. But we have some other ideas for you. Shauna will explain.' I rubbed my hands together, experiencing an adrenaline dump as I plotted the beginning of our defense. 'So I think you'll be our first witness, Doctor. That's my current thought. The trial starts next Wednesday, December first. You'll be first after the prosecution rests. So it will be probably early the following week – probably about that next Tuesday or Wednesday – that we'll need you.'

Dr Baraniq was wagging a finger at me. 'I do want you to recall, I have an obligation that following Tuesday after the trial begins. I mentioned that to you.'

That stopped me. I'd forgotten. 'Something you can't break,' I recalled.

'A religious obligation.'

Shit. It was possible, depending on what we could turn up in the meantime, that Dr Baraniq would be one of only two witnesses, and I needed him to go first. The order mattered to me. If the prosecution rested by Tuesday, or even midday Tuesday, I needed Dr Baraniq ready.

'I'm sorry, but I thought I reminded you,' he said again.

Apparently my frustration was evident. I flapped my arms. 'Well, if you can't do Tuesday, you can't do Tuesday.'

Once again – shit. But it reminded me of something. I excused myself and pulled Shauna out of the room with me. We huddled in the hallway.

'He told us about this commitment back when we first met with him, Jason. But I think it should work out just—'

'I don't care about that,' I said. 'So listen. I want you to find a way to get his religion in.'

She drew back. 'You want him to testify that he's Muslim?'

'Yes, I do. It adds to his credibility.'

She didn't get that. 'First of all,' she countered, 'it has nothing to do with anything. And second of all, if anything, we might get someone on the jury who doesn't like Muslims. You may have noticed, there are some bigots in the city. You and I grew up with some of them.'

She was right about that. But she was missing the point. I shook my head. 'Anyone who doesn't like Muslims will love an American soldier fighting in Iraq like Tom. They'll want to help him. So I'm not worried about that. But more than anything, it shows the strength of the doctor's convictions. Why would a Muslim who clearly takes his religion seriously want to go out of his way to help one of the soldiers who was occupying a Muslim country?'

Shauna thought about that. 'So he must feel very strongly about what he's saying. That's your point?'

'That's my point.'

'And my point is it's condescending to the jury. It's

259

insulting. It might look that way to the jury. If we overplay that hand—'

'Then don't overplay it. He's your witness, Shauna. Do it smoothly. Hell, use the Tuesday thing as an excuse. Ask him why he couldn't be with us on Tuesday and he can tell you why. Or find a way to bring it in subtly.'

She played this over and came back with the same reaction. 'I don't like it.'

'We need to do it.'

'Jason!' Marie was standing in the hallway.

'I'm against this,' said Shauna. 'I don't want to do it.'

I leaned in to her, so Marie couldn't hear me. 'Shauna, I don't have time for a lecture on political correctness or stereotypes or making this world a better place, okay? I have a guy with his life on the line. This is a fucking murder trial. So man up and get it done. If you can't, I'll take the witness and do it myself.'

'*Man up?*'

I didn't want to hear it. I didn't have time to hear it. And regardless of what I'd just said, Shauna was going to take this witness, not me. And I knew her well enough to know that she was going to do only what she wanted to do.

'What, Marie?' I said, walking away from Shauna.

'You have a phone call,' she said. 'Someone named Sasha?'

I didn't recognize the name.

'She said she was Lorenzo Fowler's girlfriend,' Marie said. 'And it's urgent.'

53

I took the call in my office. 'This is Jason Kolarich,' I said.

'Mr Kolarich.' It was a woman's voice, thick with an Eastern European accent. Russian or something like that. *Mee-ster Kolareech.*

'My name is Sasha Maldonov. Do you know who I am?'

I only knew what Marie had told me. 'You knew Lorenzo Fowler.'

'Yes. I loved him. When he was . . . When they shot him, he'd come from my apartment.'

I didn't know that. The police wouldn't tell me what Lorenzo had been doing on West Arondale the night he was murdered.

'Go on,' I said.

'I am in danger. I know this. I cannot stay at my home. They think that Lorenzo told me things. Things I . . . should not know.' There was background traffic noise on her end of the phone. She was on a cell phone or a pay phone, if pay phones even exist anymore.

'Did he?' I asked, my pulse kicking up.

She paused. 'Can you . . . protect me?'

'I'll protect you,' I promised, which was a bit reckless of me. 'Tell me what you know.'

'I know many things. Lorenzo knew I would not tell. He knew I would keep his secrets. But now . . .' Another, longer pause followed. Car horns honking.

'You're afraid they want to kill you for the same reason they killed Lorenzo,' I gathered. 'So the best thing for you to do is testify for me. Once it's said publicly, there's no reason to kill you.'

Clearly, she'd come to the same conclusion. 'Can we meet?' she asked.

'Yes. Anytime,' I said. 'Right away.'

Another pause. I had a moment of pause myself. I had to be sure this woman was legit. 'Prove to me you're who you say you are,' I said.

'Prove this to you? Lorenzo told you about me, no?'

'No,' I said.

'Ah. Well . . .'

'Why are you calling me?' I asked.

'Because Lorenzo went to you. He did not want to speak with the usual lawyers that he was given. He wanted someone who was not connected to the . . . family.'

That was true enough. 'What did we discuss?'

'He told you . . . that he could provide the identity of someone. He wanted protection.'

'Whose identity?' I asked.

Another pause. 'Not over . . . the phone,' she said.

I suppose I couldn't blame her. And I didn't want to push her too hard. I didn't know where she was, and she could hang up this phone and disappear forever. It was a delicate dance, and I was getting desperate. She needed me, but I needed her more.

'Gin Rummy,' she said. 'He told you he had proof.'

I closed my eyes. Lorenzo Fowler had said those very words to me – he had proof.

'Are you now satisfied?' she asked me.

'Tell me where you are,' I said eagerly. 'I'll leave right now.'

54

Traffic was light on my side of the commercial district, given the unofficial holiday of the day after Thanksgiving, plus it was just after four in the afternoon. The sun was close to setting, but among skyscrapers in the city, it was, for all practical purposes, nightfall already. I steered clear of the east and north sides, where the stores were presumably swollen with early Christmas shoppers. I didn't like to think about Christmas. It reminded me too much of my wife and daughter.

I avoided the expressway on the western border of the commercial district and took side streets south. Sasha Maldonov wouldn't tell me where she was staying, but she told me where she wanted to meet. She wanted a public place, she said, but not too obvious.

The street was zoned commercial, but the stores weren't exactly bringing in the early shoppers. The city's southwest side didn't attract Nordstrom and Neiman Marcus and Macy's. This street had consignment stores and payday loan services and convenience shops.

I pulled my SUV into the parking lot of the boarded-up restaurant on the southeast corner. There were no working lights, and by now the sun had set, so visibility was poor. To the east of this building was a big-and-tall store that also advertised secondhand clothing. Its neighbor to the south was another vacant building that used to be a shoe store, I think. But in between the two vacant buildings was an east-west alley.

And standing on the street, next to the alley, was a woman in a long black coat and baseball cap. Sasha Maldonov. Tall, attractive, long dark hair spilling out beneath the cap. She said she'd be in a dark coat and red baseball cap. I couldn't make out the color of the cap in the dark, but there was no doubt we'd connected.

I nodded to her. She nodded in return and turned down the alley.

I approached the alley with caution. I looked down it before committing. The alley wasn't a through-and-through; it dead-ended about a hundred feet down. There were garbage dumpsters along the right side and at the far wall. The lighting was poor, provided mainly by a streetlamp across the street. Sasha stood near a door that was part of the now-vacant restaurant. She gave me a curt wave, urging me to get away from the street and farther into the alley.

I kept my approach cautious. I had a tape recorder in my pocket. I didn't have a gun. I didn't make it a habit to carry it and lacked the permit to do so. I probably should have stopped home to get my weapon, but I hadn't.

I passed the garbage dumpsters and got within maybe fifteen feet of her. She seemed apprehensive, and I didn't want to rush anything.

'Mee-ster Kolareech,' she said to me in a thick accent, as I approached her. 'I can be sure you were not followed?'

'I wasn't followed,' I said, though I wasn't sure of that fact at all. I raised my hands in a calming gesture. 'Tell me how you want to do this.' I took another step toward her.

Then the door next to her burst open. A man stepped out, and Sasha – or whatever her name was – stepped inside, disappearing. Now it was me and this guy, who was wearing a leather jacket and a turtleneck.

And holding a Beretta in his right hand, aimed directly at me.

Then I heard noise behind me. Another guy, similar in look and build, had been hiding behind one of the dumpsters. He had a gun, too. He stepped out behind me. One in front of me, one behind me.

I did a double-take, then something registered with me. These were the two guys from Vic's who were harassing Tori the night I first met her. The guy in front of me was the one I had clocked and sent to the ice outside.

'We meet again,' he said, giving me a wide smile.

It didn't make sense. But this was no time for logic games. I had to assess and do it quickly. He was too far away for me to reach him, to kick out or lunge for him. But it seemed like that was my only play here, because of the second guy behind me. There was no way I could turn and run, as goon number two had cut off my exit. My only chance was to charge the first guy and hope that the second guy opened fire on me, missed, and hit his partner. The odds of success were right up there with lightning striking each of them dead simultaneously.

All of these thoughts passed within a second or two. I didn't have too many more seconds to spare.

'How's the shoulder?' I asked, to buy some time, at least make him want to say something wise in reply, at which time I could make my move and pray.

'Oh,' he replied, 'it's doing much – what the—'

I started my lunge forward, but his eyes had moved beyond me and then an explosion impacted his right shoulder, followed rapidly by one to his chest that sprayed me with his blood. His gun fell from his hand with the shot to his shoulder. His body collapsed with the chest shot.

Instinctively, I altered my direction from a lunge forward to a dive to the left, hitting the ground hard, pain shooting through my kneecap and confusion reigning in my brain. This didn't make sense. The second goon shot his partner?

Another shot fired, and then I heard the guy behind me drop, too.

I waited for a count of one or two seconds before I raised my head. Both of them were down. Neither was moving. I got to my feet and realized I had totally fucked my left knee in my dive. I limped over to the first goon, who was dead beyond any doubt. Still, I kicked his weapon far away from him. I dragged myself over to the one who'd been behind me. The bullet had entered his left temple. Presumably, he'd turned to look back toward the street and was shot before he could complete a pivot, much less fire his weapon. His gun had fallen behind him, but I kicked it away, anyway.

I had more questions than ever. But I was unbelievably lucky to be alive, however odd the circumstances. So sore knee and all, I decided not to press my luck any further and got the hell out of there.

55

'Lightner,' I said into my cell phone, once I was back inside my car. 'Get over to the law firm. Someone just tried to kill me. Shauna and Bradley and Marie are sitting ducks over there.'

'Jesus, what the hell happened?'

'Can't talk now. Just get over there. I'll see you soon.'

I punched out the phone and dialed Tori's cell phone.

'Hello?'

'Tori, it's Jason. Where are you?'

'I'm at my condo. I'm working on an Internet search—'

'Listen, you still have that gun you used five years ago?'

She was silent for a moment. 'What kind of a question is—'

'You could be in danger,' I said. 'Lock your door and don't let anyone in. They saw you with me yesterday at Summerset Farms. They just tried to kill me, and you could be next. I'll be there in less than half an hour. Okay?'

'Okay, sure. Are *you* okay?'

'I'm fine,' I said.

'What about everyone else? Shauna and the others?'

'I just talked to them. They're still at our office. Joel's going over there.'

'Maybe I should, too.'

That wasn't a bad idea. Keep us all together. 'Can you get to your car safely?'

'I – sure. My condo building's secure. We have a doorman, and the garage is underground. You'd have to go through the lobby to get to it.'

'That doesn't fill me with confidence, Tori.'

'It'll be fine,' she promised. 'I'll leave right now. I'll go straight to the law firm.'

'I don't know. . . .'

'I think you're being paranoid,' she said. 'Why would someone want to kill me?'

56

I sat in a chair in the conference room, staring up at the ceiling.

'Well, this is just insane,' said Shauna. 'We need to go to the judge. We need to tell him that we're obviously onto something here, and our lives are at risk. We need a continuance of the trial and protection.'

Bradley and Joel Lightner were sitting here with me. Tori had just arrived and had taken a seat, too. Everyone was tense. This was turning into something nobody had expected.

'You're forgetting something,' I said. 'You're forgetting I left the scene. There are two dead bodies and I'm nowhere to be found. Hell, I could be a suspect.'

In hindsight, it was probably dumb of me to flee. It was an instinct. Someone had just tried to kill me, and getting as far away as possible, as fast as possible, had seemed like a pretty swell idea at the time.

'It's only been an hour or so,' said Shauna. 'Let's call the cops now and go in.'

I shook my head. 'I could get tied up for days with those guys. I don't have those days. I have a client who needs me to be focusing on his trial.'

'But think about it, Jason. You tell them what happened, and the judge will have to delay things. Wendy Kotowski would probably agree.'

That might be true. But I couldn't trust Judge Nash. He was too unpredictable, and I was on his shit list now. And my story was a real crowd-pleaser. Some mobsters tried to kill me because I'd uncovered a plot between the Mob and a wealthy downstate CEO to kill Kathy Rubinkowski, but the ambush was thwarted when someone miraculously saved me. Who, I have no idea. Yeah, that was a real winner. Until I had something more to back it up, I'd sound like a paranoid freak. I sure as hell couldn't count on help from our judge.

Tori said, 'Are you sure they were the same guys who were hassling me at Vic's that night?'

I'd left things a little strangely with Tori on Thanksgiving night, after we'd slept together. I wasn't sure how it would work out going forward. But any awkwardness was erased by the turn of events tonight.

I nodded. 'No doubt. The one guy said, "We meet again." And when I asked him how his shoulder was doing, he started to answer. That was just before he got shot.'

Tori shook her head. Nobody had a ready explanation.

'They've been watching me all along,' I said. 'The Mob. The Capparellis. That was back when all this started. When Lorenzo Fowler came to see me. They must have been wise to it. They were afraid he was going to tell me something. So they wanted to keep an eye on me.' I threw my hands up. 'That's the best I can figure.'

'So, if the Capparellis wanted to kill you,' said Joel, 'who came to your rescue tonight?'

I had no idea. 'Someone who's a pretty good shot,' I said. 'I know, Joel, I know. You're thinking it was the infamous Gin Rummy. But Gin Rummy works for the Capparellis. Gin Rummy, if anything, should want me dead. He wouldn't try to save me.'

Nobody knew what to say. It was getting easier and easier to draw up a list of people who wanted me dead. But not so easy to think of who would want to rescue me.

'Okay, listen up,' I said. I sat up and looked around the table. 'Starting right now, each of you has permission to drop off this case.'

'I needed your permission?' Lightner asked.

I ignored him. 'Go on vacation or something. I know our witnesses and I know their witnesses. I can handle it. I don't need anyone's death on my conscience. No foolin', guys. This is my problem, not yours.'

The room went quiet. They were probably thinking it over. They should. I was serious. They'd done enough prep work for me. I could try this case alone. I didn't want to have to worry about the health and safety of two lawyers, a private eye, and Tori.

'I'm not going anywhere,' said Shauna.

'Me, neither,' Bradley added.

'Six weeks of work without pay, and now someone's going to shoot at me, too? Count me in!' That was Lightner's attempt at humor.

Tori shrugged. 'I don't know how much help I am, but I want to stick around.'

'Okay, so we're all very courageous,' I said. 'Then I say we stay together in groups.'

'Right,' said Lightner. 'That way, they can save time by shooting us in bunches.'

Shauna said, 'Report this to the police, Jason. Get it out in the open. It will make it harder for the Mob to come after you a second time if you've already publicly accused them of trying to come after you once.'

I'd considered that. But I didn't think these guys felt a whole lot of fear. They had ways of killing people without leaving a lot of fingerprints. And like I said, my story would sound too far-fetched.

And as much as I might appreciate a delay from a tactical point of view, I was beginning to wonder if we weren't better off going to trial in a few days.

'No cops,' I said. 'We go forward. And we start by asking who the hell was it who saved my ass tonight?'

57

Patrick Cahill watched the majestic sight of the Saturday-morning sun appearing over the lake, while he clutched in his hand the gun that he would use to kill Jason Kolarich.

He stood at ground level, near the grass embankment to the highway, keeping his breathing even, awaiting the word through his earpiece. He had stretched and restretched his limbs. He was on high alert, realizing that he'd only have about thirty, maybe forty-five, seconds' notice that Jason Kolarich was on his way down the ramp and through the tunnel, coming toward Cahill.

His partner, Dwyer, was serving as the marker. He was parked on Ash a half-block down from the ramp. Dwyer would tell Cahill via the earpiece when he first spotted Kolarich, and then when he was heading down the ramp.

The tunnel was where it would happen. The cover of darkness and complete privacy made it the perfect choice. Cahill would start jogging into the tunnel from the direction opposite Kolarich. If Kolarich saw him standing still, essentially lying in wait, it would raise his radar. But seeing a fellow runner come jogging into the tunnel would seem perfectly normal to him.

Cahill hopped around, did some high-knees in place, worked out the nerves. He checked his watch. It was just after seven now. The sun had reared its head, bathing him in warm light, the color of the sky beginning with a burst of orange at the horizon and fading into pinks and reds as it moved upward.

By seven-fifteen, the sun had fully shown its shape over the water. By seven-thirty, the sky reminded him of rainbow sherbet. But where the fuck was Kolarich?

'Sleeping in on a Saturday?' Cahill said.

'*Maybe.*'

By eight o'clock, Cahill didn't give a flying fuck about the sunrise anymore. By eight-thirty, he wasn't sure what to do, because the lakefront was beginning to swell with joggers and bikers and skaters and speed-walkers. Didn't they realize it was thirty degrees out here?

'Dammit. This is all fucked now.'

'*Should I go by his house?*' Dwyer asked.

'What good would that do?'

'*Okay. Then what's plan B?*'

'There isn't a fucking plan B. I was told this guy is like clockwork, running along the lake at dawn. You think he took a different route?'

'*I don't know. Probably we should wait, right?*'

Cahill looked around. Joggers and bikers and skaters and walkers aside, the tunnel would still be dark and, hopefully, empty, thus remaining viable as a kill spot. He'd have to improvise. Once he got word about Kolarich from Dwyer, he'd have to quickly assess the situation and determine whether it was still workable.

At nine o'clock, Dwyer said into Cahill's earpiece, '*There's a traffic lady handing out tickets. I have to move. It's thirty-minute parking here.'*

'Great.'

'I'll do a lap and come back around.'

Yeah, thought Cahill, and let's hope Kolarich doesn't choose that window of time to come barreling down Ash and through the tunnel.

At nine-thirty, a police squad car lazily cruised along the beach, passing directly by Cahill about fifty feet away. Cahill made a big point of stretching to not arouse their attention.

'Enough,' he said. 'Come pick me up, Dwyer. It's time to come up with a plan B.'

58

'Hi,' Tori said, answering the phone, presumably seeing me on caller ID.

'Just checking to see if you're still alive,' I said. 'Are you still alive?'

'I am. Are you?'

'I think so.'

'How's the knee?'

'It's seen better days.' I had my left leg up on a chair in my office. Keeping it straight kept it from stiffening up. When I got out of bed this morning, I couldn't even put weight on it. I had to hop on one foot into the shower. I wasn't really sure how I'd hurt it – I was a little preoccupied with bullets flying past me and ducking for cover – but I was hoping it was just a sprain and not ligament damage or anything.

I hated immobility. I tweaked a hammy my freshman year at State and could barely walk for a few days and I went crazy. Today, I missed my morning run for the first time in weeks, but worse, I'd have trouble pacing, which was how I did my best thinking.

Tori said, 'And you're positive those guys from last night

were the same ones who bought me those drinks and grabbed me at Vic's?'

'I'm sure, Tori.'

'That's so weird.'

'Not really. It tells me the Capparellis were looking at me. I checked my date book. That friendly encounter at Vic's came after Lorenzo Fowler had called to make an appointment. It was before we actually met but after he'd set up the meeting with my secretary. So they knew he was coming my way and they were watching me. They've been watching me the whole time.'

'I guess that makes sense,' she said.

It did, but something about it still felt wrong. I wasn't sure what.

'Be careful,' I said. 'We're all here at the firm if you want to join us.'

I hung up with her and returned my attention to the motions in limine that the prosecution had filed. As much as I hated paper and preferred the give-and-take of witness testimony, pretrial motions could have a devastating impact on a trial. You prepare for months or years for a trial and in the final days, the other side takes a shot at excluding your prime piece of evidence or your best argument, and you hold your breath and pray for the right outcome. The wrong result can fundamentally redirect your defense on virtually the eve of trial.

The principal bomb that Wendy Kotowski had dropped was asking the judge to exclude any evidence of Tom Stoller's heroic military background and, thus, the testimony of Sergeant Bobby Hilton, his friend. Now that the defense of post-traumatic stress disorder had been excluded by the court, she argued, Tom's military biography had no relevance to whether he killed Kathy Rubinkowski.

She was right. But getting sympathy out of the jury for a war hero who lost everything when he returned home was one of the only arrows I had left in the quiver. So we had our work cut out for us to convince the judge to allow the evidence, and Bradley John's first draft of the defense's response, which was due Monday, wasn't satisfactory, to my mind.

If Judge Nash was a normal human being, he'd feel like he owed me one at this point. That's how most judges think – if they stick one side with an adverse ruling, they try to restore the equilibrium with a favorable ruling on something else. They want to finish a trial knowing that they screwed over each side about the same.

All told, Wendy had filed no less than sixteen motions in limine. It was a routine tactic to inundate the other side with these motions so they spent their last days before trial tied up in paper and legal research. It was a tactic of which I disapproved. I deplored it, in fact. The adversarial system wasn't intended to be a game of one-upsmanship but, rather, a sincere search for the truth.

Which was why I filed only fifteen motions on our side.

Either way, it was going to be a long weekend.

My office phone rang, my direct line that almost nobody knows.

'Yeah, hello?'

'Yeah, hello,' Joel Lightner said. He was back at his office, doing his digging on Randall Manning and those other shady characters. Another investigator was helping him. He'd warned me that he'd have trouble getting to some information until

Monday, when everyone returned from the long holiday week-end, so I hadn't expected magic from him yet.

'You don't answer your cell now?' he complained.

'Oh, sorry.' It was sitting on my desk, but somehow I'd missed the buzzing.

'So I got something.'

'On that one thing?'

'No, the other thing.'

I'd grown paranoid since someone tried to ice me last night, so I was assuming the worst – including that my phones were tapped. Thus, the code-speak.

'The new thing?' I said.

'Right,' he said.

The new thing. My heart did a flip.

'You free for lunch?' I asked.

He said, 'Just what I was thinking.'

59

Patrick Cahill and his partner, Dwyer, had spent the better part of the last hour walking the block of Jason Kolarich's townhouse. The lawyer lived on a relatively isolated residential street near the lake, and the sidewalks weren't heavily traveled with the temperatures in the mid-thirties, all of which made the two of them conspicuous standing out here, not doing much of anything but studying the townhouse.

Cahill didn't have a better idea. Kolarich had aborted his run this morning. Cahill didn't know why. Maybe it was a one-off, an exception, and tomorrow he'd return to his routine. Maybe Cahill could wait that one more day.

But he needed a plan B. And he hadn't come prepared with one. It wasn't like he'd spent weeks planning this thing. It had all happened pretty fast: the guy was nosing around, he had to be eliminated, they knew he went for jogs along the lake – Patrick, get rid of him. Okay, well, now Patrick had to improvise.

He knew where Kolarich worked, but it was a downtown high-rise building, and it wasn't the easiest or cleanest thing in the world to go after someone in a building like that. There were cameras and locked doors and security guards and people in relatively confined spaces. It would take lots of preparation and planning, and Cahill had time for neither.

But Kolarich had to come home at night. It was only noon right now, so that was hours away, especially for a lawyer getting ready for a trial in less than a week. Maybe he wouldn't come home until two in the morning. But he'd come home. And they had to be ready.

'The garage,' said Cahill. Next to his brick townhome with white trim was a brick garage with white trim. It was a one-car job but presumably had some room built in for movement.

'Two possibilities,' he said. 'We break into the garage and wait for him inside. But I'm not sure how we get in there. There isn't a window. The door's automatic, so it won't lift manually. So the better idea is we wait for him outside. He pulls into the driveway, he opens the garage door, as he pulls the car into the garage, we slip in before he lowers the door.'

'So we're doing it inside a closed garage. Good,' Dwyer agreed. 'And where do we wait?'

The answer, Cahill thought, was blindingly obvious. Cahill pointed to a thin strip between Kolarich's townhouse and the one next to it to the east. It was technically the neighbor's property, a walkway that ran the length of the townhomes and dead-ended into a gate accessing the neighbor's back patio. God, these city people didn't have much real estate. Cahill was sure he could stand on that walkway, extend his arms, and touch both houses.

'We can squat down there,' he said. 'We'll pick a spot so we can see his car coming, but as he pulls in, the angle will be so he can't see us. Not that he'd be looking.'

'Right.'

'Then we move forward and once he pulls his car in, we

scoot inside. He hits the garage door button without thinking. It closes up and we make our move.'

'And this is still supposed to look like a robbery?'

'Forget that.' Cahill shook his head. 'Mr Manning said dead was the most important thing. I'm done screwing around with this guy. We should be back home getting ready, and instead we're wasting another full day on this lawyer. I'm going to put more holes in that grunt than a piñata.'

'Good. Sounds good.'

Cahill checked his watch. 'No sense sitting around now, freezing to death. He's not coming home for a long time.'

Cahill and Dwyer walked down the block to where their car, a blue Ford Explorer, was parked. They got in and drove off. Aside from getting some food and whiling away a few hours, Cahill wanted some long underwear and extra layers of clothing and a thermos of hot coffee for what could be a long night of recon. It felt good to him, like old times, he thought, when he was in the military.

It was going to feel even better when he could tell Mr Manning he'd solved the problem.

60

'Okay,' said Bradley John, reading over the last of our responses to the prosecution's pretrial motions. 'I see what I wasn't giving you the first time around.'

'You did a good job structurally,' I said. 'Really. You cited the cases, you gave good legal reasoning. But it didn't have any heart.'

'Heart?'

'This is a murder trial, Bradley. Somebody died, and a second person's life is on the line in this trial. The stakes are high. Emotions are high. Judges aren't immune to that. Look, some of these motions are routine. But the one on the prior military history, that's the whole ball game for us, right? So right there in our response, we need the judge to read about Tom's military background. I think he's going to feel bad excluding it. We start there, with the psychological aspect. Not too heavy or it feels like pandering but enough to gain his sympathy – hopefully.'

'Okay.'

It was an important lesson, one too many lawyers forgot, and too many young lawyers failed to appreciate. Judges are human. The law – statutory language, court decisions – are obviously important, but if the *facts* make them want to rule your way, their brains will start working in that direction. They'll want to believe you're right. They'll try to find a way to rule in your favor, even if they don't realize they're doing it. Now, that won't win every argument every time. If you're way off, you'll still lose. But in a close case, when it could go either way, judges want to feel good about themselves. They'll want to feel like they're doing a good thing. Even Judge Nash, I hoped.

And then, once you get them wanting to be on your side, you give them the case law to support your position, so they can feel good about being on your side. You're telling them, here's backup for your gut feeling. Here's legal support for what you really want to do in your heart.

When I was done explaining all of this, Bradley looked up at me. 'I see that now. Thanks, Jason. Really, this is helpful.'

I wagged my finger at him. 'Don't ever forget the human side of this, young man.' I looked at my watch. 'Now, it's almost midnight. Probably best we head out. We can finish these up tomorrow. Let me just check a couple of things.'

I glanced again at the newspaper, the story in the Metro section about the deaths of two men in an alley on the southwest side who were reputed figures in the Capparelli crime family. That made three dead Capparellis, counting Lorenzo Fowler, and the paper speculated about a possible war brewing between the Capparellis and the Morettis.

I dialed Lightner on my cell phone. 'How we doing?' I asked.

'Good,' he said. 'No change.'

'Good. I'm leaving now.'

I hung up and dialed my friend Ross Vander Way.

'Hey, Ross, it's Jason.'

285

'Hey, man.'

'Still all good?'

'Sure, yeah.'

'Okay. I'm leaving now,' I said.

I walked down the hall to Shauna's office. She was typing up a cross-examination on her computer. She was wearing her reading glasses, which I thought was kind of hot. Which I thought was kind of weird, since she was like a sister to me. Which I thought was bizarre, because I used to sleep with her once upon a time. Anyway.

'Ready to go, sweetheart?'

She stretched her arms. 'Sure, probably a good idea. This is a marathon, not a sprint, right?'

'Yeah, plus, y'know – we should get going.'

She nodded grimly. The simple task of leaving the office and walking to our car, these days, was a hazardous activity. I had my gun with me just in case, but I wasn't much of a shot.

Anyway, I was relatively sure we were safe for the time being.

Bradley, Shauna, and I – the lawyers of Tasker & Kolarich – headed down the elevator to my car.

61

Patrick Cahill and his partner, Dwyer, squatted down in the small walkway between Jason Kolarich's townhouse and the townhouse next door. It was past one A.M. now, and they were tired and cold, having sat in this spot for the better part of seven hours now. But the later it got, the more likely he was to show up any minute.

They were lucky, too. This was a uniquely advantageous hiding place. It was right next to the garage, it was poorly lit, and it was such a tiny space – no more than five feet wide – that Kolarich almost assuredly wouldn't even think to look for them.

And the neighbor, whoever he or she or they were, didn't have a window on the ground or even the second floor that overlooked this walkway. There was a window directly above them on the third floor, but the occupant would have to go out of his way to stick his head out the window and look all the way down at the walkway, and even then the visibility would be relatively poor.

They'd purchased thermal underwear and black hooded sweatshirts and extra pairs of socks, and they wore all of them now. It was cold regardless. The temperature was probably in the teens. But they were doing okay. Their biggest problem was that their legs were getting cramped. Every half-hour, one of them walked up and down the walkway between the houses to keep himself limber.

Above them, for the first time, they heard the voices of the neighbors. Muted sounds, presumably coming from the third floor and traveling through the window to their ears. Dwyer nudged Cahill and they listened.

'Disgusting. That's disgusting!'

It was a woman's voice, shouting.

'You're overreacting!' a man called out.

They heard the scraping and shifting of wood, the unmistakable sound of the window opening directly above them on the third floor. Cahill and Dwyer braced themselves and tucked in their chins, froze in their crouch, doing their best to conceal themselves. But they were probably okay, Cahill thought. These people were just arguing. Someone would have to look straight down, three stories, into the dark, to see them crouched down.

'It's not that big a deal,' the man called out. 'Calm down.'

'You want me to be calm? I'll be calm when it's out of my house.'

'Honey, listen!'

'No!'

Another sound, something close, right by the window. Cahill looked up just in time to see something at the window, maybe a – a bucket? –

It hit them in one sudden, heavy splash, so hard it knocked them into each other and to the asphalt.

'What the fuck—' Dwyer began, but Cahill squeezed his arm.

'*Shut up!*' Cahill ordered in a harsh whisper. 'If you can hear her, she can hear you.'

'You don't think this was on purpose?' he whispered back.

Cahill had no idea. But it sounded like a domestic dispute.

'There!' came the woman's voice from the window. 'It's gone now!'

'You threw it out?'

'I sure did. And that better be the last time I see that in my house!'

Was this – oil? He could hardly see his hand in front of his face so he couldn't tell – he didn't dare taste it – but that smell.

It's fucking motor oil! Dwyer hissed.

'Keep your voice down, God damn it.'

It was oil. That lady had just dumped a bucket of motor oil on them.

'What the hell is going on?' Dwyer whispered. 'Why the fuck did she dump motor—'

'Shh. I don't fucking know. Keep your mouth shut.'

Above them, they heard the man and woman continue to argue.

'Why are you always getting on my case?'

'Why are you such a slob?'

Then they heard the familiar grinding and whining of gears as Kolarich's garage door began to lift. Cahill grabbed Dwyer and motioned to him. They both heard it. They moved back against the brick wall of Kolarich's garage and saw the head-lights of a truck bounce as the truck came off the street and onto Kolarich's driveway.

Cahill was still stunned, and now everything was happening at once. He didn't have time to worry about the oil covering his head and shoulders. Jason Kolarich had arrived home.

'Game time.'

But the truck didn't move farther up the driveway. It stayed back near the sidewalk, the headlights trained toward the garage.

Why?

Cahill and Dwyer didn't move, didn't breathe, for a long time.

'You think he spotted us?' Dwyer whispered.

'Don't know.' Cahill was still in a daze from the oil dumping on him. He wasn't entirely sure *what* the hell was going on right now. Did that lady deliberately dump oil on them?

At the base of Kolarich's driveway, where the truck remained idled, the driver's side door opened, and the driver exited and sprinted west along the sidewalk, quickly out of their view.

'What the—'

And then Cahill heard another sound from above. He looked up and was hit smack in the face with a heavy powder that invaded his nose and mouth and caused him to gag.

He fell back against the wall, Dwyer on top of him.

Sand, he thought, as he coughed.

She had just dumped a bucket of sand on them.

'Fuck!' Dwyer shouted. 'What the fuck!' He jumped to his feet. 'Let's go get this asshole!' he shouted. He first pointed the gun up at the window, but hesitated, unsure of where to direct his fury. Then he turned around and ran toward Kolarich's driveway.

Cahill didn't know what the hell was happening. More than half his body was covered with motor oil and now sand particles were embedded in it.

Dwyer had already begun to run down the driveway after Kolarich. He should have known better. They'd both seen Kolarich run before. There was no way they were going to catch him, wherever it was he'd run. Cahill coughed again, spat, and got to his feet.

What the hell had just happened? Were those neighbors working with Kolarich—

The truck, he thought. They could use Kolarich's truck, which was idling in the driveway, and give chase.

When Cahill stumbled to the driveway, he found Dwyer standing still, staring at the truck, his gun at his side.

Dwyer looked totally ridiculous, doused in thick black oil and then with a healthy coat of sand on top of it. Cahill assumed he looked equally preposterous. Were they – where was Kolarich?

Dwyer pointed at the truck. Only then did Cahill realize that this wasn't a vehicle that Jason Kolarich owned.

This was their Ford Explorer.

'Fuck me,' he mumbled, as he approached the truck.

Every window had been busted out completely. The paint was scratched badly. It looked as if words had been scratched into the paint, but the lighting wasn't that good, so it was hard to make out.

'What in the motherfuck is going on?' Dwyer said.

Neither of them knew where to start with all of this. Cahill looked back at the neighbor's townhome. Hard to believe that it was just a coincidence that they dumped all that shit on them but if not, it meant they were on to them, and—

Dwyer started marching toward the neighbor's townhouse. Cahill grabbed his arm. 'We need to get the fuck out of here, Dwyer.'

'They're in there. I fucking know it, and I'm going—'

'Then they've called the cops, you moron. We have to get out of here.'

Dwyer couldn't bring himself to disagree. Things hadn't gone so well up to now, and there was no reason to expect their luck would improve by sticking around.

Cahill got behind the wheel, Dwyer the passenger seat. Dwyer was unhappy to discover that he had sat in a pile of broken glass. So had Cahill, but he wasn't going to delay their exit over that.

'All right, Kolarich, score one for you,' he mumbled. 'But I'm going to find you, and when I do, I'm going to cut your fucking head off.'

He put the car in reverse, backed out of the driveway, and headed west. Who knows, maybe their luck would change and they'd see Kolarich running—

Headlights popped on a car behind them, and then flashing lights on the dome overhead.

A cop car. A fucking cop car.

'Fucking Kolarich,' Cahill said. 'I'm going to rip out your eyes and piss in the sockets.'

'You're stopping?' Dwyer asked.

'Do we take our chances?' Cahill wondered. He had to make a quick decision here. He looked over at Dwyer, draped in black oil and brown sand. He looked like a fudge sundae.

'Let's do it,' he decided. He gunned the engine and started flying west down the street.

Then another cop car, with flashing lights, turned onto the street from the other direction and came toward them.

'Fuck.' Cahill hit the brakes and threw the car angrily into Park. He was cut off. This was a narrow street with parked cars lining each side, and now he had squad cars at his front and rear. Could he and Dwyer win a shootout with the police? It was possible. They were surely better shots than these mutts. But backup would be called in, hell, neighbors would call 911, and even if they managed to take out the four officers, there was no physical way they could get their car free and drive off. They'd have to leave it behind, and they'd be the most wanted men in the state. They'd be drawing all kinds of attention to themselves and, more important, to the Circle.

He had to keep his eye on the prize here. He was needed a week from now. He'd trained for more than a year and he wasn't going to miss it.

'Fuck,' he said again.

From both the front and rear, the squad cars activated their searchlights into his vehicle.

'*Turn off your engine and put your hands on your head,*' one of the officers called out through his speaker.

'Do it,' Cahill said, gritting his teeth so hard he felt physical pain. He killed the engine and put his hands on top of his greasy, grimy head.

He looked over at Dwyer, who was fitting his fingers around his gun.

'Don't be an idiot, Dwyer. We have a job to do on December seventh. Just let this happen and Manning will bail us out.'

Dwyer thought a moment, then complied. He reached down and placed his weapon on the floorboard, like Cahill had done previously when he started driving. Then he put his hands on his head.

A pair of cops from each direction approached the vehicle, their weapons drawn, Maglites directed toward the interior of the vehicle. They took their time, walking around each side of the vehicle.

'Do you have firearms in the vehicle?' called out one of them, his own weapon trained on Cahill. '*Do you have firearms in the vehicle?*'

'Why would you say that, Officer?' Cahill said in a less than respectful tone. Cahill was not a big fan of law enforcement, or government in general.

'Well, for one thing, it's scratched on the rear panel of your vehicle. It says, "We have guns in here." Right next to "Fuck you, cops."'

Cahill closed his eyes. Fucking Kolarich. He was going to rip out his tongue and feed it to him.

'You're going to keep those hands on your head, and you're going to slide out of the vehicle.' An officer on each side opened the car doors. 'Slide out right now, each of you.'

They complied, though it wasn't easy with their hands on their heads.

'What is that you got on you?' the cop asked. 'What the hell have you boys been doing?'

Cahill put his hands against the car and spread his legs.

'Sightseeing,' he said. 'I love this city.'

With the car bathed in light from every fucking direction, Cahill could now read what had been scratched on the driver's side panel: *We are assassins.*

'Weapon on the floorboard, driver's side,' said one of the cops.

'Weapon on the passenger floor, too,' said another.

An officer pulled Cahill's hands behind him and slipped cuffs over his wrists.

'You look like you've been tarred and feathered,' one of them said.

'You look like something out of a Bugs Bunny cartoon,' another opined. The threat now contained, the two suspects now in handcuffs, the cops began to enjoy themselves.

'"Die . . . fucking . . . pigs." "Cops . . . suck . . . dick."' One of the cops was doing a walk-around with his flashlight, reading all the messages scratched into the Explorer's paint.

'Someone stole the car,' said Cahill.

'And then gave it back to you? They must be nice car thieves.'

They popped the rear of the car. Cahill already knew what they would find. There were rifles and knives and rope and a body bag.

One of the cops got close to Cahill's ear. 'Whatever the hell you boys have been up to,' he said, 'you're in a lot of trouble.'

62

We watched it all from the front bedroom window on the third floor of Ross Vander Way's townhouse.

'Can't thank you enough,' I said to Ross.

'No prob, man. It was pretty freakin' twisted.'

And I was pretty freakin' sure that Ross was pretty freakin' stoned.

Ross was a trust-fund baby. His parents owned a cruise line, and Ross had never worked a day in his life. He was partying his way through a master's degree in business and living in this townhouse, which he'd converted into the best bachelor pad I'd ever seen.

Lightner was talking on the phone with one of his employees, the one who had been assigned to covertly watch my house after the first attempt on my life. It had been Joel's idea, a pretty obvious security measure in hindsight, to have someone watch my house, and it had paid off for us. Joel's associate had seen these two guys staking out the place earlier today, then head over to their Ford Explorer and leave for several hours, then return around seven tonight, setting up shop on the side of my garage, awaiting my return.

I'd considered just calling the cops, but these two would

have gotten away. So Lightner and I came up with some thoughts at lunch, and he'd gone shopping for motor oil and a pound of sand. We wanted to make sure that a getaway would be tough for them, so in addition to the oil and sand, we did some work on the Explorer ahead of time, too, with a couple of screwdrivers.

Bradley had volunteered to drive the vehicle onto the driveway. That was nice of him. Normally I would have insisted on doing it myself – there was an element of risk at that point – but I couldn't run to save my life right now with the bum knee.

'Shauna, you play a great nagging wife,' I said.

'And you the shitbag husband.'

I thanked Ross again and Joel, Shauna and I left the same way we came in – surreptitiously out the back door of Ross's place. We found my car and picked up Bradley John on the corner.

'They won't get before a judge until Monday,' I said. 'I'll bet they add resisting for driving away before they got cut off. And rifles and a body bag? That's going to be an interesting bond hearing.'

Everyone was buzzing from what had just happened. It was great fun, no doubt, and a welcome release from the long hours we'd worked. But we all realized that for the second time in two days, somebody had been concerned enough about this case to attempt murder.

'Okay, screw this,' I said. 'From here on out until this trial is over, we have to stay away from our homes. And we hire bodyguards. Shauna, Bradley – go home and pack. We're not making ourselves an easy target. Joel, you got someone we could use for personal security?'

He did. His company had done some of it, too.

'We stay at different hotels and always with a security escort. Okay, you two? You can say no, but then you're off the case. No fooling.'

Shauna asked, 'Who might be funding this endeavor, Counselor? Last I checked, we had a client who didn't pay.'

'I am,' I said. I still had a little money tied over from when I was a big-firm lawyer. My wife and I had been saving every penny for a single-family home that I now didn't need.

'Then Ritz-Carlton, here I come,' Shauna announced.

'I'll make some calls right away,' said Joel.

'Here's a question,' Shauna informed us. 'If *we* figured out that they might try to kill you a second time, why didn't *they* figure out that we might be waiting for them?'

I nodded. The same question had been on my mind, too. And I thought I had an answer.

'They didn't *know* about the first attempt,' I said. 'The first group was the Capparellis. The people who killed Kathy Rubinkowski. These guys tonight? Ten to one says they're with Manning. They don't look like mobsters. They look like corn-fed white Aryan supremacists.'

'So now you got two different groups wanting to kill you,' Lightner said. 'That's a lot even for you, Kolarich.'

298

63

Peter Ramini listened respectfully as Father DiGuardi's homily wore on. The guy could talk. He was good people, and Lord knows, he'd heard a lot from Ramini over the years – not everything, and not in detail, but plenty. But damn if his homilies didn't go on.

'Our readings today alert us to something great about to begin,' he told the packed Mass. 'Night is ending. Dawn is at hand. Stay awake. Put on the armor of light. Let us begin waiting today in joyful hope for the coming of our savior.'

Ramini's eyes drifted next to him, to Donnie. This was the first time he'd seen Donnie in a church. Ramini, he came most Sundays. He never quite challenged himself about why.

Donnie didn't look happy. Why would he be? Two of Paulie Capparelli's best men, Sal and Augie, died in that alley, trying to take out Kolarich.

'We must ask questions during this Advent season,' said Father DiGuardi. 'Are we listening? Are we paying attention? Are we looking to what will be – or are we already there?'

The time between the homily and communion felt like the same amount of time Moses spent with his people in the desert.

But soon the congregants stood, row by row, and shuffled out to receive the bread and wine.

Neither Ramini nor Donnie moved. They were in the back pew, nobody behind them, and for the moment nobody in front or next to them, either.

Donnie pulled a candy bar out of his jacket pocket, opened it, and took a bite.

'Don, for Christ's sake. We're in the house of God here.'

It didn't seem to move Donnie. He leaned into Ramini. 'You wanna wait on Kolarich?' Donnie said. 'Paulie says okay. For now, we wait.'

Ramini nodded.

'For now,' Donnie repeated. 'You're sure Kolarich killed Sal and Augie himself?'

'I'm sure,' said Ramini. 'Who else woulda done it?' He looked at Donnie. 'I saw it with my own eyes, Don.'

It was the only story Ramini could tell the boss. The truth was out of the question. He knew Paulie would greet it with skepticism – Kolarich was just some lawyer, not a trained killer who could take out two attackers – but in the end, he figured Paulie would give Ramini the benefit of the doubt. Ramini had earned that respect. But he was running out of rope, he knew.

'For now, we wait,' Donnie said. 'But two things, Petey. Okay?'

'Okay, two things.'

'One: If you think this lawyer's getting close to us, no more waiting. If you gotta shoot him in fucking *court*, you do it. Right?'

'Right. And second?'

'Second,' said Donnie. 'When this thing's over, the trial and whatnot, and we're all happy? Well, Paulie still ain't so happy, see what I'm sayin'? Sal and Augie were good earners. Nobody kills two of our boys and walks away. Can't have that. Right?'

Donnie finished up the candy bar and crunched the wrapper in his hand. The parishioners were starting to return to the pews in front of them, so the conversation would end.

Donnie leaned in to Ramini again. 'What happens when the trial's over, Pete?'

Ramini sighed. 'Kolarich dies,' he said.

'And who dies if he don't?'

Ramini nodded. 'I do,' he said.

'You and everyone you love, Pete. You know the rules.' Donnie patted Ramini on the knee and walked out of the church.

64

Judge Nash was yelling at Wendy Kotowski and me before we even made it to the lectern to argue the pretrial motions. He thought the volume of our submissions was too great. He was right, but it wasn't that unusual an amount, thirty-one motions in all. I was hoping that he would direct his wrath more at the prosecution, which technically had filed more than me, but that was wishful thinking.

A few years ago, Judge Nash put a hard limit on the number of pretrial submissions by each side. But the appellate court slapped him down. Criminal cases invoke the Bill of Rights, constitutional protections against the state unfairly throwing people in prison, and when a defendant's liberty is at stake, arbitrarily limiting the amount of arguments he can make was viewed as a nonstarter.

But that didn't mean Judge Nash had to like it. His official limitation became an unspoken one, and when lawyers exceeded it, they heard about it.

The judge began to bark out rulings. Without oral argument, only the papers we submitted, he was rattling off rulings on evidentiary objections and testimony limitations. The prosecution couldn't use their fancy computers during jury selection to look up the criminal histories of potential jurors unless they provided those same resources to the defense. (Score one for me.) The defense couldn't raise Kathy Rubinkowski's criminal record – which I had no intention of doing, given that her crime was criminal trespass, a PETA protest of an animal testing lab when she was a freshman in college. The prosecution tried to limit what I could say to the potential jurors during voir dire, because Wendy Kotowski knew me well, but the judge shot her down and said he could decide objections as they came.

It went like that in bullet fashion. Twenty-five of our thirty-one motions were decided in the space of five minutes, as the judge read through his rulings.

I scribbled down his rulings as best I could. My head was foggy. The hotel bed I was sleeping on these days wasn't to my liking, and I woke up this morning with a stiff neck and a headache, which was nice because it gave my bum left knee some company.

The judge allowed oral argument on some of the big issues. He gave me a full hearing on our motion to exclude Tom Stoller's so-called confession. My principal argument was that Tom didn't knowingly waive his right to counsel. In the video-tape, the coppers asked him whether he understood his rights, and he nodded vaguely. He never spoke aloud. I argued that the consent should have been verbal or at least unequivocal. Tom Stoller had nervous twitches, as one could clearly see from the videotape and as my expert would testify, and a nod of the head was about as rare for Tom as taking a breath.

The judge glanced over at Tom, sitting in the detainee holding area to his left, during this argument. Tom incessantly licked his lips and wiggled his fingers to no end. His head would move a decent amount, but as he sat here today, more or less unconcerned with what was taking place, his head was relatively still. It was when he was nervous that he bobbed his head more.

We went back and forth for a long time on that. I knew my opponent well, and I could see that Wendy Kotowski was nervous. She thought she was vulnerable on this one. I hadn't expected to win this argument, but as I listened to the give-and-take between the judge and Wendy, I suddenly gained hope.

But then the judge shattered my illusion in the space of ten seconds. 'I will allow the videotape but give the defense full leeway on this one. The defense is free to revisit this issue at a later time.'

'Judge, we had requested an evidentiary hearing,' I reminded him. I wanted the court, before trial, to hear from the police and maybe even Tom on this topic. I'd spent much of yesterday – Sunday – preparing for a hearing.

'We'll proceed as I indicated,' said the judge.

I hated it when judges deferred rulings. He was going to let the evidence in and then decide afterward, after hearing all of the evidence, whether Tom had consented to questioning. By then, the jury would have heard Tom's statements. The judge would then have the choice of granting our motion, which would require him either to instruct the jury to disregard the evidence – yeah, sure – or to erase the trial and start over at square one with a new jury. Or he could deny my motion and move the case to verdict and get this case off his docket. It didn't take Nostradamus to predict which option he would prefer.

Most judges would have granted me an evidentiary hearing.

But the old saying around the courthouse – *Judge Nash ain't most judges* – rang truer than ever now. If I'd had this case from the start, I would have requested a substitution. Every litigant gets the right to switch judges at least once, as long as it happens before a substantive ruling takes place. But I was long past that by the time I jumped into this case.

My phone buzzed. We were supposed to turn off phones, but I kept mine on vibrate. Wendy was in the middle of something, so I covertly removed the phone from my pocket and read a text message. It was from Tori:

> Story online. Bruce McCabe found dead this morning.
> Apparent suicide, hanging in his garage. No further details.

McCabe was dead? I wondered what it meant, other than further confirmation that I was onto something here. But he was going to be one of the surprise witnesses I might call, if the judge would ever allow it, and now he was unavailable to me. Still, this could be an opportunity for me as well. Dead witnesses can't contradict you. I could point the finger at him without any denial in reply. A suicide, in fact – if it really was a suicide – could suggest that he was doing a thing or two he shouldn't be doing and felt remorse. It got my juices flowing, but I had to temper it with a reminder that Judge Nash had not, to date, heard a single thing about Randall Manning or Global Harvest or Bruce McCabe or any of this other stuff. And he typically welcomed surprise witnesses about as much as he welcomed hemorrhoids.

Wow. Okay. I shook my head. I had to refocus on what was happening in this courtroom.

The judge reserved Wendy's biggest argument for last. She

went into a long recitation of how Tom Stoller's admittedly distinguished military career had no relevance to this action. It would serve only to pander to the jury's sympathy.

'The defense asserts that Tom Stoller didn't confess to this crime,' I said, when given the chance. 'He was talking about the incident in Mosul, not the shooting of Kathy Rubinkowski. His statements to the police line up almost verbatim with Sergeant Hilton's description of what happened in that underground tunnel. If the defense isn't allowed to present this information, they'll simply believe that Tom confessed. That's about as unfair as it gets, Judge.'

The judge invited Wendy to add anything further she'd like. Usually, a judge gives a party that right before he rules against her. He wants the record to reflect that she was given every opportunity to state her case, then he knocks her down. I felt a small measure of relief as the judge prepared to rule, while Wendy was finishing up her argument.

My relief was short-lived.

'Sergeant Hilton didn't see the shooting in Mosul,' said the judge. 'He saw the aftermath, as the state has pointed out. So testimony concerning that shooting, and its similarities to Mr Stoller's statements to the police, can only come in through Mr Stoller himself. Sergeant Hilton's testimony is excluded, as is any reference to the defendant's military honors or background, other than what might be required during Mr Stoller's testimony, should he choose to testify. And absolutely no mention of post-traumatic stress or insanity. The specific events in Mosul may come in but only through the defendant. So you'll have a decision to make, Mr Kolarich.'

It was like a hard slap to the head. The judge had given me a Pyrrhic victory at best. I wanted to put on Sergeant Hilton first, then Dr Baraniq to say that Tom was reliving a PTSD-induced episode during the interrogation, and then probably rest.

Now, Hilton was out, and Baraniq would be able to testify only if Tom did first, laying the factual foundation. I had to put in this evidence through a witness who could barely articulate his daily life, much less recount to the jury something he'd never recounted to me. And I couldn't put him on the stand without asking him the most obvious question – did he shoot Kathy Rubinkowski? To which Tom would reply, *I don't remember.*

Tom was mumbling to himself over in the cage. He had no idea what was happening.

What was happening was that we were getting our nuts chopped off.

I had virtually no defense case on the current record. And I had no way, at this moment, to explain how Tom had the murder weapon, and the victim's purse and other items, in his possession following the murder. I had a videotape which included an apparent confession by my client, but practically speaking no way to explain that, in fact, it wasn't a confession.

This was all coming down to Randall Manning and Stanley Keane and Bruce McCabe and the Capparelli family. I had a handful of days to figure out what was going on with them, or Tom Stoller would be convicted.

And all of this assumed I could stay alive long enough to solve this puzzle.

Other than that, things were going really well.

BOOK TWO

December

65

Game time. Thirty people in a box. Some of them would be deciding Tom Stoller's fate. Some of them would be bounced by the judge for cause, and some of them would be excluded by either the prosecution or me for whatever reason.

'Juror number seven,' I said to the woman in the first row. 'That civil case on which you served as a juror, I take it the bottom line there was about money?'

'That's right,' she said. 'They wanted money. But it didn't matter in the end, because we found for the defendant.'

'I like you already,' I said, getting a cheap laugh. 'And so I assume the burden of proof in that case was preponderance of the evidence? That it was more likely than not that somebody did something wrong?'

'I think that's right.'

'And do you understand, ma'am, that because this is a criminal case, the burden is proof beyond a reasonable doubt?'

'I understand.' Everybody knows that.

'So a preponderance standard is "more likely than not" – like a fifty-one percent probability.' I set a bar with my hand at my waist. 'And a reasonable doubt standard means more than "I think he probably did it" – it's more like, "I'm so sure he did it that there is no reasonable basis for thinking otherwise.'" I raised my hand over my head, as far as I could reach. A peak compared to a valley. A skyscraper compared to a doghouse. I figured it would take Wendy Kotowski a nanosecond to object.

It took about one whole second. The judge sustained.

My cell phone buzzed in my pocket. Four short buzzes, meaning a call, not a text message. I touched it just to be sure, but I couldn't answer it right now.

'I mean, usually in our everyday lives, we don't judge things by a reasonable doubt standard,' I said. 'We see someone hand-cuffed by the side of the road by a police officer, we think to ourselves, they did something wrong. Right? I know I do. I figure, they found drugs in his car, or he was driving drunk or something. But does anyone disagree that your job is differ-ent here today, if you're asked to serve? That you will hold the government to a far higher standard?'

No hands raised. No objection from Wendy, who probably didn't want to seem too sensitive about this topic. So I kept going down that road. Tom is presumed innocent, just because the government charged him doesn't make him guilty, et cetera – things that everyone knows but are worth reinforcing right now. Wendy couldn't possibly object. These were some of our nation's founding principles.

'Anyone disagree that one of the things that makes this the greatest country in the world is that we *don't* take the govern-ment's word for it – that before they imprison one of our citizens, we make them prove it, and we make the government meet the highest possible standard of proof? Anyone disagree?'

Nobody disagreed. I didn't expect them to. I was making part of my closing argument, but I was couching it in perfectly permissible voir dire questioning.

My cell phone buzzed four more times – another phone call.

I was almost done. I'd asked a series of personal questions of each juror, based on the questionnaires they'd filled out. I'd spent a good ten minutes on self-incrimination – how wonderful our country was that we didn't force defendants to testify, and raise your hand if you'd convict because the defendant did not take the stand in his own defense? I actually got a couple of the venire to admit that they would have some doubt about a defendant who didn't stand up and declare his innocence. The judge would have no choice but to excuse them on his own.

And I'd given them the rah-rah-Constitution pitch. The only thing I had left was what I called my holdout questions. I only needed one juror, after all.

'Does everyone understand that as a juror in this case, you have the complete freedom to vote the way you think? That you are under no obligation to go along with the others, just because you've been outvoted? Raise your hand, please, if you don't understand that.'

Nobody raised a hand.

'Is there anyone who would feel pressured to vote a certain way – guilty or not guilty – if everyone else is voting that way, even if you personally disagreed with it?'

Nobody, apparently, would feel pressured.

'Does anyone disagree that in a system that requires a unanimous verdict, that it's your sworn constitutional *duty* to vote your conscience, even if you're outvoted eleven to one?'

Nobody disagreed. But my cell phone buzzed again.

Somebody wanted my attention. If it was about this case, I assumed the news had to be good, because it couldn't get any worse.

313

I huddled with Shauna, and we decided to use six of our ten peremptories, the automatic challenges we are allowed to bounce potential jurors. We didn't want to use them all, because it was unlikely that we'd draw our jury completely from this pool. There would be another thirty-person pool next, and we wanted to reserve some peremptory challenges for them.

We gave our list to Wendy, who gave us hers, and we submitted them to the judge. We'd go back to his chambers now and see how many of these thirty people made the cut. Then we'd grab another thirty and do the same winnowing process until we had fifteen – twelve plus three alternates.

But I had a moment to check my phone. Bradley John had called me four times.

'Those initials,' he told me when I called him.

'Yeah? You figured out who AN and NM are?'

'No,' he said. 'I figured out *what* they are.'

66

Judge Nash kept us in court until after five o'clock, and with the third thirty-person venire panel, we completed our set of fifteen jurors, three of whom would be alternates. Of the twelve regular jurors, eight were women. Five were African-American. One was Pakistani and another half Chinese. They ranged in age from nineteen to sixty-one. One was a podiatrist, one a caterer. There was a waitress and an industrial painter, two stay-at-home moms, a daycare operator, a human resources manager, an accountant, a pharmaceutical salesman, a product manager for medical supplies, and then my favorite, Jack Strauss. He was retired.

Retired military, that is. A colonel in the U.S. Marines who saw action in Grenada and limited time in Operation Desert Storm in the early nineties.

Wendy had run dry of her peremptory challenges with the second venire panel. She'd gambled that we'd be done after that panel, but she lost – four spots remained, the twelfth spot on the regular jury and the three alternates. And when we opened up the third panel, juror sixty-one was Jack Strauss. Wendy did her best to probe for bias, but the guy wasn't exactly a shrinking violet, and there was no cause to exclude him. It was the first break I got in this case to date.

I had to find a way to get Tom on the stand to talk about Iraq. I needed Colonel Jack Strauss to know that Tom was a war veteran and a hero.

Shauna and I made it back to the office by a quarter to six, with Shauna's security detail, a guy who looked like a pro wrestler, along for the ride. (Cowboy that I was, I didn't have a security guy; then again, I also owned my own gun.)

Bradley John was waiting for us in the conference room.

'She was an organic chemistry major,' he said to us.

'What?'

'Kathy Rubinkowski. She was getting a master's in organic chemistry, right? I never factored that in.'

Bradley had a copy of Kathy's handwritten scrawl on the back of the document she mailed her father:

AN

NM

??

'The symbol AN stands for ammonium nitrate,' he said. 'It's the primary compound in fertilizer.'

'Which Global Harvest sold, obviously,' I said.

'Right. And NM stands for nitromethane,' said Bradley. 'Nitromethane is used in drugs, cleaning solvents, pesticides. But here's the really big thing: You put ammonium nitrate together with nitromethane and you get one of the most powerful mixtures of explosives known to man.'

I looked at Shauna. 'Explosives,' I repeated. 'Jesus.'

I checked Kathy Rubinkowski's note again. It made sense. A chemistry student would have used the shorthand terminology.

'*That's* why the federal and state governments monitor sales of fertilizer,' said Bradley.

I steadied my hands. My juices were flowing, but I had to synthesize this into a formal presentation in court. 'Let's take this slow,' I said. 'Ammonium nitrate, there's no doubt Global Harvest sold it. I mean, that's their business – fertilizer, right?'

'Sure.'

'But what about nitromethane? Does Global Harvest sell *that*?'

He shook his head. 'Not as far as I can tell, no.'

'Then – where's the connection? Why did Kathy write down NM at all?'

'I don't know, Jason, but we have to assume that if she wrote—'

'No, no, no. We can't *assume* anything, Bradley. All we know right now is the universally acknowledged and entirely unsurprising fact that Global Harvest International sells fertilizer. I can't roll with this. Connect some dots for me and I can use it. See what I'm saying?'

He looked downcast, but he wasn't giving up. 'I do, yeah.'

I shook his shoulder. 'This could be what we're looking for, my friend. But I need more. Start with Summerset Farms. They were the ones receiving the fertilizer. Maybe they were getting the nitromethane, too.'

'I'm on it.'

'Oh, and Bradley,' I called to him. 'Remember I said it's a marathon, not a sprint?'

'Yeah?'

'Now it's a sprint.'

'Got it.' Bradley left Shauna and me standing in the conference room.

Shauna raised her eyebrows at me. 'Look at what we're getting into,' she said.

'After the other night, seeing them doing target practice, I thought they were gunrunners,' I said. 'I figured the fertilizer shipments were some kind of cover for smuggling of weapons. But maybe I have it wrong.' I looked over the symbols scribbled by Kathy Rubinkowski.

'Maybe they're building a bomb,' I said.

67

Inside the domed building on the property of Summerset Farms, Randall Manning and Stanley Keane stood on the small balcony overlooking the ground-level floor space that typically housed the farming equipment. Tonight, some of the equipment had to be moved out, because there was work to do. Manning and Keane watched as their six soldiers – they were eight before they'd lost Cahill and Dwyer – got down to business.

The You-Ride rental trucks drove in. They had been rented by Bruce McCabe last week, before his unfortunate passing, using a fictitious name and bogus corporate credit card. McCabe had even worn a disguise in case a security camera was present. The You-Ride trucks were, as far as Manning could determine, entirely untraceable to him or the Circle.

They started with the first You-Ride truck. With a cordless electrical drill, a soldier bored two holes in the truck's main cabin area in a concealed space under the seat. Then he ran a cannon fuse through each hole, sending the fuse through the floorboard and underneath the truck itself, where it spooled onto the concrete floor. The fuse was wrapped in plastic tubing conduit to protect it while in transit.

Then he got out of the cab and slid underneath the cargo

area of the truck. He drilled two more holes into the floor of the cargo space. He reached over and took the plastic tubing that dangled beneath the cab area and pulled it over to him. He fed the tubing into the cargo area and slid back out from under the truck.

The cabin and cargo areas of the truck were now connected by the two fuses.

The soldier then climbed into the rear cargo area and attached each fuse to a blasting cap. To the extent there was slack in the tubing – they had measured carefully, but it was better to overestimate than to underestimate – he duct-taped the tubing against the cargo wall to prevent the accidental detachment of the fuses from the blasting caps in transit.

Now for the fun part.

From flatbed trucks, the crew unloaded two hundred fifty bags of high-grade ammonium nitrate fertilizer weighing fifty pounds each. They unloaded seven fifty-five-gallon drums of liquid nitromethane as well.

The crew carted empty fifty-five-gallon barrels into the rear cargo areas of the truck. They nailed boards onto the floor to hold sixteen barrels in place. They loaded into the cargo area one hundred bags of the ammonium nitrate fertilizer and three of the nitromethane drums. They mixed the chemicals using plastic buckets and industrial scales and filled each of the barrels with the cocktail. Each barrel would ultimately weigh about five hundred pounds.

The soldiers looked over their work with professional pride. They were not quite done, but the final touches would take place the day of the operation, December 7. They would attach the blasting caps to explosive 'sausages' that would snake through the barrels to ensure their detonation.

When it was all said and done, it came to this: From the front cabin, the driver could ignite the fuses that would set off the blasting caps in the cargo area, which in turn would ignite the massive drums filled with explosives. The driver, without much more than leaning down into a concealed area beneath his seat, could set in motion an explosion that would level the nearest building at a minimum, and send tremors throughout the entire commercial district.

Now it was time to repeat the process with truck number two.

Manning, who had watched the preparation of the first truck with rapt fixation over several hours, now pushed himself off the balcony railing. It was exciting, no doubt. It was finally happening. But it was tempered by a threat that had presented itself.

They'd planned this over eighteen months, carefully selecting and recruiting men from underground hate groups, purchasing the necessary materials, planning and rehearsing this operation, without a single bit of attention from the outside world – with the exception of that paralegal Rubinkowski, who had started asking her boss, Bruce McCabe, some pointed questions about ammonium nitrate and nitro-methane. But they had taken care of that. They had outsourced her murder to the Capparellis, and their performance had been bravura. Not only did they get away with it, but someone else was implicated in the murder. An Army veteran, which was truly regrettable, but life wasn't perfect.

Still, that minor hiccup aside, everything had gone astonishingly smoothly.

And now, with a week remaining – this. This lawyer Kolarich. First asking questions, getting closer than anyone else had.

And now his two best men, Cahill and Dwyer, whom he'd dispatched to take out the lawyer, were in custody on weapons charges. Manning had the money, naturally, to afford any bail, and he'd worked cash through the channels so that someone unconnected to him could post the bond. But the bond hearing had gone badly. Each of these men came from the White Aryan Nation, and that background, coupled with possession of high-powered assault rifles, knives, and a body bag – a body bag, for Christ's sake – while in a city that was two hours from their homes, had given the judge pause. Bond was denied. Cahill and Dwyer would remain locked up pending trial.

His two best men – the two men he was going to use for the most critical facet, the part nearest and dearest to Manning's heart – were now out of the picture.

Manning and Stanley Keane walked into the conference room for some privacy. They walked sluggishly, their minds heavy with anticipation and responsibility.

'What are the odds Cahill or Dwyer give us up?' Stanley Keane asked, once they were inside.

Manning shrugged. You learned not to predict too much about human behavior. These men, he was informed by the lawyer he hired for them, could soon find themselves transferred to federal custody, where weapons charges could land these men in prison for ten years. What would they be willing to do to shave off some or all of that time?

'Cahill, hard to see,' Manning said. 'Dwyer, I guess I don't know.'

He looked up at the diagram on the wall. It showed the city's commercial district, including the government buildings north of the river. The federal building, housing federal law enforcement, other agencies, and the federal courts, was three blocks from the river over the Lerner Street Bridge. One block north and one block west was the state building, which held virtually every state agency and the offices of the governor, attorney general, secretary of state, and the like.

And to make it even better, the county building was immediately across the street from the state building and held dozens of county agencies and the civil courts. Connect the buildings on a map and they linked together in what looked like a squared-off number seven. The civil engineers who designed the city in the early 1800s never thought about terrorist attacks. They had no clue about the impact of truck bombs like the ones they were assembling.

The Pearl Harbor Day procession, led by Governor Trotter, U.S. Senator Donsbrook, and Mayor Champion, would arrive at the federal building for the outdoor commemoration at approximately 12:45 P.M. to one P.M. That was when the trucks would hit. One at the federal building, one at the state building. The impact would be felt throughout the downtown, but particularly in the government buildings. If timed properly – and the team had spent countless hours and days on this point – the blasts would hit simultaneously.

Thousands would be killed, including the chief executives of the state and city, plus one of the two U.S. senators. It would make the Murrah Building in Oklahoma City look like kids throwing firecrackers. It would dwarf even September 11 in terms of casualties.

It would finally get the government's attention.

'We're not going to get away from this clean, are we?' said Keane.

Manning studied him for a moment. This question might sound like cold feet, but he didn't think so, not with Keane.

McCabe had proven weak, and Keane had his faults as well, but commitment wasn't one of them.

'I don't know what Kolarich is going to accomplish before December seventh,' he said. 'But I know I can't afford to send anyone else after him.'

'And now they have Cahill and Dwyer,' Keane noted. 'Cahill is one of your employees. They'll sweat him like it's Guantánamo Bay.'

Manning had considered that as well. 'They'll tie him back to me. Not necessarily you, Stan. What did you do, after all? Your company sold nitromethane to Summerset Farms. That's no crime, and there's no evidence you were a part of this.'

'We have our men,' Stanley said. 'Not just Cahill and Dwyer but the six downstairs. You're that sure we can ensure their silence?'

Manning gave him a patronizing look. 'You think these men expect to get out of this alive? They're not going to survive, Stanley. On the surface, they're soldiers aware of the risk of death and accepting those risks. But deep down, I think they know the odds are well against them. They'll be damn lucky if they even make it into the subway tunnels. And they'd be even luckier if the tunnels don't implode, too.'

Keane didn't respond. This couldn't be a surprise to him.

Manning put his hand on Stanley's shoulder. 'I'd hoped to continue this fight beyond December seventh,' he said. 'I won't be able to do it. I hope that you can. Nobody's going to find our additional supplies. There will be enough for several more December sevenths.' He nodded to Stanley. 'Stay away from this. Go to work. Whatever. Just make sure you stay away from the city's downtown. I'm counting on you to carry the mantle going forward.'

Keane nodded gravely. The two men shook hands. Given the threat that Kolarich, and now Cahill and Dwyer, posed to the operation, it was no longer safe to house the trucks in this dome or anywhere on the property. Tonight, the crews would scatter into designated remote locations. The crews wouldn't communicate with the others. They would lie low and prepare for the attack.

Manning and Keane would never see each other again.

'God bless, Stan,' said Manning, cupping his second hand over Keane's. 'Don't ever forget why we're doing this. No matter what happens, don't waver in the face of doubters. We are changing the course of this nation, my friend – you, me, and those six martyrs down there.'

Manning walked to the doorway of the conference room, looked back once at Stanley Keane, and disappeared.

68

I sat on the hotel room bed and read over some notes I'd made on the witnesses the prosecution would call tomorrow, the first day of the trial. I liked to outline my cross-examinations by topic matter only. If I write down specific questions, I become wedded to them. Regardless, the endeavor wasn't a difficult one. I didn't have much I could do with the prosecution's case. The responding police officer, the forensic pathologist, the ballistics expert, the detective in charge? Those were probably the only four witnesses Wendy Kotowski would call. They would be all she needed before she punted the case to me.

It was a circumstantial case. But it was a pretty decent one. Tom was found with the murder weapon and the victim's possessions. He ran when the police confronted him, though it wasn't particularly hard to explain away. He admitted the gun belonged to him and, according to the state, at least, he confessed to the murder. And the place he carved out as his home in Franzen Park was nearby, so it's not like he had to travel long and far to commit this crime.

What made their case better was the lack of a defense. My client wouldn't deny killing Kathy Rubinkowski, and I couldn't explain away his lack of memory on post-traumatic stress disorder because the judge wouldn't let me.

Jeez, the judge had really screwed me on that ruling. He had a little law on his side, but I really thought he made a mistake. The appellate court would take a hard look at that one, I felt sure. But no defense lawyer made his money counting on a reversal of a murder conviction.

I jumped at the sound of a knock at my door. It was ten o'clock, and I hadn't ordered room service. I reached into the nightstand and removed my gun. Then I walked over to the door.

I stood away from the frame of the door and called out, 'Hello?'

'Room service,' said a woman's sweet voice.

I was pretty sure I recognized the voice, even in disguise, but I checked the peephole.

I opened up the door. Tori was wearing that wonderful long white coat and, yes, another pair of knee-high boots.

'Hello, Ms. Martin.'

She raised her hands in mock surrender. 'Please don't shoot me. I come in peace.'

'We'll see about that.' I let her in and returned my firearm to the nightstand.

'Nice digs,' she lied. One room, plus a bath, crappy view, and peeling wallpaper.

Bradley was staying in a hotel a block away. He had a suite, and his security guard slept on the couch. Shauna also had a suite but with a locked door between her and her detail. Me, I had this crappy room, but I'd slept in worse places, like my house growing up.

I had offered Tori the same deal as Bradley and Shauna – a

hotel and bodyguard – but she had declined, because her condo was very secure and, she noted, I couldn't threaten to take her off the case if she refused, since she wasn't really on it to begin with.

Since the night Tori broke down and gave in to my irresistible charms, things had been weird between us. She was still helping out on the case but the wall had gone back up. There was some remorse there, I sensed, or fear, or both.

She stood near the bed – it was hard to stand anywhere in the room and not be near the bed – and looked a little awkward as she gathered her thoughts. 'I wanted to . . . say something,' she said.

'Shoot.'

She walked over to me, took my face in her hands, and planted a warm kiss on me. It started as something quick, but then it lingered, and our mouths parted, and then our fingers were running through each other's hair and we were tugging at clothes. Actually, I was only wearing a T-shirt and boxers, but she required more work. As I've mentioned, I normally enjoy that part, the undressing, but this time the clothes seemed to be an annoyance. I lifted her onto the bed and pulled down her panties and wasted little time exploring every wonderful angle and curve of her body.

I'll bet it was the best seven minutes of her life.

Afterward, we caught our breath and stared up at the ceiling, her head tucked against my chest. There was a berry scent to her hair that stirred a memory I couldn't place, but it was a happy one. Her body was like an electric blanket against mine.

'Please don't cry again,' I requested.

She laughed. 'I've been acting weird. I do realize that, if

you're wondering. I'm not sure how to handle this. I just want to be careful. That's really all I came here to say. I know everything starts tomorrow and you need to focus.'

'Focus is not my problem,' I said. 'Lack of evidence is. Lack of time is.'

She adjusted herself, turned so she was facing me, supporting her chin with her hands. 'Would you like me to stay?'

I looked at her. 'I would like that very much, Tori. You may not have noticed, but I'm not as conflicted as you are about our relationship.'

She took that in without comment.

'Okay, okay,' I assured her. 'Not meant to pressure you.'

A smile crept across her face. She didn't seem too comfortable with happiness, but I got the sense she was warming to the concept. 'You want to order some room service? You can bounce ideas off me or whatever. That's fun when we do that.'

It was fun. It had been the best part of this case, and not just because I was insatiably attracted to her. The truth was, Tori had helped this case immensely with her comments and ideas.

The truth was, I had to admit, I was letting this woman get inside me.

69

'Kathy Rubinkowski was a twenty-three-year-old college graduate who wanted to be a research scientist. It was her passion. And so while working a day job as a paralegal at a law firm, she went to school at night to get a master's degree. She was like so many other young people living in our city – ambitious, dedicated, hardworking. She was chasing her version of the American dream.'

Wendy Kotowski was dressed in a simple gray suit. She spoke slowly to the jury in her opening statement, with her customary blend of nine parts clinical and straightforward, one part emotion and outrage. She had to make sure the jury saw that she cared about what happened to Kathy Rubinkowski, but otherwise she didn't want to be the focus – the facts would be.

'January thirteenth of this year should have been no different than any other day. Kathy woke up that morning in her condominium in Franzen Park, at the intersection of Gehringer and Mulligan streets. She went to work at her downtown law firm and stayed until five-thirty. Then she went to her organic chemistry classes at night school from six to ten.

'She drove home and parked her car at some time

approximating eleven that night. We'll never know exactly what she had planned for the rest of that evening. Maybe she was going to study. Maybe she was going to veg out in front of the television. Maybe she was going to sleep. Or maybe she was thinking about tomorrow, which would be her twenty-fourth birthday, and the plans she had with her friends.

'But as I said, we'll never know. Because she never saw her twenty-fourth birthday. She never saw her condo again. She barely made it past getting her bag out of the trunk of her car. Because on January thirteenth, at approximately eleven o'clock at night, Kathy Rubinkowski was accosted by that man, the defendant, Thomas Stoller.'

Wendy pointed at Tom, who was sitting next to me. His aunt Deidre had purchased a suit at a secondhand store that fit him, more or less, and I had thrown in a tie that I haven't worn in ten years. I wanted him to look decent so he didn't appear disrespectful of the proceedings, but by no means did I want him to look polished or buttoned up. It was one of the many artifices of the courtroom. The jury was forming initial and perhaps lasting impressions of Tom based on an appearance that bore absolutely no resemblance to reality.

'The defendant robbed Kathy Rubinkowski on that dark, lonely street,' Wendy said. 'The defendant took her purse. He took her necklace. He took her cell phone. And he took something far more valuable. He took her life. He shot her in the head. He shot this defenseless woman right between the eyes.'

Most of the jurors winced or reacted in some way to those last sentences. She had delivered them well, for maximum impact. I would have said *he shot her in the face*, which sounded even worse. But Wendy was always one for understatement.

I paid close attention to how she phrased it. *He took her purse, her necklace, her cell phone, her life.* She implied that the robbery came first, then the shooting, but she didn't explicitly detail an order of events. She wasn't boxing herself into one particular theory. I knew what she thought – that Tom killed her first, then stole her possessions. The evidence lined up that way. But she had some problems with that theory and obviously knew it, so she was keeping things general for the time being.

Wendy recited the facts that would support her case. The murder weapon found in Tom's possession, and the other things the police found with Tom: her purse, her cell phone, her necklace with the clasp broken, presumably yanked from her neck. Wendy brought each of these out individually, as if item after item implicated him ever further. I, on the other hand, would try to make them a package deal in the jury's mind – if one link failed, the whole chain did.

She completed her opening statement in twenty minutes. Her case was pretty simple and straightforward.

'She didn't mention the confession,' said Shauna.

Right. She was saving it. Understating her case. That was Wendy's style. It would be a pleasant surprise, I guess.

The judge gave me the opportunity to give my opening. I'd already indicated that I would defer my opening until the defense case, because I wanted the element of surprise. I had lost Sergeant Hilton as a witness, but I had an idea as to how I could still use Dr Sofian Baraniq, my expert. It was a gamble, but it was all I had.

'I'd like to defer my opening,' I told the judge. On balance, I thought, it was still the smart play.

I looked behind me. I caught Aunt Deidre's eye, but that wasn't the one I was looking for. I found him in the back row of the courtroom: Special Agent Lee Tucker of the FBI.

'Judge, I wonder if we could take a short break,' I said. We'd gotten a late start today, and it was coming up on eleven, so he probably wouldn't give it to me. Lee would have to wait.

'Let's try to get in a witness before lunch,' said the judge. 'Ms. Kotowski?'

Wendy Kotowski stood.

'The state calls Officer Francis Crespo,' she said.

70

Officer Francis Crespo was a ten-year veteran of the city police department. He was built like a brick house and had dark features and a mustache. He was one of the patrolmen in the area when reports came in of the shooting on Gehringer Street.

'We weren't the first to arrive,' he explained. 'But we got the nod when the call came through about a sighting of a homeless man running through Franzen Park with a gun.'

'You "got the nod"?' Wendy asked.

'We were dispatched by the detective-in-charge on the scene to investigate. My patrol and Officer Downing's. Cars eighteen and twenty-three.'

'Go on, Officer.'

'My partner and I proceeded by vehicle to Franzen Park.'

'Why a vehicle?' Wendy asked. 'Wasn't Franzen Park just a block away?'

'That's correct, ma'am, but it's a city block wide and long. So the northeast end of the park was a quarter-mile away. It made sense to drive there and be mobile by vehicle once there.'

'Fair enough, Officer. Where did you travel?'

'Officer Downing's patrol took the south end of the park, and my partner and I searched the north end. When we searched behind the park district building, we found an individual sitting between two dumpsters. He had—'

'Excuse me, Officer. Do you see that person in court today?'

'That's correct, ma'am. It was the defendant, seated there.' He pointed at Tom.

'Stipulate to identification,' I said.

'Go on, Officer.'

'Ma'am, he – the defendant had a purse in his lap and was rummaging through it. I shined my Maglite – my flashlight – I put my flashlight beam on him and announced my office. I saw to his immediate left a firearm sitting in the grass. A Glock pistol. My partner and I drew our weapons. I told the subject to raise his hands where I could see them.'

'His hands were in the purse?'

'That's correct.'

'What did he do when you told him to raise his hands?'

'For a moment, nothing. I ordered him again to remove his hands from the purse. He did not.'

'But then—'

'But then his right hand came free and he looked up into the flashlight beam. His gun was to his left, so he wasn't a threat to go for that weapon.'

He was covering his ass here.

'And then in one very quick motion, he lifted a two-by-four sitting next to him and threw it at me. Kind of a boomerang throw. He hit me in the chest and knocked my flashlight out of my hand.'

'And what happened next?'

'I fell backward, ma'am, and my partner had been circling around me from behind, so I fell into her.'

'The defendant got away on foot?' Wendy said, helpfully.

'That's correct, ma'am. It's embarrassing. But he got away. He ran west, and we chased him. He jumped the fence and ran north on Gehringer Street for approximately three blocks. We had radioed for backup, and two squad cars cut him off.'

'And then what happened?'

'The subject – the defendant – dropped to his knees and put his hands behind his head.'

'You took him into custody.'

'That's correct, ma'am.'

Wendy took the officer through the retrieval of the evidence – the murder weapon, the purse, the necklace. They also found where Tom 'lived,' so to speak, in Franzen Park, but they didn't find anything related to the case there. Finally, she questioned him on the process of submitting the evidence at the police station.

The direct was finished at a quarter to noon. I was eager to talk to Lee Tucker, so I hoped the judge would recess.

'Cross-examination, Mr Kolarich?' he asked.

'It will take us past the hour, Your Honor.'

'Cross-examination, Mr Kolarich?' he repeated.

I got to my feet. A searing pain shot through my knee. I liked to move around the courtroom as I cross, but today it would be painful.

'Officer, in your search after arrest, you ultimately found that my client had a small living area staked out in the park, didn't you? Blankets, some canned foods, that kind of thing.'

'That's correct, sir.'

'And Tom's living space was on the southwest corner of that park, true?'

'That's right.'

'It was right up against the fences, right? The southern and western fences? That corner?'

'Yes, sir.'

'The corner nearest the crime scene.'

'That . . . That would be correct, sir.'

I looked at the jury. 'Less than a *block* from the crime scene.'

'Correct.'

I realized this cut both ways. It might make a crime of opportunity more likely. Tom was hanging out where he lived, saw someone and robbed her. But it also went to my theory.

'Someone walking, or let's say jogging – someone jogging from the crime scene to the southwest corner of Franzen Park – could get there in seconds, right? Less than a minute?'

Officer Crespo gave that some thought. 'No more than a minute, probably.'

'Someone could have robbed Kathy Rubinkowski after killing her and, in less than a minute, dumped those items and the murder weapon basically over a fence and into Tom Stoller's lap.'

'Objection.' Wendy Kotowski got to her feet. 'Calls for speculation.'

The judge removed his glasses and wiped them with a cloth. 'The witness will answer.'

Surprising. I would have sustained. But Judge Nash ain't most judges.

'I guess that would be possible,' said Crespo. 'But that means he also could have reached the victim within seconds and killed her and robbed her.'

'Glad you brought that up,' I said, which is what I typically say when I'm *not* glad somebody brings something up. It deflects the zinger, the initial impression that the other side

337

has scored is momentarily abated, and by the time I'm done drawing out the issue, hopefully the jury has forgotten.

Only this time, I really was glad. 'The park was north of the crime scene, right?'

'Right.'

'And Kathy Rubinkowski's assailant shot her while standing from the south. He was south of Kathy when he shot her, true?'

'Objection,' said Wendy. 'Foundation.'

I flapped my arms. 'Your Honor, I don't think anyone disputes this point. Kathy Rubinkowski was facing south when she was shot head-on. Her assailant must have been south of her. That's what the state's going to say, and I won't disagree. Do I really need to recall this witness or can we stipulate?'

The judge liked my idea. 'Ms. Kotowski?'

'Fair enough, we'll stipulate,' she said.

'Might we waive a written stip in lieu of testimony?' the judge asked her. If there isn't testimony on a stipulated fact, you have to write it up for the jury. The judge was suggesting we skip that step if the state was going to introduce oral testimony on the point.

'Absolutely, Judge,' she said.

I agreed as well. Then I turned to the officer again. I had to restart my momentum. 'Officer, if your idea held water, that would mean that my client left his living space at the corner of the park, traveled south *past* the victim, and then came back up north on the sidewalk and shot her. Isn't that true?'

'Well, maybe he was casing her, checking her out to make sure she was an easy target first. Then, when he decided she was, he came back around and attacked her.'

That was a pretty good answer. Maybe I shouldn't have gone this route. But still time to make lemonade out of lemons.

'That would entail a little forward thinking, right? Some planning?'

He chuckled. 'Not much.'

He was right. He was a more worthy adversary than I'd expected. Still, lemonade was within reach. 'So then, under your theory, he robs her and then heads *south*, away – *away* from the park, and turns around and shoots her?'

I wouldn't normally kick around ideas with a witness like this – a good cross-examination is all about control, getting yes or no responses, knowing the answers before they're given – but in a case like this, about all I had going for me was that the state couldn't pin down exactly how the murder took place. So I was willing to do this back-and-forth all day if Wendy didn't object.

But she did. She popped to her feet. 'Now we are going far afield,' she said. 'This is rampant speculation. There is no foundation for this, and we don't stipulate.'

'Judge,' I said, 'does the state claim that the victim was shot first and then robbed, or robbed first and then shot? Because if they'll tell me which way it happened, I'll adjust my questions accordingly. Otherwise, I completely agree – and would be willing to stipulate – that the prosecution's theory is entirely speculative.'

'Your Honor, this is ridiculous—'

The judge raised a hand. 'The objection is sustained. Ladies and gentlemen of the jury, please disregard Mr Kolarich's speech to you. Closing arguments are a few days away. Now move on, Counsel.'

'Yes, Your Honor. One more line of questioning. Officer, you called out to Tom to remove his hands from the purse, correct?

You identified yourself as a police officer and ordered him to show his hands, didn't you?'

'That's correct.'

'And he didn't react in any way, did he?'

'No.'

'Your voice was rather loud and commanding, I take it?'

'I would hope so.'

'Right, because when you give orders, it's important that you're taken seriously.'

'Correct.'

'So? He didn't respond to your clear command?'

'He did not.'

'And then you said it all over again, right?'

'I . . . yes, a second time.'

'And again, he didn't react in any way?'

'Object to relevance,' said Wendy. 'Could we have a sidebar?'

She knew what I was doing. I was portraying Tom as mentally ill, in his own little world, oblivious to the shouts of an approaching police officer.

'I think the ship already sailed, Ms. Kotowski,' said the judge, before Wendy could get her sidebar. I'd gotten two answers on that topic already, he meant. She missed her chance. 'Overruled.'

'Officer? A second time, Tom was unresponsive?' Since I had a clear shot now, I might as well use a more clinical word, make Tom seem like he was comatose.

'That's correct.'

I was done. I hadn't accomplished much. Wendy got all she needed from this guy, and I didn't put any meaningful dent in him.

Prosecution 1, Defense 0.

71

'I don't think you did much to that cop.' Lee Tucker was dressed comfortably as always in his standard look, a blue sport coat, white shirt, and jeans. He had a scrappy look, a wiry frame and rough complexion, long dishwater-blond hair.

I'd worked with Lee before. He'd been the case agent assigned by the FBI to me during the investigation of Governor Carlton Snow. That was a long story; suffice it to say the two of us generally got along but had the occasional rock in the road.

Lee had agreed to meet me here, and the county attorney, who had offices in the criminal courthouse, had given us a room on the eighth floor during the trial's lunch recess.

I laid out everything I knew to date: Kathy Rubinkowski, her cryptic notes, what I'd learned about Global Harvest and Randall Manning and the associated companies.

'I think these guys might be building a bomb,' I concluded.

Tucker wasn't assigned to counterterrorism. He handled political corruption, always a booming business in this city. But he'd been around the block and digested the information quickly.

He perused the notes he'd taken. 'So this company sells

ammonium nitrate fertilizer to another company it purchased. And they register the sales with the state and federal governments. So that's perfectly legal, right?'

'Yes. I think there might be something unusual going on with those sales, because they were so sensitive about them—'

'Right, no, I got that. And you don't know if they even sold that company nitromethane, the other ingredient?'

'I don't. Trying to find out.'

'So right now, all we can say is this company legally sold a product to another company.'

I nodded. 'Same thing I told my associate, Lee. I get it. Maybe this doesn't give you PC to search—'

'It sure as hell doesn't.'

'—but you can knock on their door, can't you? I mean, maybe if they know you've noticed them, they slow down what they're doing. And we build a case, meanwhile.'

'We,' he said. '*We* build a case.' He nodded generally to the door. 'Could I be so bold as to assume that this is going to help you with that case you got going there?'

'I don't deny that. Yes, it will. But these guys might be building bombs, Lee. It's bigger than my case.'

He accepted that but with skepticism. I think it's fair to say that he'd learned, after our last go-round, not to underestimate me. He thought I was using him to make my case, that I'd call him as a witness to testify that the FBI was actively investigating a terrorist threat regarding Global Harvest, that kind of thing.

'Lee, there's a time to bullshit and there's a time to get fucking serious. This is the get-fucking-serious time. These people are scary customers. A paralegal and a lawyer are dead. They've tried to kill me. I'd bet my law license they're up to something big here.'

342

He thought for a moment. 'You get any photos of them firing those assault rifles?'

I shook my head. 'They confronted me before I could do it. I screwed up.'

Tucker folded up his small notepad and wagged it at me. 'Okay,' he said. 'Okay. I've got the information.'

I love how these guys talk. Reveal absolutely nothing. Not even a simple *We'll take a look*. Just a simple confirmation that he heard what I said.

Which meant, if my history with the FBI was any guide, that they would do whatever they were going to do and keep me completely in the dark about it from start to finish.

Still, I exhaled with relief. I'd done what I could do. I'd handed this over to the experts. I'd keep doing my own investigating, but the feds had resources I couldn't dream of.

I knew Randall Manning and those guys were up to something.

I just hoped the FBI would take me seriously.

72

The prosecution called the forensic pathologist next. Dr Mitra Agarwal had been with the county coroner's office for more than thirty years and currently served as the chief deputy medical examiner. She was old friends with my mentor, Paul Riley, and I'd known her professionally and personally for several years. She testified for me twice when I was a prosecutor. Juries liked her because she had no flash, no spin. She was as straitlaced as they came. Her gray hair fell to her shoulders without style. Her now-weathered brown skin was freckled. She was stooped a bit with age but still spoke with a strong voice.

I didn't know why she was handling this case, but my assumption was that she was next in the rotation when Kathy Rubinkowski's body was wheeled in. As the top deputy, she could have passed on autopsies altogether, but the thought probably never occurred to her. She was a workhorse.

All of which made her a good witness for the prosecution and a terrible one for me. The only good news was she was a complete straight shooter – to a fault if you asked prosecutors. But in the end, there wasn't much to get here. The cause of death was beyond dispute. I would have considered stipulating but we needed a couple of things from the witness, and the prosecution wanted to introduce graphic photographs through her, which I was unable to exclude during pretrial motions.

Wendy Kotowski let her second chair, a woman named Maggie Silvers, handle the witness. She probably figured Dr Agarwal was a safe witness. The prosecutor took the jury painstakingly through the pathologist's credentials and then the autopsy she performed.

'The bullet penetrated the skin and musculature of the forehead,' said the doctor, pointing to a diagram of a human skull. 'It penetrated the glabella and continued front to back, impacting the occipital bone, where it came to rest.'

'And the blood, Doctor?' asked the prosecutor, pointing to the pool of blood that had formed at the victim's head. 'This was caused by the gunshot?'

'Yes, surely so. The sphenoid and ethmoid bones were shattered. It would cause a large episode of bleeding. Remember that even if brain activity had ceased, the heart would have continued beating. It could have gone on for a good five minutes, while she lay prone on the street.'

'All right,' said the prosecutor. 'You mentioned the ceasing of brain activity. In your expert opinion, how did that happen?'

Dr Agarwal nodded. 'The bullet produced a shock wave that essentially ended all brain activity. Her brain activity would have ceased almost instantly upon impact. That explains the injuries to her knees and the side of her skull.'

'Explain, that, please. Is this what we call a "dead drop," Doctor?'

'That's a term that is used. She died upon impact of the bullet and fell straight to the street. Her right kneecap was fractured in the fall, and she received significant contusions to the skull on the right side as well.'

'She was dead before she hit the ground?'

'Correct.'

'And the blackening of her eyes, Doctor?'

'Yes, you see here.' The doctor pointed to a close-up photograph of the victim, whose eyes had blackened. 'Her orbital plates shattered from the pressure wave from the bullet. But as I said, her heart kept beating, so blood ran into the tissue around her eyes.'

'So, Doctor, the fractured kneecap, the blackened eyes, the contusions to her skull – these were all the result of the gunshot?'

'Without question, yes. The single gunshot caused her death. There is no evidence that she was otherwise beaten or attacked physically.'

The witness appeared to have jumped the gun, anticipating the last question of the prosecutor. Without the final question she'd planned, she fumbled for a moment with her notes. 'Thank you, Doctor,' she said.

A little rough with the ending, but she got the job done. She wanted to establish that the only thing that attacked Kathy Rubinkowski was a bullet between the eyes. No punching or kicking or the like, because no evidence of such was found on Tom Stoller. He didn't have bruising or blood on his hands or shoes. She had done her job, I thought. It was one single shot that dropped the victim.

Shauna was handling the science in the case so she took the cross. 'Doctor,' she said before she got to the lectern. 'Where the bullet entered the victim's skull – there was no charring of the skin around the site of the entry wound, was there?'

'No, there was not.'

'And there was no tattooing or spotting, either, was there?'

346

'No, there was not.'

'No soot or powder stippling, correct?'

'Correct.'

'So to a reasonable degree of medical certainty, you can say that the gun muzzle was not within three feet of the victim's skull, true?'

'True.'

Shauna paused for effect. 'So the shooter was more than three feet away, wasn't he?'

'That appears so, yes.'

'That's what you think, right?' Shauna doesn't like it when witnesses equivocate. It's one of the things I love about her. It makes her a pain in the ass when we argue, though.

'That's what I think.'

'It's possible that the shooter was ten feet away, true?'

'I can't say it's *im*possible.' Another equivocation.

'Meaning it's possible.'

'Yes, it's possible. I only say that—'

'You've answered my question, Doctor.'

I couldn't get away with that. I'm not sure if it's just a gender thing or my relative size compared to the diminutive witness, but I've never felt like cutting off a witness played well with the jury. I'm also pretty sure that the judge wouldn't let me get away with it, but the old goat seems to like Shauna.

'In fact, wouldn't you agree, Doctor, that nothing in your findings would contradict the possibility that the shooter was ten feet away from the victim?'

Dr Agarwal paused. She wasn't typically argumentative, but she didn't completely agree with Shauna. We all knew that the spent shell casing from the murder weapon landed in the soil of a planted tree on the sidewalk and that the strong

347

likelihood was that the weapon was fired from ten feet away. But it was possible that the casing rolled on the sidewalk, so there was a little bit of leeway in the estimate on either side of ten feet.

Shauna was baiting the witness.

'If common sense and experience are included in my findings,' the doctor answered, 'then I would say that I am not totally convinced that the gun was fired from ten feet away.'

'Why would you say that, Doctor?' Shauna said. You never ask open-ended questions on cross-examination unless you're sure that any answer will suit your purpose. Shauna had a pretty good idea of how the doctor would answer, but she wasn't sure.

'In my experience autopsying homicides,' Dr Agarwal replied, 'most gunshots from the Glock handgun used here are not so precise that one could hit someone between the eyes from a distance of ten feet. It's obviously possible, but it's difficult.'

'The shooter would have to be very good at what he did,' said Shauna. 'He'd have to be an experienced shooter of that weapon?'

'Objection,' said the prosecutor, Maggie Silvers, but she was a little late objecting to this line of questioning and the judge told her so.

'I would think so, yes,' said the doctor, after Shauna repeated the question.

We wanted the shooter to be as far away as possible, to show both the bizarre nature of the prosecution's theory and that it would take a very good shot to hit a victim between the eyes from that distance. The prosecution had an answer for that, of course – First Lieutenant Tom Stoller was a trained shooter in the Army Rangers – but to bring in that evidence, they had to bring in Tom's military background. And they didn't want to do that, especially since we landed a retired colonel on the jury.

Shauna killed another twenty minutes with the doctor and the prosecution redirected with just a few questions. We had scored one simple point, but the jury had seen several close-up, gruesome photos of the murder and heard graphic descriptions of the violent end to Kathy Rubinkowski's life. When it was all said and done, it was another good witness for the state.

Prosecution 2, Defense 0.

73

Tori was in the courtroom at the close of the day and caught my eye as I packed up. She was telling me she had something significant.

First, I had to do the customary wrap-up at the end of the court day with Aunt Deidre and Tom. Tom had actually been pretty composed in court today, to my chagrin, as I wanted the jury to see a guy who was clearly suffering from some mental problems. Instead, for some reason, Tom had remained relatively calm and still.

We conferred in the holding room they gave us for post-court discussions. I told them about what we'd found so far with Global Harvest and my talk with the FBI earlier today. 'We're pursuing this with everything we've got,' I said. 'If there's something there, hopefully we can come up with it over the next few days.'

Tom seemed like he was listening to me, but he didn't say anything. For all I knew, he was contemplating his dinner in county lockup tonight. Deidre's expression could best be described as downcast.

'Remember,' I told them, 'this is a circumstantial case. They can't put Tom at the scene, and they don't have him firing the weapon.'

'Right,' said Deidre. She'd heard this before but, I'd come to learn, the repetition comforted her. We said our good-byes in the lobby, where Tori awaited me. As always, she wore that long white coat, only this time I didn't have to fantasize about what it would be like to undress her.

Now was not the time to be thinking with that part of my anatomy. I needed my brain more. 'Whaddaya got for me, kid?' I asked her, trying to give it a platonic feel. It sounded forced. It sounded ridiculous.

'Kid? Now I'm "Kid"?'

'Your new nickname.'

'Well, okay, Daddy-O.'

'Nice.'

We made it out of the doors and into the cool air. It felt good.

'So do you want to know what I came up with?' she asked.

'I do.'

She looked at me.

'I found Kathy's e-mail address,' she said. 'And I hacked into it.'

74

Tori and I went into my office, where she opened her laptop. I thought, under the circumstances, this was a discussion best held in private.

'So this is what you lawyers would call unethical,' said Tori.

'Not to mention inadmissible,' I added. Even if we discovered gold in Kathy Rubinkowski's e-mail inbox, I wouldn't be able to use it. On the other hand, if I found something really useful, I could subpoena her e-mails and pretend to discover the e-mail for the first time.

I really should record these thoughts and play them back to myself during a moment of reflection. The rules of ethics in my profession, last I checked, weren't optional. When did I start treating them that way?

Oh, that's right – when an innocent man was on the verge of going down for murder.

'So here it is.' Tori showed me the computer screen. 'This is Kathy's personal e-mail, not work.'

'This is her inbox?' I asked.

'Right. As you can see, she's still getting a few e-mails, a year later. Mostly ads. But the real traffic ends on January thirteenth, when she died.'

We sat next to each other on my couch. She handed me the laptop. I scrolled through the messages she received. Most of them appeared to be sent to friends. Many of them at the top of the screen – the most recent chronologically – revolved around plans to celebrate her twenty-fourth birthday, which would have been the next day after her death. It hit me at that moment, something palpable in my gut, the sense of loss. This woman didn't make it to twenty-four. What I was doing, trying to solve this puzzle, wasn't solely for my client. I owed it to her, too.

'Check out January eighth,' Tori said.

I had to move to the second screen to do so. I pulled up an e-mail dated Friday, January 8, 1:31 P.M.:

I Need Some Advice
From: 'Katherine Rubinkowski' <KRubinkowski@ DLMlaw.net>
To: 'Thomas J. Rangle' <TRangle@DLMlaw.net>
BCC: 'Me' <Rubes@Intercast.com>

Tom, something is bothering me and I wanted to lay it out for you. I think we should keep this between us for now.

Remember I told you about the LabelTek / GHI lawsuit, and how I listed Summerset Farms as a buyer of the GHI fertilizer and someone removed them from the interrogatory answer? Recall I complained to Bruce but he brushed me off? Well, apparently LabelTek found out about Summerset on its own, probably from the Dept. of Ag database. The thing is, the moment they issued a subpoena to Summerset, GHI suddenly settled the case.

Okay, so that's strange, but it gets weirder. I
handled the Summerset acquisition when we first got
GHI for a client. Summerset's a small operation, and
GHI is selling them way more fertilizer than they could
use. I know this sounds paranoid – but it's like
Summerset is stockpiling this fertilizer.

So far, this was tracking with what I knew. It actually laid
out what we'd discovered in a concise fashion. She sent this
e-mail from work – the 'DLMlaw' e-mail address surely meant
Dembrow, Lane, and McCabe – but blind copied her personal
e-mail. She was keeping a record of this e-mail for herself.

And the e-mail continued:

And remember that other acquisition we did – SK
Tool and Supply? Right at the same time GHI
acquired Summerset? Well, SK just sold basic industrial equipment, but now, all of a sudden, they sell
nitromethane, which has a lot of uses, but one of
which is explosives. And when I was over at SK the
other day on the Secada lawsuit – ok, I know I
shouldn't have done this – but I looked at their sales
invoices and it turns out, SK sells nitromethane to one
and only one customer. Guess who? Summerset.

So I know this sounds like an Oliver Stone movie,
but it seems like a lot of transactional work has gone
toward sending fertilizer (ammonium nitrate) and nitromethane to one company in large quantities.

When you combine ammonium nitrate with nitromethane, you get a potent explosive. It's pretty much
what Timothy McVeigh used in Oklahoma City.

Tell me if I'm totally paranoid, but this is freaking
me out a little bit. I know Bruce brushed me off before,
but now that we know about the nitromethane, too –
should I raise it with him? Or . . . and I can't believe
I'm saying this . . . should I go to the police?

Thanks, T.

K

'Who's Tom Rangle?' I asked.

'The head paralegal at the law firm,' Tori said. 'Kathy's boss.'

I read the whole thing a second time. I always miss something when I'm reading fast.

'Jesus, Tori.' I looked at her. 'This is the motive, right here.'

I got up from the couch. My left knee screamed at me to slow it down. It was gradually improving but still hurt whenever I breathed. I lapped my office – limped was a better term – and found my football as I ruminated.

'A few days before her murder, Kathy connected the dots,' I said. 'Global Harvest bought a company to use as a front to gather two chemicals used to make a bomb – fertilizer and nitromethane. Global Harvest sold the fertilizer but didn't sell nitromethane. They didn't want to be too obvious about picking it up as a new product, so they did the next best thing. They purchased another company, SK Tool and Supply, that sells industrial products and had *that* company sell the nitromethane to Summerset. Nobody's paying attention because it's not like they're selling these things to Al Qaeda or something. They're selling it to a farm, for Christ's sake. A farm that needs fertilizer to grow wheat and nitromethane, I don't know, probably for pesticide. Bradley said that was one of its uses, right?'

'So Summerset Farms is the perfect front.'

'Perfect,' I agreed. 'We already know from this e-mail that Kathy talked to Bruce McCabe about Summerset Farms being removed from that interrogatory response. So McCabe was on notice that she was suspicious. And by the time this e-mail was sent – what was it, January eighth? – Kathy had put even more pieces together. She probably told McCabe that there was a possible terrorist operation going on.'

'She probably did,' Tori agreed.

'And that connects us to Randall Manning. McCabe could have just told his client that his paralegal was asking questions.'

'And just a few days later, Kathy is murdered,' said Tori. 'Just enough time for Manning to hire the Capparellis to kill her.'

We looked at each other. This was it.

Tori said, 'But you can't use this. It's inadmissible, you said.'

'I can't tell the judge I hacked into her e-mail, no. But I can subpoena her e-mails and act pleasantly surprised.'

I thought about that. There had to be another way.

'Better yet,' I said, 'let's talk to Tom Rangle.'

75

Friday, December third. I looked at my watch. We'd gotten a late start for court today, as Judge Nash had to handle a few matters – or, if you prefer, mercilessly berate some lawyers – before we reconvened the trial. I was hoping the delay would give Tori enough time to find Kathy Rubinkowski's boss, Tom Rangle, and see what we could put together. For the time being, I had to be here at trial, because today was going to be the heart of the prosecution's case and these were my witnesses.

Thus far, the prosecution had established the murder weapon, plus the victim's possessions, were found with Tom within an hour after Kathy's murder. They had proved the obvious, but necessary, fact that the bullet between the eyes was the cause of death. And they had published a number of grisly photos to the jury.

Today, they would present a ballistics expert to match the bullet found in Kathy Rubinkowski's brain to the Glock 23 found in Tom's hand. Then they would put on Detective Frank Danilo to testify that Tom Stoller confessed to murder in the interrogation room.

And that was going to be it. They had no eyewitnesses to

the shooting. But they probably didn't need any. Tom was caught with the gun and stolen items. And even if Tom took the stand, he wasn't going to deny shooting her. He was going to say he didn't remember.

I still had my ace in the hole, though. When the prosecution introduced evidence of Tom confessing to the murder, I would argue that he wasn't confessing to Kathy's murder but to the shooting in Iraq. I was going to back-door the post-traumatic stress disorder evidence. The judge had barred the defense, but I wouldn't be raising it as a defense – I'd raise it simply as an *explanation* for the supposed confession.

Wendy, I thought, wouldn't see that coming. With the PTSD defense knocked out by the judge, she probably assumed Dr Sofian Baraniq had no basis for testifying. But the judge hadn't specifically barred Dr Baraniq as a witness.

It was a quarter after ten when the jury came in. Where the hell was Tori? I prayed that Tom Rangle wasn't on vacation or something.

Wendy's second chair, Maggie Silvers, put the ballistics expert on and got through his direct in about twenty minutes. I told Shauna to do what she could to draw this out. We had no basis for denting his testimony, but I needed time. I didn't want the prosecution to rest today, and if they did, I didn't want them to rest until the end of the day.

I needed the weekend. I needed at least a couple of days to put all of this together.

Shauna did what she could, but the examination was completed before eleven.

Normally we'd take a mid-morning break, but with the late start it made no sense. The judge told Wendy to call her next witness.

'The People call Detective Francis Danilo,' she said, just as Tori walked into the courtroom with another man.

Tom Rangle, I presumed.

76

I worked on a matter with Frank Danilo once when I was a prosecutor. He was a good guy. Pretty nondescript appearance – average height, average build, short brown hair – and cool under pressure. And overall, a pretty fair guy. I ran into him in the hallway about six weeks ago, while each of us was working on another matter, and he even told me he hated like hell that an Iraq War vet who was obviously messed up in the head was going down for this.

But I remember working an interrogation with him, and he had the suspect so scared that he threw up on Frank's shoe.

Danilo was dressed today in his Sunday best. He didn't look comfortable in a shirt and tie. But he did look comfortable on the witness stand. He was the kind of cop juries liked.

I looked over my shoulder at Tori, who was now seated a few rows back next to the man who came in with her, presumably Tom Rangle. I was more interested in what she had to say than what Danilo did, but the judge wasn't going to give me a break right now, because he'd want to give Wendy Kotowski the chance to complete Danilo's direct testimony before lunch.

Wendy started with the basics, getting Danilo's bio before the jury. He'd been a detective first grade for more than seven years now in the robbery-homicide division. He'd investigated over a hundred murders.

Danilo did a chronological tour of the night Kathy Rubinkowski died. The call came in a few minutes after midnight. Danilo and his partner, Ramona Gregus, responded to the shooting of a female DOA. Danilo was the DIC – the detective in charge – who oversaw the handling of the crime scene in every aspect. He and Wendy did an impressive show of how the evidence was collected, but in my opinion they went on too long. I say that because they ultimately didn't find anything incriminating, so it only highlighted this point. But most jurors these days have watched *CSI* and expect these kinds of investigatory procedures. In fact, Wendy spent most of the voir dire making the point to the potential jurors that *CSI* is just fiction – that, in fact, finding fingerprints, for example, is remarkably harder than you'd think from watching TV. Prosecutors around the country face these unfairly high expectations from juries. I feel really bad for them. But that wouldn't stop me from doing my '*CSI* cross,' pointing out all the tremendous resources available to them but the lack of any physical evidence against my client.

By the time Wendy had gone through all of this and chain-of-evidence testimony – establishing that the evidence was collected and stored in proper fashion – the hour of noon had passed. That was okay with Wendy, who wanted to elongate this testimony because Danilo would probably be the last witness. And it was okay with me, for whom the end of the day could not come too soon.

But Judge Nash wanted to keep going, so Wendy didn't miss a beat.

'The interview with the defendant was conducted by myself and Detective Ramona Gregus,' said Danilo.

'Did you record the interview, Detective?'

'We did.'

'Did you read the defendant his rights?'

Danilo nodded. 'I informed him of his right to remain silent and the right to counsel. He indicated he was willing to speak with us.'

'And did he speak with you?'

'Yes.'

Wendy Kotowski retrieved the murder weapon from the evidence table and asked for permission to approach the witness. Most judges have dispensed with that formality but not Bertrand Nash.

'Showing you People's Number Six,' said Wendy. 'Did you show this firearm to the defendant?'

'I did.'

'And what happened next?'

'Without any prompting, he said, "That's my gun." He said it twice. "That's my gun." '

'And after the defendant twice indicated to you that the gun belonged to him,' asked Wendy, following the time-honored tradition of repeating helpful information, 'what happened next?'

Danilo said, 'I asked him where he got the weapon.'

'Did the defendant respond?'

'No, he didn't.'

Wendy nodded and reviewed her notes. She obviously wanted to save the confession for last, and wanted to make sure she'd gotten everything else from the witness.

Then she looked up at the judge and said, 'Nothing further for this witness.'

Nothing further?

I jerked in my chair, a surge of electricity passing through me. Wendy wasn't going to ask him about the confession?

I played it out. She had established that Tom claimed the gun as his own, so she would take that – without any statement to the contrary from Tom – to mean that Tom had owned that firearm for some time before the shooting. If left unchallenged, that would kill any argument I had that the weapon was planted, dumped into his lap by a fleeing murderer.

And that, she had decided, was good enough for her.

Because she had figured out my plan.

She knew Tom's confession was shaky. She knew that a jury would watch the videotape and see Tom squaring off against an imaginary foe, shouting orders to 'drop the weapon' and bursting into tears. She knew it would give me an opening to introduce my PTSD argument and Tom's military history.

So she wasn't going to argue that Tom confessed. She was going to take his claimed ownership of the gun as enough.

It had never occurred to me that a prosecutor with a confession on tape wouldn't use it. When she didn't mention the confession in her opening statement, I thought she was just holding back. I hadn't realized what she was doing.

Wendy Kotowski had outsmarted me.

Judge Nash banged his gavel. 'The court will recess until one-thirty,' he said.

I looked at Shauna. Her expression showed that she had worked through the same calculations. 'Smart move,' she whispered to me.

I looked over my shoulder past Aunt Deidre to Tori, who nodded eagerly. I nodded back.

And hoped she had something really good.

77

At a quarter to two, I rose to begin my crossexamination.

'Detective,' I said, 'upon arresting and booking Tom Stoller on the early morning of January fourteenth, you didn't find any of Kathy Rubinkowski's blood on his hands, did you?'

'We didn't, no.'

'You didn't find any of her blood on Tom's shirt, did you?'

'No.'

'Or on his shoes?'

'Correct, we did not.'

'You searched the area where Tom lived, so to speak. Where he slept. At the southwest corner of Franzen Park. And you didn't find any of Kathy Rubinkowski's blood among his possessions, either, did you?'

'Correct.' He was answering matter-of-factly, as if these were not significant facts. He was a well-trained witness.

'Gunshot residue,' I said. 'GSR. That's residue of the combustion components of a firearm after it's fired, right?'

'That's right.'

'When a gun fires, it creates an explosion – combustion of the primer and powder.'

'True enough.'

'Gunshot residue is the residue of the combustion. Little particles, or residue, can be found on the arm or wrist or body of an individual after they've fired a gun, right?'

'It can be, sometimes. Not always.'

A good answer. He was going to say that on redirect, anyway. 'You tested Tom Stoller for the presence of gunshot residue, didn't you?'

'Yes, and we didn't find any.'

'Nor did you find gunshot residue on anything else among his possessions in the southwest corner of Franzen Park, correct?'

'We did not.'

'So you didn't find any physical evidence that Tom Stoller fired that weapon, did you?'

'We didn't find any GSR, as you said.'

Equivocation. Dumb. A chance for me to repeat and emphasize.

'GSR or anything else, Detective – you didn't find a single shred of physical or forensic evidence that Tom Stoller fired the murder weapon, did you?'

'That's correct, sir.'

I paused for a segue, and to let that quick rat-a-tat of favorable information soak into the jurors' minds.

'Now, in the course of collecting evidence that night, you found the spent shell casing from the Glock 23 on the sidewalk, in the soil of the planted tree?'

'That's correct, Mr Kolarich.'

'A distance of ten feet and one inch from where the victim was lying dead.'

'That's correct.'

'A Glock semiautomatic expels its casing to the right, true?'

'True.'

'Not forward or backward.'

'Correct.'

'So it's likely that the weapon was fired from ten feet away.'

Danilo shrugged. 'Hard to say. A shell casing could be moved.'

I looked at the jury. 'You're saying someone might have moved the shell casing?'

'It's possible, I'm saying.'

'Well, did you find a fingerprint on the shell casing?'

'No, sir. But it was wintertime. People wear gloves.'

'Did you find gloves on my client's hands when you arrested him?'

He paused, then smiled. 'No, we did not.'

'So you have no evidence that the shell casing was moved, do you?'

'Just as you have no evidence it wasn't.'

'But I'm not trying to prove my client innocent beyond a reasonable doubt, am I? *You're* trying to prove him *guilty* beyond a reasonable doubt. Isn't that your understanding of how this works, Detective?'

'Objection. Argumentative,' said Wendy.

The judge overruled. Danilo conceded the point. 'I have no evidence the casing was moved.'

'And if the shell casing wasn't moved, that would mean that the shooter was ten feet away from Kathy Rubinkowski when he shot her.'

'If the casing wasn't moved, yes.'

'Detective, have you ever fired a Glock weapon?'

'Yes, I have.'

'Hitting someone with a shot between the eyes from ten feet away with a Glock pistol – that's no easy feat, is it?'

366

'It's good marksmanship,' he agreed.

'It's *excellent* marksmanship, wouldn't you agree?'

He gave that a moment. 'Yes,' he said.

'And the street lighting on Gehringer Street was rather weak, wasn't it?'

'I'm not sure I would characterize it that way.'

I walked him through the high-powered flashlights and the remote-area lighting equipment he brought in to conduct the crime scene investigation that night. I drew it out in a series of questions to overstate my point, which was that the shot from the Glock was not only impressive because of the distance but also the relative darkness.

'But since you raised it, Detective.' I moved from the podium now. I didn't even feel my knee. 'In your experience, why would someone move a shell casing?'

Danilo thought for a moment. He probably hadn't expected that question. 'To throw off the measurements,' he said. 'Criminals alter crime scenes to make the story look different than it was.'

That was what I needed. 'Criminals try to alter things to hide their crimes, yes?'

'Of course.'

'For example, some killers pick up their shell casings after firing their weapon. Yes?'

'Yes.'

'And in your experience, you've seen instances where killers robbed their victims after killing them to make their motive appear to be robbery. You've seen that, haven't you? They had a different motive but they wanted to conceal it, so they made it look like a robbery? In your twenty-two years on the force, you've seen that?'

Danilo had no way out of that. 'I've seen that happen. It's not the norm.'

'But you've seen people use a purported robbery to cover up their real motive.'

'Objection, Your Honor. Asked and answered.'

'I'll withdraw,' I said. 'Kathy Rubinkowski was a paralegal at a law firm, wasn't she, Detective?'

'Correct.'

'Do you know how many criminal cases she worked on?'

'I don't, no.'

The answer was zero, but *I don't know* was what I wanted.

'Well, then describe for us generally what cases she worked on.'

He shook his head. 'I'm not able to do that.'

'You didn't investigate the cases she worked on?'

'I didn't consider it necessary, no.'

'Did you check her e-mails?'

'No, sir. I didn't consider it necessary, given that your client was found with the victim's personal items and the murder weapon, which he claimed as his own.'

'Did Tom say how long that gun had been in his possession?' I asked. I asked it as an open-ended question only because I knew the answer; the entire conversation was captured on tape.

'No, he didn't,' Danilo conceded.

'He didn't say, "I've owned that gun for ten years."'

'No, sir.'

'He didn't say, "I've owned that gun for ten *hours*."'

'No, sir, he did not.'

'Detective, you've had some experience with homeless people as both a beat cop and later a detective, yes?'

'Yes.'

'And isn't it fair to say that homeless people are often possessive of their things?'

'They can be. It's not a hard-and-fast rule, but I take your point.'

Nice of him. 'So isn't it possible that when Tom said, "That's my gun," that he had only possessed that gun for an hour before he was arrested?'

'That would surprise me.'

'But it's possible.'

'Possible, I suppose.'

'So it's possible that someone dumped that gun over the fence – the closest fence to the crime scene – and Tom was there. He picked it up, and in his mind, *voilà*, it was now his gun.'

'Objection. Calls for speculation.'

'It's no more speculative than the prosecution's theory,' I protested. That wasn't a valid response to the objection, and every lawyer in the room knew it. It was my closing argument.

The judge sustained and admonished me.

Good enough. I wanted to get back to my larger point. 'Did you talk to Kathy's co-workers about whether anyone had a problem with Kathy or would want to hurt Kathy?'

Danilo looked up and sighed. 'I don't believe we interviewed them, no.'

'What about her friends?'

'No, sir. As I indicated—'

'It wasn't necessary. Yes, Detective. So you would have no way of knowing whether Kathy Rubinkowski had expressed some fear for her life? Fear that someone wanted to hurt her. You would have no way of knowing that?'

'Objection.' Wendy got to her feet. 'This is all rampant speculation.'

'Your Honor, I'm simply inquiring into the depth, or lack thereof, of the investigation.'

Judge Nash paused, then overruled the objection.

'We had our guy, Counselor,' said Danilo.

'So you can't tell this jury, one way or the other, whether Kathy sent e-mails to friends or co-workers that she was afraid for her life.'

'He said he didn't review her e-mails, Counsel.' This from the judge.

I glared at him and then moved on. 'And as the lead investigator on this case, Detective, that would be kind of an interesting thing to know, wouldn't it? That the victim thought her life was in danger?'

'Objection. Argumentative and speculative, Your Honor.'

'Overruled. The witness will answer. But Mr Kolarich,' said the judge, peering down at me over his glasses, 'don't belabor this.'

'Yes, Judge.' I looked at Shauna, who nodded back at me. She was right. It was probably time.

'Detective,' I said, 'isn't it true that Kathy Rubinkowski was about to blow the whistle on what she believed to be serious criminal activity only days before she was murdered?'

'Objection!' That was the quickest I'd seen Wendy leap up. 'May we have a sidebar, Your Honor?'

The judge waved us up. I'd thought about going to the judge first, showing him everything I'd come up with to date, and begging him to let me introduce this evidence. But I liked springing it better. No matter how Judge Nash ruled on this, the jury heard it at least once.

The judge stepped down from the bench. We met him off to the side. He gave me a long look.

'This better be good, Mr Kolarich,' he said.

78

The prosecutors, Wendy Kotowski and Maggie Silvers, were speechless. Judge Nash, sitting behind his desk in his ornate chambers, was likewise dumbfounded. My client, Tom Stoller, sat quietly without showing any reaction.

Wendy Kotowski said, 'Judge, I have to assume this is some kind of a joke.'

'I know it's late, Your Honor,' I said. 'Believe me, I know. But this is the first time I've had something concrete to show you. If I'd come to you before now, I don't think I would have had much chance at succeeding.'

'And you think you have a chance now?' asked the judge. Out of his robe, his bony shoulders and stooped posture made him appear frail. But he still had that cannon of a voice.

'I would hope so, Your Honor. I know all about procedural rules, and I take them seriously. I've been working around the clock to compile this evidence so that I could give you something more than speculation.'

'It's *still* speculation,' said Wendy. 'This company – Global Harvest – sold fertilizer to one of its subsidiaries? Another company sold another product, also perfectly legal, to that same subsidiary? Kathy Rubinkowski came up with a theory that this meant someone is building a bomb, and she was murdered to silence her?'

The judge pointed at Wendy but looked at me. 'Beyond the fact that all of this information is untimely, it's also unconvincing,' he said. 'If you think these individuals are up to something like you're saying – some kind of terrorist activity – then you should talk to the FBI.'

'I have,' I said.

'All right, you have.'

'Judge, the victim in this case stumbled upon the information and ended up dead less than a week later. And when she sent an e-mail to her boss at the law firm, that e-mail never made it to him. We just spoke with the individual, Tom Rangle. He never got the e-mail. Which means that someone at the law firm was monitoring Kathy's e-mails and deleted them. And then killed her only days later. I have more than enough to take to a jury on this.'

'Putting aside the timeliness. Or lack thereof.'

I gripped both arms of the chair in which I was seated. 'If Tom were convicted, and I came up with this information months or years later, I could get a post-conviction hearing on newly discovered evidence. I'm doing better than that. I'm discovering it right now and asking for the chance to get this into the record before a verdict. Give me that chance, Judge.'

'Your Honor—' said Wendy, but I cut her off and kept going.

'The end here is justice, Your Honor,' I said. 'I mean, that's what we're all doing here, right? We have rules and protocols, but at the end of the day, nobody – not you, not me, not the prosecutor – should try to stop the truth from coming out. That's why you wanted to wear a robe on day one. That's why Wendy and I became prosecutors. We wanted to do the right thing. And I'm telling you that, even if it took me a while, I've come upon information that I believe in my heart will exonerate my client. I'm telling you that the state has the wrong man. And I can't believe some deadline is going to prevent me from showing the jury that.'

The judge was actually considering my argument, which was more than I'd expected.

'Your Honor, I'm not looking to sandbag anybody. If the prosecution wants some time to digest what I have to offer, that's fine with me. My client will stay locked up. She can have all the time she wants. Hell, I'd *welcome* her involvement. It might lead us to the right result. And it might prevent a terrorist attack. I don't want that on my conscience. Do you?'

The judge was taken aback by that last comment. But that was my very point. I needed a little shock value, because while I'd been living with this information for a few weeks, this was the first either of them had heard of it.

I didn't know how any of this was going to sit. Truth and justice, ironically enough, were words seldom uttered in this courthouse, filled with lawyers whose idealism had been eroded over decades of experience. No practitioner – judge, prosecutor, defense lawyer – mistook what happened in this building as justice. It was simply the closest anybody could come. The old line was that the United States had the worst system of justice in the world, with the exception of every other one.

In some ways, I sounded like an idealistic, first-year law student. But Judge Nash knew me well enough to know that I wouldn't give this speech without some basis.

'Judge,' said Wendy. 'Judge, this is absurd. And if, by some stretch of the imagination, it's not, then Mr Kolarich has alerted the authorities. It's possible to take him seriously *and* proceed with this trial. And if by some chance he is ultimately right, then he has correctly pointed out his remedy of a post-trial motion.' I began to answer, but she raised a hand and, for good measure, her voice as well. 'If trials were halted midstream every time a lawyer said he thought maybe, just maybe, he was about to connect some dots on a theory of innocence he has never *once* given us a hint about, then nobody could run a courtroom.'

I looked over at the court reporter and had one more thought. 'I'd like to say one more thing for the record, if I could, Judge. Only days before we went to trial, you barred my insanity defense. I know you think you made the right decision, but regardless, you left me in a very difficult position. I was planning on asserting an affirmative defense and you took it away. You left me with nothing to argue but innocence, with only days to do so. So that's what I did. And I'll admit, at first I was clutching at straws, but for the love of God, it turns out that we've uncovered evidence that exonerates my client. I was as surprised as anyone. But here it is. I followed your instructions and came up with this evidence and now, if you bar *that* evidence, too – how can we possibly say this was a fair trial? Every avenue I turn, you shut me down?'

For the first time, I was stretching. The truth was, I was considering a dual defense all along – insanity and innocence, figuring I might settle on one eventually, most likely inno-cence, but keeping both options open. But Judge Nash would never know that. The story I just laid out was unassailable, and as Judge Nash watched the court reporter type these words, he was thinking about the appellate court reading this tran-script. *You took away his insanity defense, then he came up with an innocence defense and you barred that, too?*

My plan had always been to put my case together airtight and then present it to the judge. I knew that if I convinced him of its viability, he'd have no choice but to allow it. That hadn't happened. I just wasn't quite there. But I was out of time. The prosecution would rest today and come Monday morning, I'd have to have a defense. So I had to do this now. I had to lay out my cards now, even if they weren't a full deck.

Judge Nash leaned back in his leather chair and bobbed for a moment. A great mind at work, or something like that. I glared at Wendy, who glared back at me. I had to admit I would probably have the same initial reaction as she, were I the prosecutor, but I'd like to think I would give it more thought and reconsider.

'Okay,' said the judge. 'Here's what's going to happen. We're going to go in there and finish this witness examination. We're going to finish that today. And then, Ms. Kotowski, I take it the People will rest?'

'That's correct, Judge.'

'All right. Come back Monday morning. Mr Kolarich, I'm going to think about this and reserve ruling for now. But understand me, Mr Kolarich, and understand me well.' He wagged a bony finger at me. 'You better be prepared to start your case on Monday. If you assume I'm going to reopen discovery and let you add all these witnesses, you are flying without a net. Don't act surprised if I deny your request and expect you to call your first witness.'

Those comments, too, were for the transcript the appellate court would read.

'And as long as we're making a record,' he added, 'we should all be clear that this information has been made known to this court and to the prosecution for the very first time this afternoon. Now let's get back in there.'

'Thank you, Judge.'

All things considered, it was the best I could hope for. The judge was giving me one chance, one forty-eight-hour period to put all of this together.

'Better than I expected,' Shauna whispered to me as we left the judge's chambers. 'Now we have two days to connect those dots.'

79

I completed my cross-examination in another hour. It was pretty predictable stuff, taking the prosecution's theory of the case and stretching it and poking holes in it wherever I could. If Tom shot her first and then robbed her – the theory which made the most sense – how did he manage to steal her purse, her cell phone, and a chain off her neck without getting any of that pool of blood on himself? And if he robbed her first and then shot her – well, first of all, why did he move south of her before shooting her, when his ultimate escape was to the north? And why would he move ten feet away from her before shooting her? If he robbed her and for some reason wanted her dead, a close-up shot would have made the most sense.

That was, in essence, my closing argument, cloaked in a cross-examination. It was broken up in pieces and asked out of order, but I'd be sure to put those pieces together for the jury in my summation.

Still, I couldn't shake the feeling that there was an overarching *so-what* feeling to this last hour. There was no blood on him because he shot from a long distance, and he was simply careful when he stole her things. And as for the sequence of events, *so what* if nobody knows exactly which came first, the robbery or the shooting? Nobody saw it happen. But that doesn't mean it didn't happen. Those precise details weren't crucial to the prosecution's theory.

These were all points that Wendy Kotowski made on her redirect. I didn't recross, and the prosecution rested. The jury went home for the weekend with a pretty strong feeling, I thought, that Tom Stoller was guilty of murder.

I spoke briefly with Tom before they carted him back to Boyd. Aunt Deidre thought my cross went well, but she wasn't exactly unbiased. I gave it a solid B-plus but the score was still Prosecution 4, Defense 0.

I spent Saturday morning with Tom and Deidre, running through a direct examination in theory, but in practice trying to get Tom to open up to me about the events of January 13. To the extent I could get him to focus, he continued with his insistence that he didn't remember. It was doubly frustrating because my client wasn't helping me and because I was wasting my time that could have been spent tracking down the Global Harvest angle.

At eleven o'clock that morning, I made a decision.

'I can't put him on,' I told Deidre outside the Boyd Center. 'He's no use to us. He won't deny he killed her. And we can't explain his lack of memory on mental illness. The judge shut us down because Tom wouldn't cooperate with the prosecution's shrinks.'

'Because he *couldn't*,' she cried. 'He can't. He's so sick, Jason.'

'I know that, I know that.' I put my hand on her shoulder. 'The judge made a bad ruling. He screwed us. But it won't do us any good crying about it now. So we focus on the deficiencies in the prosecution's case. They have plenty. And I do

379

whatever I can do between now and Monday morning to tie up everything I'm chasing down with Global Harvest.'

She searched my face for any semblance of hope. 'You think the judge will let you use it? You said he's considering it.'

'I do think he's considering it. I do. But the stronger the case I give him, the better our chances. So I'm going to run now and see what my lawyers and investigators have come up with.'

She nodded silently. She needed more but the best thing I could do for her and her nephew was to get back to my office.

I called Shauna's cell phone while driving. She didn't answer but called me within thirty seconds.

'Sorry, didn't pick up in time,' she said.

'How's it going?'

'So far, not well.' Shauna was over at Bruce McCabe's law firm with Kathy Rubinkowksi's immediate supervisor, Tom Rangle, the man to whom Kathy had sent that long e-mail that somehow got intercepted and deleted before Tom could ever read it. She and Tom were trying to re-create what happened the day that e-mail was sent – where Bruce McCabe was that day, who opened and read that e-mail and where, in office or remotely.

'Keep at it, Shauna, and get us something good. Somebody kept that e-mail from making it to Tom Rangle. It must have been McCabe.'

When I got back to my law firm at noon on Saturday, we were thirty-six hours from the opening of the defense case. And I was now pinning Tom Stoller's fate entirely on what we could find between now and then.

80

'Bruce McCabe,' I repeated into the phone. 'M-c, capital C, a-b-e. He was one of the name partners.'

On the other end of the phone, Wendy Kotowski let out a sigh. 'I'm not saying yes.'

But she wasn't saying no. Unless she wasn't the person I once knew, Wendy Kotowski was one of those prosecutors who preferred a just outcome over a victory. She had to have some seeds of doubt in her mind after today. She knew I was prone to stunts in court, which made her initially skeptical, but I'd gone beyond mere theatrics and she knew it. I didn't know if she believed what I was saying, but I think she believed that I believed it.

'They won't talk to Joel Lightner,' I told Wendy. 'They're stiff-arming my investigator. So please – just check yourself, even if you don't tell me. Ten to one says the cops are suspicious of McCabe hanging himself. A dinner at Marley's, Wendy, if they don't suspect it was a murder staged to look like a suicide.'

'Kolarich, whatever else, don't play me for stupid, all right? You and I both know if I ask the question, and I get that answer, I'm duty-bound to tell you.'

She was right, of course. 'And you and I both know that what I'm asking you to do is the right thing to do. This is the guy that Kathy Rubinkowski went to see about Summerset Farms. This is the guy who brushed her off. And I'll probably never be able to prove it, but he's the guy who erased Kathy's e-mail from Tom Rangle's computer before he could read it. And now that I'm sniffing around, the guy suddenly offs himself? I mean, how many coincidences do we need before you stop calling this smoke and mirrors?'

'I don't need preaching from you, Jason.'

'No, you don't. You know what the right thing to do is. So do it.'

I punched out the phone.

'That was harsh,' said Tori, sitting next to me in my SUV.

It was. But I had faith in Wendy. And if she didn't talk to the detectives investigating Bruce McCabe's suicide, I would subpoena them and ask them myself. She knew that, too, which made our entire conversation somewhat contrived. Contrived, but necessary. It was better if Wendy felt like she was doing this voluntarily. It would invest her in the result.

I made a right turn and headed west. 'I don't know why I let you talk me into bringing you,' I said.

'Because you love spending time with me.' Tori put a hand over mine, resting in my lap. 'Because you aren't as conflicted as I am.'

'This could be dangerous, Tori. This isn't a joke.'

'I'm not laughing.'

No, she wasn't, but she was in a good mood. Playing cops and robbers always seemed to elevate her spirits, from the first time we visited a crime scene together to checking out

Summerset Farms to now. It took the focus off of our relationship. Maybe that should tell me something.

I watched the street addresses and slowed my vehicle as we got closer. When it appeared we were about a half-block away, I pulled the car over to the side of the road.

My cell phone rang. Caller ID said it was my scrappy associate, Bradley John. Or John Bradley. Sometimes I forget.

'Hey, Pretty Boy,' I said.

'I found it. It's the state police, believe it or not. The state police tracks sales of a number of chemical explosives. Nitromethane among them. SK Tool and Supplies sold nitromethane to Summerset Farms.'

'Boy, that's a great system we got. The department of agriculture tracks the sale of fertilizer and the state police track sales of nitromethane?'

'Our government at work,' he agreed. 'One hand *not* talking to the other. And Kathy's e-mail was right – SK didn't sell that product to anyone but Summerset Farms.'

If there was any doubt, that confirmed it. Randall Manning bought two companies at the same time, Summerset Farms and SK Tool and Supply. SK would sell the nitromethane, Manning's company would sell the ammonium nitrate fertilizer, and Summerset would be the recipient of both, the front company.

I was still missing the 'why.' Why would a multimillionaire like Randall Manning want to build a bomb?

'It'll be interesting to hear how Stanley Keane explains this,' said Bradley.

'Yeah. I'll let you know what he says.'

I hung up the phone and nodded to Tori. We got out of the car and walked toward Stanley Keane's house.

81

Stanley Keane lived in a small town called Weston, more than a hundred miles southwest of the city. He lived on a corner lot in a two-story Victorian brick house. The houses were well spaced, and Stanley had an impressive backyard filled with trees that were naked this time of year. We walked to the street corner and looked at the front of the house. There was a light on upstairs. The front porch had an awning and a sconce that produced orange light.

As far as I knew, Stanley Keane lived alone. He was fifty-five years old and he was the only registered voter at this address, so that probably ruled out a wife or adult children. His age probably ruled out younger children, but I couldn't be sure. We were doing everything on the fly, and this was the best we could do.

I'd figured out a few things about Stanley Keane, but I didn't know enough. I didn't know, for example, if he knew me, if he'd recognize my face. I didn't even know if he was a part of this thing, but the odds were decent and I was out of time to dance around subjects.

It was eight-thirty, cold, and dark, so the streets were otherwise deserted, which helped. It was Saturday night, but this was a residential street. We'd passed a few busy taverns on our way here. They were a mile away easily.

Tori and I did a lap around the block. There was a back door into Keane's house and the front door, of course. I thought about how this should play out.

We went back to the car. I drove it around the corner and parked in front of his house. I had considered a back-door entry, maybe using Tori at the front door to distract him. But I decided, in the end, to play it straight.

Well, kind of straight, anyway. I clipped my badge to my coat so it showed outward. It was my prosecutor's badge. I'd lost it back when I was on the job, which was an extreme no-no, because in the wrong hands it could create all kinds of havoc. The job gave me a replacement badge, of course, and docked me pay as a penalty, which I had no problem with. When I later found the original in my overcoat at the dry cleaner's, I figured I'd paid for it, so I'd keep it.

'You should stay in the car,' I told Tori. 'I know you wanted to come and I thought I might use you, but I think this is better one-on-one. If I'm law enforcement, who are you? You look like a runway model, Tori.'

'I'm too short.'

'Okay, a short runway model.'

'You look less threatening with me at your side,' she argued. 'Otherwise, you're this big bruiser guy all alone. I'd be less worried about you if a woman were standing next to you.'

She had a point. Okay, fine.

We got out of the SUV and walked to the front door. I rang the bell and stepped back off the porch, beyond the awning, and held up my badge to the lit window on the second floor. A silhouette appeared, and then the window slid open.

I held the badge at an angle to obscure my face. He probably didn't have a terrific look at me, anyway, but it didn't hurt to make it more difficult.

'Mr Keane?' I called out. 'County sheriff's investigator.'

He stuck his head out through the window. 'It's late. Can't it wait until tomorrow?'

'If it could wait,' I said, 'I would have waited.'

He nodded and closed his window. If Stanley Keane were an innocent guy in all of this, he'd come to the door. If Stanley Keane were a guilty accomplice in all of this, he'd come to the door. Right? If he was part of a plan for a terrorist act which obviously hadn't happened yet, why would he risk himself and his plan by starting some controversy on his front doorstep with a law enforcement officer? What was he going to do, shoot me?

I would soon find out. I followed a trail of lights turning on in the house as he made his way downstairs. A light near the front door came on and I braced myself. He might know my face, after all.

He opened the door slowly. I held out my credentials for him to see clearly, which was pretty standard protocol for a nighttime visit from law enforcement. He poked his head out and his eyes went first to the badge. If he had good eyesight, he was probably wondering what a guy with a county investigator's badge from the city was doing down here in Fordham County.

But he wasn't wondering that. I saw it immediately in his eyes when they locked with mine. He knew who I was.

I lunged for the door and threw my shoulder against it just as he was closing it. A second later and it would have been shut. I could feel the dual impact of my thrust against the

386

door and then the counter-push against his body when it collided with him. Turns out, I'd knocked him to the floor.

'Here, Stanley,' I said, throwing an envelope like a Frisbee onto his chest. 'You've been served with a subpoena.' That threw him off temporarily, as his mind raced, mentally bracing for danger and then hearing me say something nonthreatening, the subpoena. I stood over him and grabbed him by the sweatshirt and lifted him to his feet. He still wasn't sure what had hit him.

Stanley Keane was in his mid-fifties, maybe six feet tall, on the thin side, with a military crew cut. He was decked out in sweats, head to toe.

I held him there, almost lifting him off his feet, face-to-face with me. He was on the tips of his toes. Fear ran through his beady eyes – yes, now he realized the danger impulse had been the correct one.

'What . . . do you want?' he managed.

'I want to know who tried to kill me. Twice,' I added. 'And I'm going to break bones until you answer me.'

His fear turned quickly into defiance. He scowled, which was somewhat of a chore for him, given that he was off balance and having some difficulty breathing.

'You'll have to do . . . more than that,' he snarled.

'Interesting, Stanley. I would have expected, "What do you mean, someone tried to kill you? I have no idea what you mean. I have no idea who you are." So I appreciate that, Stan. The honesty. That's a good start.'

I threw him against the nearest wall but kept my grip on him.

'See, Patrick Cahill and Ernie Dwyer – you remember them, the Aryan brothers who got picked up in the city after they tried to kill me? They say it was you, Stan. They're putting this all on you and Bruce McCabe.'

'Like . . . hell,' he said through his teeth.

'Personally, I think it was Ronald McDonald or . . . what was his name? Oh, yeah, Randall Manning.' I hurled my right knee into his groin. He doubled over, but I was there to catch him. His body was collapsing, but I hadn't had any exercise since I hurt my left knee – which, by the way, was holding up nicely, thanks to the adrenaline pump – and I could prop him up with help from the wall. Some kind of physics thing. I'd ask Tori later.

'Jason, what are you doing?' Tori asked.

'I'm obtaining information. Why don't you go upstairs and see what you can find? That okay with you, Stan, if my associate pokes around?'

'Fuck . . . you.'

'I'll take that as a yes.' I nodded to Tori, careful not to use her name. 'Poke around. Look for a computer, a cell phone, any papers, that kind of thing.'

I waited until Tori had run up the stairs.

'I'll kill . . . both of you,' said Stanley.

I used my left hand to brace him. With my right, I hit him with a shiver into the shoulder. The linemen at State used to practice that move all day long, and I would join in after practice. I always liked the shiver, the quick thrust that came almost out of nowhere, no windup.

The pop to Stanley's shoulder was either sickening or enjoyable, depending on your perspective. Stanley cried out in pain and gnashed his teeth. Angry guy.

'That's a separated shoulder, Stan. So I said I was going to break bones, and here I've just kneed you in the balls and taken out a shoulder—'

His right hand rose up in a vain attempt at a punch. I grabbed his hand with both of mine. I bent his fingers back, putting all my weight forward. I figured I broke at least three fingers, based on the number of snaps I heard. It was hard to tell because they all came at once.

Keane fell to the floor, his left hand clutching his right. He was screaming, and this was a quiet neighborhood, so I came down on him and pressed my hand over his mouth.

'It's going to get worse, Stan. I'll break every bone in your body if I have to. So let's cut to the chase.

'Stanley,' I said, 'tell me about the bombs.'

82

'Jason, you have to stop this.' Tori came bounding down the stairs, holding a blue canvas gym bag. 'You're going to kill him.'

'You don't die from a separated shoulder,' I noted, my knees pinning down Stanley's arms. 'Or broken fingers. Or a broken wrist. Does that wrist seem broken to you, Stan?'

I figured a fractured right wrist worked nicely with broken left fingers, making either hand unusable for a weapon, now or later. Stanley's eyes were squeezed shut and he was moaning with pain. He was probably approaching shock. Tori was probably right.

'You're going to give him a heart attack,' she said.

'Stanley. Stanley.' I smacked at his cheek lightly. 'The bombs, Stan. What are you planning to bomb and when?'

Stanley Keane was fading in and out now. He was probably in excruciating pain. I'd gone overboard. I'd let my anger take over. But I didn't care.

'Stop this, Jason. I may have found some things. Let's go,' Tori said. 'Please.'

'Go to the car,' I said. 'You don't need to be around for this.'

'No. I'm not leaving without you. Let's go.'

'Not yet.' I got off Stanley and dragged him into the living room and propped him up in a chair. I went into his kitchen, grabbed a glass and filled it with water. When I returned to the living room, he was slumped forward, his chin resting on his chest, his breathing shallow.

I took a drink of the water, because I was thirsty. Then I threw the rest in his face.

It helped a little. He shook his head and managed to raise his eyes to mine.

'You decide when this ends,' I said. I removed the slippers from his feet. 'Next up, I'm going to smash your toes into ground beef,' I said, showing him my boots.

'No, Jason. Stop this!' Tori shouted.

'You have . . . no idea,' Stanley mumbled.

'I know your company sold the nitromethane and Randy's company sold the fertilizer. I know you're building a bomb. And so do the feds. You know how the G is, Stan. You've probably given this a lot of thought. They're a step or two behind, because they're building a case for a search warrant and all that, but they'll get there. You're done. They're on to you. There's no way you and Randy and whatever nutjob group you're a part of is going to get away with this. So tell me what you're planning to do, and when, or walk with a limp the rest of your pathetic life.'

'I . . . don't . . . need to know.'

I paused. So he was saying there was operational security, and only the game-day players would know the details. Always a good strategy to maintain confidentiality.

'You know plenty, you piece of shit.' I gripped his shirt. 'I'm not leaving until you tell me.'

I didn't really want to smash his toes. But this was my chance to learn some things. Maybe my only chance. So I threw him another shiver, reminding him of how much his shoulder hurt.

He let out a low cry, something primitive, a wounded animal, then he fell against the arm of the chair, seething through his teeth. Now, I thought, I was hitting the limit. He wasn't even crying out anymore, just panting and moaning. Too many things hurt all at once.

'You're going to tell me. Since it looks like you're about to pass out, I'm going to cut to the finale. The finale is I go to the kitchen, grab a butcher knife, and cut off your balls. You'll bleed out on this chair while I watch.'

I looked at Tori, who stared at me with her mouth hanging open. She wasn't sure what she was witnessing, or *whom* she was witnessing. I wasn't either, not at that moment.

I gave her a faint shake of the head, indicating I was bluffing. It didn't change the expression on her face.

Stanley swallowed hard, then his eyes grew vacant. For a brief, panicked moment, I thought he had died. But he hadn't died. He'd simply grown calm.

'I'm . . . sorry,' he mumbled. 'So . . . sorry I wasn't . . . there for you.'

'Sorry about what?' I asked, shaking his arm.

His face contorted. Tears came from nowhere and rolled sideways down his face, as his head lay on the arm of the chair.

'I miss you so . . . much,' he said. 'I'm coming . . . to you . . . I'm coming . . .'

'He's going into shock,' Tori said. 'We need to get him to the hospital.'

I looked back at Stanley, who was looking in my eyes. 'Kill me,' he said, with a surprisingly strong voice. 'It doesn't mat . . . matter any . . . anymore.'

'Tell me, Stanley. Whatever you're doing, it has to stop.'

My tone had instantly changed from punitive and taunting to a plea. This man, I now realized, wasn't going to talk. I could waterboard him and he wouldn't crack. Whatever he was doing, he was committed to it.

What was he talking about? Some tragedy in his life? I didn't know. But I did know that I wasn't going to get him to talk, and I couldn't just leave him here.

I scooped him up in my arms and headed for the door.

83

Tori found the nearest emergency room with her iPhone. I burst in and got someone's attention right away. I told them my uncle had tried to move a refrigerator down to the basement by himself and he'd fallen down the stairs. I figured fractures to the wrists and hands, and a separated shoulder, told that kind of a story.

Stanley could tell a different story if he wished, but I couldn't see him doing it. His hands were pretty dirty. Why call attention to himself?

I took the medical paperwork with me to a chair and then walked out of the place. Tori had the SUV running outside, and I jumped in.

'That . . . wasn't right,' she said to me.

'I agree.' I looked right at her. 'You shouldn't have stopped me.'

'That's not what I—'

'I'm trying to save lives, Tori. This guy's plotting to bomb something. I don't have time for touchy-feely ACLU bullshit. You're feeling sorry for that asshole?'

'That's not the point—'

'It most certainly *is* the fucking point. What, you think I enjoyed that?'

She didn't answer. Which was an answer in itself.

'Okay, so now I'm the sociopath,' I seethed. 'I beat up a homegrown terrorist and I'm the bad guy. Lock me up, but let him plot a mass murder.'

She looked away. 'Let's just go home,' she said in a more subdued tone.

'Yeah, let's do that. Thanks for coming along, Tori. You were a real help to the cause.'

She didn't respond. There wasn't much left to say. I wasn't the least bit sorry for what I'd done. I only regretted that I didn't get more out of him. In fact, I got basically nothing, other than confirmation that I was on the right track.

We drove awhile, back onto the main roads, and then the highway. I was exhausted from the adrenaline drain. My head was pounding, and my knee suddenly remembered how much it hurt.

'What's in the gym bag?' I asked. 'What did you get from the upstairs?'

'Anything I could sweep off his desk,' she answered. 'A pile of papers that I didn't have time to look at.'

'What about his cell phone or computer?'

'He didn't have a laptop that I could see. Just a desktop that I couldn't have carried if I wanted to. No cell phone that I could see. Really, I didn't have time, Jason. It sounded like you were killing him downstairs.'

I didn't have the energy to rekindle a civil-liberties debate. I just prayed like hell that she had found something good.

84

When we got back to my hotel room, I dumped everything out of the blue gym bag Tori had taken from Stanley Keane's office upstairs. My initial optimism quickly dimmed as I pored over Stanley's telephone and cable bills, a letter from his health care provider, a summary of year-end payroll for his company, and a notice from Publishers Clearing House informing him that he may have just won a million dollars.

But before I got to a second makeshift pile that appeared to contain similarly irrelevant stuff, my heart did a flutter. Among the pile was a pocket-sized map of the city's downtown.

I unfolded it and spread it out on the table. It was limited to the commercial district, bordered to the west by the north-south bend of the river and to the east by the lake, covering twelve city blocks with the east-west leg of the river cutting it roughly in half.

I saw markings in red pen. There was a red X near the southern boundary of the district, by the Hartz Building at South Walter Drive. Next to it was the handwritten number 12. Then a red marker traveled north along South Walter to River Drive, then across the Lerner Street Bridge, and stopped at the federal building. There was an X placed at the federal building, as well as another X two blocks away at the state building. Next to both the state and federal buildings was the number 1.

'This is it,' I said to Tori, who was seated on the bed next to me now. 'They're going to blow up the Hartz Building and the state and federal buildings downtown.'

'The Hartz Building?' Tori said. 'What's that? Who's in there?'

'No idea. I know a couple of law firms there.' I traced the route with my finger. 'Assuming twelve and one are times, they're going to hit the Hartz Building at noon – or midnight – and then hit the government buildings an hour later.'

That seemed odd. I'd never planned a bombing before, so admittedly I had little on which to base this, but I didn't see why a multiple-strike attack wouldn't occur simultaneously.

'The question is when,' said Tori. 'Tomorrow, a month from now, when?'

That wasn't the only question. But neither of us knew. And Stanley Keane was no longer available for our questions. Had we handled things differently at his house, we might have had time to review this map and then ask him about it.

But that was over now. No sense relitigating that battle.

'I'm calling the FBI,' I said.

I looked around and found my cell phone. As I reached for it, it began to buzz. I hate it when that happens.

But maybe not this time. The caller ID said it was Wendy Kotowski, my opposing counsel.

'Tomorrow morning, nine A.M.,' Wendy said to me. 'The M.E.'s office. You're one minute late and I lock the door.'

85

Wendy Kotowski, Detective Frank Danilo, and I huddled around a table in the office of the chief deputy medical examiner for the county, Dr Mitra Agarwal.

'These,' said the doctor, 'are photos of a man who hanged himself three weeks ago in a mental institution.' She pointed to the bruising on the decedent's neck, which angled downward from each side of the neck to a point at the center of his throat.

'The force of gravity from the fall off the platform – this decedent jumped off a ladder – causes the ligature mark to form this V shape,' said the doctor. 'His neck wasn't broken. A hanging almost never results in a broken neck, certainly not from a fall of six feet or less. This decedent suffered no hemorrhaging in the strap muscles of the neck, which is consistent with a suicide. And here.' She showed another set of photos. 'You see no ancillary bruising near or surrounding the ligature marks that would indicate any kind of a struggle. Not cuts or abrasions.

'This,' she concluded, 'is a classic suicide by hanging.'

Okay. Fair enough. Now, I assumed, we were going to talk about our favorite dead lawyer, Bruce McCabe.

'And here are photographs of the decedent under examination, Mr . . . McCabe.'

She dropped down two photographs, from slightly different angles, of Bruce McCabe's neck and shoulder. My heart did a leap.

'Note the ligature marks are a straight line across his throat,' she said. 'In addition, the decedent suffered a broken neck. And we found internal hemorrhaging into the sternohyoid and thyrohyoid – the strap muscles of the neck.'

She threw down two more photos.

'And finally,' she said, 'you see some other bruising and cuts near and around the ligature marks, including some on the chin and cheek. Evidence of struggle. He was desperately grabbing for the rope around his neck.'

I looked at Wendy, then at the doctor.

'Bruce McCabe didn't commit suicide,' I said.

'Bruce McCabe was strangled from behind.' The doctor nodded. 'He was dead long before they strung him up and hanged him.'

'Oh, come on, Wendy,' I said outside the M.E.'s office. It was a rare December day that the sun was out. A little snow had fallen last night, and it lit up under the sunlight. 'The lawyer who tried to cover up what Kathy Rubinkowski was uncovering shows up dead just as I'm sniffing around? These guys are covering their tracks, circling their wagons.'

Wendy stood with her arms crossed and made sure I was finished before she answered.

'You've had this information for a while, Jason. You never said anything, wanting to maximize the element of surprise

– but now, *now* you spring it on me and expect me to immediately embrace it? To lap it up like a dog?'

I shook my head. 'I expect you to carefully consider it,' I said. 'I expect you to evaluate it and realize that your cops may have rushed to judgment on my client. I'm not asking you to drop the charges, Wendy. I'm saying take a damn breath. Let's suspend the trial or go in together and ask for a mistrial without prejudice. You have more than a good-faith basis to believe that you're prosecuting an innocent person. I'll have to go back and re-read the Constitution, but I think that's something you're not supposed to do.'

She shook her head. 'If you'd given me the information sooner, I might have been able to process it, to investigate it. I would have done that, Jason. But you decided to hold this back and spring it—'

'You know damn well that if I brought my evidence to Nash before it was in solid shape, he would have bounced it in a nanosecond. With you cheering him on,' I added. 'I couldn't introduce this until I had more than speculation. I would've preferred to wait a little longer, but you rested your case and it was now or never. Every day I learn more, Wendy, and every day it supports what I'm saying more and more. Look at what you just showed me in there.'

'You're welcome, by the way.'

'Yes, thank you for doing your job, even though we both know if you hadn't, I would have subpoenaed Mitra and let the judge know you refused to help me.'

I probably shouldn't have said that. We both knew it, anyway, but it made more sense to make her feel like she was doing this of her own free will. It enhanced her cooperative spirit, kept her from going into her corner, and me into mine, before we came out duking.

'Look, Wendy. A guy I'm looking at hard for complicity in murders and maybe something worse shows up dead before I can subpoena him to trial. A murder staged to look like a suicide. So we wouldn't see it for what it is – more evidence of a cover-up.'

She knew all of this already. I was just trying to crystallize it for her. It was a guilt trip of the highest order. Here was the knockout punch:

'Doesn't a guy who put his ass on the line for his country, and got totally messed up for doing so – doesn't the government that sent him there at least owe it to him to take a careful look at the evidence before they put him in prison for life?'

'Okay.' She waved him off. 'That's quite enough. You have a theory, I have mine. I still believe that your guy is the doer. You don't. Fine. Let's go to war. If I wasn't ready for trial, I don't think your shoulder would be available to cry on.'

'Our jobs are different, and you know it. You have a higher obligation.'

She pointed a finger at me. 'Don't you ever again tell me what my obligation is, Jason. I'm sick of your preaching. I've got my guy and I've got my case. I'll let the judge decide about continuances or mistrials. I got you access to this information about the autopsy, and now you have it. I've gone over and above. Now do your job, and I'll do mine.'

She walked off in a huff. I'd never seen her so angry. But it was still time well spent. I didn't get what I wanted from her, but I knew she would keep thinking about it. However much I was getting under her skin, she was right – she did know her obligation, and it was higher than winning a case. It was about justice. I still held out hope she'd take my side tomorrow morning.

Speaking of. I looked at my watch. It was high noon on Sunday. We'd be back in court in twenty-one hours.

My cell phone buzzed. It was Joel Lightner.

'I'm at the firm,' he said to me. 'Where the hell are you?'

I sighed. 'Me? I'm at the beauty salon having my eyebrows plucked.'

'Well, get your ass back here, gorgeous,' he said. 'I've got something for you.'

86

I made the twenty-minute drive from the medical examiner's office on the south side to my law firm. I was trying to focus but it was difficult. I was sleep-deprived. Tori and I had been up most of the night poring over the information taken from Stanley Keane's house. I think I dozed off somewhere around dawn this morning. So I was the dictionary definition of tired and wired.

When I reached my law firm, Joel Lightner was waiting for me, looking fresh and eager. He called down to Shauna that I was back, which meant it was time for him to break the exciting news to us together. Bradley John joined in and we all took chairs in the conference room, giving Joel the floor.

'Okay,' he, framing his hands. 'We know that in June of 2009, Global Harvest International purchased the stock of two companies – Summerset Farms and SK Tool and Supply. We also know that Manning went back on plans to take Global Harvest public that same month.'

'Right.'

'So the question was, what happened in June of 2009?'

'Right,' I said again. 'And the answer?'

'The answer,' said Joel, 'is nothing happened in June of 2009.

403

But your enterprising private eye extraordinaire – y'know, the one who couldn't track a bleeding elephant through the snow?'

'I think I apologized for that.'

'But you didn't seem sincere. So anyway, the question is what happened in *May* of 2009?'

'Okay,' I said. 'What happened in *May* of 2009?'

'In May of 2009, Global Harvest International completed a joint partnership with a company called Verimli Toprak, a Turkish company. Southern Turkey, the . . . Çukurova? The Çukurova region in southern Turkey is apparently some of the most agriculturally fertile land in the world. So, big company, globalizing, international partnerships, all that. Right?'

'Right.'

'Okay, then after the deal is cut, and the first shovel goes into the ground and the ribbon-cutting and all that – after that, Randall Manning returns to the United States and leaves his son, Quinn, behind to run the business, the joint venture. Quinn Manning has a wife, Julie, and a daughter, Cailie. Also, Randall Manning's wife, Bethany, stays there, probably just for a while, to hang with the son and the granddaughter, right?'

'Right.'

'The city where they're staying is Adana. Adana, Turkey.' He looked at us.

'Oh, Adana.' A gasp escaped Shauna. 'The . . . what did they call it? The Adana Massacre or something?'

I was a little behind. It rang a bell, but I've had my head up my ass for quite some time now. Some would say a *long* time. Others would say always. 'Help me out, someone,' I said.

Joel was glad to oblige, proud of his investigative work. 'The first week of May 2009, there's some kind of European soccer tournament in Adana's main stadium. French, Spanish,

Italians, Germans – all kinds of foreigners flooding to Adana for the tournament. That brings us to May sixth, 2009.

'May sixth, 2009, the Brotherhood of Jihad terrorist group attacks the Sahmeran Adana Hotel. A truck loaded with explosives drives up to the steps of the hotel and detonates. It rocks the building and destabilizes it. A lot of people die inside. But some don't. Some manage to escape. And – you remember this now? The terrorists are waiting for them outside. They open fire on people trying to escape. They pick them off like it's a video game. And they have machetes, too. They behead some of them. I mean, it's fucking medieval.'

'Jesus,' I said.

'More like Allah.' Joel nodded. 'Manning's wife, son, daughter-in-law, and only grandchild are staying there. They all die. Randall Manning's whole family dies.'

Holy shit. I knew something about losing a wife and daughter. But I had nobody else to blame, except maybe myself.

'Bruce McCabe,' said Joel. 'McCabe's wife worked in international sales for Global Harvest,' he said. 'She was only in Adana temporarily. She died, too.'

'Wow,' said Shauna.

'And Stanley Keane?' I asked.

Joel nodded gravely. 'His son was some big high school soccer star. He caught on with a Belgium team that was playing in Adana that week. I can't tell if he was staying at the hotel, but I know he was in the hotel that day. He died, too. And so did his mother, Stanley's wife.'

Unbelievable. That explained Stanley's mumblings about how he was sorry he wasn't there, how much he missed his family. His wife and son, blown up in a building by Islamic terrorists.

405

'Over three hundred people died that day,' said Joel. 'Seventeen were American.'

'So it wasn't viewed so much as an attack on America.'

'Right. Most of the victims were European. Americans died, but this was an attack on the infidels, the nonbelievers,' said Joel. 'Nonbelievers invading their soil.'

Shauna threw up her hands. 'So there's the connection.'

'The connection is that they're pissed off at our government,' said Joel. He shook his hand, which held the remote for the television and DVD player in our conference room.

He hit Play and the television came to life. 'This was very hard to find,' he said.

It took me a moment, but it was Randall Manning, standing before a bank of microphones. He was dressed down and his hair was uncharacteristically messy. His face was contorted in anger.

'Why isn't our government invading this country?' he said. 'Why aren't we going after the headquarters of the Brotherhood of Jihad? When Al Qaeda bombed the twin towers, we invaded Afghanistan and hit them where they live. Why not now? We know the Brotherhood of Jihad is in the Sudan, we know it's in Yemen, and we know it's here in Turkey. What are we waiting for?

'Three thousand casualties is unacceptable, but seventeen is okay? What amount of American lives is an acceptable level of casualties before this administration will act? I know we're all very heartened that the administration is "gravely concerned" and "investigating diligently." But where is the justice?' He looked around at what I assumed were gathering reporters. 'Where is our government when the citizens need it most?'

The picture disappeared and the television went black.

Nobody spoke. A part of me agreed with the guy. These guys are attacking us, go attack them.

'So he's not real happy with our government,' said Lightner. 'He organized an online petition and got over a million people to sign it and urge the president to bomb Brotherhood of Jihad facilities in Yemen, Sudan, and Turkey.'

'It's not that simple,' said Shauna.

Maybe not, but that wouldn't assuage Randall Manning.

'He's going to replicate it,' I said. 'He's got explosives and assault weapons. He's going to bomb those buildings and shoot anyone who tries to flee.'

87

Randall Manning always closed his eyes when it came to mind, as if that would shut out the imagery. He recoiled from it but pursued it at the same time. He'd promised himself he'd never forget.

The Brotherhood of Jihad had posted the video following the attack at the Sahmeran Adana Hotel. Someone had had the sense to take it down shortly thereafter, but Manning had a copy. He didn't play it every day. Only once in a while. Like when he was having any second thoughts, any residual doubt, about what he was going to do.

Like today, when he got this text message on his prepaid cell phone: *The FBI was looking for you this morning.*

He had to admit it had crossed his mind to abort the plan. He was only human. Bruce McCabe had harbored similar thoughts. But the feeling had been fleeting. All Manning had to do was hit Play on the computer and watch that video for five seconds.

Chunks of the building falling to the ground. The torso of the building buckling as it struggled to remain standing. Innocent people jumping from windows or scrambling out from the lobby. Terrorists shooting at them, chasing them with machetes, which they swung without mercy, without regard to man, woman, or child.

He remembered the bodies coming back from Turkey on a military plane. He remembered the inconceivable sense of loss. He remembered asking the funeral director, an old family friend, if it was possible to reattach his son Quinn's head to his body for the visitation, and bursting into tears when the answer was no.

He remembered the image of Jawhar Al-Asmari, the leader of the Brotherhood of Jihad, speaking into the camera, a white mural behind him, hiding like a coward from an undisclosed location, praising the attack on the Sahmeran Adana Hotel and vowing more of the same.

He remembered a president with nothing but words. Diplomacy and justice didn't belong in the same sentence.

He remembered the runaround from the Department of State, a lot of political doubletalk about a complicated menagerie of interests and considerations in the Middle East.

He remembered how desperately he wanted the head of Jawhar Al-Asmari, and how desperately he wanted his government to want the same thing.

He remembered promising his wife, Bethany, his son, Quinn, his daughter-in-law, and their only granddaughter – he remembered promising them, as he stood over their dead bodies, that he would never forget.

He'd met Bruce McCabe and Stanley Keane on the military plane on the way to Turkey. They lived close enough together that they shared the same government transport. They were all shell-shocked, wounded and numb and completely at a loss. They spoke then in only general concepts – this can't go unanswered, our government has to respond, someone has to pay.

They'd traded phone numbers and agreed to keep in touch.

It didn't have to come to this. But the goddamn government was so sensitive about anything concerning Islam, more concerned about the rippling effects of international action, than they were about making it clear what happened to you if you killed Americans. The president didn't face much political pressure at home on this. It didn't happen in America, it wasn't aimed at Americans, and few American casualties resulted. Seventeen Americans, in the scheme of things? Not a big deal. Shake your head, make an off-color remark about Muslims, and flip over to the latest reality television show.

He remembered his old fraternity brother from the Ivy League days, now a defense contractor with good ties to the CIA, who put Manning together with someone who could help. He remembered the agent who agreed to give him the straight scoop – for a fee, of course. Costigan was his name, a man with loads of information and twin girls who wanted the same expensive Ivy League education Randall Manning had received.

He remembered what Costigan had told him, two weeks later. He'd always remember every single word that Costigan told him.

He remembered several weeks after the bombing, calling Bruce McCabe and Stanley Keane. Manning was firmly committed to the idea, but he danced around it initially with the two of them. He didn't know if they'd go along, if they'd need some coercing, or if they'd simply say no. He wasn't sure what he would have done if they'd said no outright.

But they didn't. They said yes.

Manning always described it to them as something they could pull off without detection. A large, international company like GHI and a smaller industrial supply company like SK could separately sell bomb components to a front company, a farm, that could justify purchases of both fertilizer and nitromethane for pesticide. Nobody would be expecting it. And nobody would suspect it afterward, if the bombings were carried out correctly. The trucks could be rented in a way that didn't lead back to them; the bomb components wouldn't be traceable; and the individuals actually carrying out the attacks wouldn't survive and wouldn't be traceable back to them, in any event.

But the truth was, Manning never really believed he'd get away with this. The federal government had ways he couldn't fathom of gathering evidence and chasing down leads. They would catch him. But maybe not Stanley, a small-business owner who would be guilty of nothing more than selling a legal product to a farm. And maybe not Bruce McCabe, guilty of nothing more than practicing law, working the financial deals that allowed GHI to purchase Summerset Farms and Stanley's company.

Manning had to cancel the public offering of GHI, naturally. The things he was going to do, he couldn't be answering to a board of directors and shareholders. No, he'd have to keep the company private, so he was the one and only boss, free to do whatever he pleased with the company. Like selling an inordinate amount of ammonium nitrate fertilizer to a small farming company. Like keeping people such as Patrick Cahill in a job, so he had the right people watching the gates and driving the trucks.

He thought the hardest part would be finding recruits, people who detested the government and were willing to take up arms against it and risk their lives in the process. He was surprised to learn that this was the easiest part.

Tuesday, December 7, was the ideal date. The symbolism was perfect, and it gave them sufficient time to stockpile materials for this attack and future ones, and to recruit and train the soldiers.

Manning stretched his nervous limbs and sat down on the bed. He looked at his prepaid cell phone again, an untraceable phone he'd purchased at a convenience store two days ago with a package of two hundred minutes. The FBI had come calling today. They didn't search the place. They just came by to chat.

So they'd gotten wind of things, probably from Jason Kolarich, but it didn't sound like they were close.

Not close enough. Not soon enough.

The attack was less than forty-eight hours away.

88

After Joel Lightner's briefing, he and I spent the next several hours with Lee Tucker of the FBI. This time, Lee Tucker wasn't wearing a patronizing smirk. I'd made some headway with him, and the information Joel and I gave him now only solidified our position.

Not that Lee gave up a single damn thing in return. He didn't confirm or deny anything. He gave no indication whether my information was news to him or stuff he already knew. I couldn't tell if he put the threat risk at low, medium, or high, or the imminence of that threat as near or far.

From his viewpoint, which he revealed drip by drip through various comments, I had a circumstantial case against Global Harvest at best. None of the sales of fertilizer or nitromethane were illegal. In fact, they were openly disclosed to the authorities. I claimed the quantities were underreported, but I had no proof of that. And my theories on how Kathy Rubinkowski and Bruce McCabe died were just that – theories. Yes, it helped my cause that two people from GHI's law firm had been murdered, and it helped that white Aryan supremacists named Patrick Cahill and Ernie Dwyer, in custody on federal gun charges, worked private security for GHI. But at the end of the day, all of my arguments were colored by the fact that I lacked a smoking gun, and I was a defense lawyer desperate to use these facts to exonerate his client.

'So this map came from Stanley Keane's house,' said Lee Tucker. 'And you take these X marks to be bombing targets.'

'Don't you?' I replied.

'And Stanley Keane is in the hospital right now with multiple broken bones, recovering from shock.'

I nodded. 'In his rush to hand me the map, he fell down the stairs.'

Tucker didn't even smirk. 'He'll tell that story the same way?'

'Lee, are we here to discuss whether I assaulted this asshole, or are we here to discuss whether he plans to detonate bombs in our city someday soon?'

Tucker thought for a long while, perused his notes, and then gave a presumptive nod. 'Okay, Kolarich, I got it,' he said.

Okay, he got it. He wasn't going to give me anything more. But I'd done my duty. Again.

Joel and I got back to the law firm at four. Shauna was in her office, busily typing. Tomorrow morning, we were going to present Judge Nash with a written motion outlining all of the evidence we had uncovered and why it merited either a mistrial or a delay. If Judge Nash denied it, I was going to file an emergency motion in the state supreme court, which has supervisory powers over every court, every case, and ask them to halt the proceedings based on this emergency development. I would make sure that Judge Nash knew of my plan B. My best chance was that, with the specter of the state's highest court looming over him and the stakes being so high, the old codger would at least grant me a small delay in the trial. Most judges would. Then again, *Judge Nash ain't most judges*.

Regardless, this written submission had to be spot-on. I needed the best written product I could muster, and that meant Shauna. She knew this stuff, but she had been focusing on forensics, so I wanted Joel Lightner around this as well. I called Tori in, too, because she'd seen much of this up close. We would need a sparkling brief and affidavits as well, supporting our factual contentions.

'Okay, do your magic,' I said to Shauna. 'And Lightner, behave yourself around these two beautiful women.'

'Yeah?' he said. 'And where the hell are *you* going?'

I stretched my arms. 'I'm going to prepare my closing argument,' I said. 'In case Judge Nash tells us to go fly a kite.'

89

I worked on two things for the remainder of the night and well into the morning: my argument on why Judge Nash should let us reopen this entire case and investigate my new evidence, and, in the event he shut us down, my closing argument to the jury on why the prosecution hadn't proven its case against First Lieutenant Thomas Stoller.

I finally cried uncle at three in the morning. Tori, who had stayed with me at the firm and even listened to my summation a couple of times, accompanied me to my hotel room.

My hotel room was a piece of shit, but I could see part of the city's north and east side where most of the young people lived, where most of the socializing took place.

Even now, at half past three in the morning. Some of these places had four A.M. liquor licenses. I remember that time, before I was married, when you didn't get started before midnight, when four A.M. meant you were done drinking and it was time to find an all-night diner or some burrito joint.

'You've done your part and then some,' Tori said to me, sitting on the bed. She was wearing a gray T-shirt and nothing else. Under any other circumstances, I would be powerless to resist. I'd be jumping on the bed.

'Maybe, maybe not. If I hadn't been so consumed with Gin Rummy, I would have had Lightner investigating Randall Manning earlier on. All this stuff that happened with him and his family – and Stanley Keane's and Bruce McCabe's families? The Brotherhood of Jihad shit? If I'd known that weeks ago, we could've made more of it.'

'You were playing catch-up all along,' she said. 'You thought this was a simple insanity case. You said so yourself. When it was handed to you, you were told it was a simple case. I mean, Jason, the guys who had this case before you – they didn't come up with any of this, did they? You should be proud of what you've uncovered in such a short amount of time.'

Down on the street, a couple blocks away, a man wearing several layers of clothing was staggering across an intersection. He looked drunk. He looked homeless.

This all started with Tom, and my promise to Deidre Maley that I would do everything I could for her nephew.

Tori climbed off the bed and came to me. She put her arms around me and wrapped her warm body against mine. We stood like that forever. I rested my head on hers and looked out over this city where I grew up, where I lived, and where I would die.

'What if we just left?' she whispered to me. 'When this is over, I mean. We could leave. I have money saved up from an inheritance. We could do it, Jason. We could leave this all behind.'

I turned and faced her. I touched her cheek and looked into her eyes, desperately searching mine. 'You'd do that? With me?'

She looked into my eyes and nodded.

'Where would we go?' I asked.

'Anywhere.'

417

Anywhere with me? I had misread her. I knew things were moving forward, but I didn't think she'd traveled this far. Had I?

'Let's get through this first,' I said.

'No, you're right.' There was an imperceptible nod of her head. It made sense. We both knew that. I had no idea how this would end. And I had no idea what would remain of me when it did.

90

I arrived at the criminal courts building early the next morning. I walked through the lobby, flashed my bar card to the deputy, took the elevator up to the seventeenth floor, walked into the courtroom, and sat down. Shauna showed up a half-hour before court. Wendy Kotowski and the prosecution team weren't far behind. 'Got your brief,' she said to me, holding it up. 'Half an hour ago,' she added, an octave lower. 'Not exactly advance notice, Counselor.'

I nodded at her. 'You gonna do the right thing today, Wen?'

'I always do the right thing,' she said, without looking up from her document.

Aunt Deidre came in just then. I conferred with her briefly, giving her little but platitudes, a pep talk. The truth, that I hated to confront, was that the judge would have a reasonable basis to deny everything I was trying to do here.

They brought in Tom at a quarter to nine. He looked a bit disheveled this morning, which seemed appropriate to his state of mind. I leaned into him and asked, 'How were the eggs this morning, Tom?'

He actually smiled for a moment, which I took as a good omen. 'Terrible,' he answered.

At five minutes to nine, the court bailiff, an old guy named Warren Olive, stuck his head into the courtroom and looked around. 'You all here on *Stoller*?'

'We are,' I said for everyone.

'Judge wants to hear this in chambers,' Warren said.

That wasn't surprising. We all trudged back to the judge's chambers. Judge Nash, having outlived every other human being on the planet, had photographs and memorabilia dating back more than seventy years. The walls of his chambers were lined with framed photos with every mayor going back as far as I can remember, a few presidential candidates on the Democratic side – I remember him mentioning he was a delegate to one of the conventions, maybe the one where they nominated Lincoln? – and all kinds of other politicos and celebrities. He received honors from all sorts of bar associations and civic groups and we got to read all about it. It looked like the inside of an old Italian restaurant in here.

Judge Nash resumed his seat in a high-backed leather chair, behind a walnut desk. Directly over his head on the wall was a flag of the United States and his certificate of honorable discharge from the U.S. Marine Corps in the 1950s after he fought in the Korean War.

Judge Nash waited for the court reporter to ready herself. When she gave him the high sign, he turned on me.

'Mr Kolarich, I've had a chance to read your lengthy submission this morning, having just *received* it this morning. You've apparently raised issues that go beyond even what you discussed with the court last Friday.'

'That's correct, Judge. We continue to learn new information. It proves more than anything that we need time to develop this evidence. When you consider—'

'Counsel, if this evidence were even remotely related to your theory of the case, I might be more sympathetic. But none of this has anything to do with your case. You're off on a story about terrorists and cover-ups. The prosecution can rightly assert that this is coming out of the blue.'

'It's newly discovered evidence,' I replied. 'As soon as we learned it, we told the prosecution.'

The judge removed his glasses and wiped them with a handkerchief. 'If I let every litigant create a brand-new case on the eve of trial—'

'This isn't every litigant,' I said, interrupting the judge. 'This isn't every case.'

He let my interruption go without comment, which was an even worse sign, because it meant he was definitely planning to rule against me and was cutting me some slack.

'Judge, I realize that the lawyer before me pleaded insanity and I was planning to do the same. But we've come up with evidence that goes well beyond a wild-goose chase. If you give me a week, I'll probably be able to prove everything I'm alleging. Just give me a week.'

'No, Counsel. If you come up with something in a week or a month or a year, you can bring a post-trial petition. But we're not stopping this trial.'

'Judge—'

'We're done. I'll give you until tomorrow, Mr. Kolarich, to call a witness or we'll just go to summations. All right, everyone? December seventh, nine A.M., Ms. Kotowski, I'll expect you to be prepared to close first thing in the morning if the defense rests.'

I shook my head and looked at Shauna. We both knew this was a possible outcome. The judge was wrong, but he wasn't going to change his mind. I stood up and stared at Judge Nash, who was already reviewing other papers on another case. I looked over his head again at the certificate of honorable discharge from the Marines. Next to that certificate was a photo of the judge in military attire, shaking hands with our city's mayor, Mayor Champion, himself a former Marine who never missed a chance to honor the military, who even held parades and memorials on anniversaries that other cities and states had long ago stopped celebrating, like D-day and . . .

Oh my God.

And Pearl Harbor Day.

'Judge,' I said, 'I understand your ruling, but could I ask for an additional twenty-four hours? If I could just have until Wednesday.'

The judge's face scrunched up the way it always did when he was annoyed by something.

'Counsel—'

'Just one more day, Your Honor. That's all I ask. I won't request any additional time.'

The judge looked at Wendy, but he wasn't seeking her guidance. He was probably thinking, after the different ways he'd screwed me, it would look good to the appellate court that he gave me that extra day when I asked.

'Good enough,' he said. 'Wednesday, December eighth, at nine A.M. We *will* reconvene at that time, and there will be no further continuances.'

With that, the judge ordered us out of chambers. It had been a bad appearance for our case but adrenaline was surging through me regardless. I had tomorrow open. And something told me I'd need it.

Because tomorrow was December 7. Tomorrow was Pearl Harbor Day.

91

'Kolarich, calm down,' said Lee Tucker over the phone.

'Did you hear what I said, Lee? Tomorrow is—'

'I got it, I got it. Listen, we need to meet.'

We worked out the details and I hung up. I conferred in the courtroom with Tom and Aunt Deidre and then spent some time huddling with Shauna on a game plan.

'Listen to me, lady,' I said, placing a hand firmly on her shoulder. 'You and everyone else at the law firm – nobody goes into work tomorrow. Stay away from downtown. No fooling. Okay?'

'God, it's that certain in your mind?' She recoiled. 'I mean, if that's the case, shouldn't we be screaming from the mountaintops about a potential attack?'

'It's not that certain. It's just my gut. But yeah, I'll be making that point to the FBI in a few minutes.' I shrugged. 'It's not my call, kid. I can't evacuate a city. But humor me on this, okay? Promise me, Shauna Tasker.'

'Okay, I promise. A firm holiday tomorrow. But only if you promise me that *you'll* stay away, too.'

'I'll be safe,' I assured her, and took off before she could press me further.

*

Lee Tucker's government-issue sedan picked me up curbside not ten minutes later. I jumped in the backseat.

'Jason Kolarich, Special Agent Barry Clemens.' Lee, who was driving, gestured to a tall African-American guy who looked like he kept in shape, who shared the backseat with me. 'And this is Dan Osborne from the Department of Justice's counter-terrorism division.' Osborne rode shotgun, an older guy with red hair cut to a crew. *Government* written all over these guys.

'That information I gave you checked out,' I said.

Osborne nodded. 'It checked out.'

'Tomorrow's Pearl Harbor Day,' I said. 'Tomorrow's when it happens.'

Lee looked at Osborne, then at me through his rearview mirror. 'Listen and listen good, Kolarich. All right? We're giving you the benefit of the doubt on this. And it's not because we think you're a great guy or the straightest shooter. It's because these days, we can't afford not to. Know what I mean?'

'I do.'

'And if you're onto something here about these guys, then you know them better than we do. But what we share with you stays between us. Agreed?'

'Agreed,' I said. I didn't know if I'd be able to keep that promise. I had a client whose defense might be aided rather significantly by what I might learn. A bridge to cross later, if necessary.

'You fuck us on this—'

'I'm not fucking around, Lee. I get it.'

He watched me a moment, then nodded. 'Tomorrow's Pearl Harbor Day,' he said. 'And I didn't even know this, but apparently our city celebrates it every year with a parade.'

'It's Mayor Champion,' I said. 'He's big on that stuff. He was a

Marine. His kid's a Marine. His father, and his father's father, were Marines. We do a parade every year. A small one, a short one, but still. He always gets the governor to come march in it, too. Oh, and shit.' I snapped my fingers. 'They start it at the southern tip of downtown. Which means it starts at—'

'The Hartz Building,' said Lee. 'At noon. And guess where it ends?'

'Either the state or federal building at one o'clock,' I said.

'Close enough. One o'clock is probably a safe estimate. The procession should get there earlier. But even if it does, there's a brief outdoor memorial in the federal plaza following the march. There will be probably a hundred people in the plaza. Who knows, could be five hundred. Could be thousands.'

We were driving now, presumably toward that very federal building. A helicopter flew overhead. I wondered if it had anything to do with this.

'So I take it the governor's coming again this year?' I asked.

'Like always, yeah.' Lee paused. 'Governor Trotter, Mayor Champion, and Senator Donsbrook are going to be there.' He looked back at me.

'They should cancel the whole memorial,' I said. 'You guys should evacuate the entire downtown.'

Osborne reacted with a bitter sniff. 'If we reacted that way based on the level of information you've provided us, do you know how often we'd evacuate the downtown?'

It seemed like a rhetorical question. 'A lot?' I said.

'A lot. Our citizens would live in constant fear. Commerce would shut down. Our economy would collapse.'

A little heavy on the drama, but I took his point. That was his job, to do the worrying for the rest of us. I didn't envy him.

Clearly, these guys had taken me more seriously than I'd

425

realized, but still – something new must have developed to make them think I was onto something. They had developed more information. 'What happened that made you guys suddenly believe me?' I asked.

A pause followed. I assumed there was rank within the car, and Osborne had it, so it was his call. 'We don't work on "believe" so much as credibility of evidence,' he said. 'But you're right. We just recently learned that three You-Ride truck rentals were made, from three separate locations, all charged to the same bogus credit card, over a week ago. We've reviewed security cameras in the stores and it was all the same guy.' He showed me a grainy black-and-white photo of a stocky guy in a flannel and blue jeans, wearing a baseball cap and a silly-looking beard. ZZ Top at a Cubs game. But I recognized the face.

'Bruce McCabe,' I said. Randall Manning's attorney, recently departed.

Osborne nodded.

McCabe rented three trucks. Carriers for bombs. 'Have you located them?'

'No. Any thoughts? Anything from what you've learned that would give you an idea where they might be?'

'Nothing off the top of my head. Except that they'd probably be parked in three separate locations.'

'Probably,' said Agent Clemens.

'And why the Hartz Building first?' I asked. 'Then two separate bombings of government buildings an hour later? It doesn't make sense. If a building went down in the commercial district, wouldn't you guys immediately barricade all government buildings?'

'Sure we would,' said Clemens. 'But does Randall Manning know that?'

'Sometimes with these radicals, logic doesn't play into it,' Osborne said. 'Or it's logical to them, but not to us.'

That was comforting.

'I would probably want the trucks close by,' I said. 'Maybe already parked here in the city. Or someplace close. If I were you, I'd search every place a You-Ride truck could be parked right now. Parking garages, alleys, whatever.'

Osborne looked back at me. He didn't seem impressed with my suggestion. I figured that was because he was already doing that very thing.

Everyone went quiet for a while.

'What about those two guys – Patrick Cahill and Ernie Dwyer? I mean, those guys probably know everything.'

Osborne was shaking his head before I finished my sentence. 'We haven't been able to crack them. Those boys are hard-core. We don't know if there's an operation at all, of course. And if there is, I'm not sure they would have operational knowledge. If everything you believe about Randall Manning is true, then he has managed to prepare this entire attack without drawing our attention. It means he's meticulous. It wouldn't shock me if the soldiers didn't *know* the details.'

We reached the federal building – known derisively by the criminal element as the 'brown building' – and drove down the ramp leading underground. I could already see a heightened presence at the perimeter of the building.

'Put on your thinking cap, Jason,' said Lee. 'It's all hands on deck. We need all the help we can get.'

92

The federal agents and I went to the fifteenth floor of the federal building, which appeared to be Command Central. I'm not usually the nosy sort, and this wasn't a tour – they were walking me along one wall and taking me into a conference room – but I snuck a few peeks around me. There were projection screens showing satellite coverage of what I assumed to be the city's downtown and near north. Agents were tapping on computer keyboards and reviewing all sorts of information and speaking into headsets.

I really didn't have a sense of the scope of this operation. What Osborne had said to me in the car rang true – they reviewed threats or potential threats all the time, on a daily basis, around the clock. Where did this one fall in the spectrum?

Inside the conference room, there were documents lying on a long table. There were dossiers on Randall Manning, Stanley Keane, Bruce McCabe, Patrick Cahill, and Ernie Dwyer. There were photographs of Summerset Farms that looked awfully familiar, as well as shots of Global Harvest International.

There were photographs of a standard You-Ride rental truck, too. It was a yellow truck with a front cabin and then a large cargo area behind. Not the longest model – not quite the size of truck you'd rent to move out of your house – but not the shortest, either. I was no expert, but there had to be plenty of room in that cabin to transport a bomb.

'Stay in here and let us know if anything occurs to you,' said Osborne. 'We'll be in and out ourselves. We'll have questions, you might have an idea. That kind of thing. Remember, the key is trying to figure out the location of those three trucks. The best outcome is that we stop them before they get anywhere near their targets.'

'I'm impressed,' I said. 'Usually you feds think you're so smart, you don't need any help.'

He stared at me for a moment, then smiled. 'True enough, Kolarich. But if you're right and something's about to go down, then we're way, way behind these guys. We've only had a couple of days, and they've probably had a year. I'll take all the smart minds I can get.' He nodded at me. 'And you can help, too.'

A nice parting jab. I spent the next two hours reviewing everything I could get my hands on. To their credit, the feds had done a pretty thorough job, on very short time, of trying to put together information on Manning and GHI and all of this. It was probably a good thing that Lee Tucker and I had some history and that, no matter what he may have thought of me on a personal level, I had established some credibility with him. From my circumstantial ruminations, they had managed to do a lot of digging in short order.

I was in a windowless room and time seemed to be a fleeting concept, which was interesting given the ticking clock with which we were working. My watch, and stomach, told me it was approaching dinnertime.

My cell phone buzzed. I didn't recognize the number, so I didn't answer. But I listened to the voice-mail message. It was Dr Baraniq, our expert, in his clipped, precise manner, wondering what the time frame might be for his testimony this week in the Stoller trial.

I'd forgotten to call him and give him the news that there wouldn't *be* any testimony. It brought me back momentarily from a terrorist plot to Tom's case, a case I felt, deep down, that I had botched. I'd been arrogant. I'd overplayed my hand.

I called Shauna to check in. I told her what I could but explained that I was being sworn to silence for now.

'So there's not going to be an evacuation or anything?'

I sighed. 'I don't know. I don't think even they've decided one way or another. I mean, we've put together some facts that look ominous, but the truth is, they don't know if this is going to happen tomorrow or if it's going to happen at all. And think what our country would be like if every time they heard some scary chatter, a major metropolitan center just ground to a halt? Think about Al Qaeda or the Brotherhood of Jihad, or homegrown lunatics. They'd set up hoaxes and watch us go crazy chasing our tails, evacuating cities and destroying our way of life. It would be death by a thousand cuts. They'd win without ever killing a single person.'

Shauna was quiet for a long time. 'Sounds like they've indoctrinated you.'

'I can see their point of view. Me, I think it's happening tomorrow. I think Manning is timing this so that he attacks our government on the anniversary of what was, for a long time, the single worst attack on American soil.'

'You'd think they would've chosen September eleventh.'

That was a good point. I wondered why they didn't. Maybe

430

because security was too high on that day? The government was far less likely to expect an attack on Pearl Harbor Day.

'Anyway,' I said, 'promise me, kiddo. Nobody goes near downtown tomorrow.'

'I promise,' she said.

I walked over to the doorway of my windowless room and looked out. Dozens of dedicated agents were trying their best to separate threats from hoaxes, imminent from distant, likely from unlikely. They were trying to locate three You-Ride rental trucks, rigged with deadly explosives, within a metropolitan population of three million people. They were flailing, grappling in the dark for something, anything.

And so was I. I'd gone through most of the documents on the table, trying to stir a thought or memory, to no avail. The only truth I knew, at this moment, was turning my stomach into a battleground, filling my chest with a poisonous dread.

We had no idea where those three trucks were located.

Lee Tucker walked into my conference room at eleven o'clock that evening. Agents had been in and out of this room over the last several hours, asking questions and throwing out ideas. I had tossed out some of my own. But I could tell, as the night wore on, that nothing I could come up with was getting us anywhere.

Lee looked over a half-eaten pizza and considered a slice. 'I should have taken this more seriously from the first time you talked to me,' he said.

I didn't reply. He was right. But these guys had a tough job, sorting through all this shit constantly.

'Well, it's over,' he told me. 'We're done looking. We've satisfied ourselves that there is no truck containing bomb material within the commercial district. Not on the streets, not in parking garages or parking lots. We've gone block by block.'

'What about private residences?'

He shrugged. 'There aren't many of those with garages that could hold one of those You-Ride trucks. They're ten feet tall. But anyway, anything we came across, we checked. We knocked on doors and got permission or sometimes didn't wait for permission.' He shook his head. 'If these truck bombs really exist—'

'They do.'

'. . . then they aren't down here yet.'

That was good news, at least. 'So, why don't you extend your search outward?' I asked. 'Go a mile or two beyond the commercial district and near north?'

'Because it would never end,' said Lee. 'Because at some point, you have to focus your resources elsewhere.'

'Like where?'

'Like on prevention,' said Lee. 'We know the trucks aren't down here yet. Now we have to make sure they don't *get* down here. We have to stop them before they hit their targets.'

Lee rubbed his eyes, which were already bloodshot and hooded.

Then he looked at his watch. 'Twelve hours from now,' he said, 'that procession begins.'

93

Randall Manning set up the framed photos of his family on the dashboard of the You-Ride truck. It was poorly lit inside this garage but he could still see them clearly. The photos were just physical manifestations, anyway. His wife and son, his daughter-in-law and granddaughter, were burned into his memory.

Would his wife approve of what he was doing? Would Quinn? He didn't know. He didn't kid himself that everybody would side with him. But his resolve wouldn't be shaken. This was no time for forgive-and-forget. His government had turned its back on the victims of the Sahmeran Adana, and he could never forgive that.

Nor could he ever forget. He'd never forget the words that changed everything, the words delivered by his CIA mole, Costigan, the balding, weathered agent who would use the hundred thousand dollars Manning paid him in cash to educate his twin daughters.

We found him. We found Jawhar.

A thrill had run up Manning's spine. The U.S. had found Jawhar Al-Asmari, the supreme leader of the Brotherhood of Jihad, the man behind the attack on the Sahmeran Adana Hotel.

Where? Manning asked.

Costigan spoke so low as to qualify as a whisper, even though nobody could possibly hear them in Manning's car in the parking garage.

I can't reveal that, Costigan said.

That response had surprised Manning, given the sum he'd paid for inside information. *So what's going to happen? When do we go in and get him?*

Costigan's eyes diverted.

Manning repeated the question.

Costigan cleared his throat. *The country where we found him – it's a potential strategic ally we've been courting for a long time. A country we've been trying to pry away from Iran, from Russia and China. We need all the allies we can find in that region—*

What are you telling me? Manning interrupted.

Costigan took a moment. *I'm telling you that the attack on the Sahmeran Adana is not viewed as an attack on America. I'm telling you that if we go in and raid that compound in that particular country, we lose that country forever.*

Manning was speechless. The man who had ordered the murder of hundreds of innocent people, including seventeen Americans – and Manning's entire family – was going to walk away scot-free?

The president just said last week that we're still hunting Al-Asmari, said Manning. *So that was all bullshit?*

Costigan nodded and sighed. *It was all bullshit. Officially, the manhunt continues. That's the line everyone will recite. Even me. But this comes from the Oval Office, I'm told: Nobody is to breathe a word about the location of Jawhar Al-Asmari, and the U.S. government will do nothing to apprehend him or kill him.*

434

Then tell one of the European countries, Manning protested. *Tell the Brits. The French.*

Costigan shook his head. *The feeling is that it will still bear our fingerprints. We're not even telling our allies about this. I'm sorry, Mr Manning.*

Then tell me, Costigan. Tell me! I've paid you handsomely—

You can have the money back, Mr Manning, if you like. I'm truly sorry. If it were up to me, we'd go get that asshole. But it's already been decided. Jawhar Al-Asmari is getting a pass on this one.

And this – this is what the president wants?

Costigan started and paused. *From what I hear, this was the recommendation from the attorney general. He's part of the brain trust on these things. He has the president's ear. There was disagreement in the room – but the AG's position won out.*

The attorney general? Randall Manning couldn't believe his ears. Langdon Trotter? Lang Trotter had been governor of Manning's state until his elevation to attorney general a couple of years ago. He'd been a law-and-order guy, a tough guy. Hell, Randall Manning had been a fundraiser for Trotter, one of the top money guys for 'Friends of Lang.' They'd smoked cigars and drunk scotch together. Manning had probably raised more than a million dollars for the man. And *this* is what he got in return?

Randall Manning rubbed his eyes and shuddered at the memory. That was the day his country, and an old friend, betrayed him. That was the day he recognized his country for the cowardly multicultural abyss it had become.

Tomorrow would be the first step in taking his country back. The Pearl Harbor Day procession. He wished like hell that U.S. Attorney General Langdon Trotter would be in attendance, part of the anniversary march, like he used to be when he was governor of this state.

He'd have to settle for the state's new governor: Lang's son, Governor Edgar Trotter, who was scheduled to lead the march tomorrow along with Mayor Champion.

After tomorrow, Lang would know how it feels to lose a son to terrorism.

94

The men recited the words from memory, by rote, as they continued their preparations.

'I understand that the cause is greater than the individual. I understand that sacrificing this life for the cause will open up a new and richer life in the hereafter. I understand that the tree of liberty must be refreshed from time to time with the blood of patriots and tyrants. I understand that revolution is not only a right but an obligation. I understand that bigotry and hate cannot be answered with tolerance but with intolerance. I understand that those who take up arms against us cannot be answered with peace but with like arms.'

The men were inside a storage unit, all of fifteen feet high, twelve feet wide, and thirty feet long. No windows, no furnishing, not even a traditional door – just an automated garage door at the front of the unit. The You-Ride truck had been stored here since they cleared it out of the silo at Summerset Farms – a bit earlier than they'd expected, because of that lawyer who Manning always complained about.

But they'd always planned that tonight – the night before the attack – they would stay here, given the proximity to the city. It was cramped and dingy, but it didn't really matter any longer. It was a sacrifice that paled in comparison to the one they'd be making very soon.

'I understand that the cause is greater than the individual. I understand . . .'

One man – Olsen – was performing a mechanical inspection of the You-Ride, checking tire pressure, the battery and engine, looking for anything that could go wrong tomorrow morning. The second man – Briggs – had the job of inspecting the equipment. He insured that the fuses were in proper and working order in the driver's cabin. He confirmed that the protective plastic tubing, covering the fuses as they traveled underneath the driver's cabin and up into the rear cargo area, were still intact. He checked the connection between the fuses and the blasting caps in the cargo area. He made sure that the slack in the plastic tubing was fastened securely against the wall of the cabin, preventing the accidental detachment of the fuses from the blasting caps in transit.

The third member of the three-man team, Roscoe, slept. They had to take turns, only one man at a time. Everyone was hyped up, wired at the prospect of tomorrow, but Manning had been clear about it – everyone had to get at least four hours' sleep at some point before the big event. Focus and discipline, a proper execution, were impossible without some amount of sleep beforehand.

It was almost midnight. It was almost December 7.

In thirteen hours, this country would change forever.

BOOK THREE

December 7

95

I stood on the Lerner Street Bridge, part of the Pearl Harbor Day procession route that would lead three blocks north to the federal building. It was a clear day but not sunny. The sky was the color of ash, which I hoped was not foreboding.

It was eleven in the morning. Traffic was light over the bridge, and it would soon be nonexistent. The city would rope off the bridge for the marchers, who would begin at noon and probably hit the bridge about twenty, twenty-five minutes later.

I had my cell phone with me, and Lee and I had promised to stay in touch, but I wasn't really needed anymore. The federal government didn't need me to tell them how to stop truck bombs.

Lee, in fact, had told me to leave the downtown, but it felt odd to me to do so. Nobody else was evacuating. Why should I?

I wasn't really sure what to do. I crossed the bridge that split the commercial district and walked north toward the federal building again. The barricades surrounding the building had been fortified, and the Army had been called in as well to defend the building. Lee had mentioned air protection, too – fighter jets, presumably. The good news, as Lee had noted, was that all this military presence would fit right in with a memorial honoring the fallen at Pearl Harbor.

Overhead, well beyond human sight, American satellites were shooting down, searching for suspicious vehicles, for three seventeen-foot You-Ride trucks.

I ambled north and then west and passed the state building, an ugly structure composed in large part of glass. It would be a great target for a truck bomb.

Then I completed my lap of the targets. I headed south. I wanted to be down by the Hartz Building at noon.

The Pearl Harbor Day marchers were gathered on South Walter Drive near the Hartz Building. Over seventy-five people had assembled, some veterans of World War II, some children or grandchildren of the fallen at Pearl Harbor. At the front and rear of the procession were Army tanks, which, again, seemed perfectly normal and symbolic in this context. Members of the military – Army, I thought, maybe Army Rangers like Tom Stoller – stood at attention in their combat fatigues, weapons aimed upward.

The politicians were absent. They'd been briefed and presumably thought better of serving as terrorist bait on this particular day. I knew this because I was part of the inner circle now. But nobody else did. The feds didn't want this telegraphed in advance, because it might get back to the bombers and affect how they operated, and we didn't want them to know that we knew. So as far as the general public knew, the mayor and governor and Senator Donsbrook were supposed to be here but for some reason weren't. So the procession would now be led solely by a retired brigadier general who had been stationed in Pearl Harbor on the day of the attack.

It felt wrong that these other marchers weren't told of what might be happening. I had to assume that the immediate area had been thoroughly searched, and there was sufficient fortification to stop a You-Ride truck long before it reached this group.

Still. The downtown was filled with people, people working in offices, people strolling the streets. It felt wrong. And I felt complicit.

I caught Lee Tucker's eye, who gave me a nasty look, unhappy to see me here.

It was ten minutes until noon. There was no sign of a truck approaching, or Lee wouldn't be standing still.

My cell phone buzzed in my pocket. I didn't recognize the caller. I looked at Lee and it wasn't him, so it didn't matter.

Five minutes to noon. Someone was herding the marchers into some semblance of order on Walter Drive. Lee Tucker was in full concentration, his index finger placed against his earpiece, but he wasn't registering grave concern. Nothing yet.

And then it was noon.

Nothing exploded. No truck came barreling toward us. I looked at Lee, who returned a blank stare back.

The march began.

96

Olsen checked his watch. It was twelve thirty-seven. About right. A little behind schedule, but he wasn't going to panic. Traffic was worse than expected. They'd accounted for a slow-down, given that certain streets would be barricaded in light of the procession, but this was worse than he'd figured. Still, he had plenty of time before one. And even if it were a few minutes past one, he wouldn't be too late. The memorial was expected to last until at least a quarter past the hour.

And hell, even if he missed the memorial completely, the federal building was still going to be there.

Don't panic. Mr Manning always said, don't panic.

He checked his side mirror. Behind him, the other two members of his team, Briggs and Roscoe, were in a Chevy sedan. They were the getaway, and the backup if things got rougher than expected.

He nudged the You-Ride truck along as traffic inched forward. Up ahead at the cross street – Miller Street – he saw a police officer directing vehicles. It didn't really make sense, though. They were still three blocks away from the federal building, and *that* was where traffic was detoured. Not at Miller Street . . .

'I don't get this,' he said, hearing the nerves in his voice.

'It's just traffic backed up,' said Briggs, in the car behind him.

'It's fucked up, though,' said another voice, McPike. McPike was the driver of the second You-Ride, the one destined for the state building. Olsen checked his side mirror again. The second You-Ride truck was . . . call it ten cars back in traffic. It was going to turn right at Miller Street, cut over, and drive south to the state building a block away, while Olsen would plow directly south into the federal plaza.

'Keep cool,' said Olsen, trying to take his own advice. 'Keep cool.'

Traffic inched forward. The cop at the intersection with Miller Street made each car wait, spoke to the driver, then released him or her to go forward. It was hard to tell why. Stupid government assholes, holding up traffic to justify their existence.

The car in front of Olsen was next up, pulling up to the intersection with Miller Street. The police officer walked up to the driver's side door and spoke to the driver. He pointed to the left and then stepped away from the car. The car drove on through the intersection.

The traffic cop then motioned Olsen forward, wiggling his fingers. Olsen took a breath and eased the You-Ride forward. The cop walked up to Olsen's window, avoiding eye contact. Olsen lowered the window.

'So listen,' said the cop. Then his hands quickly raised up, a firearm in his hand. He fired a rubber bullet directly into Olsen's face, knocking him unconscious.

It happened in coordination: Army tanks came from each side of Miller Street to cut off the You-Ride's forward route. U.S. Special Forces converged from behind buildings on each corner of the intersection and charged both the You-Ride and the vehicle behind it, Briggs and Roscoe. The satellites had been following the You-Rides long enough to know that there was a backup car immediately behind.

Briggs and Roscoe grabbed their assault rifles but didn't even get out of the car before a barrage of rubber bullets pelted them. The Special Forces subdued them almost instantly, without firing a single incendiary round of ammunition.

The process was identical for the second You-Ride truck driven by McPike, except that the Special Forces had approached from the rear. Before the two team members backing up McPike knew what had hit them, assault weapons crashed through the front windows and fired rubber bullets into their temples. McPike hadn't fared much better, reaching for his sidearm instead of trying to access the fuse to his feet to begin ignition of the bomb. In any event, the Special Forces had smashed through his window and knocked him unconscious before he could spell his own name.

They didn't know what to expect in the cargo area, other than the incendiary devices, but it turned out there were no humans inside, just the bombs. Specialists jumped inside each cargo area and detached the fuses from the blasting caps, so that even if the drivers had managed to engage the time-delayed fuses before being subdued, the fuses wouldn't be connected to the blasting caps anymore.

'Truck number one clear!' the specialist in Olsen's truck shouted into his microphone.

'Truck number two clear!' said the one in McPike's truck.

The bombs were defused. The trucks were in custody. The terrorists were subdued.

Two trucks down, one to go.

The time was twelve forty-four P.M.

97

I stood in the plaza of the state building, looking up at the all-glass building, wondering if it would still be standing in fifteen minutes, when my cell phone rang. It was Lee Tucker.

'Two trucks down, no casualties,' he said. 'You were right, Jason. You were right all along. They had enough material to take out half the downtown. Time-delayed fuses hidden under the seats, state-of-the-art blasting caps, very sophisticated stuff. But we got them. We fucking got them!'

My heart pounded. Relief swept over me, followed by the churning of my stomach as the obvious statement hung out there between us: 'Where the hell is the third truck?' I asked. We'd thought the third truck was destined for the Hartz Building, but that hadn't come true. So where was it?

'I don't know. Satellite hasn't picked up anything. We don't know. I'm out.'

I hung up my phone and stared, helplessly, at the screen. It showed a missed phone call from eleven fifty-one this morning. Right, I remembered that. I was pretty sure it was another call from Dr Baraniq, asking about scheduling of the trial this week. I'd forgotten to call him yesterday.

I stared a little longer.

Dr Baraniq had been concerned about the scheduling this week because he had a conflict.

A religious obligation, he'd said.

My body went cold. I clicked on the number that had called me at eleven fifty-one as my heart started pounding.

'This is Sofian Baraniq.'

'Dr Baraniq, Jason Kolarich.'

'Yes, Jason, oh, I wanted to know when you—'

'Doctor,' I said. 'Doctor. Is today that religious obligation you had?'

'Yes, it is, as I mentioned.'

'What is that religious obligation?' I asked, as I started walking.

'You want to know – what is the particular obligation?'

'I do.'

'Well, it's the first day of Muharram, which is the first month of our calendar,' he said. 'We have a different, shorter calendar than the American calendar. This year it's December seventh on your calendar.'

I broke into a jog. 'What are we talking about, Doctor? Some big deal?'

'To some, yes,' he said. 'Not so much for the Shia—'

'Where are you, Doctor?'

'Where – well, I'm parking my car near the mosque.'

'That giant one on the west side where they protested after Nine/Eleven? The al-Qadir mosque?'

'Yes, of course.'

'There's some kind of service?'

'Yes, Jason. But why—'

'Starting at one o'clock?' I asked, the panic unmistakable in my voice.

448

'Yes,' he said, picking up on my concern.

'Tell everyone to get out, Doctor! There's a bomb! Do you hear me? Tell everyone to evacuate *right now*!'

I punched out the phone and dialed Lee Tucker. By now I was in a full sprint westward.

'Lee,' I said when he answered. 'That giant mosque . . . on the west side,' I managed, panting as I ran. 'On . . . Dayton?'

'Yeah?'

'That's truck number three, Lee. Get over there now!'

'How do you know?'

'It's the largest mosque in the entire Midwest, Lee—'

'But how do you know the attack is there?'

I split through two people on the sidewalk and ran over the bridge that spanned the western leg of the city's river. I was now about two miles away from the Masjid al-Qadir.

'Because today isn't just Pearl Harbor Day,' I said. 'It's the Islamic New Year!'

98

I ran with everything I had, but my knee wouldn't permit my best effort, no matter how hard I tried. I cut across plazas and diagonally across streets but I couldn't run two miles in ten minutes or so. I wasn't going to make it by one P.M.

The Islamic New Year, a different day every year of our American calendar. How did I miss that? I didn't even know that was celebrated. It was the perfect day for Randall Manning. Two birds – the government and a large gathering of Muslims – in one coordinated attack.

I hit Dayton, which was one-way east – the opposite direction from my route – and came up to an intersection where traffic was idling. A guy on a motorcycle was two cars back from the front of the intersection. I didn't have the element of surprise, as he saw me approach, so I compensated with aggression. I barreled into him high, up at the head and shoulder area. I'd hoped to keep his bike upright but failed. The guy fell off the bike, but it toppled down on top of him, and me on top of it.

'I have to take this bike,' I said. 'I'll kill you if I have to.'

The guy was stunned a moment, not sure of what he was getting with me.

I righted the bike, hopped on, threw on the spare helmet for passengers, and sped away as he called out in protest. I drove forward and then did a U-turn and went onto the sidewalk and took off westbound.

My watch said it was four minutes to one. Surely they would wait until all of the Muslims had entered the mosque before they'd hit it. Why not maximize casualties?

But maybe my watch was slow, or theirs fast.

It had been a long time – college – since I'd driven a bike, and I surely didn't know all the ins and outs of this one, but I knew how to go forward, and that was about all I needed to master. I sped through traffic, narrowly missed an oncoming car traveling northbound at an intersection, and silently prayed that I wasn't too late.

99

Randall Manning pulled his truck out of the storage unit he'd rented, in cash, over six months ago. The unit was directly north of the target, ten blocks away. He was about two miles directly west of the commercial district.

The first intersection he hit was Rovner Street. It was a red light. Manning stopped the vehicle, saw nothing unusual ahead of him, and reached between his legs, under the driver's seat, and engaged the first fuse, the five-minute fuse.

He hit the timer on his watch to correspond: 4:59 . . . 4:58 . . . 4:57 . . .

He closed his eyes for just a moment and thought of each of them, one last memory that lingered above all others. His son, Quinn, at a Little League baseball game, crashing into the catcher at home plate and crying when he realized he'd given the catcher a concussion. His wife on their wedding day, so pure and sweet in her white gown, the way her eyes lit up when she squeezed his hand and said, 'I absolutely do.'

He remembered Langdon Trotter, back when he'd just been elected governor, and how he shook Manning's hand and said, 'Randy, I couldn't have made it here without you. If you ever need anything, I'll be there for you.' That was before he became the big-shit U.S. attorney general, where he breathed the Washington air that polluted a man's soul, turned him into a coward, allowed him to forget the debt he owed to Manning and led him to decide not to chase a jihadist who had murdered Americans, including Manning's son.

Payback is a bitch, Lang. Let's see how you feel after your son is blown to bits today.

The light changed and Manning moved his You-Ride truck forward. Unlike the other trucks, which were canary yellow, Manning had painted this one fire-engine red and put a corporate logo on the side. But he wasn't delivering flowers today.

If, in fact, the government and that lawyer had gotten far enough to be on the lookout for an assault today, Manning hadn't given them anything to play with. His vehicle was disguised, and it hadn't appeared in the open until just now, just five minutes before the truck was going to explode. Even if they were on top of their game, they probably couldn't stop him.

He did wish he had Cahill and Dwyer, though. The others were three-man teams and he'd wanted one, too. Especially him. Because unlike the other teams, who would try to escape before the bombs detonated, Manning had no intention of leaving. He – and if they hadn't been arrested, Cahill and Dwyer – planned to pick off anyone who tried to escape, just as the Brotherhood had done to Manning's family and others at the Adana Hotel.

He'd even brought a machete.

The five-minute fuse having been triggered at Rovner, all that remained was the two-minute at Dodd Street, just a block away from the mosque at Dayton Street.

453

His heartbeat ratcheted up as the truck passed street after street, catching a couple of lights.

'I understand that the tree of liberty must be refreshed from time to time with the blood of patriots and tyrants. I understand that revolution is not only a right but an obligation. I understand that bigotry and hate cannot be answered with tolerance, but with intolerance. I understand that those who take up arms against us cannot be answered with peace but with like arms.'

When Manning hit Dodd Street, a red light, he began to lean down to access the two-minute fuse. Up ahead, movement caught his eye. The mosque, a block away.

People were running away, fleeing as if –

As if someone had called in a bomb threat.

'No!' he cried. He slammed his foot on the accelerator, driving through the red light at Dodd and picking up speed as he headed toward Dayton Street and the Masjid al-Qadir. There was another red light at Dayton. As he got closer, Manning could see more clearly than ever the congregants fleeing from the mosque, running onto the grass and up the sidewalks.

There were still plenty of them to hit. And the blast – well, it wouldn't kill everyone, but the numbers would be high enough.

Then he made a decision. Forget the fuses. Forget about picking them off as they fled. He was going to crash the You-Ride directly into the building and blow the whole damn thing up in an instant.

He floored the accelerator and held his breath. He steeled himself as the truck ran the red light at Dayton. As he approached he saw a spattering of people pouring out the front door of the mosque, a man carrying an elderly woman in his arms – a white man . . .

Kolarich?

Kolarich.

Manning pushed down with all his might on the gas pedal and cried out for his wife, his son, his entire family.

BOOK FOUR
The Aftermath

100

I woke up in the hospital with a start. Two beautiful women stood in my room. And Joel Lightner was no Robert Redford, but it was nice to see him, too.

I tried to take a deep breath but it hurt. Every part of my body hurt. But I still had two arms and two legs, and I could feel all of them, so it could have been worse.

'What happened?' I asked. 'Did the . . . bomb go off?'

They looked at each other. 'You don't remember,' said Shauna.

Tori was hanging back, letting Shauna and Joel hover over me. Actually, it seemed like Shauna had sort of boxed her out.

'The bomb went off,' she said. 'The mosque was leveled.'

I took another pained breath. 'Casualties?'

Shauna shook her head. 'Lots of injuries. A few people in critical condition. So far, no deaths.'

My head fell back on the pillow. I closed my eyes and felt myself spin. 'That's . . . amazing.'

'They have a theory,' said Joel. 'He didn't use as much fire-power in that truck as in the others. He didn't need to take down some huge government building. Just a one-story mosque. Just a really big house, basically. And they think he didn't want to blow it to smithereens, anyway.'

'He wanted people . . . to survive and . . . try to escape,' I mumbled. 'So he could pick them off . . . as they fled.'

'Just like the hotel in Adana,' Shauna said. 'But apparently he changed his plan when he saw everyone evacuating the mosque. So he drove the truck straight into the entrance. The truck was three-quarters inside the foyer of the mosque when it detonated. The blasting radius – that's what these guys call it – the blasting radius wasn't particularly wide, especially when the mosque itself absorbed much of the blow.'

Joel said, 'So people closest to the mosque, like you, Superstar, got the worst of it, but nobody got blown up. Just knocked off their feet. You came down on your head and had a nice five-hour nap.'

'The woman you were carrying out,' said Shauna, 'the one in the wheelchair, broke her leg and has some scrapes and bruises, but she's otherwise fine.'

'But everyone got out, Jason.' Lightner again. 'You called Dr Baraniq, apparently. The people in that mosque had about a twelve-minute start. Over a thousand people evacuated a mosque in just over ten minutes.'

A doctor came in and wanted to check me out. My vision was cloudy, and it hurt when I moved my eyes right to left. Or when I closed them. Or when I stood still. I noted that my left leg was heavily bandaged, my left arm less so.

'We're going to leave you now.' Shauna pressed her lips against my forehead. She got off the bed. 'C'mon, Joel.'

'See you later, tough guy.'

I opened my eyes again. Not everybody was leaving. Shauna was giving Tori and me some privacy. That felt . . . I don't know what it felt like.

When the doctor finished with me, Tori came over and took the spot on the bed where Shauna had been. She took my hand in hers and brought it up to her face.

'Sleep,' she said. 'I'll be here when you wake up.'

101

Deidre Maley and I waited on the top floor of the Boyd Center at the reception area. Tom Stoller came walking down a hallway, unescorted for the first time in about a year, holding a small bag of personal possessions.

He looked at each of us briefly before his gaze went beyond us. That was Tom. Maybe it wouldn't be someday.

The day after the bombing, Judge Nash declared a mistrial in the matter of *State v. Thomas Stoller*. Two days later, Wendy Kotowski called me with the news that the county attorney would not re-try Tom Stoller for the murder of Kathy Rubinkowski and was dismissing the case with prejudice. Randall Manning was dead, but there was more than sufficient evidence to suggest that Kathy Rubinkowski had uncovered evidence of the terrorist plot and had died because of it.

The media, hungry for any angles they could find on the December 7 events, had taken up Tom's cause. He was featured on cable news programs and even *60 Minutes*. He was headed now for a private home that would give him the care he'd needed since he left Iraq. We hoped it wouldn't be long before it was outpatient care, so he wouldn't have to spend his life in some institution. For now, all that mattered was that things were finally starting to look up for the guy.

We took the elevator down together and stopped in the lobby. Deidre was going to drive Tom to the facility now, and I was heading back to the office.

Deidre had been on the verge of breaking down all morning, since she first saw me. Apparently she wasn't good with good-byes. I wasn't, either, which was why I had made plans with Deidre to have lunch next week at Tom's facility. It wasn't good-bye. It was see you next week.

'Well, we did it,' I said, clapping my hands together. I put out my hand for Tom. 'Lieutenant—'

Tom came forward and wrapped his arms around me tightly. I didn't really know how to respond. This wasn't how it usually worked with us. Deidre, who by now had turned on the water-works, joined us and made it a three-person hug. It had been a pretty bumpy ride, no doubt, and Tom had defied some pretty serious odds.

Finally, Tom released me. He stepped back, nodded without looking at me, and walked away. Deidre kissed my cheek, said, 'See you next week,' and followed after him.

102

I returned to my office after leaving Tom and Aunt Deidre. I was moving slowly these days. I lost a lot of skin on the left leg and some on the arm, too. And my left knee hadn't been doing so well even before that time. The doctor at the hospital told me I probably could avoid surgery but I had to avoid stress on that knee for two months.

When I walked into my office, I found everything from the Stoller case in boxes. Marie, our office assistant, had apparently decided to put in a few hours of labor.

Someone had left today's *Chronicle* on my desk. Yesterday, the U.S. attorney's office had announced the indictments of Stanley Keane and eight others for murder, mayhem, and lots of other things you're not supposed to do, like providing material assistance to a domestic terrorist organization. Manning had used the cover of his corporate entity, Global Harvest International, and Stanley Keane's SK Tool and Supply, to slowly stockpile an astonishing amount of bomb material. They had armed two trucks, headed to the federal and state buildings, with one hundred bags each of ammonium nitrate fertilizer and three drums of liquid nitromethane. Each truck was part of a three-person team. The driver, traveling solo, would smash the truck into the building. The other two team members would follow in a car as a backup. Once the truck penetrated the building – if it didn't detonate on impact – the driver and his partners were supposed to race to the nearest subway station, head underground, and try to avoid the blast. The driver would have set the five-minute fuse in advance and the two-minute as well, so the driver was likely doing a suicide run.

The third truck – Manning's truck – was different. It was armed with only fifty bags of ammonium nitrate, half the amount of explosives, because its target was smaller and less sturdy – a mosque as opposed to a multi-story building. And because Manning didn't want to level the mosque. He wanted to destabilize it, just like the hotel in Adana, Turkey, where his family perished. He wanted people to run from the mosque, so he and his two helpers – Patrick Cahill and Ernie Dwyer – could pick people off like the Adana terrorists did.

Manning, everyone had acknowledged, had been smart and disciplined. Had that bomb material been purchased in bulk, or had it been purchased by individuals, the federal government likely would have noticed. But under the cover of legitimate corporate transactions, and over time, Manning had stockpiled enough material to blow up ten more buildings besides those on December 7. Only yesterday the feds found the remaining stockpile in an underground facility several hundred miles away.

According to Stanley Keane, who was cooperating with the authorities, Randall Manning hadn't expected to survive December 7. Nor had he expected his soldiers to do so. But the other two 'brains' of the operation, Bruce McCabe and Stanley Keane, were expected to carry on the mission. The way Manning figured it, no roads led back to Keane or McCabe, and they'd be free to conduct further attacks. That, of course, was before he killed Bruce McCabe, for a reason that isn't yet clear.

The federal government had missed all of this. They should have noticed that Summerset Farms was buying a hell of a lot more ammonium nitrate than it needed, but on paper the farm had the size to justify the purchase. Had anyone bothered to go out and notice how little of that acreage was actually being used for farmland, they would have become suspicious immediately.

And they missed the part about December 7 being the Islamic New Year, too. But for that much, I can't really blame them. For one, Lee Tucker and that guy Osborne didn't have much time to think about all of this. I'd only given them the info a few days earlier, and nobody knew for sure that December 7 was even the target date until the day before. Plus, the Islamic New Year isn't some major holiday for most Muslims. But it was close enough from Manning's perspective, allowing him to combine a day that commemorated an attack on our soil with a day that was significant to Islam.

The good news for me was that my name had been kept out of it, as much as possible at least. The reporters know that I was Tom Stoller's lawyer, but that's the extent of it.

I saw a large three-ring binder in one of the boxes and didn't immediately recognize it. Then I remembered. Joel Lightner had put together a dossier on the identity of Gin Rummy, the guy nobody could ever identify. For a short time during this investigation, it had been my focus, but Tori had correctly noted that it wasn't really going to help me, in the end. Even if I identified the guy, it wasn't like I could drag him into court and get him to confess. Finding out his identity wasn't going to help me win Tom Stoller's case.

It brought me back to Kathy Rubinkowski, the first one to speak up about suspicious activity taking place at Global Harvest. She was now a heroine in this entire saga, the one who started the ball rolling.

Her murder was technically unsolved. Everyone figured Randall Manning's guys did it. Maybe one of those guys picked up ahead of time, Patrick Cahill or Ernie Dwyer. Maybe another one. Close enough. It wasn't a critical detail in the scheme of things. I could tell the police about Gin Rummy, but to their mind, it would be like telling them the Easter Bunny did it. Nobody knew his identity, and nobody really cared anymore about Kathy Rubinkowski's murder.

For no particular reason, I opened up Joel's lengthy work. He had identified a number of people within and outside the Capparelli crime family who might qualify as Gin Rummy. Joel even had an executive summary, the kind of thing his corporate clients would like:

Approximately four years ago, federal authorities first heard the name 'Gin Rummy' transmitted over a wiretap by two known members of the Capparelli crime family. Since that time, a number of killings have been attributed to Gin Rummy, but his identity has remained a mystery. It is believed that, in the face of increasingly invasive surveillance by federal agents, the Capparelli family has entrusted its most important work to Gin Rummy, including the murder of top crime boss Anthony Moretti, and has deliberately kept his identity known to only a handful of people. Federal agents believe, in fact, that his identity is known only to Paul Capparelli, his sole confidant Donnie Mancini, and Gin Rummy himself. We believe, of course, that Lorenzo Fowler also knew that information, and was willing to trade on it before he was gunned down, probably by Gin Rummy himself.

Right. I recalled that odd conversation with Lorenzo, right here in this office, when he first mentioned 'Gin Rummy' to me. *A hit man?* I asked. Close enough, he said. *An assassin?* Right, he said. I never got the answer to my follow-up question: What's the difference between a hit man and an assassin?

And I probably never would. Joel, for his part, had given his best guess in the following paragraph of his executive summary:

The most obvious suspect is Peter Gennaro Ramini, a.k.a. 'Pockets,' who served as the primary assassin for the Capparelli family under Rico Capparelli, before Rico's arrest and imprisonment left his brother Paul Capparelli in control.

I finished reading the executive summary and let out a sigh. Some questions don't get answered. Who knows? Maybe I'd keep looking for the elusive killer.

Or maybe, at some point, he'd come looking for me again.

Or maybe not. Maybe I was done with this. Maybe Tori was onto something in her apartment, the night before December 7. We could leave here. We could ditch everything and run away, start over. Was I ready to do that?

I looked at the photographs on my desk. One of my deceased wife, Talia, clutching our newborn child, Emily. Talia would always be the love of my life. That spot was permanently filled.

The other photo was Shauna and me, mugging for the

camera in the bleachers last summer at a ball game. I stared into her frozen eyes and felt my heartbeat ratchet up. I didn't know what that meant. I didn't know what *we* meant. I wasn't sure I had the courage to find out.

Exhale.

I decided not to confront that particular topic at this time and, instead, flip through Joel's report. I'd had enough drama in my life for one year.

103

Peter Gennaro Ramini waited on the corner, his hands stuffed in his coat, watching his breath freeze. The town car arrived on time. Say this for Donnie and his brother Mooch, they were punctual.

He got in and felt a spasm of nerves, which went nicely with the stench of fried food.

Donnie kept him in suspense, which was annoying but sometimes part of the drill. He was really just a glorified delivery boy, but he liked to feel important.

Finally, after the town car had traveled several blocks, Donnie patted Ramini's knee.

'Even Paulie knows when to pull back,' he said. 'He says to me, get this: "We kill the prick now and we paint a target on our back."'

Ramini deflated with relief. He'd hoped that Paulie would see the sheer stupidity of killing the man who had helped thwart a terrorist attack on this city. Even if the general public didn't know the extent of what he did, the feds sure did. If they whacked Kolarich now, the feds would rewrite the Patriot Act to target the Mafia.

'He understands that we're in the clear now,' Donnie went

on. 'We dodged a bullet. We go after Kolarich now, we go right back to being in the soup.'

'Great. Thanks, Don.'

'Now, he did kill Sal and Augie.'

Actually, he didn't, but Ramini had been forced to lie about that to Paulie and Donnie. The Capparellis couldn't know what really happened in that alley with Kolarich.

'So what does that mean?' Ramini asked.

The town car was now pulling back to the same corner where Ramini had jumped in.

Donnie said, 'It means we don't forget. It means we wait. It means, someday, the lawyer might get a visit from us. It means Mr Jason Kolarich, Esquire, better never stop watching his back.'

104

I was the last in the office, past six-thirty. I was looking out the window at the cityscape when I heard her footsteps down the hallway, the familiar *clack* of her boots.

'Hey,' Tori said.

'Hey, yourself.' Down below, Christmas shoppers filled the streets. I used to love Christmas when I was a kid, because it was one of the only days that my dad was in a good mood. And it was the only time when our family seemed normal. That used to matter so much to me, when I was a kid – feeling like I was normal. Feeling like I belonged.

'Did you mean what you said before?' I asked, my forehead planted against the glass window, still looking down at the street. 'About us just leaving this city? Leaving everything behind?'

'Of course I did,' she said. 'Would you . . . do that?'

I didn't answer. I breathed onto the glass and watched it fog up.

'What's wrong, Jason? Did something . . .'

Her sentence trailed off. In the reflection off the window, I could see her standing by the couch. Joel's treatise on 'Gin Rummy' was resting there, open to the executive summary.

'I thought seriously about saying yes,' I said. 'I really did. I love this city, but I would have considered leaving it for you.'

'You still can,' she said.

True. I still could, after everything.

'I have unfinished business,' I said. 'Gin Rummy is still out there. I have to find Kathy Rubinkowski's killer.'

'That's not your job. You did yours. Leave the rest to someone else.'

I nodded. That was the same thing I'd been trying to tell myself.

'Help me out here,' Tori said to me. 'Because this is sounding suspiciously like an excuse to blow me off. And if that's what you want to do, I'd rather you just said that.'

I could see where she might think that. I've heard a lot of women complain that men are afraid of confrontation when it comes to breakups. They hide behind stupid reasons. But that wasn't the case here.

I watched her in the reflection. It was somehow easier to do it this way. She reached down and picked up the three-ring binder Joel had put together.

'Joel got me started,' I continued. 'He identified a long-time hit man named Peter Ramini. Apparently he was a big deal when Rico Capparelli was the boss. He would still make the most sense, even with his brother Paul at the helm.'

'So I'm reading,' she said, holding the summary in her hand.

'Right. But ultimately, Joel rules him out,' I said.

Tori didn't answer. She was reading what Joel had written.

I had a copy of the executive summary rolled up in my hand. I unrolled it and read the pertinent part. '"Nearly five years ago, Peter Ramini was diagnosed with a disorder known as 'essential tremor,' an involuntary shaking disease that, in his case, has left him with a nearly permanent tremble in his hands. Ramini's nickname, 'Pockets,' stems from the fact that he almost never lets anyone see his hands. In fact, federal agents believe that his disorder is unknown to virtually everyone within the Capparelli family."

'So,' I said, 'it's not Peter Ramini. He probably can't even hold a gun in his hand.'

'So it seems.' I saw Tori toss the binder back onto the couch. 'Tell me what this has to do with you and me.'

I turned and faced her now. 'Funny thing. Joel did bios on the main suspects in the body of the report. According to Joel, ol' Peter never married or had kids. He had a brother Joey who died young. Joey left behind an eight-year-old daughter. Peter's niece.'

Tori blinked. She started to answer but thought better of it. Her eyes darted about the room and into the hallway.

'She'd be twenty-seven today,' I said.

'You don't say.'

'Her name is Ginger,' I said.

The temperature dropped in the room. Tori watched me for a long time. Her features had hardened. She was still wearing the long coat and her hands were hidden inside the pockets.

'No, it isn't,' she said. 'It's Victoria. Victoria Virginia Ramini.'

She removed her right hand from the pocket and produced a handgun.

'Unfortunately, my aunt was also named Victoria, so they called me Virginia. And "Virginia" became "Ginger." I always hated that nickname, for the record.'

'And now you're Tori Martin,' I said. 'So "Tori" comes from "Victoria." What about "Martin"? Just a name you dreamed up?'

'My mother's maiden name.'

'Ah. Came in handy. Let me see if I have this right. You killed your husband, went into a little spiral, then came up for air with a new name – Tori Martin – and better yet, a new job helping Uncle Peter kill people. He gets the contracts, but he can't fulfill them personally with shaky hands, so he farms them out to you. Nobody knows it's you. Nobody would even suspect you. And the cops and the FBI, they may like Peter for the various murders but they can't prove it. No prints, no trace evidence – hell, Peter's probably twenty miles away with an alibi when the hits go down.'

Tori studied me before answering. 'Actually, he likes to watch. He's weird like that. I don't know if he's protective of me or he wants to stay close to things, even if he can't pull the trigger himself. But he watches every one of them. Do you want to psychoanalyze my uncle some more, Jason?'

I didn't. Tori kept the gun at her side but watched me closely. I was behind my desk. She knew I owned a gun. She didn't know where it was. Not that she seemed particularly worried. She had proven herself to be an expert shooter. She could put one between my eyes before I could get anywhere near my desk drawer.

'So the Capparellis see that Lorenzo Fowler's getting nervous, maybe getting some loose lips,' I say. 'They find out he's made an appointment with me, an outside lawyer, someone the Capparellis don't use. So they want someone close to me. Someone who can find out what I know. And that someone is you. You and those goons stage a little scene at Vic's so I can intervene and play the hero. And then you do a masterful job of playing hard to get, but ultimately you and I become close. I share everything with you. I tell you everything, and you tell them everything.'

I laughed at a memory. 'You even saw me investigating the identity of Gin Rummy and talked me *out* of pursuing that angle. I actually *thanked* you for your intelligent insight. You must have thought I was the most pathetic mark you've ever—'

'Don't say that.' Tori's eyes welled with tears. 'You don't know how I feel about you.'

'You're right, I don't. Because everything was a lie.'

'Not everything.'

I took a couple of deep breaths. I moved slightly to my right, within reach of the desk drawer. I couldn't tell how closely Tori was noticing.

'Why did you tell me you shot your husband five years ago?' I asked. 'That was true, right?'

She nodded.

'Why did you tell me that? Why would you reveal something truthful about yourself that could expose your secret?'

She cocked her head, blinking away tears. 'Because I wanted to share it with you.'

She said it as if it were an obvious answer. I shook my head. I was furious and humiliated and confused.

'If you're going to tell me that my actions didn't make sense, Jason, I won't disagree. I didn't plan this nearly as well as you think. I was supposed to become your friend and keep an eye on things. Everything that happened after that, it just happened.'

'Bullshit.'

'Move away from the desk, Jason. And keep your hands where I can see them. Don't make something happen here that doesn't need to.'

'I'm turning you in,' I said.

'No, you're not. You could have already done that.'

'I still can.'

'If you call the police, I can't protect you.' Tori walked toward me, cutting the distance between us in half before stopping. 'Do you have any idea how hard it's been for me to keep you alive? My uncle pleaded with Paulie to spare you. And when he couldn't stop it from happening, *I* stopped it. I've known Sal and Augie most of my life. I killed two of my *friends* in that alley.'

I took a breath. Anger and embarrassment had clouded my thoughts, but I did see her point. She did save me in that alley when those two goons tried to kill me. Clearly, she had gone against the Mob's wishes there. The top brass had ordered a hit on me and Tori had jumped in and stopped it.

'This job with Uncle Pete – I only killed people who deserved it,' she said to me. 'People who robbed and murdered and cheated and did all kinds of bad things. Anyone I killed shouldn't have been too surprised when it happened.'

'Kathy Rubinkowski,' I said.

She nodded. 'I was told she was blackmailing her boss, that she'd found damaging information and was looking for a million dollars. I didn't know anything about Randall Manning or Global Harvest. I just took the assignment from my uncle. As soon as I found out the truth, I did everything I could to help you figure out your problem.'

'Everything but turn yourself in. You could have just raised your hand and the case would've been over.'

'And if I had, the worst terrorist attack in the country's history would have taken place.'

I laughed harder than was warranted. My emotions were riding a roller coaster now. I was raw and exposed and looking for a way to make it hurt less. But as my mother used to say, I was born at night, but not last night.

'So you're the killer with a heart of gold.'

'No,' she said. 'I'm someone who made bad choices that I have to live with. Someone who wants things to be different now. I can be different, Jason. I . . .'

I waited her out. I was pretty much done with my end of the conversation.

'I love you,' she said.

'No.'

'Yes. I do, Jason. You're strong and decent and ethical and, yes, you're damaged but you have this tremendous heart, this sense of right and wrong that I've never known. All I've ever known in my life are people looking for an angle, people who hurt and kill you if you don't go along with them. But not you. I didn't know people like you existed. I can be that person, too. I'm more than what I've been so far. I can be better at – at life, I guess.'

'That's touching.'

'What you won't read in some silly little report is that I was totally messed up after I shot my husband. I started into drugs – painkillers at first, then cocaine. I was a train wreck. I could only do one thing well, and that was shoot a gun. I'd been shooting since I was seven, and I could do it better than anybody. So my uncle's career was falling apart when he got diagnosed with tremors, and my life was falling apart. Okay? So we helped each other. He got me straight, and I kept him in business. But he promised me it would only be bad people. Only people who were already dirty. And now I want a new life, and I want you in it.'

'You killed Kathy Rubinkowski, and you framed Tom Stoller—'

'I didn't frame anyone. I had nothing to do with that. I just

478

pulled the trigger and kept walking. I was told to leave behind the spent shell casing so it wouldn't look like a professional hit. So I did that. The rest – taking her valuables and dumping them in the park with a homeless guy – I didn't do it and I didn't know about it.'

I thought about that for a moment. 'Then who?'

'It was Lorenzo,' she said. 'At my uncle's direction. He knew this shooting would draw some attention, I guess. A nice white girl in a yuppie neighborhood? So he took extra precautions to make it look more like a garden-variety robbery gone bad. Lorenzo, he already knew about my arrangement with Uncle Pete. Only he and Paulie and Paulie's errand boy Donnie knew. So he had Lorenzo cover my tracks. I didn't know, Jason. I swear.'

I shook my head. 'But then you *did* know. And you were going to let Tom—'

'No,' she interrupted. 'I was never going to let him go to prison. If it had come to it, I would have confessed. Or something. I would have done something. I would *not* have let that poor guy go to prison.'

I watched her carefully, trying to read her, sure that my normally reliable instincts had failed me. 'That's easy to say now.'

She wiped tears away with the back of her hand. Her left hand. The gun hand remained still at her side. 'You don't believe me,' she said. 'If you don't believe that, then I guess we're done.'

I didn't answer. My throat was full and my stomach was churning.

She let out a bitter breath. 'I wondered if this day was going to come. Believe it or not, I thought if it did, I could make you understand. I thought you'd give me a chance.' She shook her head and took another breath. 'I guess that was dumb.'

I reached for the desk drawer.

'Don't do that, Jason. Please.'

I opened it up.

She raised her gun.

'Jason, don't.'

I removed a business card for Detective Frank Danilo, the lead on the Rubinkowski murder. I placed it on the desk, picked up the receiver of my office phone, and dialed the number.

When the police station operator answered, I said, 'Detective Frank Danilo, please.'

'Hang up the phone, Jason.' Tori stared at me, the gun trained on me. We watched each other as I waited for Danilo to come on the line – probably just a few seconds but elongated by the tension. A twitch of Tori's finger and my life was over.

'Please don't do this,' Tori said. I stared into the barrel of the gun as the voice of Frank Danilo came over the receiver.

'Detective, this is Jason Kolarich,' I said.

Tori's eyes narrowed. Her gun held steady. I'd be dead before I realized she pulled the trigger.

'Yeah, Jason. What's up?'

I loved Tori, too. I knew that for certain this afternoon, when I put everything together. I always measured love by pain. What I felt when my wife and daughter died was so consuming that it crushed me and rebuilt me into something vaguely resembling my former self. This was not that kind of pain. This was poison through my blood, something that grabbed and twisted my insides and stole my breath. I loved her, and at this moment I believed that she loved me, too. That was supposed to make it easier. It made it worse.

'Kathy Rubinkowski's killer is named Victoria Virginia

480

Ramini,' I said. 'She's the niece of Peter Ramini. She now goes by Tori Martin. She's Gin Rummy, Detective.'

I slowly placed the phone back in its cradle. Closed my eyes. Took a breath.

When I looked up, Tori Martin was gone.

ACKNOWLEDGEMENTS

Many thanks to Dr Ronald Wright, forensic pathologist extraordinaire, for his delightful explanations of how people are hanged, shot, strangled, and otherwise fatally maimed – and doing so with an infectious laugh. Thanks to Dan Collins, my favorite federal prosecutor and friend for life, for telling me as much as he could about domestic terrorism without having to arrest me. Thanks to everyone at Putnam and Berkley, all of whom are charged in some manner with the task of putting up with an author who misses deadlines and is sometimes spacey: Ivan Held, Leslie Gelbman, Neil Nyren, Rachel Kahan, Victoria Comella, Michael Barson, Lydia Hirt, and my new discovery, Sara Minnich. You guys rock.

And to my life partner, mother of my children, beauty queen, sex goddess, and tirelessly patient and loving wife, Susan, for making everything worth it.

Read on for a taste of Jason's Kolarich's next case:
this time, he's on the stand

THE
LAST
ALIBI

THE TRIAL, DAY 1
Monday, December 9

1

Jason

Judge Judith Bialek, from her bench overlooking the court, peers down over her glasses at the defense and prosecution. Until now she has been businesslike, efficient, carefully instructing the twelve jurors and three alternates as to their duties in this case. But this particular case gives her pause, as she is familiar with the parties and tries to emit some kind of acknowledgment of this fact: a grim smile, lips tucked in, a brief nod in the direction of the defense table.

'Please remember, above all,' she says, 'that the defendant has pleaded not guilty, and he is presumed not guilty unless proven otherwise beyond a reasonable doubt.'

Everybody knows that, of course. You've only made it as far as Judge Bialek's courtroom if you've uttered those two words: *Not guilty.* Not guilty by reason of insanity. Self-defense, maybe. But always *Not guilty*!

How many times I've stood in a courtroom like this one, the grand, ornate walnut molding and finishes, the overdone lighting, the walls practically bleeding with the fears and horrors they've absorbed during the seven decades that this building has stood. *Not guilty* are the only words the exhausted and terrified defendants utter prior to trial, but so many more lie just beneath the surface, at the backs of their throats, yearning to gush forth: *I didn't do it. I was set up. This is all a misunderstanding. It's not like it seems. I'm not a criminal. Please, please, before this goes any further, just please hear me out!*

I've lost count of the number of times I've stood here. Over three hundred cases, if you count everything from third-chairing a trial to being the top dog, while I was prosecuting. Nearly fifty cases, surely, as a defense lawyer, standing next to a weak-kneed defendant watching the machinations of the criminal justice system begin to churn against him, the enormity of what is happening crashing down upon him – the judge in a black robe, the steely prosecutor, the sheriff's deputy waiting to handcuff him, the United States flag waving over a courtroom of the public, spectators watching him stand accused by the government, peering at him with a combination of morbid curiosity and vicarious thrill.

'We will now hear opening statements from the prosecution. Mr Ogren.'

'Thank you, Your Honor.' Roger Ogren is a lifer at the office, probably close to twenty-five years in by now. I knew him when I was there. I was surprised, in fact, to learn that he was handling this case. And I was unhappy, too. This is a man who has seen everything, who is surprised by nothing.

He is slim, unusually so to anyone who knows him, after a long illness that many thought would end his career. No longer fitting into his old suits, Roger is wearing new stuff, fashionable threads his wife must have picked out.

As Roger Ogren approaches the podium to address the jury, Shauna Tasker very subtly places her hand over mine. I turn and offer a grim smile. Shauna is my law partner. She is my best friend.

And for this trial, she is my lawyer.

'Ladies and gentlemen,' says Ogren, 'we are here today for one reason and one reason only. This is a murder trial, and the defendant is Jason Kolarich.'

Ogren turns and points his finger at me. I always advise my clients to be ready for that, to have earnest, nonthreatening looks on their faces, and to return the stare. I now understand just how difficult it is.

And again I hear the cries of the thousands who have sat in this chair, their silent, desperate wailings: *It wasn't me. They have the wrong guy. You don't understand what happened, just let me explain, please don't do this to me!*

But I say none of those things. I just look at the jurors with my *I didn't kill anybody* face – yes, I practiced before a mirror – searching their eyes, wondering what it is they are seeing in me.

I will probably testify. When I do, I'm not sure it will be convincing enough to establish reasonable doubt. I'm not sure it will do more good than harm.

I'm only sure, in fact, of one thing: When I testify, I will not tell the truth.

SIX MONTHS BEFORE TRIAL
June

2

Jason

I stand up in the courtroom gingerly, still hesitant with the knee, more out of habit than necessity. My mouth is dry and sticky, so I slide the glass of water near the podium in case I need it. Once I start, I don't like interruptions unless I choose one for tactical advantage. It's all about strategy once I walk into a courtroom.

This is war, after all. No other way to look at it. The cop sitting on the witness stand arrested my client for possession of two grams of crack cocaine. My job at this hearing is to show that he had no probable cause to search my client, and therefore the product of that search – the cocaine – must be excluded from evidence. This is technically a preliminary hearing prior to trial, but everyone knows that this is the whole enchilada. If the crack is found admissible, my client is toast; he has no defense left other than claiming that the plastic bags fell from the sky into his pocket, which usually doesn't work. But if, on the other hand, the judge excludes the crack from evidence, my client walks.

My client is William Braden, a nineteen-year-old high school graduate from the posh suburb of Highland Woods who's 'taking a year or two off' before college. Exactly why Billy decided to come down to the city's west side to buy his drugs is anyone's guess. Surely he could have found them at the high school or other places up there; the lily-white, wealthy suburbs are no longer immune from hard-core drugs. But people do dumb things. If they didn't, I wouldn't have a job.

I cast a glance at Billy's parents, John and Karen, doctors at a prestigious downtown hospital each of them, who are seated behind the defense table, wearing expressions I see all too often – they are overwhelmed, they can't believe this is happening, this isn't where people of their ilk are supposed to find themselves. Not wealthy white people from the suburbs.

I wonder if they know that their son is more than a user – he's a dealer. I certainly can't tell them. And the cops didn't find enough drugs on Billy to charge him with possession with intent to distribute. So to all the world, Billy is simply a clean-cut kid who was experimenting, taking an ill-advised walk on the wild side.

I reach the podium and stop. Three months ago, this small exercise of motor skills would send pain skyrocketing up from my knee.

'Detective Forrest,' I say, 'my name is Jason Kolarich. I represent Billy Braden.' Billy, not William. A kid, a stupid boy, not an adult criminal.

'Counsel,' he says. Nick Forrest has worked undercover narcotics for almost four years. He is thick through the chest and shoulders and maintains a formidable posture. He must, if he works the city's west side.

'You arrested my client walking down Roosevelt Avenue on December eighth of last year, correct?'

'Correct, sir.'

'He was walking west between Girardi and Summerset.'

'That's . . . that's correct.'

'He was alone, as far as you could tell.'

'As far as I could tell.'

'But there were other people on the street, on Roosevelt, yes?'

'There were a few. It was getting close to dusk. People wander out less when it gets to be dark around there.'

'It's a dangerous neighborhood.'

'It can be.'

'Lot of gang activity, right?'

'That's right.' Detective Forrest nods.

'And Billy – Billy was wearing a black wool coat as he walked westbound.'

'He . . . That's right, yes.'

'It was cold out that day, true?'

'It was.'

'Below freezing, you could see your breath, that sort of thing?'

'That's right.'

'Nothing unusual about wearing a black wool coat on a cold day, correct?'

'I didn't say it was unusual.'

I pause. Sometimes judges like to interject when witnesses elaborate, especially at the beginning of their testimony. But Judge Goodson remains mute, his chin resting in his left hand.

'You agree with me, it wasn't unusual.'

'I agree,' he says.

'His hands were in his pockets, correct?'

'I believe they were, yes.'

'Nothing unusual about that, either.'

497

'Correct.'

'You were in an unmarked Chevy Cavalier, parked on the south side of the street.'

'That's right. I was doing a drive-around.'

Judge Goodson, a former prosecutor, knows what that means, but I have to make my record for the appellate court. 'You were driving around Roosevelt, looking for someone to stop and sell you drugs in your car.'

'Correct.'

'Okay, Detective. And you were in the driver's seat.'

'I was.'

'So you're on the south side of Roosevelt, looking north?'

'That's correct.'

'So Billy, walking west on the opposite side of the street, came up from behind you, so to speak. He wasn't walking toward you, he was walking away from you.'

The detective clears his throat. 'I observed the suspect in my rearview mirror, walking westbound. Then he passed by my line of sight and continued walking away from me.'

'The suspect,' I say. 'You called him a suspect.'

'Well, the—'

'He was already a suspect, the moment you laid eyes on him in the rearview mirror. That's your testimony.'

Detective Forrest leans forward in his chair, a bit of crimson rising to the surface of his cheeks. Surely he's been warned, over and over again by the prosecutor, not to let me get a rise out of him.

'The block in question is where Buildings A and B of the Eagleton Housing Projects are located,' he says. 'They are known drug houses. It's been well documented that people go to Eagleton to buy crack cocaine.'

'Okay, so he *was* a suspect the moment you saw him walking down the street in a black wool coat with his hands in his pockets.'

'You forgot that he *ran*, Counselor.'

'No, I didn't. I'm not there yet, Detective. I'm at the point in time that you first saw him, in the rearview mirror. For the third time, Detective . . . '

It's always nice to remind the judge that the witness isn't answering your question.

'. . . was Billy a suspect at that point in time, or wasn't—'

'And I already told you, Counselor, that he was walking along a route that is known for drug activity.'

'Just walking down Roosevelt? You didn't see my client come out of Building A or B, did you? You were just doing a drive-around when you saw my client, correct?'

He lets out a sigh. 'Correct.'

'So you're saying that simply walking down Roosevelt, between Girardi and Summerset, made Billy automatically a suspect for drug possession.'

'I didn't say that.'

'Well, you've already agreed that there were other individuals walking on Roosevelt at that time. Were they all suspects, too?'

'I didn't say that, either.'

I look at the judge, as if I'm bewildered. Judge Goodson actually smirks. My theatrics play better with a jury than with a judge who has seen this act a thousand times.

'So Billy was one of several individuals walking along a *known route for drug activity*,' I say.

'He's the only one who ran,' says Detective Forrest.

'He's the only one you followed in your car,' I answer. 'Right?

You drove along after him for almost an entire city block before he started to run. Isn't that true?'

It may or may not be true, but it's what he wrote in his police report, so he's glued to it.

'Yes, that's true.'

'What was so different about Billy versus the other people walking up and down Roosevelt Avenue at that time, Detective? He was wearing a black wool coat and kept his hands in his pockets in the dead of winter. What was so different about him that made you follow him and only him?'

As a technical matter, we tell young lawyers not to ask open-ended questions like this on cross-examination. You're supposed to control the witnesses by asking your preferred questions and getting *yes* or *no* responses. But we're going to get to this point one way or the other when the prosecutor gets to ask him questions, and I want this Q&A on my terms.

Plus, I have his police report, and if he adds facts that weren't contained in that report, I'm going to crucify him. That would make matters even worse for him.

'He was walking quickly and looking around, like he was nervous.'

'Walking quickly in the dead of winter. Looking around nervously while he walked alone in a neighborhood you agreed was dangerous and gang-infested. Walking quickly and acting nervous while an unmarked car, with unknown occupants, *followed* him. *That's* what you're telling the judge struck you as suspicious.'

The detective glances at the judge.

'Anything else, Detective? I'm giving you the floor here. What other facts, Detective, gave you probable cause to believe my client was carrying drugs?' I tick off the points on my hand.

'He was walking on Roosevelt Avenue like several other people, he was wearing a winter coat like several other people, he had his hands in his pockets like several other people, he was looking around nervously and walking quickly while some stranger followed him in a beater Chevy. Is that *it*, Detective?'

The heat has fully reached the detective's face. I'm sure he's the combative sort ordinarily. He'd like to have it out with me behind the courthouse, if he had his druthers.

'He fit a profile,' he answers with a bit less bravado. 'It's a known fact that suburban kids come here to buy drugs.'

'Ah,' I say, like I've discovered gold, like we've finally arrived at the truth. 'He looked like a suburban kid.'

'He did.'

'Because he is white.'

'Because – he looked like a suburban kid.'

I drop my chin a notch and look up at the detective. 'Among the several individuals who were walking along Roosevelt Avenue at that point, isn't it true that Billy Braden was the only white person?'

'I don't recall,' he snaps.

'You picked him out because he was a white kid in a black neighborhood.'

'I didn't.'

Of course, he did. Billy looked like someone who didn't belong. It's not that Detective Forrest was acting illogically. It was somewhat logical. But when it comes to racial profiling, the police department gets very sensitive. They don't want to admit that they single out a white kid in a black neighborhood any more than they want to admit that they single out a black kid in a white neighborhood.

And no judge wants to condone racial profiling, either. Judge

Goodson is a temperamental sort – if he weren't, he'd have his own felony courtroom by now – but he isn't stupid. Unless the prosecutor cleans this up, the judge will have to toss this one. And I don't think the prosecutor can clean this one up.

He doesn't, not very well at least, during his examination of the detective. I do a recross and lay the racial thing on pretty thick. I don't particularly enjoy doing it, but guess what? My client doesn't pay me for what I enjoy doing. He pays me to win the damn case. And this is the most effective route to winning it.

At the end of the hearing, the judge takes the matter under advisement. We'll find out what he thinks soon. The Bradens thank me more profusely than I deserve. The adrenaline from the court hearing begins its slow leak, my interest in being here along with it. Actually, it's more like the balloon has burst.

I have to leave. I have to get out of here.

Then I hear a woman's voice behind me. 'Mr Kolarich.'

I notice a change in both of the men, father and son alike, their eyes growing, their posture straightening.

I turn. It's the court reporter. The prosecutor's office likes to hire an independent court reporter for these suppression hearings, because when they lose – when their whole case goes in the dumpster because of an evidentiary ruling – they like to appeal the case right away, and the county's court reporters aren't the most reliable.

I quickly understand the reaction of the Braden men. The court reporter has cropped black hair with Cleopatra bangs and large, piercing eyes the color of teal or aqua. Her face is finely etched into a V, with a nicely proportioned figure, from what I can see in her blue suit.

Those are the vital statistics, but there is something more there, something haunting, something electric. Her very presence feels like a dare, a challenge. Like she understands me. *I know you. I know what's wrong with you.*

She hands me her card. 'That has my e-mail and cell on it,' she says. 'I'll have the transcript to you by the end of the week, is that soon enough?'

I look down at the name. *Alexa Himmel.*

'Okay, Alexa Himmel,' I say. Just saying her name makes me feel dirty.